# Chasing Normal

## A Novel

Tara Fuselli

iUniverse, Inc.
New York   Bloomington

**Chasing Normal**
**A Novel**

iUniverse books may be ordered through booksellers or by contacting:

iUniverse
1663 Liberty Drive
Bloomington, IN 47403
www.iuniverse.com
1-800-Authors (1-800-288-4677)

ISBN: 978-1-4401-7743-9 (sc)
ISBN: 978-1-4401-7741-5 (dj)
ISBN: 978-1-4401-7742-2 (ebk)

Printed in the United States of America

iUniverse rev. date: 10/27/2009

For Mark.
My own happy ending.

And for Erica.
Who first shoved a romance novel in my face then suggested I write
one.

There is nothing like returning to a place that remains unchanged to find the ways in which you yourself have altered.

NELSON MANDELA, 'A LONG WALK TO FREEDOM'

# Acknowledgements

I wanted to include a special thanks to all of you out there who have taken time to support my adventures in writing.

Family, friends, coworkers and writing groups. You have read, edited, sent your thoughts and careful critique, listened while I rambled on endlessly about one character or another; you have shown a genuine interest and encouraged me to push forward with something incredibly close to my heart.

Jessica, your endless hours of editing saved me when I thought all hope was lost in getting this thing to fruition. Big Hugs.

My husband, Mark, my two wonderful kids, Kait and Ben…thank you for the time you gave, allowing me to spend hours face down in a book or delving into a manuscript. I wouldn't be here without you. Love you so much.

This has been quite the adventure, and though I've been writing for nearly ten years, I feel as if it is just beginning.

So here it is: the first one in print. Please enjoy! And don't hesitate in passing my name along so that one day I might find myself on a bookshelf next to the big ones!

# Chapter 1

## Eve ♀

I will never look at the color yellow with the same eyes. I think it was the *taffeta bridesmaid dress* part of it that changed me and unfortunately for Yellow, my mind is predisposed hereafter to want to scream at the sight of it.

My mother picked out the dress which explains a lot—it's neither my color nor style. Honestly, who can make an enormous bell-shaped gown look flattering aside from Scarlet O'Hara?

I wonder, too, if the dressmaker plays practical jokes in her spare time, adding bits of straw to the hem of her dresses; it's been itching my thighs all afternoon. Though I am mere steps away from parading down the aisle in front of the congregation and risk someone seeing my underpants, I can't resist the urge to lift the layers of frills and scratch.

Things could be worse, couldn't they? I mean, it could be polka dots. No, on second thought, I think taffeta truly is the worst of the worst and considering recent events in my life, yellow taffeta is just the icing on the enormous cake of my existence. Minus the plastic groom on top.

I eye the aisle from around the corner. The pews of the small church are filled with townspeople, watching from either side as the organist begins the music.

My cue.

My sister, Maggie, nudges me to step forward. I groan again at the taffeta and take a step, nearly tripping over the fringed hem.

Yep. I am, once again, *not* the bride but the bridesmaid at someone else's wedding. This time it's my sister's day of wedded bliss. I can see my mother watching me with an eye roll that says, "Get that unmarried behind of yours moving, Eve. You're holding up the ceremony."

Let the music begin…

Okay. So I've fallen in love more times than I'd like to count—with a playboy, a gay guy and a juvenile man attached to a beer keg. At least life can be adventurous that way. My name is Eve Whitting. Yes, like of the Adam and Eve, and yes, my mother tells me that I live up to the name quite well, though I'm never quite sure how to take that. I know it has something to do with the sinning part. And probably the temptation.

While my mother's ideals differ from mine at the best of times, my family has never hesitated sharing their opinions. Whether a help or hindrance, they make it their life's work to meddle and fix and advise—experts that they are.

…"Do you take this woman to be your lawfully wedded wife?"

Maggie smiles wide and Brock answers, a tear clinging to his eye as he swallows it back with an, "I do."

The guests in the audience let out a collective, "Awe."

I just groan and return to my inner dialogue…

From *my* perspective, my life has been more or less simple of late. It's had its ups and downs and roller coaster turns, I'll admit; even this recent plunge into monotony is like one of those long, deep falls before the next rise. But I've found myself at a crossroad. Stuck. In need of something or some*one* to say, *Wake up, Eve! This is where you belong!* before the next turn of adventure hits.

…"I now pronounce you, husband and wife. Brock, you may kiss your bride."

More collective noises of applause, sighs and blowing into tissues.

I'm sweating and wonder to myself, how noticeable are sweat stains on yellow taffeta?…

I *am* feeling stuck and I don't want to be forever staring at a NEXT STOP: MONOTONY! road sign with my flashers on, but it seems that temporarily trading in my roller coaster life in the city for my average and normal hometown is the best option just now. Just for a pause. The funny thing is I've spent years running from Normal. And where did that get me? A long stint on those hectic fairgrounds for one.

I recently returned to this land of Normal; a town where young girls marry their high school sweethearts and families still gather for annual pig roasts. Where women flock to weekly gossip groups, the men to trade secrets about ranching and farming and everything agriculture.

I returned and now stand in the churchyard. The ceremony was long, the church was hot and I've scratched a raw patch on my thigh. If not for my sister's wedding, I wouldn't have come back to this old town. I took Maggie's hand in mine with a squeeze, our last few moments alone before the guests descend on the new bride.

"So. Jackson didn't come with you to my wedding," she said. The simple statement came with a deep prodding yet subliminal question of "what's *really* going on here, Eve?"

"No. He didn't come to the wedding."

Maggie linked her arm through mine and we walked, her wedding dress swaying at her feet, swishing around my ankles. In the moment, this seemed the closest I would ever get to marriage so I enjoyed the swishing like a little girl watching her first bride walk down the aisle, her impish face full of awe and jealousy and utter happiness all rolled into one. Even for a tomboy like me.

"I ended things with Jackson," I finally said. "Two months ago."

"You broke up with Jackson and never told me?"

"You were planning your wedding. Of course I didn't tell you."

"What happened?" she asked, in that careful, concerned tone.

I kept our slow pace, arm in arm, down the long, gravel driveway and shrugged. "My heart didn't exactly skip a beat around Jackson anymore. I didn't lay awake thinking about him every minute of every day. I liked him. He made me smile. But honestly, Maggie, we didn't love each other. I think we did at first. But while you are here doing it for real, I only played house with Jackson, pretending we were happy."

"So what next?"

I shrugged my shoulders. "I thought I'd just live your life for a while in the *Land of Normal*." I sighed with the thought. I would be moving into Maggie's house for four months and while it might be the answer to finding my place in life, it also meant moving back home, a place I ran from the first chance I had out of high school.

Her eyes glimmered for a moment.

"You are my sister, Mags, and my best friend. I love you to death. But before you get any ideas, remember you don't get the privilege of picking apart my love life."

"You're right. The picking apart is Mom's job." She had to bite her lip to avoid any "advice" flowing out of it.

"Speaking of Mom, you didn't tell her I was staying at your place, did you?"

"It might have slipped out in conversation." She winced an apology.

"Ugh."

"She also might be coming by with a green bean casserole Tuesday evening around four thirty."

Huge sigh.

"I've gotta run," she said and knocked her forehead on mine. "Brock is waiting for his bride. Are you sure you don't mind staying this long to watch my place? It might be the whole four months, you know."

"Which should have been no problem except now Mom knows where to find me."

"She'd have found you sooner or later. And don't be so hard on yourself. Mom'll be there soon enough to do that for you."

"You are a joy, Maggie, you really are. Have a great trip." I squeezed her tightly in my arms, the vulnerable part of me still wanting to cry on her shoulder over Jackson, and watched her glide toward the vintage Chevy.

I watched the wedding car pull away from the church. The strident sound of the tin cans clanging against the dirt road made me certain I wasn't ready for marriage just yet. The same went for the confetti littering the lawn at my feet and sticking to the hairspray in my fancy up-do, which I never do on a regular day. In a sudden urge to grasp at my youth, I threw an outstretched arm into the air and waved at the car, jumping up and down like we used to do when we were kids. Maggie blew a kiss back with a dazzling laugh through the window.

This would be the last of those sister-to-sister moments and I suppose I resented Brock just a little for taking Maggie away. Only because my own love life hovered in the midst of a landslide and no one stood next to me just now to drag me up off the dirt. Even in that moment, I recognized this as self-pity, but other people's weddings sort of did that to a girl. One of those *always a bridesmaid* things.

So there I stood, alone in the churchyard. And though Mrs. Pollard's angelic wedding march still droned from the organ inside and the reverend shook hands with guests, his black robe kicking up dirt at his feet, the light breeze carrying whisperings of *a lovely day for a wedding*, I didn't feel the serenity, didn't breathe the hallowed air around me with pious glee.

I simply felt numb.

I lingered alongside the wedding guests, people from my distant past, fake-smiling the best I could until we finally left for the farmhouse. The moment I stepped down from Dad's old pickup truck onto home ground for the reception, I sighed. A bittersweet sight lay before me. The yellow house had a fresh coat of paint, the white detail of trim and trellises shone bright and every windowpane glimmered with the rays of welcoming sunshine. Trailing vines clung to the porch posts at even intervals, rosebushes flanking the stairs in a haven of scent and color, bright crimson a contrast to the yellow walls as its backdrop, blue sky its canvass. In the distance stood tall silos of grain, a small matching yellow barn and the far off call of the Holsteins, the lulling baa of a herd of sheep. This canvass of beauty and the symphony of sound that was the farm were sweet.

The surrounding and still arriving clusters of people sent the bitterness up my throat. And my mother. Who, I reminded myself again, did love me in her own way. With that thought, I let out an audible groan.

"Eve," called my mother. "You've lost your smile again."

I put on an over exaggerated one.

She shuffled next to me in her floral print dress and wide-brimmed hat. Both fluttered in the breeze, her hand moving quickly to the top of her head to keep the hat from flying away, the flowers that crowned it now squished and wilting.

"Eve, put on a happy face for your sister for Pete's sake." She tugged at the puffed sleeve of my yellow taffeta dress and ran her thumb over my bottom lip to dull the bright lipstick I'd added for color. For bold, yet natural color as opposed to the bright blue eye shadow and clumping mascara applied to my face by Miss Brooks in the local salon that morning.

I eyed the poor disheveled excuse for my mother's hat then focused back on the slowly crowding yard. "I'm trying to smile. But come on, Mom. Even you have to admit it's been a long day. Flower arranging and rearranging, primping over these dresses that, really, what are the chances they're going to improve? Maggie sucked back antacids, you, your "nervous pills" and Dad's still waiting for the moment everyone will leave his house so he can put his feet up in the old recliner."

"On my way there already," said Dad as if on cue, darting toward the house in what looked like a blur from the corner of my eye. Thinking on that heavenly recliner was like building castles in the air, this being only the first few minutes of a long evening reception that lay between my dad's ass and that comfortable chair.

There was room for another sigh, but I held it back for the sake of my mother.

"Oh no. You're not going anywhere Mr. Whitting," she said, following Dad into the house.

Saved by my father and his aging Lazy Boy.

The primping and preparing for the ceremony—not to mention my mother's worldly advice—had come to an end, but the crowd was sprouting roots around where I stood. Not all was lost, I thought, eyeing the perimeter of the Whitting land. There were many secluded places on the farm, little cubbies in the trees, small crevasses and coves along the fence line where the neighbor's farm and ours met, a cluster of birches weaving it one side to the other.

I found one of those sacred spots in the birches, hiked my dress to my knees and swung a leg over the waist-high wooden fence. I propped myself on the rail, feet dangling and kicking in the cool, shaded air, my high heels kicked off and hidden somewhere below in the tall grass. Memories of a small pond hinted from the recesses of my mind, somewhere not far from where I sat. I could hear it croaking with frogs, just out of sight. Here, listening to the quail skitter near the water, the sparrows in the tall treetops, trilling their song, I found my peace and solitude of home. But it wouldn't last long before I had to reappear for dinner, smile for Maggie and pretend to heed my mother's advice.

By the time I wandered slowly back through the yard, the reception was well on its way inside the house. I breathed deep, took in the scents of home. Some of them had me yearning for a comfort that remained stranded somewhere in my youth: the earthy soil, fresh, clean air, even the manure toiled into nearby wheat fields and the smoky oil from the tractors that toiled it. But the sounds of the people, the echoes of the local Ladies Social knee deep in gossip, had my stomach churning. And I just didn't feel I'd ever fit in here again.

I lasted three hours. Aside from the giant buffet style home cooked meal—everything from pot roast, ham and rosemary grilled chicken to vegetables, casseroles, salads and cakes—I managed to avoid mingling more than necessary and nod my way through one-sided conversations, slowly slipping unnoticed to the next. Eventually, I inched my way to the front drive and ducked out before the first few guests made their departure, sometime around eight thirty in the evening. The sound of my Jeep engine turning over was a welcome one.

It was less than an hour drive south into town from the farm. Hopefully the sun drummed a warmer beat there. Drops of rain hit the windshield in heavy plunks and being early spring, the warm days became fast chilled as night fell. I cranked the heater to high and blasted the music on the radio.

I felt a twinge of guilt at having left the reception early. But only a twinge. Nothing brought out the high spirits of the town and most of its *folks* that still lived there like a blissful country wedding. The perfect time to leave. Besides, if my mother really did plan on visiting this Tuesday, I would have all the time I needed to fill up on advice about relationships.

As I glanced around town now, the dim streetlights pulling me toward my destination, the crackle of gravel on the quiet roads lulling my tired eyes closed, I thought about home. This really would be my home, though a temporary one.

Despite the changes that had occurred, time appeared to have stood still in Tayton. My first impression, as I finally pulled down Vine Street, swarmed over like a cool breeze; the sky looked clear, stars shone through the blackness and it felt peaceful. Second, it had been a draining day and I felt as tired as a workhorse. Instead of unloading my crap from the car, I threw an overnight bag over my shoulder and trudged up the dark, lonely walk to the house. The house looked peaceful tonight, too, as it usually did. A quiet neighborhood in the suburbs of town.

I had to laugh at Tayton's "suburbs" after living ten years in the city. Here, birds chirped in the day, crickets hummed at night, stars shone brightly, not dimmed by city lights like the ones I had grown so used to. The smell of flowers from newly planted and sprouting gardens hung in the air. Suddenly, the clanging neighbors, barking dogs and honking horns of the big city reminded me of my many bad decisions. This would be nice. Four months of peace and quiet. Four months to shut out the mistakes.

It didn't feel so bad to be back.

I slammed the door behind me, kicked my shoes into a corner, peeled out of the country-frilled bridesmaid dress and hit the pillow.

## JOEL ♂

I dragged myself out of bed early, only because some idiot slammed a fist on my front door at what felt like three in the morning. The clamor of voices outside and the heavy footsteps on the front porch confirmed my suspicions. It was an idiot. More than one idiot. And I felt like shit.

My name is Joel Powell. I work as a heavy-duty mechanic, fixing equipment around town and the surrounding area. When someone needs it fixed, I'm the guy to do it. Growing up, I tinkered with everything and I guess I never tired of moving parts, metal on metal— the sound of my first rebuilt engine turning over for the first time was like an orgasm. More so in recent years since my time to spend with women in that department had shriveled to a stand still. How sad was that? Welcome to the life of Joel Powell. At least I wasn't sucking dirt in the family plot.

The light shone through the slats in the bedroom window blind. Laundry piled high in two corners of the floor, books and organized junk in the others. It wasn't tidy, but it was clean. A failed marriage had left me the perfect picture of a bachelor. And my otherwise chaotic life left me an excuse to live up to the title well sometimes. This week was exactly one of those times, the lack of sleep still not caught up.

The banging continued on the front porch. I threw on a pair of old jeans, the first I could find from the heap in one of the corners, and appeared at the door, eyes squinted and in a foul mood. The cool air cut my bare chest the minute I threw open the screen door.

"What?" I asked with my best bear growl. Two of the sorriest looking sons of bitches stared at me; my closest friend Raif stood behind them and none of them moved from the doorway.

"New neighbor," said one of them, named Tal. He slugged back the last of the beer he held in one hand.

"So?" I asked. I was not in the mood.

They snickered as if I'd missing something and Tal leaned in with a whisper. "It's a woman."

"A woman used to live there before, too," I said with feigned excitement. I turned back into the house and slammed the door behind me. I should have locked it.

It flung open and I heard the lazy shuffle of Trey's cowboy boots.

"I brought beer," said Tal.

"Well, it looks like moving day. There's a bunch of shit in her Jeep out front. We came to check it out," explained Trey, which explained everything. Tal plus beer plus the chance to gawk at a woman equals a good time for Trey. Easy math.

Tal and Trey were the least likely looking small town men. Both were lanky with overgrown blonde hair. Trey—taller and blonder—still lived with his family most of the time, one of us the rest, working one job after another. He never caught on at how to fit in; cowboy boots and the old tattered straw cowboy hat permanently affixed to his head fit in. The homeboy jeans and gigantic peace sign around his neck did not. But he'd be there without question if you needed him. Peace sign and all.

Tal fought the small town cowboy appeal and clung more to the trailer park persona, where he spent a lot of his time trying to wheel a girl named Cammy in and out of a relationship on a regular basis. He went to school in town a few years behind the rest of us and moved down the street with his sister five years ago when his parents were killed in a flood disaster three towns over. He lived life with the goal of holding a job for at least twenty-four hours. He's family, a distant cousin, so he fast became my responsibility. If someone didn't keep an eye on him, he'd be dead or in prison by now.

"Are you seriously drinking beer at this time in the morning? Great. Have yourselves a party," I said and flung myself onto the sofa, legs outstretched. My muscles ached and the light I tried to squint away made my brain explode with more pounding. I had plans today. Do shit-all and possibly sleep in until noon. There weren't many of those days in my life so I cherished them.

Trey pulled open the blinds and I raised my arm to block the sunlight pouring in from the bay window.

I could feel Raif's presence across from me in an easy chair. I always could. Even when he didn't speak, I knew he was there. Chances were, he hadn't joined the other two in a beer and he'd come for reasons other than interest in the new neighbor girl.

Raif and I had known each other since his family moved from the big city in grade school. I taught him how to fight like a farm boy and he introduced me to his older sister. A match made in heaven for a thirteen-year-old kid with raging hormones; she wore a size D bra and taught me everything I wanted to know about french kissing. Raif and I became inseparable.

I felt him stare from across the room and knew he was smirking. "What?" I asked.

"Hard night drinking?" asked Raif.

"No. Working. I got in after midnight from the ranch. You aren't joining the party over there?"

"Nope. I came to see if you were up for a drive, but apparently you haven't joined the world of the living yet. I just found these two on your doorstep when I pulled up." He nodded in the direction of Tal and Trey who were perched at the window, eyes glued to the neighbor's house.

"What kind of a drive?" Something always came attached to a drive. It usually meant the use of my pickup.

"I need to haul a tractor out of the mud pit."

The mud pit was a baron field at the edge of town, usually used for racing dirt bikes or any other manly competition of testosterone involving a variety of motorized vehicles to run over the hills and through the mud, one or two a week getting stuck, sometimes permanently; also known as the Metal Graveyard for the same reason.

"A tractor? I shouldn't even ask why or how you lost a tractor in the Graveyard."

"No, you shouldn't. But it wasn't mine. It was my brother-in-law who has a brain the size of a cockroach."

"I have some lumber to haul out to the ranch. You help me with that and I'll pull out the tractor." I didn't need to ask why he wasn't using his own truck. I drove an old beat up blue pickup. Raif thought of his as a baby and it didn't go anywhere near the graveyard.

"Do I have to build a fence or anything?" he huffed.

"Maybe. Depends how bad you need the tractor," I shone him a smile.

"It's my dad's tractor."

"Then you'll be building a fence."

"Hey, Joel, keep it down," whispered Tal from the open bay window at the front of the house. He peered back through the window where it angled toward the blue house next door.

"Jesus," I said to Raif. "They're like teenagers."

"Nearly. Their brains definitely stopped growing after high school."

Tal sat on the floor with his eyes glued next door and Trey sat in the chair next to him, leaning over the armrest.

"Tell me you didn't wake me up at nine in the morning just to stare out my window. What the hell are you two doing up so early anyway? This is the first time I've seen you outta bed before noon on a weekend."

"I got up to go to work at the lumber yard this morning. Thought it was Saturday. Of course, they're closed today and I missed yesterday seeing as how my week has got all messed up. So I got fired," said Tal. Trey laughed and chugged back a beer. "Then I needed a beer."

"Glad you thought to come here," I muttered from the sofa.

# Chapter 2

## *Eve* ♀

I woke abruptly to the sound of banging and yelling coming from the neighbor's door and pulled a pillow over my face with an outward moan, willing the noise to stop.

I rolled onto my stomach and mumbled, "I thought this was supposed to be a quiet town. It's noisier than the freakin' city," face down in my pillow.

Trying to sleep became futile, so I hauled out of bed with plans to unpack the Jeep. I stood in front of the mirror and cringed at the sight of my hair. The up-do I'd worn to the wedding hung down at the sides, pins sticking out in all directions and hair spray glued it down in the front where I had apparently slept face planted on the bed for a solid eight hours; a longer stretch than I had in two months. Mascara smeared my eyes like a raccoon and suddenly I felt like I might just fit back into the small town hick look pretty well.

I pulled out the hairpins—which is painful by the way, when they're super-glued to your head—and strong-armed a brush through my mop of hair until it resembled a half decent style, though not exactly one I'd choose to wear on an average day. My blonde hair, complete with dark brown chunky streaks—the perfect example of yet another attempt at avoiding normal by looking the city girl—hung in short curls at my neck with a stiff swoop across my forehead this morning. The best I could do without a shower first, and my clothes were still in the trunk. No one would see me anyway. I laughed at the thought of trying to impress any of the cowboys in the first place and trudged to my sister's closet to find something to wear.

Maggie's room, along with the rest of her house, looked as if a garden full of wild flowers had puked in it. Yellow walls were accented with pink and blue floral borders, hand painted details of the same at the windows, the curtains puffs and piles of floral fabrics. Wainscoting of spring green lined every wall except where a doorway sat; those were trimmed with more flowers. The white bedroom furniture, trimmed in gold, reminded me of the canopy bed and suite Maggie adored as a little girl. The only difference being this one accommodated two now that she was married. Trinkets of stuffed animals, dolls, old water pitchers and basins also painted with flowers, sat on every surface between mismatched frames of family photos. And aside from the odd animal head attached to wall in the living room and a picture of poker playing dogs added by Brock to man up the place, the bedroom, like the rest of the house, pretty much screamed "*Maggie!*"

I looked from the closet to the bridesmaid dress lying in a heap on the floor and considered my options in getting dressed. There weren't any, it seemed. I didn't care who saw me today, but I couldn't bring myself to pull on the yellow taffeta dress again. Burn it, maybe.

I finally settled on a pair of khaki pants that hung two inches too short and a baggy white t-shirt covered in glittering daisies. Maggie stood three inches shorter than I did, a few inches of comfortable padding wider, so I rolled up the pant bottoms to sit mid-calf and belted them at the waist where they hung below my belly button.

It was awing that *I* grew up the tomboy.

A country girl who spent most of her childhood with the farm hands and horses, roping and branding cattle, building fences, driving herds to slaughter—certainly the tomboy. I even delivered a calf with my own hands at age eleven. I also learned to cuss, spit, fight and yell, squish frogs under my boots and shoot squirrels with a pellet gun. The excitement and fondness of the last two memories has turned more toward remorse in my adulthood. I spent as little time as possible indoors playing with dolls and a toy oven like Maggie had. Of course, that's where my mother lays the blame for my lack of manners and foul mouth. At the end of the day, I look past most of my mother's opinions without being too hard on myself. I like who I am, tomboy and all, and have come to realize my mother and I will never see eye to eye.

I started a pot of coffee brewing and tromped outside with a plan in my head and the keys to my Jeep in hand. I stopped midway down the walk and slapped a hand to my forehead with an inward groan. You know that feeling that hits you upside the head when you know there's something you were supposed to do? And you aren't sure what it is exactly, but there it is, that daunting aura of importance surrounding it. Well one of those came over me and the doom crept in.

"Shit. I was supposed to do something...Think, Eve. Think. Think. Oh God! Feed the cat."

An epiphany.

"But where does Maggie keep the cat food?" I walked halfway back toward the house and stopped again. "Shit. Where's the cat?"

*...Deep pit wrenching through stomach...images of country bumpkins taking shots at Maggie's cat running through my mind...*

## JOEL ♂

"Oooh, she's a doozy, this one," said Tal, watching my new neighbor emerge from the house.

"What's she doing?" asked Trey.

"I don't know. She's slapping her forehead. Now she's turning around again. Nope. Stopped on the sidewalk. She looks confused."

"You're confused," muttered Raif as moved toward the window, unable to keep from looking. Boys will be boys, after all.

Enough was enough. I wanted some sleep and wasn't going to get it with these clowns gawking out my window. I got up from the sofa to shoo them away.

"Get away from there and leave her alone. It's just Maggie's sister, Eve," I said. Then I saw her, standing in complete disarray. Or maybe this is just what she called "fashionable". She hesitated on the walkway then turned back toward the Jeep parked on the side of the road.

"She doesn't look much like Maggie, does she?" asked Tal in a near whisper, lost in thought.

"She must be from the city," said Raif.

"Why do you say that?" asked Trey.

"No one wears make-up like that here. Or stripes in their hair. And what's with the rolled up pants?" he asked.

Tal just said, "Hot hair." And meant it.

She reached for a box in the back of the Jeep. Very nice back view, I thought, but kept my thoughts to myself. Unlike the idiots.

"Look at her bend over. Oooh-eee," said Tal. All four of us leaned in closer and followed her, eyes glued, back toward the house carrying the box. She stumbled part way up the walk and adjusted the box against her waist. Her shirt had ridden up to her bra line exposing a flat stomach and generous curve at the hip.

"Sugar and spice, little darlin'," said Trey.

I stopped fighting the urge to walk away and instead stood silently as part of the immature gawk session. It was awing; she stuck out like a beacon in the middle of town.

"Didn't Maggie grow up here?" asked Raif.

"Yeah, on a farm off the East highway," I said.

"Then so did Eve."

I knew most everyone in town but I didn't know this one. Not any more. I remembered Maggie's sister as a kid; straggly and tomboy came to mind. She beat up the youngest Miller boy once and he was twice her size.

"Maggie said she left right after high school for the city. She's been back to visit periodically but never stays long," I said, almost in a trance myself. This was not the lanky kid I remembered. No one paid her any attention when she left for the city or noticed that she hadn't come back.

"Have you seen her around here, Joel?" asked Trey.

"Nope. She only ever came on the weekend, always when I was out at the ranch."

"Here she comes again." Trey nudged us to keep quiet, eyes trained with all of ours on the womanly vision of "Sugar and Spice" in the front lane.

"Damn, she fixed the t-shirt," said Tal.

She leaned deeper into the back into the Jeep. We all leaned with her to the left to get a better look but kept quiet, hoping she wouldn't hear us as she carried another two boxes and came back one last time to throw a duffle bag over her shoulder and strained to haul a heavy suitcase, the last of the luggage. She struggled, wiped her brow and bent to the ground a few times, giving us an eyeful. Her loose pants shifted down lower around her hips; Trey let out a low whistle of awe—which we all thought but didn't act on—and she stopped to hike them up again.

She paused then, partway up the walk, and stood frozen, glancing cautiously around her before continuing into the house.

Tal and Trey exchanged a humble but still hormonal glance.

"Uh oh. I think she saw us."

"She didn't see us."

"She glanced over here."

"She can't see us. The sun is shining in the wrong direction."

"And there's a glare on the window."

"I swear she looked right at me."

"Yeah?"

"Yeah."

"Hot."

"Uh huh."

"What color are her eyes?"

"Christ," I finally said. "You guys act like you've never seen a woman before." *Obviously* far more idiotic than I.

"You're getting in on the view, too, Joel, so shove it," said Trey.

I folded my arms across my chest without a word. Arguing would mean walking away from the window. What guy in his right mind would leave this scene willingly? We watched a while longer, waiting for her to reappear.

"Do you have any binoculars?" asked Trey.

I didn't grace Trey with an answer, only sighed at the thought that these were actually my friends. I ran a hand through my disheveled hair and headed back toward the sofa.

Raif turned toward me and asked, "So, when are we going for the tractor?"

# EVE ♀

I stalked along the side of the house, nostrils flaring, a fire lit at my feet. I held a water hose and nozzle in one hand, my other balled into a fist and thrashing at my side as I moved up the side of the house. What the hell kind of immature little boys sheepishly watch a woman from the window? And binoculars now? Didn't get a good enough look?

Little bastards.

Two of them leaned against the window screen. I could hear them shuffling around then one of them pulled back the screen and poked his head around the corner. "Nope, she's not coming back out," I heard him say.

"Damn. And we didn't even get a full show yet."

"What did you expect?" called someone from inside. "A wet t-shirt contest or mud wrestling?"

My aggravation heightened. Steam may have shot from my ears.

The idiot closest to the window yanked his head inside the second he saw me. Fast reflexes for a little shit, I thought. The other, not so much. I pointed the nozzle inches away from his forehead and he reacted as if I aimed a loaded Glock at his face. Idiot.

"Holy sh—!" he barely said before I pulled the trigger and a gush of water hit them both in the head, soaking their clothes and everything beneath them. They scrambled to their feet cursing me up, down and sideways. Of course, that didn't faze me. I could curse right along with them if I'd wanted to, so I kept spraying.

I didn't let up until they were drenched, aiming next at the two figures standing behind the first, in the shadows. I shone a huge smart-assed grin through the window before finally letting up with the spray nozzle.

"Oops," I said. "Did I get you?" I laid the sarcasm on pretty thick and my grin even thicker. Then I rolled my eyes and quickly found the scowl I'd grown so proud of as a stubborn tomboy of a little girl.

The front door opened and I jerked around toward it. Damn. I hadn't thought about someone coming *out* of the house.

A tall, bronzed, bare-chested man stared daggers at me. His jeans, though tattered and frayed, hugged him in all the right places. His dark hair flicked in the breeze and it looked like he'd had a day of growth on his face. His eyes sparkled in the sun but held nothing in the way of humor.

He glared at me where I stood on the front lawn, his eyebrows arched in with a wrinkle forming between them. I could have studied that wrinkle for hours.

"Oh crap," I muttered to myself, partly because I hadn't considered that I might be breaking a trespassing law, and partly in awe of this man on the doorstep. I hate to admit it, but my heart sped a patter.

"I beg your pardon?" he asked in a gruff voice. Sarcasm noted.

I pulled my jaw up from drooling and the stare down began. Back to reality, I thought, and pushed the vision of him from my mind. And the fast heart rate that accompanied it.

"What are you doing?" he asked, still gruff and apparently less than impressed. His eyes fell to the nozzle in my hand where it dripped water in a puddle at my feet, then back to my face. He held my glare.

A second man joined him on the front porch with raised brows. This one laughed behind his silent expression, but only a slight grin escaped on his face. His blue eyes twinkled in the sunlight, blonde hair hung in curly locks on bronzed skin, a shade lighter than the first Adonis. What a vision these two were first thing in the morning. Might have to trespass more often.

"What am I *doing*?" I asked, contempt returning. "I was unpacking my stuff when I heard what I thought were a bunch of little boys snickering from the window."

"You look surprised to see me standing here," said the bare-chested one.

"No. Only shocked that you aren't the twelve-year-old boy I assumed from the way you were acting. Or you," I said and nodded toward the other one. He held up a hand to wave hello and stuck it back in his pocket. "You," I glared at the blonde one harder, "seem to be enjoying yourself. The show wasn't good enough; you have to come have another look?"

I looked back at the first one again. He held that cold glare but his eyes were laughing, as if trying to hold back a smile. He leaned casually on the doorframe and crossed his arms as the other two poked their heads through the doorway behind him. Soaked from head to toe, they dripped water all over the floor like a couple of long faced bloodhounds just returned from the hunt empty-handed.

"Oh, my mistake!" I yelled. "There are the twelve-year-old boys!"

"We're not—" started one but he stopped himself when I pointed the *Glock* at his already sopping head.

"Hey!" yelled the bare-chested Adonis. "Put it down. You've done enough damage with that thing already."

I turned my aim on him out of pure protective instinct, threatening to pull the trigger; I *so* should have been a cop.

Damn, but he didn't even flinch.

I lowered my weapon. "Oh, my deepest apologies for any damage done. And thanks, by the way, for watching me carry the heavy boxes into the house by myself while the four of you amply able men sat back for a gawk session. Very neighborly. And I'll make sure to wear my string bikini next time. And douse myself in mud when my friends are over in our white t-shirts!" I glared at the blonde one.

"Hey, they were just being typical men," said the bare one.

"Men? I hate to argue, but under the circumstances, buddy, they are nowhere near men. You included!"

The Adonis smiled now and eyed me up and down once more with folded arms. A shiver brushed over me the same time as his eyes danced over my skin.

How dare he! He was ogling! Could he seriously be this bold? Of course, I had to ignore the shiver that presently crawled across my skin.

"My mistake. Look, I'm sorry if we offended you." He watched me carefully still and the other one laughed outwardly now. I felt like ripping someone's head off.

"Hey!" yelled the soaked kid, "You just waterlogged Joel's floor!" This one seemed to lack a few smarts upstairs.

"And which one of you dumb-ass's opened the window?" I asked.

He gaped at me with a dropped jaw.

"So, you must be Maggie's big sister," said the bare Adonis with a smirk.

"And you must be my new immature dumb-ass neighbors!" I yelled and took two steps away. I turned back then with a grin. "Nice to meet you," I said in my sweetest most sarcastic voice and sloshed back to

Maggie's house through the mushy grass. I tossed the water nozzle to the ground, still leaking a thin stream of water at my feet.

I organized my suitcase into empty drawers and hung jackets in the closet of Maggie's bedroom. Disgust still sizzled in me at the thought of the egotistical men next door, particularly the one eyeing me while I lectured the four of them. My cousins were no less mature at the wedding last night trying to sneak a peek up everyone's dress. They were only eleven.

Frustration subsiding, I slouched onto the bed. "Ugh. Nice introduction to the neighbors. First day in town and I'll be the laughing stock after being seen in this stupid outfit. Except with the mentality of those guys, they likely rated this get-up as stunning eveningwear. Maybe I'll be the center of attention in my country bumpkin pants and raccoon make-up job. A trend setter, even." I wondered if this counted as one of those occasions I should have controlled my temper like my mother always told me.

Maggie's gargantuan cat, now satiated on the last can of tuna from a sparse kitchen cupboard and a bowl of fresh water, slunk through the bedroom purring and occasionally snaking back and forth between my ankles. He had only three paws—missing one front passenger side—and could only see through one eye so he walked lopsided most of the time and bumped into walls on a regular basis.

I have never found a use for cats. Cats, dogs, hamsters, they're all more work than I ever wanted and nothing small, fuzzy, yappy or with carpet pooping potential were allowed in my apartment. We already had rats. And trust me; they do not make good pets.

"Well, Stumpy," I said to the cat who purred louder than my Jeep engine. He let out a half-meow, half-growl, intended as affection even though it sounded more of a dejected groan. "You'll have to introduce me to Mr. Self Important next door. It seems I may have ruined his carpet and will need to make up for it. With my piles of money I have saved up over the years and recent lack of a job." Stumpy purred, did another lap through my legs, meowed again and crashed into a wall. "For that reason alone, this was definitely one of those times controlling my temper would have been much more beneficial."

I made a grilled cheese sandwich doused in ketchup for dinner after traipsing through town for groceries. I even baked a lemon cake, pleased with myself for pulling that one out of my ass. I didn't bake often but my mother's lemon cake recipe seemed to filter into my knowledge base even though I don't tend to absorb most of her other lessons on being a proper housewife. I showered, my hair now damp with relaxed blonde curls hanging softly just above my shoulder. I guessed that the wispy fringes dangling across my forehead would eventually annoy me—my hairdresser said they were sexy but he knows nothing about comfort—so I pinned them back behind my ears. I slapped on my usual make-up—eyeliner and lip-gloss—and pulled on my own clothes. Heaven.

I hadn't been happy about the make-up job and hair-do Maggie had insisted on for the wedding, but shone a grin through the grueling process for Maggie's sake. She'd been so excited and I remember the beaming smile she'd had while she watched the curls being fluffed and teased—who teased anymore, really?—and pinned up on my head in what I saw as a God-awful attempt at country girl hits a windstorm. I don't know how I managed it, but I cringed through, kept my mouth shut and allowed Maggie to enjoy the morning. It had been her wedding day after all.

I scooped up a canvass bag, which now wafted the smell of lemon cake into the air, added a tub of chocolate ice cream and walked out the door. I hesitated at the front step, tempted to walk across the lawn in a diagonal toward the neighbor's house, but chose to walk down Maggie's walk to the street and back up the other a few feet away. Be neighborly, Eve, I kept telling myself between deep breaths.

I stood halfway up his walk and stared at the house; a perfect clone of Maggie's blue bungalow barring its cream colored siding. Porches stretched the front face of both homes, a door on the right of Maggie's, the left of the neighbor's, where they shared a property line. Each boasted a stoop near the door with an uncomfortable willow chair. I imagine you could jump from one rail across the couple of feet expanse the houses were so close. Both homes were well kept, Maggie's with more flowers and trimmed shrubs, the other plain with fresh mowed grass.

As I looked down the street, it seemed there were other clones; only slight differences in bay windows, color of siding, shrubs and the odd gnome pushing a wheelbarrow full of annuals to set one apart from the next. Cozy and homey. Normal. Come to think of it, I still hadn't felt the nauseated pit wrench in my stomach since returning home. Until now. But I had a feeling this pit was owing to the biggest hangdog of all walks of shame.

I rapped on the front door to the cream-colored house and bobbed up and down on my feet trying not to glare as I eyed the window where the four idiots had been gawking. The same man, still bare-chested but now with a towel around his neck and a fresh pair of snug fitting jeans stood in the doorway. He smiled and eyed me up and down again. Nervy of him but my stomach defied my stubborn streak and fluttered. I took a deep breath and forced an enormous smile as the door opened.

# JOEL ♂

She seemed happy enough now from where she stood on my front porch, but she fumed behind those wide, revealing eyes. The same fire she'd shown earlier had reignited as if at the sight of me. I couldn't help but enjoy it.

An image of this woman had stuck in my mind all morning. Hair that could only have been styled by a chipmunk on Prozac, wide black circles around her eyes, pants rolled in floods to her calves, contrasting strappy heels on her feet, soaking wet and grass stained.

And a tiny waist with a deep, seductive curve at her hip that tempted from beneath the hem of her shirt.

All but the tiny waist and deep curve had gone, replaced by sexy, voluptuous and edible. Not that I noticed.

"Well, hello there, neighbor," I said.

"Hi," she said, still smiling large.

I watched her closely, gave her a minute to collect herself as I towel-dried my hair. She seemed to be searching for something momentous to say.

"So," was all that came out of those full lips. She wore tight jeans that flared at the bottom and a fitted bright green t-shirt. A pair of pink sunglasses sat atop her head in a mess of curls blowing in the wind.

"So."

Nothing momentous seemed to reveal itself to either of us.

"Are you going to invite me in, or what? I brought a peace offering of ice cream and cake." She raised the bag and smiled brighter. If that was possible. "Sort of a huge apology for your floor. I'll pay for it as soon as I can. In installments would be better. I just quit my job and haven't exactly been raising a cash cow here. Have you got an estimate on the repairs yet?"

"Repairs?" I asked. She baffled me. And distracted. She had the brightest smile I'd seen in a long time and her personality shone through it between the angry fire she seemed to be trying to keep at bay as she eyed the window again.

"Repairs. To your carpet. Water damage." She grinned with what looked like a hint of embarrassment now though she didn't try to hide anything in her expression. She was as bold as she accused me of earlier.

"Come on in," I said, reluctant to see her walk away any time soon. And though women were more of a complication in my life lately, it never hurt to look. Or smell their hair with your eyes closed as they brushed past.

I heard her feet tread lightly behind me as she assessed the damage in the living room. It didn't look too bad, though the wood spat up dust when you walked on it, spots and splashes of water stains clung to the grain, lines of glue stuck to the edges, carpet tacks along the perimeter. I still had glue under my fingernails after spending all afternoon ripping it out. The rest looked as usual: an old green sofa with a tear down the side. Plain patchwork, hand-me-down green curtains hung on either side of the bay window, a beanbag chair and overstuffed arm chair shoved into he corner next to a small television unit. On better days, I organized the room to watch sports with the guys or pull up a table for poker. For now, my entire living room had been shoved to one side until the work on the floor could be completed. A bachelor pad to say the least. Not even a picture hung on the faded, pale cream walls.

"You tore out the carpet?" She looked mortified. Price tags might as well have appeared over her head, credit cards retreat deeper into her purse.

"Yup."

"You could have had someone suck out the water or something. Don't they do that? Why didn't you do that?"

"I don't know. But we tore it out this afternoon."

"I'm sorry about the water. I should have thought before I—I really didn't think about ruining your floor." She began pacing.

"Let's see that cake and ice cream. Did you make it yourself?"

"Yes."

"If it's any good, we'll call it even. I owe you an apology, too. We could have helped you carry your bags inside."

"They were boxes. And they were damn heavy." Arms now crossed, one eyebrow rose.

"Boxes? How long are you staying for?"

"Four months. You mean you were so infatuated with my sexy wardrobe you didn't notice the boxes?" A sexy grin drew up the corners of her mouth.

"No. I was on the sofa trying to kill a headache after the *twelve-year-olds* woke me up this morning to stare out my window."

"Oh God. You weren't even hanging out the window staring like an ape and I wrecked your floor."

"I stared a little. Do you want a drink?"

"Sure. Whatever you've got."

Before I could offer her a seat she pulled the ice cream from the bag, then the cake. She set it on the table and stood in search of plates and cutlery. Drawers banged, cupboards opened and closed as she shifted from one to the next. I turned around and watched as she made herself at home, rifling through my kitchen. Then she froze, drawing her hands quickly away from an open cupboard door.

"Oops. Sorry. I was looking for plates. I tend to forget my manners. I was raised by wolves," she grinned.

"Make yourself at home, Mowgli. I'm going to get dressed."

## *Eve* ♀

He spoke with a drawl the same as that of my family's and the entire town's. Similar to mine I hate to admit, except that mine faded in and out. In, when I grew befuddled; the angrier, more frazzled state I found myself in, the bigger the drawl. I usually cringe when I hear the accent in my family. Annoying at best, it reminded me of a place I chose to walk away from as a teenager. Today, his, left something of a comfort. Not to mention a lingering quiver in my nether regions.

"No need to get dressed, really," I whispered to myself and watched him walk back around the corner feeling an urge to let go a long, low, whistle behind him. He had a killer smile and sparkling eyes that on first meeting him were cold, boring a hole through me and my garden hose. Now, they shone with laughter and intrigue. His build, strong but not steroid enhanced, had me guessing he probably did a lot of hard labor outside with his shirt off by the look of his biceps and the bronze of his skin. Not just sexy. Strong, virile maleness positively oozed from him.

# JOEL ♂

I returned to Eve sitting at the table, one leg tucked beneath her with two large pieces of cake set out on plates. She scooped ice cream with a salad spoon, letting it slide to the plate and slick into a pool as it melted. She licked it from her fingers as it dripped down the handle. The best thing about women and ice cream: the sticky wet mess. Even better when they needed a hand with clean up. I began to make a move to reach for her hand, lick it from those fingers myself, then paused when I realized we hadn't even introduced ourselves yet.

She gave me a saucy glance with raised eyebrows toward my chest. My first thought sprouted from my masculine ego with the assumption she was sizing me up. Then I followed her eyes to my green t-shirt—old, faded and one size too small because I'd outgrown it sometime in the last fifteen years since I first bought it, the words *John Deere* written across the chest. Drops of water sprinkled my shoulders from damp hair and I hadn't shaved in two days. What a prize.

I looked back at her between strands of wet hair then brushed them from my face.

"I suppose we should formally introduce ourselves. I'm Joel Powell."

"Eve Whitting." She held out a hand and shook mine with a surprisingly firm grip. Her arm even shook up and down with force. Then she wiped her hands on her pants; they were still covered in ice cream and I eyed them. I couldn't shake the urge to want to suck on her fingers.

"Nice to meet you, Eve," I said instead. I felt a jolt of something move from her fingers to mine when they touched. I ignored it and changed the subject, shoving my hands into my pockets. "So you're here for four months? What happened to Maggie?"

"She's on her honeymoon."

"Yeah, I knew she was getting married. But where are they going for four months?"

"Sailing around the world on Brock's yacht." She dug her spoon and half of her forearm back into the ice cream bucket, twirling a bite of it around her tongue.

"I didn't know he was finished the yacht. Or that it was a yacht." I moved an inch closer while she scooped.

"It's not a yacht exactly. He's always had this dream to go sailing so he bought a boat years ago and has piddled away fixing it up. It was finally ready to take out and he came into his inheritance, which was more than enough to cover four months of frivolous sailing, so they decided to make a huge trip of it."

"I can't see Maggie on a boat for four months."

"I know. But she'll be fine because Brock is there. Romantic, you know."

"You don't sound so sure."

Eve set the spoon down and grinned between bites of ice cream. "I love Maggie to death. And she has met Mr. Wonderful. But it's strange to think of her cooped up on boat. Do you know Maggie well?"

I shrugged. "We've been neighbors for the past two years and I'm away a lot. But I see her around. And your mom stops by frequently."

"I know." She rolled her eyes and I smiled at her carefree attitude.

"You aren't looking forward to the daily visits?"

"Daily?" She actually looked pained. "No. Ugh. I dread just the weekly visits. I hadn't even thought of daily. I am very different from Maggie. And my mother thinks Maggie is a goddess. That leaves me as the unmannered, still single and aging daughter that moved to the city out of spite."

"You moved out of spite?"

"According to my mother I did. Really, it was a preventative move for fear I'd find a man and get married straight out of high school like everyone else. I thought I should escape while I still had a chance, and then find a career and a man that could keep me away from here. Which has worked out *extremely* well. Now I find myself back here without a job *or* a man and my mother lives just a short drive away."

"I see. So you ran away from marriage did you?"

"Yes. That sounds pretty stupid, huh?" She glanced up with an ambivalent smile. "I didn't even have anyone to chase me away. I'm sorry, Joel. I'm talking away about marriage and you're probably married." Her face fell and eyes widened. "Oh my God. You probably have a wife and here I am in her kitchen eating cake and ice cream after dousing her floor with water."

I chuckled at the thought. "No. No wife. I just have two immature friends that like to think they can live here part time."

"Ah. The gawkers. Must be a life of living hell. And I thought there were four of you, not three."

"Just two. The other two of us are completely mature."

"So, what are you renovating?"

"I don't know yet. I didn't have a plan because I didn't expect to start so soon until someone destroyed my carpet." I don't know why I still felt a need to turn the knife a little harder, but it amused me to watch her squirm. Eve didn't seem the type that usually did the squirming, more the one with a tight grip on the knife.

"Right. Well, that someone didn't make you tear it up. It could have been fixed and left a much smaller dent in that person's credit card."

I took a bite of cake and raised my brows with a grin.

"Great. How much do you think it will cost?" she asked with a wince.

"Your decorating advice."

"My what?"

"I have no idea about color schemes and decorating." Which I didn't. No idea. I could start the shit out of a tractor after rebuilding the engine; I've raised barns, fixed toilets, re-shingled a roof or two... tore out a carpet. Decorating has never been my area of expertise and I do not intend to change that.

"And you trust that I have any sense whatsoever about that kind of stuff?"

"Either that, or you'll have to pay someone to come in here."

"Ugh. Fine. When do I start?" She sounded as if this were the lesser of two evils. I would have taken the easy way out and refinanced my house if tables had been turned.

"Now," I said. "We can start now."

"Now? I really don't like the idea of redecorating."

"Why not?"

"Because how do you know if I have a single bone in my body dedicated to interior design?"

"I'll take the chance. It'll be more than mine. And you owe me, remember?"

"I really don't know if I'm up to the task."

"What did you do at your place?"

"My place was my place. I had rats. Rats don't care about floral, plaid or paisley."

I shrugged, giving her only a wide grin and no option out of her predicament.

"Well," she said and walked toward the living room to assess the damages. "You could start by having the floor refinished and polished."

"You wouldn't put new carpet down?"

"Nope," she said and shot me a scowl. "It'll just be ruined the next time someone decides to aim a garden hose through your window."

"So have you heard from the temptress next door?" asked Raif as he unhooked the toe hitch from the tractor. It sat atop a muddy hill, dripping wet but free from the puddle. Nearly two days had passed since our plan to save it; how it hadn't become a permanent fixture in the graveyard was beyond me.

"She came by yesterday evening and she's anything but a temptress." I hauled my ass out of the pool of mud, covered in black to my knees and splattered everywhere else. I brushed an arm across my face and felt more mud streak through my hair and forehead.

"Uh huh. Brazen maybe."

"Yep. I'd say you could definitely call her brazen."

"So what are you doing about the floor?"

"I'm having the hardwood cleaned and polished and ordering in some throw rugs for starters."

"Throw rugs?" Raif stared and I slammed the driver's side door closed on my old truck three times before it latched.

"Yup."

"Who talked you into throw rugs? I thought you'd re-carpet."

"I have Eve convinced she has to help me redecorate. And she is not happy about it," I grinned at the thought of the fun I would have while putting her through hell.

Raif tipped back his head with a chuckle. "You're playing games with her?"

"I need a new floor. I've wanted to do something about it since I moved in, so I figure that if she feels she owes me, I should take advantage of it. And you should have seen her face. She has about a much decorating sense in her as I do and it's eating her that she has to use it."

"There's no way the carpet could be damaged enough to pull up after a morning of flooding."

"I know that and you know that, but Eve doesn't. So she's decorating."

"Not to mention she's not so hard on the eyes."

"And, she's not so hard on the eyes," I grinned. "Besides, it'll be one less thing to worry about the next couple of months while I get the ranch ironed out."

"How are things going, anyway, at the ranch?"

My mother's ranch, the same one my grandfather built, my father worked, I grew up with, went up in flames a month back. It still pained me to think of all we lost. "Well, the fence is almost up and ready to paint. And the new barn's going up in two weeks."

"Is the old one cleaned up from the fire?"

"Almost. We're just clearing out what was left of the old timbers we could salvage."

"Is your mom still looking for a buyer?"

"Yeah. She's found some interest with the land and the house but nothing's panned out. I'm hoping the new barn and fence make a difference."

"Let me know if you need any help."

"We will. Everyone's coming out to bang up the new barn and Mom's putting together a feast with the Ladies Social."

"I'll be there no question if she's cooking."

"Speaking of which, I'm going by for dinner tonight and she asked if you'd come."

"Great. I get to be your date again."

"Yeah, right. She's just itching to get me hitched so she has a woman to invite over for dinner. For now you'll have to do."

"That means when you find the next Mrs. Powell I'm out of home cooked dinners."

"That won't be happening any time soon. It's too busy at the ranch to search for women."

"You don't need to look far. Why don't you bring that spitfire Eve over one night?"

"Yeah right. She'd rip Dale's head off for looking sideways at her and eat my sister alive."

"Your brother-in-law is an idiot. And Dale's too infatuated with your sister anyway to notice another woman. But you're right. She scared the hell out of me yesterday."

# Chapter 3

## *Eve* ♀

Tuesday had come. The day my mother would "drop by" so disaster preparations commenced. I had a sudden urge to find an instant job, an instant man and start having instant children. Too bad you couldn't pop a box in the microwave and BANG! Usually, I didn't let my mother's ideals get to me. But standing in the eye of the hurricane meant I'd be surrounded by the storm of my mother's ideals far more often than I'd like, which made it hard to ignore.

I raced around inspecting the house. It astounded me that in a couple of short days it could look like a windstorm blew through with only me and Stumpy living in it. Maggie would never keep her house like this. It would be spotless, cleaned top to bottom twice a week. But I wasn't Maggie. And maybe if the house were in chaos my mother would focus on that and not on my finding a job, a man and children. Not necessarily in that order. She had, after all, grown desperate.

The house finally tidied, I stood on Joel's porch with a measuring tape outstretched across the bay window, a notepad between my teeth and a pencil stuck over my ear. I had fast shifted into working mode. The quicker I got started, the quicker it would be over.

I leaned across the porch on my hands and knees writing down measurements, balancing ass-in-air. The tape measure kept snapping back, impossible to hold while writing down numbers. I had gnawed the pencil to bits at the end—yellow flakes of paint still stuck in my teeth—after a long half hour of staring and debating over the front window from the porch. I wondered how much longer it would take before I snapped and forgot about this crap. Rebuilding the freakin' living room myself would be easier than designing and decorating it.

# JOEL ♂

"What the hell is she doing?" asked Raif. We sat in the truck staring aghast at the scene on my front porch.

"I have no idea."

"She's sure making herself right at home. You'd about think she moved in."

I stepped out of the truck, once again awed at this phenomenon of a woman. I nearly took back what I said about her having more talent for decorating than I did. But the view was extraordinary. She hunched over, sticking her nicely rounded bottom in the air, one arm outstretched, the other holding something in her hand. And she hadn't seen us pull up in the truck.

Raif stepped out of the passenger side and slammed the door closed. The sound alerted Eve who popped up from behind the porch railing and waved. A hissing noise sounded followed by a snap and a shriek from Eve when the tail end of a measuring tape hit her in the arm and she dropped it to the ground.

Her hair had been blown back to disarray, brown-streaked blonde curls tucked behind one ear and falling into her eyes from behind the other. The wind tossed them and a bright smile shone through the strands as she walked toward us.

"Hey," she said and stumbled over an uneven block in the walkway. She stared us down with those quizzical eyes and I wondered if she had fallen back into her snarkiness, surveying us while she readied a defensive comment. It wasn't until then that I felt the stretch of dried mud pull at my cheek as I smiled and wiped a hand across it. I got the worst of the mess from the looks of Raif who stood spotless except for his hands. But then I, not Raif, had lowered myself into the sinkhole to attach the tow strap and chains to the tractor. His brother-in-law really was a dumb ass.

"What are you doing?" I asked, bringing my attention back to Eve.

"Taking measurements. What the hell happened to you?"

"We pulled a tractor out of the mud. Measurements for what? New windows?"

"No. Not new windows. How did you get a tractor in the mud?"

"I didn't. Raif's brother-in-law did. I got it out. So, what are you measuring if not new windows?"

"What do you use the bay window for?"

"You mean besides for looking out of?"

"Yes. In the alcove there, smart ass."

"Nothing," I said. "I usually stick a beanbag chair in it. Or old newspapers. Or a tool box and work stuff."

"Just like a man," she said and strode back to the porch to peer inside.

I exchanged a confused glance with Raif. "Here we go," I said and walked toward the steps preparing for Eve's tongue lashing. There just had to be one coming.

"What do you think about a window seat?" she asked.

"A window—no. No window seats."

"Why not?"

"Because with window seats come frilly pillows and lace curtains."

"I would never put frilly pillows, even in my house." She rolled her eyes.

"And I wouldn't know that because I don't know who the hell you are, do I? Which makes me wonder why I insisted on you decorating my living room."

"Because I doused it with water and you were trying to trap me into doing the work for you even though we all know that carpet didn't need tearing out in the first place."

Presumptuous thing, she was. And as sexy and edible as she looked in a pair of cutoffs, she was damn annoying. Even though she was right. Raif stifled a laugh and I would have slugged him in the shoulder if she weren't looking.

"You remember Raif," I grumbled.

"Nice to *formally* meet you." She shook his hand with her strong arm, Raif vying for the control of the handshake, and shot him a grin. "I take it you're the other mature one."

"That I am," said Raif. He could charm anyone, did charm most women, with a just a simple grin which Eve would have noticed. Most women noticed Raif because he wasn't your typical townie. Well kept, as close to city for a country boy as you could get without packing up and moving there, Raif seemed to have a knack for acting the sweet and sensitive guy to lure the girls. Sex charmer through and through.

A car drew Eve's attention abruptly away as it pulled up in front of Maggie's house. Her expression changed to an icy glare, the soft curve of her smile evaporating as her lip curled and the look of agony drew across her face. "Oh crap," she muttered.

We all watched as a middle-aged woman, heavy around the hips from many homemade farmer sized meals, and a stare, strong and stubborn and similar to Eve's, parked the car. Strange I hadn't really noticed the resemblance before.

"Hi Mrs. Whitting." I waved as Vivian Whitting stepped out of an old brown sedan.

"Hi Joel. Nice to see you again. And Raif. I see you've met Eve, my *rebellious* daughter. I hope she hasn't been too entertaining since she arrived." She leaned her cheek toward Eve who kissed it reluctantly and withdrew. Eve crossed her arms at her chest and her face turned sour. She shrunk back, her shoulders hunched, suddenly lacking the boldness she'd shown in the past two days.

"Nice to see you, too, Mom," she muttered beneath a pout.

"How have you been Mrs. Whitting?" I asked.

"Just fine, Joel. Maggie's wedding was wonderful. We had a great turnout at the farm for dinner and a regular old barn dance. It's too bad you couldn't make it. Your mom sent your warm wishes. Wasn't the wedding nice, Eve? That's what you get to look forward to one of these days, honey. When you find yourself a man. Except you left early so you missed the end."

"I was there for dinner," she huffed.

"Well, at least you showed up. Unlike at your cousin's wedding where you didn't even make an appearance."

"Mom, that was ten years ago. I was in school writing exams and I couldn't make it. He had the whole freakin' wedding planned last minute anyway." Her accent became thicker as she spoke.

"Honey, don't say freakin'. It sounds trashy."

Eve rolled her eyes. I half expected Eve's spirit to shrivel before us the way her mother carried on. But instead, she just seemed to lose some of her crispness; her shoulders, instead of hunching like a defeated dog, just rounded a bit as her mom flipped out her opinions. It seemed Eve could go full boar with her mom when she had to. Fire raged in those eyes. The flames licked and tempted but out of some kind of respect, she took it. Must be those old country values.

I felt a twinge in my chest; a pang of sympathy or something, I suppose. And respect. Eve had the strength of ten women, probably more than any woman next to my own mother and what, after meeting Eve two days ago.

Mrs. Whitting eyed the rolled up carpet lying across my front porch. The waterlogged stench still clung to the air. "Are you doing some remodeling, Joel?"

"Yeah," I said and glanced at Eve. "Eve has agreed to help me redecorate."

"Well, that will be a sight. I hope you have an open mind, Joel. She is a smart girl but certainly lacks the good taste of her sister."

I imagined Maggie's floral print everything and bit my lip to stop from smirking. "Actually, Mrs. Whitting, she's had great ideas so far. We're measuring for a window seat right now and I'm leaving the choice of rugs to her, too. It's looking better already." I smiled brighter and Eve perked up a little more at the mention of the window seat. There seemed to be no stopping Mrs. Whitting. Funny that in the many times I'd met her before, she left nothing more of an impression than that of a small town farmer's wife. But that had always been in the presence of Maggie. Her *non*-rebellious daughter. Was that a warning I steer clear of this one for my own good? Jesus.

Mrs. Whitting continued. "Well what on earth happened to your carpet in the first place? Far as I knew, this place was only built eight years ago," She eyed the heap on the porch. "I reckon it's not due for remodeling yet."

"I had a flood," I said bluntly.

"Oh," she said, apparently at a loss. "You boys should come for dinner to Eve's. I've brought a casserole."

"Thanks, Mrs. Whitting, but we're going to the farm tonight. And we've already been invited to have dinner at Eve's place tomorrow night." No we hadn't. I held back a laugh.

Eve grit her teeth, forced a smile and nodded. "Right. I'd almost *forgotten* about supper. Good thing you so kindly reminded me, Mr. Powell. Tomorrow night? Is that when I had *invited* you?" asked Eve.

"See you tomorrow, Eve," said Raif. "Thanks for extending the invitation." Raif could never turn down a home cooked meal.

Eve cringed and I reveled in it, keeping the teasing going at her expense. But as her frustration raised so did her spirit. "And Tal and Trey say thanks for the invitation, too. Those are the twelve-year-olds. Remember them? We'll all be there around seven," I called as we walked toward the porch.

"Great!" she called back. "I'll see *y'all* then. The neighborly thing to do, Joel Darlin', would be to bring by some nice wine and dessert," she barked in a thick drawl.

Wine and dessert. Of course.

## EVE ♀

I huffed and turned toward the house, my mother two steps behind me. I should have known Joel's defending me would be laced with payback the moment he said it. I just hadn't expected it in the same conversation.

"Bunch of jackasses." I trudged heavily up the porch stairs.

"What's that?" asked my mother, her Godly ears perking up at the curse. She would probably have heard it if I'd said it to myself.

"Nothing."

"Eve, have you found something to eat since you got here? I doubt Maggie would have left the kitchen dry, but nothing that would spoil, of course, so you probably don't have milk. I hope you bought milk. At least the basics. You at least need the basics."

"I bought a bunch of crap this afternoon, Mom. Thanks. I know how to get groceries."

"I'll put the casserole in the oven for dinner." She didn't take a breath, already fishing through the cupboards to inspect the results of my shopping spree at the One Stop Food Shop. "And don't say crap, Eve."

"I know. It makes me sound trashy."

"It's nice to see Joel is doing so well. After the fire an' all. You've got dishes in the sink."

"What fire?" I asked casually. I sensed a story full of gossip in this one.

"The fire at the ranch. The Powell place. You must have heard. Oh, right," she tsk-ed. "You live in the big city now so you don't hear all the news of this insignificant little town. That's what happens when you're in the big city and you forget all about your family way out here."

I'm in the big city "now"? *Now,* as if I hadn't been gone for over ten years already. "The fire, Mom, what happened?" Redirection was always in order when my poor, pitiful life choices got in the way of conversation.

"Oh, there was a whopper." She filled the sink with sudsy water and started scrubbing the one pot, two dinner plates and a mug. "Took the barn and the two nearest Quonsets to the ground. Everyone got out all right, but poor Amy will never be the same. That's Joel's mother. Amy. Nice enough lady. She joins the Ladies Social every now and again and brings cobbler. It's not as cakey as mine, but it'll do in a pinch. And Joel's father passed on few years back now. The ranch was his baby and Amy will be sad to let it go, if only for the memory of Mr. Powell. At least she has that ranch hand, Henry, or Hank or—I don't recall his name just now—"

"Go where?"

"She's selling. Imagine the cost to repair it and keep it running on her own is too much. Or she's just had enough of the farm life after all these years. She wasn't born to be a farm girl. She's like you, that one. Feisty as anythin' when I first met her years ago. Thought she had a few screws loose. But then the farm life gone and got under her skin like it does everyone around these parts. Except you, Eve. A nice farm boy would do you some good. Maybe straighten up your manners for a start."

The general assumption was, anyone not happy in small town utopia "had a few screws loose".

"How do you do that, Mom?"

"Do what, honey?"

"Bring the conversation back to bashing me."

"Oh, now, I'm not bashing. I love you to bits. I want to see you happy is all. And you can't tell me you're happy out there in God knows where with that Jackson boy. I mean, really, Eve."

"Mom it's *the city*, not *God knows where*." I guess I had dodged the Jackson conversation long enough. Apparently, Mom wasn't aware of our recent detachment and I paused to contemplate how to enlighten her. There never came a bad time to bring up my falling apart life for some good motherly advice; I just avoided it when I could. "And Jackson and I aren't together anymore."

"Good. Hoped as much. He was a bum." She drained the sink and picked up a tea towel.

"Mom!" Now there was a shocker. True, but a shocker coming from my saintly mother who wanted grandchildren at whatever cost. And where the hell is the sympathy when your daughter just lost the love of her life? Okay, not exactly the *love of my life*—enough with the melodramatics—but really.

"Sorry dear. Are you alright after the break up and all?"

"Yeah. Fine. And he was kind of a bum. And I want to say right now that though my life choices seem devastating to everyone else, they were right for me at the time. Even Jackson. And leaving Jackson." She handed me dishes that I set into cupboards while we talked. "And probably, it all comes of my strong bull headed ways, leading me to making choices that don't always turn out perfect. Bull headed and stubborn like you, Mom."

She snorted as she dried off a plate. "You got that from your father."

I just rolled my eyes. No point in arguing.

"Stubborn can be a good thing, Eve."

"Or it can get you into trouble."

"Keep your chin up, chipmunk. You were too good for that man," she said, tousled my hair and planted a firm kiss on my forehead.

"Thanks," I said with a stare of awe.

"Don't act so surprised," she said and waved off the rare moment of nurturing. "The fear of God blew into me I'd have a son-in-law with a last name for a first."

# Chapter 4

## JOEL ♂

I heard pounding at my front door for the second time in three days but this time it had been invited. Still, I hesitated opening it. I hadn't decided if I welcomed dinner with Eve or not. Tal leaned in to peer through the window with a goofy grin plastered across his face and Trey followed, wearing his tattered cowboy hat pulled down low over his brow, peace sign glistening in the sunlight. What a pair. But as much as I complain, they're good guys, just full of hormones and an attitude that hadn't yet matured, likely never would.

Why I maneuvered an invite for these two I'll never know. Yeah I would. Another bee in Eve's bonnet and the damn window seat was reason enough. And don't forget the frilly pillows that, though she denied it, would eventually make their way into my house. Not all was lost. It wasn't as if she had moved in.

"Tell me Joel, are you serious about going for dinner next door, or just pulling our leg?" asked Tal.

"Serious. Did you bring wine?"

"Yep. Well, not wine exactly."

"What does "not wine exactly" mean?"

"They were out of the box kind. Sawyers were havin' a dinner party thing and bought up the last five boxes. Too bad. They were dirt-cheap. So I bought this stuff and a case of beer just in case." He lifted a bottle out of a brown paper bag. Even Trey lifted his eyebrows in mild disgust.

I just took the bottle and heaved a sigh. "Cooking sherry?"

"It was the best I could come up with. There were a few bottles of that crap wine from France, but I figure if you can't read the language it must be shitty. And it was dusty an' all. I ain't paying that kind of money for dust."

"France would have been better. Bring the beer. I only hope Eve prefers beer to cooking sherry."

I lifted a large canvass bag—the same one Eve had carried over with cake and ice cream two days before—and made my way toward the door.

"What's in there?" asked Trey, eyeing the canvas bag and sniffing at the air.

"Pie."

"What kind?"

"Paws off," I said and knocked Trey's hand away. "They're apple pies from the ranch."

"Ooh. Your mom made pie."

"Yeah, and you don't deserve any for buying cooking sherry."

"I didn't buy it. Tal did."

"Were you there?"

"Yeah."

"Did you stop him?"

"No," he huffed.

"Then you don't deserve any either, but Eve will probably be nice and share with everyone. If you're lucky."

We found Raif standing on the front porch when we traipsed outside.

"You didn't want to go over without us?" I asked him.

"Are you kidding? I value my life," said Raif.

"She's not that bad." I made my way down the walk with Raif and Trey. Tal stayed behind and climbed up on the porch rail, balancing both feet on the edge facing Eve's place, arms out like a lanky totem pole at his sides.

I peered through the living room window and rapped on her door. Eve answered and the smell of roast beef and gravy wafted toward us.

"Hi," I said, feeling a twinge of hunger roll through my stomach. And a twinge of something else below the belt. A hot woman and a home cooked meal meant absolute heaven in my books. "We're here."

"I see that. Come on in," she said. A loud bang sounded on the front porch and we all turned to see Tal stumble after jumping from my porch to Maggie's. I shot him a grin. Eve just rolled her eyes and walked inside.

"Thanks for the invitation," I said.

"No problem whatsoever, gentlemen. And I say that lightly. I'm just doing my part to be neighborly. I managed to throw a dinner together between all of the unpacking and setting up the place, like I had nothing better to do than make a couple of immature men some dinner. Hi Raif," she said as he closed the door behind him.

"Hi. Smells good."

"Thanks. And you two must be Tal and Trey," said Eve, staring at the two bozo's ogling her from the doorway.

"Sorry, I forgot introductions," I said. "This is Eve. My new neighbor. Eve, meet Tal and Trey."

"Nice to meet you," said Tal. He ogled Eve some more, this time with an obvious sleazy grin which I would guess wasn't the best idea based on past experience.

"Eyes up front, buddy," she said. "I still have that hose hooked up in the yard and I'm not afraid to turn it on you." A drawling fluctuation came through in her voice that made my insides melt.

Tal's eyes shot up to her face and he took a step backward into Trey who didn't dare continue his glance down Eve's slender body.

She wore a striped blouse, the top few buttons open to expose enough cleavage to be sexy and classy at the same time, the rest of it fit the length of her to her waist; a pair of jeans began just below her belly button, followed her curves the rest of the way; curves in all the right places—wide hips, nice breasts, tiny waist between. I managed to notice without the obvious ogling. So did Raif. Tal and Trey attempted their best behavior, which finished below acceptable in most women's books, just not the women these two hung out with.

"Make yourselves at home. What does everyone want to drink?" Eve called from the kitchen.

"We brought drinks," said Tal. He made a move to step into the kitchen then stopped, overcome by an obvious fear of God—or Eve—and instead set them on the floor in the hall.

I set the canvas bag on the counter next to a pile of dishes and glanced over the rest of the counter top. Chunks of mashed potatoes and splashes of gravy dotted the surface, what could have been every pot and pan available trembled on hot burners or filled the sink as part of a communal heap. Something still steamed and might have been burning a hole through an old potholder on one end while smoke filled the air from the oven.

"Excuse the mess. I can cook a half-decent meal but I suck at clean up. I'm not overly organized. Especially on short notice," she scowled at me to drive the point home and let the oven door slam closed after wafting the smoke from her face with an oven mitt. "What's in the bag?"

"Dessert. From the ranch. My mom did some baking."

"Oh? My mom told me about the fire at the ranch. I hope everyone was all right."

"Yeah. It was a month ago now. Clean up is almost done and we're nearly ready to start rebuilding."

"I thought she was going to sell."

"She is. But no one wants to buy a ranch with no where to house the horses."

"I guess not. Joel, why don't you run the ranch, or someone in the family?"

"Just didn't work out that way. I don't have that kind of money, not yet, and there is no other family that would. So, what are we having?" I asked to change the subject. I wasn't comfortable reliving the ranch fire or my complicated circumstances as to why I couldn't buy it myself.

"Roast beef, potatoes, veggies…the usual stuff." She leaned over a stockpot on the stove to mash potatoes.

"Can I help with anything?"

"You can serve drinks if you want. Everything else in here is under control." We both eyed the disaster zone from counter to floor. "Okay, so wrong choice of words."

"Where do you keep the glasses?" I smiled—couldn't help but smile—and reached toward the cupboard she motioned to.

"I think they're in there. I'm still getting used to where everything is." She reached to open the door and my arm brushed across her shoulder. Both of us stilled and I took a step back.

"I'll get the drinks." I had smelled her hair. A sharp pain lurched in my chest which I think was similar to the twinge in my pants earlier. And damn, she smelled like strawberries. Had it really been so long since I'd stood so close to a woman that I went to mush at one inhale?

We exchanged a glance over the beer can as I cracked it and rested a gaze on the bottle of sherry.

"Is that your interpretation of wine?" she asked.

"This is Tal's interpretation of wine. I don't drink wine. So you're stuck with cooking sherry or beer."

"Beer is fine. Thanks."

Raif appeared in the doorway. "Can I do something?" he asked.

"Joel's getting the drinks but I forgot to set the table. You can do that." Eve eyed the table set with two placemats and a vase of artificial flowers. There wasn't room for a roast dinner, much less five adults to sit around it. "And pull out the table. There's probably a leaf somewhere." She moved toward the table and leaned over to look for a leaf beneath it. "Actually, I have no idea if there is one or where it would be. We might be eating on the floor."

"I'm on it," said Raif and he left in search of a quick table fix.

"So, how is your mother?" I asked when we were alone again. While thoughts of strawberries and Eve's curvy hips flashed through my mind, so did her short fuse and how easily it was set off. I supposed a sly grin attached to a little idle chitchat about her mother might set her off, but I shot her one anyway. At least it would keep my mind from the strawberries.

Eve shook her head with a grimace, then a chuckle. "Thanks for mentioning it. And she is just peachy keen fine. Up to her usual insults and jabs implied with an I-meant-nothing-by-it tone. I guess I should thank you for saving my ass yesterday, even though it meant inviting yourselves to dinner. My mother isn't always tactful when it comes to me."

"I figured as much." I helped her fill serving dishes with food. We stood close next to the counter and our arms brushed against one another setting off more sensations I tried to avoid.

"She gets along real well with Maggie, but then Maggie is a townie. I'm the daughter that avoids family like the plague."

"So you aren't planning to move back permanently anytime soon, then?"

"No. It will stay temporary. It was supposed to be a relaxing break from the city but now I'm hoping it'll be a fast four months."

"And then back to the big city where you can forget about this wee little town."

"I see you have the bug, too," she grinned with raised brows.

"What bug?"

"Everyone from this town thinks there's no life *outside* of this town and that everyone who doesn't live here is living beyond the outer walls of utopia."

"It is a pretty great place. But I'd rather not live here either."

"Where would you live? I hate to say it Joel, but I doubt you'd make it in the city."

"Not the city. On a farm or ranch not far from here."

"That doesn't count. That's still like town."

"No it's not. It's peaceful and quiet and your own space."

"Well, I had plenty of my own space in the city."

"Uh huh. Space like a huge back yard, land, trees—"

"No, not that kind of space. Enough space."

"I bet there isn't quiet in the city."

"There's enough. I'm not used to this quiet. It gets ghostly quiet sometimes. It's creepy."

"What's creepy?" asked Trey, sauntering into the kitchen. I tossed him a can of beer and he cracked it open. He adjusted his cowboy hat up, then down again over his forehead.

"Eve thinks the town is creepy," I explained.

"I never said that."

"It is creepy," said Trey.

"See, I'm not the only one that feels out of place here," said Eve.

Oh, let's just see where this conversation goes, shall we? I turned my back to lean on the counter and sipped my beer like a nice neighbor.

"I'd like to move to the city," he said. "One day."

"You've said that for the last seven years since you were out of high school, Trey," I cut in then went back to sipping.

"How old are you Trey?" asked Eve, watching him from her pot of potatoes.

"Twenty seven. Almost twenty eight."

"Then why wait? When is there a better time?"

"I don't know. I should. I have plans, you know." He shot me a glare.

"What kind of plans?" she asked.

"I thought I might go back to school. Learn somethin'."

"Like what?"

"It's stupid." Trey pushed his hat lower on his forehead.

"Nothing's stupid," Eve tilted her head to the side, a very small movement but one that came from a natural empathy and kindness.

"I want to learn how to build stuff. I'm good with my hands."

"So, construction?"

"No. Motorbikes. I saw these guys on TV called the Tuttles. Have you heard of them?"

"Yeah. American Chopper, right? Very cool stuff."

"They build choppers and take 'em out on the open road. And I've worked with Joel some so I know a bit about mechanics."

"Bikes. That's not so stupid. It's something. And something is better than doing nothing about your dreams." She went back to the dinner on the counter, muttering to herself, having half her own conversation. "Or else you'll just get stuck where you don't want to be, in a place where you aren't happy. Then you lose track of what your dreams even are and you live some life that you thought you should be living when you're really only there because it's comfortable. Not that comfortable is *bad*, but come on. A person can only do comfortable for so long."

"Prob'ly," said Trey and swigged back a gulp of beer. He'd already forgotten about city life as we watched Eve mash the hell out of those potatoes.

We served our own plates from pots and dishes that lined the stove and countertop, some still bubbling and the burning smell hadn't gone but we appreciated the home cooked meal. Raif hadn't come up with the table leaf or any better option so we moved the table-for-two out of the way and huddled around on cushions on the kitchen floor, eating from our laps. It lent a cozy, bachelor feel. A small part of her mother must have rubbed off on her somewhere down the line because Eve turned out to be a pretty good cook and hostess in the end.

I lay back, propped up on one elbow and observed the odd group around me. I marveled on first sight of this woman and how she might fit in with our bunch, but she did. Watching her now, laughing with her mouth full of food when Trey told his stupid jokes, had me smiling. No one got Trey. Not *really* got him. And it egged him on the more she laughed.

Tal updated us on his latest conquest; always a good story but I can't keep track of the women at the best of times. I didn't exactly have many "women stories" myself to tell these days.

Raif acted his usual sweet and sensitive self as he does in the presence of women, the last of us to slip into real-guy conversation. Raif is the expert at how to treat a lady, whatever capacity that came in.

Eve gulped back the last of her beer and slouched into the cushion on the floor.

"Thank you for dinner," I said, catching and holding Eve's eyes. "It was good."

"You're welcome." She grinned back from behind her bottle of beer. "Just don't expect a neighborly dinner too often. Unless you're cooking. I'm worn right out after spending a couple of hours in the kitchen and won't be doing that for a long time."

"More time than I've spent in a kitchen in my whole life," said Tal.

"More time than you spend out of bed everyday," muttered Raif.

"Piss off. I work. Sometimes."

"Does "sometimes" pay the bills?"

"Almost. Pays most bills. Sometimes."

"Well, it was nice to have the company. The wedding was a nightmare." Eve rolled her eyes and I could tell she felt more at home on the floor with a bunch of small town boys than at her sister's frilly wedding just by the glimmer behind her eyes.

"The reception was at your mom's house?" I asked.

"Yeah. How come you guys weren't all there? I thought the whole town came out for these things."

"Not the whole town. Unless it's big news."

"I was there. For the wedding, at least. With my sister, Lacey," said Raif.

47

"I don't remember seeing you. But I mostly just kept my eyes trained on the floor or hid out in the backyard. It was easier that way," said Eve.

"Come on, this ol' town is charming," I teased and shone her a grin. She grinned back. Eve's smile oozed sugary sweet and feisty all at once.

"Yeah. Charming," said Eve. "Is that what you call it? Do you know how many people were trying to figure out what I was doing there until the conversation quickly jumped to *oh my God, that's not Maggie's big sister, is it? The one that beat up my Timmy at age eight…the one that left town for the city…is she back? When did she get back? Is she staying?*"

"Yeah," said Raif. "I heard a few of those."

"And yet, here you are. To stay," I said to Eve and leaned back against the cushion with my feet outstretched.

"Not permanently. Just a three or four month sentence."

"It's not really that bad," said Raif.

"No. Not exactly. But I have this daunting feeling it will get much worse before my time is up."

"It just might," said Trey. "At least you know us, now, so all is saved." He winked at her, tipped the battered straw cowboy hat up, and back down on his head.

"My greatest of appreciation granted, oh great knights," she laughed. "At least I can take comfort that I will never have to take on this whole town by myself."

"Not the whole town. Maybe some of it," I said.

"Thanks for the confidence, Joel."

"Well, if you had to, I'm sure you'd manage. But you haven't met Lacey yet."

"What's wrong with Raif's sister?"

"Nothing at all," I grinned and hid behind my beer.

"Lace likes to think she's Queen 'round these parts," said Raif. "You might have stepped into her turf and she won't like it depending on how much noise you make."

"If you sit back in the sidelines, you'll be fine," I said.

"I'm not here to hone in on anyone's turf. But I've never been good at keeping quiet and out of everyone's way. I have a habit of making a bad name for myself. Just never on purpose."

"So, what are you going to do while you're here?" asked Trey.

"I haven't figured that out yet. I've saved some money for a house in the city that I never bought and won't for a long time now, so I'm going to live meagerly off of that for the time being then invest the rest. Or spend it all on shopping," she grinned.

"On shopping?" I winced.

"Invest?" winced Trey.

And Eve asked, "Why not?"

"Not very exciting," Trey said and let out a low whistle.

"Shopping's too frivolous. And why aren't you buying a house anymore?" I asked.

"Because that plan fell through when I broke up with Jackson."

"Tell us about Jackson. Boyfriend?" asked Tal.

"Ex boyfriend. Ex loser and I don't want to talk about it."

"Alright. So why not still buy a house for yourself?" I asked.

"I will. One day. Maybe I'm not so sure where I want to settle just yet. Like what if I want to stay on Vine Street and make a little home near Maggie," she said. And for a minute, I believed her. "We could have matching kitchen curtains and I could get some nice floral print sofas…and get a dog with two legs, one eye and no hair."

"Why a dog with two legs?" I asked.

"Maggie already has the broken cat with one eye and no sense of direction or balance. They could be friends and then Stumpy wouldn't feel so bad."

"He's not that bad," I said.

"Stumpy? Have you met Stumpy?"

"I've seen him around outside."

"Outside there's not so much to crash into. Let's get him. I'll show you," she laughed and stood up. Eve wandered around the house whistling and clapping her hands in search of the morbid sounding cat. A minute later, a huge black and orange ball of fur came tearing around the corner and smashed into the wall with a bang. He rubbed up against Trey's leg, gained some attention and made rounds to the rest of us in turn, purring louder than the old Chevy in back of my shop.

"Wow. That's some cat," I laughed.

"Cute, isn't he? He's kinda like me. A bit of an outcast. Stumpy and me are going to stick together." She sat back on the floor and scooped him into her arms.

"So, you're a cat person," said Raif.

"Not before Stumpy here, but he kind of grows on a girl," she grinned. "And he's nice. Clumsy, but nice. At least he helped me with the boxes when I moved in." That earned us another scowl.

# Chapter 5

## Eve ♀

I sat on the front porch tying my shoelaces and squinting the sun from my eyes. The morning had begun with a warm breeze, refreshing, and damn it but I found myself enjoying the quiet of the street. I could actually hear birds chirp instead of the odd sound of unidentifiable nature muffled by the noise of morning traffic, blowing horns and blaring music.

"Good morning," I heard from next door. Joel stretched in an old willow branch chair with his feet propped up on the railing of the porch, elbows resting on the chair arms. There must have been a sale because Maggie had the same kind of chair on her porch and it was freaking uncomfortable.

"Good morning," I said and smiled in his direction.

His eyes sparkled in the light, his grin shone. He looked so relaxed, feet outstretched with a mug of coffee cupped in both hands. His damp hair flicked in the light breeze. "You're up early," he said.

"Not that early. It's already nine thirty in the morning. I thought we'd get a head start and beat the rush at the hardware store, get a start on that living room of yours."

"How long did you say you've been away from town?" he chuckled.

"Why?"

"The hardware store never has a rush. And they don't open until noon. It's the weekend. We're lucky they're open at all today."

"I forgot small towns died on the weekend."

"They don't die. Just, those that do open don't open until later."

"What about Sunday? I suppose everything's closed Sunday."

"Yep. It would be sacrilege to be open on Sunday. Except the bakery that Arnie runs and he goes to service on Saturday night instead of Sunday morning."

"There's a Saturday service now? In this small town?"

"Yep. Arnie stays open Sunday to bake for the churchgoers and the "Good Reverend Love-Joy". They made an arrangement years ago. This way, the Reverend can get his Sunday morning coffee fix and the Ladies Auxiliary can get baked goods at a discount for the after service social."

"Really." I smirked.

"It's a win-win situation for God and business." He waggled his brows.

"Right." Joel was brilliant, I decided. A smart-ass, but brilliant nonetheless. "I forgot all about church. Suppose my mother will drag my ass there for penance tomorrow. I'm sure I have a lot of catching up to do."

"Oh, well. Not everyone's perfect. And all will be forgiven."

"So, are you serious or just mocking me? Because either way, you're probably going to hell for that one."

"I should go with you to church tomorrow, then, and give my penance."

"Do you usually go to church?"

"Only since the fire. I go to church with Mom and I can't very well stand outside. Besides, it's nice."

"I don't mind the church part. I'm sure it is nice. It's the listening to my mother part that I have trouble with."

"Wasn't it you who used to get kicked out of Sunday school every two or three weeks?"

"Yes. You remember that?"

"How could anyone forget that fiery temper?"

"Well, the temper hasn't changed, so watch yourself buddy."

A huge smile drew across his face and his eyes glanced over me again. All of me. And I shivered, a bit of the fire turning my insides to molten liquid.

"I will. So, do you want a coffee while we wait for the store to open? Then we can get there a few minutes ahead. To avoid the rush."

"Shut up," I mumbled and tromped across his front lawn toward the porch stairs.

Joel went inside and I sat into the oversized willow chair. Then shifted to find a spot where branches didn't stick into my ass.

"Cream and sugar?" he yelled from inside the house.

"Cream and one sugar," I called back. He returned with two cups of coffee and sunk into the enormous chair next to me. I slouched comfortably into it with my mug cradled in my hands much the way a person would cradle a precious treasure. I soaked in the feel of the warm mug, steam rising to my face, the aroma of fresh brewed coffee beans mingling with cream. Absolute heaven.

"Have you run into anyone around town?" asked Joel.

"Not yet. I only recognized a few people at Maggie's wedding and did my best at avoidance. But I never made friends as a kid to hang onto long enough and beat up the ones I had." I shone him a smirk and he laughed. "We lived on a farm west of here and I avoided coming in whenever possible. Only since Maggie moved into town have I returned to visit. And not often. It's amazing how foreign your own home can feel."

"I know what you mean."

"You find it foreign here?"

"Yeah. I'd rather be out at the ranch."

"So why aren't you there?"

"Because we're selling the ranch."

"Why are you really selling the ranch, Joel?" I asked. It may have sounded like prying but truthfully, I had a keen interest in what Joel had to say.

He grinned and looked away toward the road, shifting his eyes around aimlessly. He took a breath then spoke in a low tone. "The fire destroyed the barn with some of the horses and an arena and everything in between. I had to convince my mom to let me rebuild at all but she won't hear of staying. She's done with ranching."

"Where will you go?"

"Nowhere I guess. Just stay here."

"But you don't want Vine Street. You said so yourself."

"Sometimes grand ideals are hindered by real life."

"But the ranching's in the blood, huh?"

"I guess so."

"Why not buy your mom's place?"

"Maybe one day. So what are you going to do when your four month sentence is up?"

"I assumed I'd go back to the city but I have no idea where. That all depends on what job I can get. I only have so much money saved and it's supposed to last me until I get back to find one."

"So you've been planning a while for this trip here?"

"Not really. I had money saved up for a big house and a potential marriage. High ideals."

"Oh yes. Jackson."

"And you're getting into harsh terrain. Subject change."

"Okay. What color did you have in mind for my living room, oh *wise designer*?"

"I was thinking red."

"Red?"

"Not tomato red. More a deep, blood red. What would you paint it? You're the one living there."

"I don't know. I was thinking white. It's neutral."

"And it shows the dirt and it's not trendy."

"And you know what's trendy."

"I know white isn't."

"I like green. You know what, I think we should stick to the color that's already there so I don't have to fuss over matching anything else to the rest of the house."

"We could do that. Do you know what color it is now?"

"Yeah, off white."

"There are probably at least twenty shades of white and off white. You're still looking at painting everything if we can't match it. And there's the dirt."

"It'll be close enough."

"Close enough?"

"For me, it'll be close enough." And he gave me a look.

We both turned to hear a loud rattle then a bang from a car that pulled up on the road in front of the house; a rusted out El Camino

54

and Trey slid out of one side through the window Duke's of Hazard style.

El Camino: Not quite a car, not quite a truck. Trey: Not quite a city slicker, not quite a cowboy.

"Hey!" he called and started up the walk.

"Mornin'," said Joel. He didn't get up.

"What's up?"

"Nothing so far."

"Hey Eve," said Trey and he gave me a hesitant nod.

"Good morning, Trey."

"Thanks for dinner last night."

"No problem."

"Joel, you need a hand at the ranch today?" he asked and tipped his hat forward on his head.

"I'm going over later on and I can always use a hand. And I need you around next weekend."

"Sure thing. Your mom cookin' dinner tonight?"

"Yep."

"Count me in."

"We're headed to the hardware store at noon and I'll be back before one if you want to hang out here until then," said Joel.

"Sure. Tal's comin' by sometime this afternoon. I'll call him from here and get him here sooner if you need the extra hands."

"I wouldn't mind. Raif's meeting us there. We can crash here later if you want. Get some beer."

"Sounds good. You coming, Eve?" asked Trey after a pregnant pause.

"What? Where?"

"For drinks later," he said.

"I don't know, I—"

"You're welcome anytime."

"Well, it's Joel's place. I'm not just inviting myself over."

"Everyone invites themselves over. Get used to it," said Joel with a grin. "I don't mind. And Trey's invitation counts as much as mine does."

Trey didn't answer or acknowledge the comment, just leaned back against the porch railing and got comfortable on the step.

"Okay. Sure." Trey caught me off guard. What business Trey had to live at Joel's house when he felt like it I didn't know. It must be some townie thing. But I'd be hangin' with the boys tonight. Mom would just *love* this.

The line at Griswell's Hardware was short. Actually, non-existent. Joel chuckled and I slugged him in the shoulder.

"Ow!"

I hate being wrong. "Listen. I've been out of this town for a long time. Yes, it's been a harsh reality coming back. Yes, I have changed while everything here has stayed almost the same. And, yes, Joel, there is no rush to get into Griswell's on a Saturday. You win."

"Hey. I was just joking around. Jeez, you're awfully bitchy all of a sudden."

"And you're looking for another welt on your shoulder." I couldn't hold back the smile any longer. But I liked that you could spar with Joel.

He held his hands up in the air. "You win. No more cracks about the store. Or the line-ups. Or getting up before dawn to beat everyone and their dog downtown for the best spot in line…"

"Joel!"

"Okay, okay. Where to first?"

I pulled a shopping cart out of the long line of *five of them*—total, as in, for the entire store—and started truckin' it down the nail aisle.

## JOEL ♂

"We need stuff for floor boards. And paint. Let's start with the floorboards." I grabbed a paper bag and started filling it with handfuls of nails.

"Don't you need to count and figure out how many boards per room and per wall, and how many nails per board or square foot or something?"

I just gave her a look.

"What?"

"I figure a few nails per every few feet, between eight and twenty feet per wall, depending on the wall—gives me about…I don't know…a few handfuls of nails." I shot her one of her own classic eye rolls.

"Right. Good measuring, Tex."

"Don't call me Tex."

"I should call you Tex. Tex. The name suits you, cowboy. You and your handfuls of nails."

"Are you done?"

"Yep. Tex."

"Jesus," I said beneath my breath. And a smile. I tossed the bag of nails into the cart and took the cart from Eve. "Now we need floor boards." I pulled a piece of paper out of my jacket pocket and started calculating the numbered measurements in my head.

"So you did measure," said Eve.

"Yeah. You can grab handfuls of nails. Not floorboards. Floorboards you have to measure."

"Thank God. I thought I'd be in there piecing together odds and ends to tack up on the walls. With your handfuls of nails."

"You won't be doing all the work anyway. You're just here for decorating advice."

"Why? I could be very useful doing handy work. Probably more useful than with my decorating advice. I had warned you about that in the first place. And I know how to use a nail gun."

"Right. Well, you aren't using mine."

"Why not?" she shrieked, making a scene. It didn't take much to get Eve going. I grinned and she punched me in the shoulder again.

"Hey! Stop that."

"You deserved it. Again."

"Alright. Let's just get paint and call it a day. You're getting dangerous."

"Fine. What color?"

"I brought a chip from the wall so we could match the cream that's already on there." I pulled it out of my pocket.

"I've been thinking that maybe you should go with a whole different color after all. Brighten the place up. The cream is kind of boring. I mean—"

"Eve," I warned.

"Okay, okay. Cream it is. Because you know best."

By the time I finished shopping with Eve and spent a day at the ranch with the guys, our bellies full of Mom's home cooking, I could have keeled over. Trey and Tal were off for a beer run, Raif to shower and change. The time alone lent too many hours to brood so my mind switched focus immediately to the barn.

Selling the ranch was the last thing I wanted. I grew up there. It was home...more than just home. Yeah, there were memories in the place all the way back to childhood; I know my sister Janet would be heartbroken to leave those behind. But you can make new memories. I just hated that the ranching life would be gone. It's what I knew, what my dad knew, my grandfather knew. Mom was a different story, though, and she didn't want to do it anymore. I couldn't blame her. And if I could bail her out, I would.

I wanted to put everything I owned into the ranch. It would fix everything. But the money wasn't there; not enough to keep the ranch functioning, anyway. Before the fire, that had been the plan and I could have made it work, even if things were tight for the first while.

But there was another roadblock. My ex-wife Meg.

We were high school sweet hearts and married after senior year. She left six years ago, we divorced after only four months separation and things haven't been the same since in the romance department. But they weren't great through most of my marriage either. Meg had a lot of shit to work out in her life and having a husband around proved to be more of a hindrance than she'd expected. Our breaking point had been Dan, a guy eight years older that looked the part of a drug lord out of a Hollywood movie. He moved in sometime before I moved out.

I remember the day I began to see Meg as a stranger. About a week before I found her in bed with Dan, getting high. Along with Dan came Meg's ever growing drug problem, rehab and, as a result of trying to straighten herself out, a new life. New apartment, new car, new job. All of which I financed and still do. I know, what idiot would take care of his ex when all she's done is cause trouble and heartache? And I wouldn't. Not for any reason except that she has no one else to yank her boots up and her existence is crucial to the life and upbringing of our son, Damian.

We didn't have kids through the marriage because Meg didn't want them. Then four years ago, we got together to try and make the relationship work. It didn't. But it turned out to be the best mistake of my life. She called a year later to say I was a father, so I was a father. Just like that. Not the way I would have planned things, but I now had a three-year-old son that I see as much as I can on a fluctuating schedule depending what crisis Meg is into at the time.

So everything I do is for Damian. The house, the money, the visits. The ranch.

Tonight, I only had one problem: staying awake long enough to have a beer with the guys. And Eve. I still didn't know what to think of her. I've enjoyed the view with her as a neighbor, but I've never met a woman as strong willed and—well, she's still a tomboy to the soul even with that deep curve to her hips. I felt torn between wanting to slap her on the shoulder like a dude and wanting to grope her.

Raif and I had shoved the TV up against the far wall. Two black beanbag chairs and the tattered old sofa cramped around it in the corner while the rest of the room stayed bare from the ceiling down to the floor tacks that I still hadn't removed. A noticeable draft wafted in and out of the front room since the carpet had come out and an echo had settled after emptying it of furniture. Still, everyone wanted to gather here. It was beyond me what they were thinking, but this had always been the hang out spot, meeting place, game room, drinking hole. Unless we were adventurous enough to head down to the local pub.

The door opened and a familiar whistle echoed through the empty living room, meaning Trey had arrived. He entered the room wearing a smile and his tattered hat. "Hey Powell."

"Trey."

"You look like shit."

"I feel like shit."

"I guess when you get old you can't do much anymore, huh?"

"Wiseass."

"Wait 'til you get a few beers into ya. You'll be sleeping like a baby." He scanned the room and walked toward the television. "Done some rearranging."

"Kind of. The carpet came out and I'm working on the floor."

"Ah. The work of Eve and her garden hose." He cracked a beer and tossed me one from the box at his feet.

"Yep. It needed some work anyway. Where's Tal?"

"He's coming. He says he might be late. I dropped him off to meet up with the new girl at the Grub 'n' Grill." Trey winked.

"When did he start dating again after Cammy? I thought she was the one who "broke his heart in a thousand pieces"?"

"That ended a week ago, Joel. Time to move on."

"After a whole week. Must have been rough."

"You know Tal. Where's Raif?"

"Coming. Went home to shower and grab a deck of cards."

"What happened to yours?"

"Destroyed in the flood."

"Ah. Like the carpet."

A rap sounded on the door then it whined on its hinges and banged against the wall. "Hey!" yelled Raif.

"Hey!" we both called back.

"We still up for poker?"

"Sure. Couple of rounds. Then I'm crashing," I said. "And Eve's coming."

"Eve?"

"Trey invited her." I slapped him on the back hard between the shoulder blades.

"She was standing right there," he argued.

"Very neighborly, Trey. We still playing then?" asked Raif.

"Why not? She can watch. Or deal," I said with a chuckle, which I regretted a second later. The door whined again and Eve stood in the doorway with another of her sour faces.

"I could always leave you boys alone. I only came by to amuse you, since you all look so unfamiliar to the domain of women."

"We are not," protested Trey. "I'm very familiar in that domain."

"You don't even know what a domain is, Trey," said Raif.

"Maybe Eve can show you, she's so eager to amuse us," I said. That earned me another scowl and an eye roll as she made herself at home, ripped open a bag of nachos and slumped into a beanbag chair.

"Shut up, Joel. So, you guys'r playing poker?" she asked.

"Yeah. I suppose you know how to play and will kick our asses."

"No, actually I don't. I could learn, though."

"And you think we'll teach you?" I asked with a smirk. She annoyed so easily.

"Why not?"

"I had to buy in double to learn," said Trey.

"Why?"

"Beginners initiation," said Raif.

"Really," she said with a scowl and shoved another chip into her mouth. She stared around the room, contemplating everyone for a moment, then stood and reached into her pocket to pull out a wad of bills. "How much?"

"We start at fifty cents small blind, a buck for the big—that's one and two for you—then start doubling as the pot grows—five for the big blind is ten to you, darlin'."

"Okay, I get the double everything for me. You lost me on the rest."

"This is going to be an easy win," muttered Trey.

"Yeah, you sucked your first round, Trey. And give her a break Powell, she's a girl," said Raif. This had been the biggest mistake yet. Eve stomped toward him and pushed twelve dollars into the palm of Raif's hand. "I can play the same stakes as the rest of you, jackass. Don't do me any favors."

"Alright, alright."

"Eve," I said, drawing her attention away. "You don't put it in all at once, sunshine."

She grabbed the money back, stuffed it into the pocket of her jeans and stuck out her tongue.

# Chapter 6

## *Eve* ♀

So I suck at poker. I lost twenty-two bucks after two rounds—which, apparently, are called *hands*—and lost track of everything else somewhere along the line, even though I thought I was catching on. I still haven't figured out much about the cards but learned a few things about the men around the table.

First: Raif is a great poker player and I wouldn't want him sitting at my table in Reno.

Second: Trey is more on my level, except that he actually understands what a Royal Flush is and when to bet, raise and fold. (By the way, I have a firm grip on poker terminology, just not how or when to use it.)

Third: A set of pairs doesn't ever beat a straight and that it doesn't matter if the King and Queen are happily married or why the clubs are called clubs and not clovers, even though I've eaten a thousand boxes of Lucky Charms in my lifetime to know a clover is a clover is a clover.

And Joel is a cocky son of a bitch when he plays poker.

But I have a plan so I will sleep well tonight. I'll be joining them from now on, even if just to sit back and watch. Once I've absorbed their masses of manly brainpower I can swindle them all out of their money and laugh my ass right out the front door.

I've never been a good loser.

I don't know what I did in my younger life to deserve the kind of payback coming to me, but it must have been something big and payback usually came in the form of my mother. Don't get me wrong. I love my mother and I know she loves me, deep down somewhere, and I keep telling myself that her obsession with my life is her way of making me into a better person.

She actually appeared on my doorstep this morning, talking to the neighbor across the railing of the veranda. And yes, that neighbor happened to be Joel Powell. So there my mother stood, leaning a sturdy hip on the railing, beaming a smile and questioning Joel about his mother and the fire. Nothing could satiate my mother's gossip circle.

I walked out the front door in my housecoat and slept-on hair. Make-up smudged across my face as usual because I don't follow "proper beauty technique" and remove it with puff pads doused in alcohol-laced remover every night before applying a thick layer of mud. I rinse mine off with water and a bar of soap after my morning coffee.

*If* I planned to go out that day.

Sometimes not.

I imagine my face looked scowling and puffy today, too, after sleeping only…what had it been? Five hours?

Joel stood on the steps to his front porch wearing a beat up jean jacket and khaki pants with a button up shirt—a pleasant surprise—and he wore his hair slicked back instead of the usual comb-your-hand-through-it-wet style. I couldn't help but notice the grease stains in the jacket, reminiscent of the black lines in his hands and under his nails that I had seen from across the poker table last night. Really, I wasn't trying to cheat and look at his cards. (Maybe just a little cheating.) And a lot fascinated by his hands and the arms attached to them…the shoulders, chest, neck. The face attached to those.

"Morning," he said when he saw me standing in the doorway. I waved and cringed a smile.

"Honey!" called my mother. "I came by to pick you up for church. I was right in assuming you wouldn't want to go alone wasn't I? Or do you usually go at all? Prob'ly you don't which would explain the housecoat. You're not even ready. We have a lot of work to do."

"I don't have any dress up clothes with me, Mom."

"You can borrow something of Maggie's. She has lots of floral print sun dresses that would look stunning on you."

Not so sure stunning best described floral print anything, but Joel laughed his ass off, waved and walked to the back of his house.

"Eve, I'll help you change. We have a few extra minutes. Thank the good Lord in heaven I done come by a bit early."

"Sure. Great." My mother had already walked half way toward Maggie's closet and fear ripped through me within seconds of her reaching it. I had already seen Maggie's "dress clothes" and once again found myself weighing the options against the yellow taffeta.

I finally settled, just to keep her quiet, on a skirt I had brought with me—flared at the bottom and fitted everywhere else—and one of Maggie's blouses because mine were *too tight, too transparent and show too much cleavage.* Unless we got into my t-shirt collection, which my mother informed me were not church appropriate. I figured God would just be glad I showed up in the first place. She set a straw sunhat on top of my head to top it all off; I pitched it at the front door without my mother noticing.

"There, that will do." She walked toward the door and added, "And you've got a little make-up around your eyes, Eve."

Of course.

I walked into church at my mother's side. A small congregation sat scattered among pews, even smaller than I had remembered. There were a few familiar faces mixed with the majority of whom I didn't recognize but all of them stared. Some offered faint smiles, others gasped. One woman even glanced down at my skirt with a "tsk". I guess my mother knew best; the skirt was too short and too tight. I smiled inwardly and gave myself a pat on the back for *not* fitting in.

There were people there I had last seen at Maggie's wedding, and not in ten years before that. Mr. and Mrs. West sat in the back row next to a herd of seven children ranging in age from terrible two's to sweet sixteen's, and the Pope's were in front of them. Both Mrs.' were exchanging comments after seeing me in the doorway. We walked up the aisle as the minister began his Sunday morning announcements and my mother finished hobnobbing with the *ladies.* We sat down next to my father in the third row back.

My father has never acted the enthusiastic parent, certainly didn't make his way to the school with a plate of cookies for special occasions; that was my mother's job. But he made an effort for the most important of the school functions and worked the farm all the rest of the time.

I gave him a kiss on his forehead and he squeezed my shoulder as we sat in the pew next to him. "Hey kid, I guess you lost the battle, huh?" he asked in a whisper, eyeing my blouse with a chuckle.

"Yep. I agreed to come on the condition I wasn't forced into community dinners with the cowboy clan."

"You enter into breaking that condition the moment you walk in here, you know that don't you?"

"Yeah, I know. I'll find a way out. Need any help on the farm?"

"Nope. Nice try."

I sat between my parents, heaved a deep sigh, glanced around while the congregation rose in prayer and—sacrilege—I didn't close my eyes with everyone else. I scanned the pews and saw Joel sitting one row up on the other side of the pulpit.

He sat next to a woman around my mother's age, petite and worn looking. A rugged man sat at her other side; a man reminiscent of a true cowboy from the movies, hardened lines on his face, tanned skin, only missing the sprouted piece of grass between his teeth and hat on his head.

Joel scanned the room, too, and our eyes met. At first, we held each other's stare with an intensity I doubt either us had expected at first. Then, just as if I were putting up a protective wall, I crossed mine and shot him an exasperated smile. He laughed quietly and winked at me. At least one familiar face kept his eyes open with mine. I could just feel my mother praying for the both of us.

After the service came the Meet-and-Greet. I followed my parents down the walk in front of the church feeling a little bit enlightened; a little bit guilty for missing more Sunday's than I could count. My father went ahead for the truck. I don't remember a day of church going by that we didn't bring two vehicles—one for us and the truck for Dad so he could leave early. I guess that was his condition on coming to church and nothing much had changed.

Don't get me wrong. My father is a religious, good man, just not a particularly social one. He came to make his peace with God every Sunday then quietly snuck out before being bombarded by the Ladies Social gossip group.

My mother chaired the Ladies Social gossip group. I walked somewhere in between today, lingering back from my mother and her figurative captain's hat, kicking at the dirt with my shoe. I crossed my arms at my chest and self-consciously pulled at the buttons on my floral blouse that hung too loose at my waist.

"Hey there city girl," said a voice behind me. It was Joel.

"Hi Joel. Nice to see you didn't stand outside this morning."

"And nice to see you've found something presentable to wear, thanks to Maggie." He eyed me up and down.

"Thank you. Nice, huh?"

"I like the skirt," he said, eyes lingering on my calves and over-exposed thighs.

"Thanks. And stop gawking, smart-ass."

"I feel awkward here, too. It's nice to finally have someone to talk to that doesn't know everything about everyone and has something to say about it."

"Well, we could make up some stories."

He laughed again, a deep laugh with his head tipped back, and ran his hand through his slicked back hair. Still an Adonis, only an Adonis in a grubby jean jacket.

"To be honest, I felt more comfortable at dinner the other night with your friends than I do here."

"Me too. I'll see you around, Eve."

"Sure."

He walked away and took his mother's arm in his to lead her to the truck parked in the gravel lot.

All in all, church didn't turn out too bad this morning. I played the Dutiful-Farmer's-Wife card on my mother and managed to convince her after another long conversation about my love life, that, really, she ought to go straight home to Dad. Saved, until two hours later when I heard a knock at the door and opened it to my mother now in her Sunday afternoon visiting clothes. Crap sandwich.

"I didn't think you'd mind if I dropped by," she said. "I have a book I want you to read about relationships, Eve. I think it might help. After our talk today I remembered about it."

Oh God. Huge inward sigh. Joel stood on his front porch with a wide grin on his face.

I shut the door with my mother still standing on the other side of it and walked into the house. I thought about locking it, too. I wouldn't have felt any remorse in doing so either except that I didn't want Joel or anyone else to hear more of my life's failed relationships, which my mother had no qualms about telling everyone. *The more people know, the more advice you receive* is my mother's theory. Mine: *Mind your own damn business.*

"Eve," she called once inside the door. "How have the first few days been going? I wouldn't usually intrude, but I want to make sure you're managing on your own here. You are on unfamiliar ground, after all. And what with breaking up with Jackson, I didn't want you wallowing in the pits of depression. They say all you need is one little push when you're in the pits and you either become suicidal or turn to the devil."

"I'm not suicidal, Mom. I'm tired."

"When you're in a depression, you sleep all the time. Are you sleeping all the time?"

"No. Just at night. Usually until morning. That's the way it works."

"Well, I was watching Dr. Phil yesterday and he was talking about women whose relationships always fail. And I think maybe you have some unresolved man issues." She made a dramatic swipe of her hand in the air as if to bat those issues away. "Those are leading to your being depressed and all and I worry that you'll do something crazy. Like playing with upside down crosses and chanting to the antichrist."

"You mean issues besides I don't want to be in a relationship that's going no where? I think Dr. Phil would side with me on this one."

"Maybe you are self destructing your relationships. Dr. Phil talks about self destructing relationships."

"How was I self destructing?" I screeched through the hall and fell onto the sofa in the living room.

"Dr. Phil knows a lot about relationships. Do you know what I think? I think you should go on Dr. Phil. He could help you resolve some of these issues."

"As much as he helps resolve issues, I think I'll manage, Mom. Thanks." Like I'm the only woman in the world that ends relationships. "I'm not self destructing, or relationship destructing, or having man issues other than I don't want to be with one at the moment."

She paused while a horrified expression crept up and plastered itself smack across her face. "Good God. I hope you don't want to be with a woman."

"No, Mom. I just want a break."

"What kind of a break? Like celibacy?"

"No."

"I hope you don't mean casual sex, Eve." This time she stuck a hand on her hip and tipped it to the side.

"No, I don't mean casual sex!"

After a long pause, the conversation seemed at a welcome end. I breathed a sigh of relief that it was over. Wishful thinking…

"Dr. Phil could really help you."

"That's right Mom. I'm gay, I'm having casual sex and it's all based on my unresolved man issues and self-destruction. And I make crosses and hang them upside down from the ceiling next to voodoo dolls of Jackson and all of the other men I left in ruin. You go see Dr. Phil and discuss your psychotic daughter. *Mother's whose daughters aren't giving them grandchildren fast enough.* Because that's the real issue here, isn't it?"

"You aren't taking this very seriously, Eve." She actually tsk'd.

"No. I'm not. I'm trying to relax and figure things out. Not search for a man that I don't want to find right now."

"Well, I'll leave this book here and you can read it. I've highlighted some pages and made a few notes for you with the Ladies Social."

"Great. Thanks."

"That book did wonders for Catherine's daughter. She thought of it immediately when I mentioned your trouble."

"Again, thanks for sharing."

"You'll appreciate my concern one day, Eve. I'll stop by tomorrow with a casserole. I can't imagine you're doing a lot of cooking in your state. Most depressed people can't even manage to feed themselves."

I waited to hear her shoes clack down the walkway then let out a loud scream into the sofa cushion and braced myself for my mother's "notes and highlights". I thought of many things I could do with the stupid book. None of them included reading it and most were bordering on unnecessary violence.

Another knock came to the door. I cringed inside, drew a deep breath and prepared myself to face my mother again. Maybe she'd forgotten some important piece of advice. Should I run for a highlighter and sticky notes?

"What more could you possibly say?" I screamed as I walked to the door. It felt good to yell through the door because I rarely did it to her face. I knew she could hear me, but I'd deny everything. "*My* life sucks! *I* need a man! *I'm* going shopping for one today just to satisfy *your* needs, then I'll watch talk shows and take freakin' notes!"

I yanked open the door and saw Joel staring at it, hiding a smile beneath his raised eyebrows. I gripped the book in my hand, still at the ready to wing it at my mother.

"Hey. Thought you might want a coffee," he said. He eyed the book and my white knuckles, and raised his eyebrows higher at the grip I held on it. "That could be dangerous."

I lowered my arm. "Jesus Christ!" I yelled and stomped back into the house.

"Can I come in?" he asked.

"Yes. Sorry. You've caught me in my depressive state of man loathing and self destruction."

"So…your mom left."

"Yes. She must have released enough of her worldly advice for one day. But she's stopping by tomorrow to unleash some more. I guess I need to get a start on reading this freakin' thing."

"Oh." He set two travel mugs on the table in the living room. "Would you feel better if you flung the book out the door?"

"Prob'ly." My pout was Oscar worthy.

He walked toward the front door, pulled it open and showed me the way with his arm outstretched.

I walked toward him, wound up and flung it straight out the door. Exhilaration filled me to watch it fly past the porch and down the walk. It landed on the sidewalk and notes of yellow paper scattered from some of the pages.

"Thanks. That felt much better," I said, huffing fast, deep breaths. I could feel my chest rise and fall and I just wanted to curl up and die. Uh oh. Hope those weren't "suicidal thoughts".

"Thought it might."

"So, why are you here?"

"I came over to save you from your mother."

"How did you know I needed saving?"

"Just a hunch. Your face earlier said a lot."

"She means well, I'm sure, but I'm still trying to figure out how."

"Want to talk about it?"

"No," I said with a pout. Really, I didn't, but I started spouting anyway. "What's really sick is that if and when I finally do meet someone she'll think it was all her and Dr. Phil's doing. I feel sorry for that man if he ever has to come face to face with my mother. She might be his biggest challenge yet." Huge sigh. "I came to Tayton to get away from all this and it seems like it's harder to hide from here than it was at home."

"Maybe you need to *not* hide from it."

"Is that what you do? Face your problems and stomp over them until you feel better?"

"Sometimes."

"What's your excuse for not being married with children and a white picket fence? Does your mother rub in your face every ten minutes?"

"I never said I wasn't married with children," he smiled. "And the white picket fence came crashing down six years ago."

"Actually, you did say you weren't married. I never asked about children."

"Ah. Well, this conversation is about your messed up life, not mine."

"At least it's a comfort to know I'm not the only one with a messed up life."

"You're not. I could totally take you on that one."

"Well, cheers, then. Thanks for the coffee. Here's to messed up lives and not hiding from them. Even though I tried my best to."

"You know, Eve...I have this book—"

"Shut up, Joel."

# JOEL ♂

I'm still trying to figure out what happened to my emotions this afternoon. I laughed at first when I saw Eve on the doorstep, her mother facing her with a relationship advice book and her head swimming with thoughts to help her daughter. The creative energy in her was palpable.

I had been on my way to work to put in some weekend hours, ready to walk around back and hop into the truck. Then I turned back and watched through the neighbor's window. Her mother paced the floor, hands on hips, and Eve looked tormented, her entire afternoon ruined. It had been her face, the way it fell when her mother approached her. Just as it had the first day I'd seen them together.

I suppose I think of my mother's endless support and unobtrusive parenting and feel sorry that Eve doesn't have that. And I think about my own soul being squashed by Meg and I sense a connection there on some level. Or at least sympathy for Eve when I see it in her eyes. And, funny enough, I've been craving strawberries lately.

The afternoon began with Eve and her mother but ended with mine. I turned down the highway toward the ranch after work, opting—after deciding throwing something in the toaster wasn't going to cut it over a home cooked meal—to run begging for dinner at Mom's. Hank's truck sat parked in the drive, so the workers weren't done yet for the day.

Hank had worked at the ranch since my grandfather started handing over some of the work to my father forty-eight years ago. Hank had only been fourteen and without a job or an education and my grandfather pitied him. He worked miracles with the horses and quickly learned everything there was to learn on the ranch.

At eight, I watched as Hank showed me how to do anything my father hadn't. Two months ago when the barn lit into an inferno, Hank pulled as many horses from the flames as he could rescue and alerted my mother to leave the house before it went up. He pulled her out before the smoke became too much—thank God it never caught fire— and landed himself in the hospital for burn treatments and smoke inhalation. There were moments during the chaos I prayed I wasn't losing a second father in three years.

Hank appeared from the house and tipped his hat as I approached. My mother stood in the doorway, tying her apron, stained red and purple from whichever kind of pie she'd been laboring over today. Dark hair with lines of gray had been pinned at the sides, the same as she'd always worn it, but cut shorter now. Her eyes shone as much as they always had though they were tired sooner in the day. She waved a hand in the air toward Hank. He pulled away from the house, kicking up dust in puffs behind his tires.

"Hi, Joel," she said and opened an arm toward me.

"Hi, Mom. How's clean up going?"

"Fine. Hank says it's about done. They're hauling the last of the rubble away in the morning and the horses seem to be managing well enough at Bert's place. One more had to be put down yesterday."

"Oh, no. So we're down to eleven."

"But still a strong eleven, Joel. They'll be okay."

"Any more offers?"

"Not a one. The interest we had three weeks ago seems to have dwindled."

"We're putting up the barn this weekend. It'll get better."

"I know. Don't you worry about it. Have you heard from Meg?" I heard the hesitation in her voice. Meg hadn't been a pleasant topic of conversation in the past few years.

"No. Not for four days."

"And it's eating you. You're worried about Damian?"

"Yeah. She should have called back by now."

"You know how she is, honey. She's probably thinking about herself again and not realizing you're sitting here worrying yourself sick."

"I just need to know he's alright. She's been out of rehab for two months. It was about two months the last time she relapsed."

"She's got family there. They're watching out for Damian, too."

"Yeah, and itching to get their hands on him. Everyone but you seems to want to forget I'm his father. Her own mother has been covering for her problems since they began. I should have full custody already the way things have gone."

"Here, have some supper. I saved you a plate in case you came by."

"How did you know I was coming?"

"A mother always knows. Besides, it's been a busy week and you looked tired at church this morning. I figured the TV Dinner & Beer Gourmet wouldn't be up for cooking." She smiled, itching to get into my kitchen and stock it with food. I think her confidence in my ability to cook stopped at opening a can or boiling water. "Is Raif joining you next weekend?"

"Yeah. We've got twenty-eight men coming. And the ladies auxiliary has offered to help with the buffet."

"I spoke with Frances yesterday. It seems all I have to do is donate a few pies. They've got everything else covered."

"Good. You could use the break. Though Raif and Trey will be disappointed. I told them you were cooking to make sure they'd come."

"They can come for dinner this week. Invite them by and let me know when you're coming. I'll let Hank know to stay a while."

"Alright."

"You haven't eaten a good meal since being here last, have you, when I sent the pies home?"

"Yes. As a matter fact, I have. We were at Eve's Thursday night."

"Oh?"

"She's staying a few months until Maggie gets back."

"I don't recall Eve Whitting being back in town for a long time."

"Rarely in the last twelve years. I imagine her mother had something to do with the avoidance."

"Oh, I imagine. I'm sure she means well. We didn't always get on very well, Vivian and I, but she's a good woman. Just the old fashioned sort is all."

"Well, Eve turned out just fine anyway."

"So that *was* her in church today, with Vivian?"

"Yeah."

"I saw you talking to her. What's she like, Joel? As I recall, she was a little hellcat as a kid."

I raised my eyebrows.

"Well, she was. Didn't she beat up that kid down the road? He was older than she was and twice her size."

"Yeah, that was her. She hasn't changed much in personality, but she sure as hell doesn't look like a tomboy anymore."

"No. That she doesn't." My mother actually turned away to hide a grin. "She's cute."

"No, not cute. Pretty, maybe."

"A city girl."

"Yeah. But she's still rough around the edges, not frilly. I think she'll have a hard time settling back in here in some ways, and just fine in others. The guys seem to like her."

"I'm sure they do. Especially around a woman that looks as womanly as Eve. I've seen Tal and Trey around women. They're like teenagers. No different from you and Raif except that you two do a better job of hiding it."

"She straightened us out quick for gawking. You'd be impressed."

"Good for her. Someone needs to keep you boys in line. Seems she hasn't lost all of her hellcat ways." I could hear her chuckling under her breath as she turned to pull two more blackberry pies from the oven.

# Chapter 7

## *Eve* ♀

Monday. As the town woke, slowly making their way toward their destinations, a sedate bustle grew through the streets, adding to the morning quiet rather than interrupting it. I ventured out myself for a few groceries and more remodeling supplies for Joel's house, a deck of cards and a book, *Poker for Dummies.* The dummy would be me.

I returned to the quiet of Vine Street for a walk; the quiet now broken only by chirping birds, the lone bark of a dog and idle chatter of the "tea ladies" at the house on the corner. They met every morning, talked about grandkids, the weather and whatever else deemed too private to talk about through an open window; that left only whisperings and murmurs. Feeling revived and refreshed from the country air, I opened the front door to Stumpy as he crashed into the table, knocking Maggie's fancy key-plate to the floor. I treated him to some Cheerio's and played "find the fur balls" after he coughed a few up.

It wasn't a particularly exciting day, but a pleasant one. That pleasantry would soon be broken; I found a note taped to the door that read: *Hoped to find you home, Eve. Can't imagine what you're up to in this insignificant town. I'll come by later. Mom*

*Insignificant town* was in quotation marks.

I expected her arrival soon, not so prepared to hear her oh-so-expert advice, so I thought I'd do my best at avoidance. I made dinner—yet another grilled cheese sandwich and soda—and spent some quality time with a few fashion magazines. Surprisingly, they no longer tugged at my city girl need for the high gloss pages of an artificial existence so I tossed it aside with a sigh of boredom.

I heard the rumble of tires on asphalt out front.

I paused, groaned and inched toward the window to peer through the slats in the front blind at the bumper of my mom's sedan pulling up street-side. A woman wearing a wide brimmed sunhat, a frown and one raised skeptical brow sat in the passenger seat next to her.

"Crap. Reinforcements." So much for avoidance. I ran out the back door, ducking under the height of the windowsills along the way and crept through the back yard. Joel had parked his truck in back, my only chance at cover. I crouched down along the driver's side and listened.

Footsteps approached from the front street, making their way toward the house. I heard their voices trail and buried my face in my hands.

And I waited.

Joel approached out of nowhere and crouched down next to me. I felt him lean in and whisper, "What are we hiding from?"

"My mother. Shush." He started to stand to get a look and I yanked him back down by his jacket, keeping a firm grip. "Don't you dare even move or she'll hear you," I whispered and stared him down. I raised a brow to emphasize the serious nature of my predicament.

"Okay, okay." He smiled and we locked eyes. I could smell his cologne he sat so close and the heat between us grew with every inch of his smile. I really tried my best to forget city life. Now I even had flutters for a cowboy.

I don't know if I would call Joel a cowboy, really. I couldn't see him in a cowboy hat and doubted he even owned one. But he had boots and that damned drawl that used to make me gag, not swoon. I guess it had been a while since I'd satisfied my womanly urges.

"Eve!" my mother called.

"Shit. She's coming into the back yard." I stared at him with pleading eyes. Very dramatic. He set a hand over mine and yanked my tight grip from his jacket.

He stood up and waved at my mother. The bastard.

"Hi Mrs. Whitting."

"Hi Joel. You haven't seen Eve, have you? I came by earlier and her Jeep was gone. It's here now and she's not answering the door."

"Yeah. She's around somewhere." I kicked his leg. He grunted and continued. "She went out for a walk after dinner with Ms. Darcy down the street."

I slapped a hand to my forehead. And Joel was loving this a little too much.

"Maybe I should just wait. I'm sure she won't be long if—"

"Actually, she just left and Ms. Darcy was looking a little feisty. If you want to give me a message I'll let her know and she can call you tomorrow."

"I guess so." She paused, assessing the options in her mind. "Just tell her I was here. I brought a lemon cake over." I heard her walking toward us. "Maybe you could—"

"Just set it on the front porch. I'm working on the truck and there's some nasty fumes over here. I'll get it to Eve later. Thanks."

"Oh." I could hear my mother sniffing the air for the fumes. "Well, I suppose. Thanks, Joel. Just have her call me tomorrow afternoon. I'll be out all morning. Be sure to remember about the cake. Eve likes her lemon cake."

"Will do."

I didn't move until she walked away and neither did Joel. She had gone, or must have, because he slid down the side of the truck next to me again. I punched him in the arm.

"Ow. What was that for?"

"For the lonely widow comment. Now she'll think she's rubbed off on me. And she'll probably check up on Ms. Darcy."

"Don't worry. Ms. Darcy left with her grandson this morning. They won't be home 'til the next day. That's usually the routine."

"So, I'll have to come up with a fun filled day with Ms. Darcy to tell my mother tomorrow."

"I could have pulled you up by your ear lobes and yelled, *here she is!*"

"Thanks for not doing that. You saved me twice."

"Three times."

"The last time didn't count. She was already gone."

"Yeah, but I brought you the best damn cup of coffee you've ever had."

"Right." I rolled my eyes and stood. Joel followed. He was tall. Not too tall, but enough I had to look up at him and he had to look down to me, and we stared into each other's eyes long to enough to feel a slow trickle of ardent awkwardness roll through my gut.

"Well. Want some lemon cake?" I asked, jumping out of his way as fast as I could.

"Sure." Huge smile, dimple, eye sparkle and shining white teeth. "Oh, and call your mother sometime tomorrow afternoon."

"Thanks. I'll be sure to do that."

"By the way, you hit like a guy," he said and rubbed his arm.

I sat on Joel's front porch and peeled the foil off my mom's lemon cake. We pulled the cake apart with our hands and ate it in crumbs like two children savoring a bowl of icing. I started to feel guilty eventually but not until half way through my fourth piece.

"I really do love my mother," I said through a mouthful.

"I know. She might be a pain the ass, but she's still your mother."

"She'd do anything for me if I asked her and I think that's the problem. I don't ask so she feels like I don't want her around. I just wish we could sit over a cup of coffee and have a normal conversation."

"So why don't you just ask her to do small things for you that are bearable to keep her helpful urges satisfied?"

"You make it sound so simple. See, I never think of those things. I just think of the negative crap and get myself all worked up."

"So, be more positive."

"Tell me about your wife."

"What?" His jaw dropped and he stared. A cake crumb dropped from his mouth.

"I just assumed after this morning's conversation you might have a wife. You didn't want to talk about it, so I'm prodding again. Probably just deflecting my own negative torment."

He raised his eyebrows and looked into the street without a word.

"I don't mean to pry. You just sound so smart about this kind of stuff, now I'm curious."

"I don't think anyone's called me smart before," he grinned. "Except my mother."

"No? Well, you are."

He held my glance for a moment with a soft smile then turned away. "Meg and I got married a year after high school. She left six years ago."

"She left? I'm sorry."

"Actually, I kind of made her leave."

"Why?"

"The usual cheating nightmare story. I found her in bed with another guy."

"I'm sorry I brought it up."

"It's okay. So, tell me about the relationship you ran from to come here."

"I was living with him; we were together for the last four months of it only because it was comfortable. I realized I didn't love him so I left. He has always had a more meaningful relationship with his drinking buddies anyway. They should be happy together."

"When did you leave?"

"Two months ago. I gave up my apartment and came out here for Maggie's wedding. I didn't tell my mother about Jackson until a few days ago."

"That was probably smart considering you were at your sister's wedding. Prime time for relationship fixing by relatives. I found that out at my sister's wedding. Right after Meg and I were separated."

"Were you in love with Meg?"

"I wouldn't have married her if I wasn't."

Stupid question, Eve. "I just mean that I almost got married once. Besides my marriage ideals with Jackson, I mean. We were going to go through with it up until the groom called it off."

"What happened?"

"He came out of the closet."

"What?" Joel laughed aloud and threw his head back, leaving me in complete shock at his reaction.

"You're laughing at my heartache?" I tried to act miffed.

"I'm sorry. How long ago was this?"

"Five years. I did love him. But we're friends now. And I think he loved me, too. Just not in a…sex kind of way." I burst out laughing and this time Joel followed.

"Wow. You win. That sucks."

"Yeah, well. What was your strangest relationship?"

"Meg. At least it is now. We're still in touch and I try to care about her in some way. Mostly feel sorry for her, I guess. And we'll always be attached on some level. There was this one girl I dated for a while that used to send me postcards from wherever she traveled."

"That's not so strange."

"We were dating for three weeks, and she sent them from one town over when she visited her grandmother, and from her sister's place in Michigan. From her best friends house two blocks away once."

"That is a bit strange. I bet you didn't even read them all, poor girl."

"No. Not after they started coming from her friends in the next zip code. We broke up. It was very emotional." He rolled his eyes.

"I dated a mime."

"A mime?"

"Yep. We used to go out in public and he'd wear his make-up, plastered white and black. When we met he seemed very secretive of his occupation. Then when he finally told me, I didn't know what to say so I told him I respected him for doing what he wanted to do. Which I did, but I didn't expect to him to do what he wanted all of the time.

"But, you know, the worst of all was this guy Bruce. He took twice as long as I did to get ready for a date and had a mirror in every room of his house. He always checked his reflection, whether it was in plates at restaurants—which he'd actually hold up in front of him—reflections in windows, and my favorite: he carried a compact in his pocket."

"A compact? A little vain?"

"A touch."

"How long did that one last?"

"Four months. But I was young, so I loved that one, too."

"What's your record shortest date?"

"Two minutes."

"Two minutes?" he chuckled.

"Yep. I sat down in a restaurant, said hi to a guy that coughed all over my water glass—there were actually droplets—then used the edge of my sweater to wipe his mouth and blow his nose. So I politely excused myself to the washroom and left. How about you?"

"You win. In a small town like this, you have watch who you date because everyone watches and everyone knows."

"So what do you do about it?"

"I don't date."

"What do you mean, you don't date?"

"I don't have time right now anyway. And like I said, things with Meg are complicated."

"So, you're still on again off again?"

"No. Never on again."

"I'm sorry. I'm prying again and I should let you get some sleep. You look tired."

"And you look like you could stay up for hours," he grinned.

"I didn't this morning. But I am getting restless in this town. Even evading my mother all day."

"Maybe that has more to do with extreme anxiety than restlessness." He gave me a therapist style raised brow then laughed.

"Maybe." I nudged his arm. "I was thinking I should start on your living room while you're at work this week."

He only stared.

"Please, let me do something before I rip my hair out."

"Alright. Here." He reached into his pocket and tossed me a set of keys. "This is the house key. Just don't do anything too heavy and hurt yourself."

"I'm not a wimp."

"Yeah, you did well with a measuring tape."

"I can manage just fine, thanks. Have a good night, Joel." I stood and walked back to Maggie's house.

"Don't you want your cake?" he called, holding out the plate.

"No. You have it. I'll tell my mother you never gave me the message. Or the cake."

"Don't get me involved, Eve."

"Don't worry. You can handle her. I'll send her over tomorrow night for the plate." I shone him a grin and walked into the house leaving him standing with a half-eaten plate of lemon cake and a confused grin. I was teasing, but I may have just solved my problem and avoided a heart-to-heart with my mother for one more day.

# JOEL ♂

The past three nights I arrived home from work to find Eve in my living room, a pot of mystery food keeping warm in the oven and her warm smile to greet me. She would finish painting or pulling tacks or measuring for fabric while I ate, then clean up for the night. It felt kind of nice, a bit homey and comfortable.

Tonight, the fourth in a row, she stood next to a floor sander with a pair of goggles on her face and her hair in disarray.

"What are you doing?" I asked. She looked up and lifted her goggles with a huge smile. Her hair stuck out in Alfalfa-like sprouts from the elastic around her head holding the goggles against her forehead.

"I'm sanding the hardwood so we can refinish it when you're not busy."

"You've been busy enough the past few days. You don't need to keep doing this, you know."

"No way. This is the perfect excuse to avoid my family. And now, because I've been missing my mother's calls and visits, she has the Ladies Social coming over with food, too, so I think by the weekend you and I will have an eight-course meal. She left a green bean casserole and pot roast today."

"I can't deny the food's been good." I couldn't deny enjoying the company either. "So, you think you can tackle this sander?"

"Of course."

"Have you done it before?"

"No. It can't be that hard."

"Yes it is. Give it to me." I reached for the handle and she grabbed it back.

"No way!"

"Yes! This is not going to be your job."

"Why not? You think I'm not capable?"

"I *know* you're not capable. Hand it over. Come on, Eve."

She didn't budge. I hadn't met anyone so stubborn. Or someone so sexy in a pair of coveralls, but that wasn't the point. Christ, a floor sander now?

"Come on, Eve. You cannot sand a floor."

"Why, because I'm a woman?"

"Eve, you can't do it."

"I can so. Let go."

I did what any man would do. I turned it on and let it shoot out in front of her, spinning in all directions, leaving a trail of dust from the hardwood spraying into our faces.

"You jackass!" she hollered above the swooshing. "That's not fair, I wasn't ready."

"That's because you don't know how to run a sander." I grabbed hold of the machine and turned it off, keeping her away with the other arm outstretched. I couldn't help but smile wide at the look on her face. She looked ready to explode. Her eyes narrowed, her face turned red and she reached for my arm.

Then she let go and let out a frustrated scream.

And body checked me to the floor.

If I'd have been ready, I would have stood up against her—no way would I let a woman take me down—but I wasn't and she did. I have to admit, aside from an elbow to the face and knee that narrowly missed my groin, she smelled great and the feel of her body pressed all over me had me wanting to wrap my arms around her and pull her tighter.

Raif appeared out of nowhere, pulled her off me and I heard Trey laughing his ass off in the corner. I stood and brushed off a thin layer of dust.

"Let me go, Raif," she said.

"No way. You're a psycho."

"So," started Trey. "We were going to grab some beers at Kasey's. You guys coming?"

If Eve had even a thought of staying home, Raif didn't give her a chance to argue. She was so keyed up over the sander, still huffing as we walked out the door, that Raif kept a hold on her arm in case she snapped again. She walked out with us and sat into Trey's car with a solid expression of hatred directed at me.

I would rather not take Trey's car. It always smelled like corn chips and I always ended up driving it home. But Trey's ocean liner of a vehicle fit the crew better than any of our vehicles did. Raif and I drove a truck. I didn't want to chance asking Eve to drive. She'd probably drop us off in a ditch to rot along a desolate highway somewhere.

I sat in the back with Raif and he shoved Eve in shotgun next to Trey who kicked the car into gear. It backfired and Eve jumped half a foot into the air.

"Nice car, Trey," she said, still scowling. "Ever think of maybe sprucing it up a bit?"

"Yep. Got it all planned out. When I win the lottery I'm taking this puppy in for a brand new paint job and a stereo system," he grinned.

"Right," she said and huffed out the window. "Where are we going anyway?"

I took the liberty to answer this one. "Kasey's. Local pub."

"Oh. And I just got dragged along for the ride, is that it? Or maybe you needed a designated driver to lug you all home in your intoxication a few hours from now."

"No. I usually drive home. You can get pissed if you want."

Eve turned to glare at me in the back seat.

"Lighten up, sunshine," I said and winked at her.

"You're pretty nervy for a guy who almost got his ass kicked," she said with a heartfelt scowl, then smiled. Raif burst out laughing and we all eased into the night. She fit in just like one of the guys.

Trey pulled up outside Kasey's and parked the car along the side of the building. Raif helped Eve from the car and we walked inside the usual haunt, the usual crowd plus one odd and out of place woman. Eve followed with her arms swinging at her sides and a large smile. She looked nervous but I knew she wasn't likely to admit that right now.

"So, what else is there to do in this small town nowhere?" she asked.

"Plenty," started Trey. He slouched back in his chair where we sat around a tall table. "You could sign up for the baseball team. Or bowling. There's league play every Wednesday. Or lawn bowling if you're into that; the seniors club meets on Thursdays. Town hall meetings are a blast."

Eve scowled across the table at Trey, a grin hidden beneath it. Eve had scowling down to a perfected art, I noticed. Along with icy glares, which I think all of us mostly avoided.

"And do you, Trey, bowl or play baseball or meet with the seniors club every week?"

"No. I come here, drink beer and play poker," he grinned.

"So what is there to do?" she asked again, this time directed toward Raif.

"I don't know," he said. "There's a barn raising this weekend. You could come to that."

"A barn raising? They still do those?" she scoffed and gulped back more beer.

"Yep."

My turn to scowl. I didn't like Raif inviting Eve into my family problems, not that the entire town didn't know my life's history and weren't showing up to build the barn at my family's ranch anyhow.

"So, you're not joking," she said.

"Nope," said Raif. Then he glanced at me.

"Are you all going?" she asked and eyed everyone around the table.

"Joel's going. And I'm going," said Raif and I wanted to beat the shit out of him just then.

"I'm goin'," said Trey. "And I'm working on you," he said and shoved a finger into Eve's shoulder.

"Might be interesting." she said.

"I'll drive you," said Raif.

"I thought I was driving you, Raif," I said, hoping to pull the too-many-people-in-the-truck excuse.

"I can drive behind you in the Jeep," said Eve. Great.

"Fine. Sounds good," I said. "I'm getting more beer." I stood and moved toward the bar.

"Need a hand?" asked Eve.

"Yeah. Raif, give me a hand," I said, fuming still. He stood and followed me to the bar.

"What's your problem, Powell?"

"Why'd you invite her to the ranch?"

"Why not? Everyone's going."

"She doesn't need to know all of the details of my life's disasters."

"Why not? It's small town nowhere remember? Everyone knows."

"She's a stranger."

"Not anymore. Suck it up, cowboy. Why is it any different for Eve than everyone else that knows about Meg and Damian? Because that's what this is about."

"It just is. It's nice to know one person in the world doesn't know and I can have a normal life for a few minutes of the day when she's around."

"So you don't have to mention Meg and Damian."

"She knows about Meg. I didn't tell her about Damian. I want people to meet Damian, he's a great kid. I just hate all of the crap that goes with it. As much as I'm frustrated with Meg I don't want to air her life all around the ranch, which it will be already. Damian doesn't need to hear how awful his mother is. And I sure as hell don't need to deal with Eve coming along for the ride of my chaotic life."

"So tell her not to come."

"You already invited her."

"And I think she's nice. It's cool to have a girl around in our crowd that doesn't act like a girl all the time. She fits in with us. She doesn't know anyone in town"

"Nice time for you to get all social and accommodating."

"It'll be a shitty four months for our city girl to sit in a small town by herself."

"She won't be by herself. She'll have her mother."

"That'll be great."

"Shit." Raif was right. I felt the pang of sympathy for Eve again.

And I wanted her to come to the ranch and raise the goddamn barn.


"So, Eve says she can't two-step," said Trey when we returned to the table.

"No shit," said Raif. I just slugged back a gulp of beer and found my seat.

"I really can't. It's been twenty years or more. Trey says you're the best to teach me, Raif."

"You want to learn to two-step? Trey's better than I am. He hangs out here more."

"Then you can both take turns getting your feet stepped on."

"Alright, alright. Let's go," said Raif. He beamed a smile. Eve stood and gave a ye-haw to embarrass everyone within earshot then bust out laughing and slugged me in the shoulder.

"Jesus," I said and shook my head in Trey's direction.

"More spice than sugar," said Trey.

"That she is."

"Having a girl in the group makes things interesting, doesn't it? It's nice."

"Christ, not you, too," I muttered and ran a hand over my weary face.

"What?"

"Raif said the same thing."

"I thought you liked having her around. You're spending more time with her than we are."

"She's my neighbor. I'm being cordial."

"You're shying away because you like her." Trey leaned back with the beer bottle at his lips and uttered a, "Heh, heh, heh."

"No I'm not."

"Yes you are. That's what you do, Joel."

"No I don't."

"Yeah, you do. You're getting all broody over there."

"I'm not brooding."

"You like our little Evie and you're brooding over her. Nearly swooning."

"You're one to talk Mr. Suave. Sugar and Spice?"

"She's cute. Like a kid sister."

"Exactly."

"And hot. Right Joel?" He waggled his brows.

I muttered, "Go fuck yourself," under my breath.

Trey paused and let out a snort of laughter. "We must have grown some tits cause this conversations sounds like we're co-hosts for a friggin' girly talk show."

Eve returned to the table with Raif, both were beaming and Raif had an arm slung around her shoulders. Again, I wanted to slug him but for different reasons this time.

"She's a natural," said Raif. "A born cowgirl."

"Your turn, Trey," said Eve. "Show me how it's done."

"I can show you a thing or two," said Trey and he slid onto the dance floor with Eve's hand in his.

"So, I suppose she's a good dancer, too," I said, sulking into my beer. I knew I was sulking. I enjoyed the sulking.

"Yep."

And that's all we said. I watched Eve dance with Trey. He stood a foot and a half taller, too tall to be Eve's dance partner. But she kept up with his wide strides, spinning around the floor in laughter. Then Trey twirled Eve back to the table.

"This is so much fun!" she said, bouncing up and down and I couldn't help but smile with her. I was shocked that the Eve we all knew outside of the bar fit in here as well as she did.

"Now you, Joel," she said and coaxed me up. "Or do you not know how to two-step?"

"Yeah, I know how to two-step. Just not as good as these guys. I haven't done it in a while."

"Well, you're still better than me. I haven't danced like that since I was about eight, in my father's barn with the ranch hands."

I laughed aloud, picturing an eight-year-old Eve two-stepping in the barn with farm hands likely three times her size.

We danced, back and forth, side to side, and she had me smiling through all of my dark hovering clouds of brooding. I don't know how, but she did it.

"See, it's not so bad. Or is it? Do I really suck?" she asked.

"No. You don't suck." Then we slowed our pace to match a change in the beat of the music. Eve fit neatly in my arms and I didn't want to let her go.

## EVE ♀

As soon as Joel set his left arm against mine, held my hand in his, my heart sped a little faster, keeping up with the slide of the steel guitar and fast paced fiddles of the music coming from the stage. I really liked dancing. All of it made me feel like a kid again, light on my feet, my heart spinning with excitement as I whirled around the floor. I hadn't two-stepped in so long I had forgotten how, which made it even more fun. Trey was the better dancer, Raif more my height so I felt less clumsy, but he moved like a pro, not like me, an ox clunking around the floor and stepping on toes. With Joel, it felt perfect.

As my eyes met Joel's a grin lit his face. I smiled back, uncertain of what to think of any of this. My heart continued to flutter, warming me from head to toe. It had to be all of the dancing. At least that was my story.

But when his arm brushed against mine and I felt his breath on my neck as he drew me nearer, I wasn't so sure this warmth was just the dancing. We moved as one to the right and I managed to keep up with Joel's simpler steps without having to focus on everyone's toes; as if perfectly matched.

The music stopped and I became suddenly aware of the quiet between us. And pulsing tension. The dancers around us clapped for the band. We heard a few "Ye-haw!"-s—these really were cowboys—and Joel kept staring. I felt myself drawn to him; I couldn't bring myself to look away until the music started up again. This time, the tune slowed and his arms slid down to my waist, bringing my eyes back to his stare. His slow touch sent a shiver across my skin and a flutter in my stomach. Boy, was I in trouble.

"Now what?" I asked. I could manage the fast pace. My heart blended well with it. This—this was painfully slow and my heart sped above the pace, beating to it's own tune in it's own world. "I don't know what to do with this." Of course, I wasn't talking just about the dancing. At least I don't think I was. What the hell was I trying to say, anyway? A few minutes ago, with Trey, Raif, I simply enjoyed the music and adrenaline rush of a bunch of cowboys on a crowded dance floor.

"Just follow my lead," he said softly. Christ, sexy voice now? This wasn't helping.

He pulled me tight against his chest and kept his stare locked on mine. Was he playing games or studying me now? Was he studying me? And what was this electric energy between us? I was on fire. Crap. Look away. Look away.

I looked away, down to the floor in a shy girl, not my usual self-confident kind of way. I usually bounded whole hog into things, even men, when I thought I wanted something. Maybe that was it. I didn't want this one. I wanted Joel to be the same to me as Raif and Trey and Tal. I wanted a friend, a brother-like pal. My body told me different. Don't listen to the body, Eve. Ignore the flutters, ignore the hot, burning spots, ignore—

"Eve, are you okay?" asked Joel. In the sexy voice.

"Yeah. Fine. Why? Am I doing something wrong?" I avoided his eyes.

"No," he laughed. "You just look distracted. Do you want to sit down?"

"No. I'm good. Unless you want to sit. Then we could sit. Whatever." Oh, real smooth, sunshine. Not showing your nerves at all. What's wrong with me?

"So you're coming to the barn raising?" he asked.

"Yeah, I guess so."

He smiled, with his lips tight and pursed this time, as if holding something back. Then something in his face clued me in.

"Joel, is this barn raising at your mom's place? Your mom's barn?"

"Yeah."

"I hadn't realized. Raif shouldn't have invited me. It wasn't really his place and if you don't want me to go—"

"No. I want you to go." He paused and held his stare again on mine. Then blurted out, "Damian will be there. And...and Meg."

"Oh?" Something new shot like fire in his eyes. Uncertainty or maybe an ache. And that electric volt heightened. I felt a bond between us, me wanting to fix whatever he felt, him needing me to. I didn't know what to do with these sorts of emotions, wasn't sure they weren't misplaced. And that small amount of awkward that could be a good or a bad thing. Good, like the fluttery kiss-me-hard kind. Bad, like get me the hell outta here. "Meg? Oh, Meg. That's going to be weird for you, then. If you guys aren't on good terms anymore?"

"A little. More weird for her, though. Most people know our story and side with me over the whole thing."

"Oh." This was definitely bad awkward. He looked like he wanted to take back the entire conversation. He glanced around the room sporadically, looking for an escape.

"So, I should invite Jackson. We could have an all around party with the exes. He's good at getting pissed drunk and making a fool of himself. And Darryl. He's the one I turned gay. They'd love him here. No one would pay attention to you or Meg. I guarantee it. Hey, I know. Invite my mother!"

He tipped his head back with laughter and all of the uncertainty suddenly fled from him.

"That would be so much better. But then you'd have to talk her. She's been trying to track you down since your last intervention. And you'd have your ex's there to fuel the relationship conversations."

"We could have a *Fix Eve's Relationships* panel. My mother would volunteer to mediate. But it'd likely turn into her version of a dating game to find me my man. She didn't like Jackson. And she's given up trying to change Darryl's mind about his sexual preference."

"She tried to change his mind?"

"Yep. She was convinced he really did want to be with me. She liked Darryl."

"Which must have gone over very well."

"You can imagine."

"Well, come to the barn raising, without Daryl or Jackson, and your mom can still come, she is part of the town after all. I'm sure she already invited herself."

"Great. So I might have to rethink coming after all."

"No, I think you should face your relationship advice and come anyway."

"Ugh. I guess I'll have to one day, won't I?"

"Yep. I'll be there for distraction if you need me."

"Thanks." I made the mistake of smiling into his eyes again and wound up caught in the same electric mess of tension we'd managed to escape, if only temporarily. And here came the awkward again. The not so bad kind that made your head spin and stomach tighten.

## JOEL ♂

I threw myself into bed as soon as I got home and willed the pounding in my head to go away. What was I doing? Staring at Eve like a lost schoolboy with raging hormones—that I had myself convinced were conveniently gone from my life lately—then blurting out that Meg and Damian might be there, as if it affected Eve in any way, except through knowing me. I was an idiot.

I was also craving strawberries again.

I hadn't felt this kind of…what was it?…not passion. I won't say passion. Sexual tension, maybe. But Jesus, with Eve? Since when did I start thinking about women like this? It had been what felt like eons and I'd been glad for the break. With so much else to worry about, I didn't need a woman on my brain. It wasn't worth the heartache and pain to involve myself in a—a relationship? No, I don't need to make this into something it isn't. Sexual tension. Healthy sexual tension. It will go away.

Might have to enlist the services of the "fist sisters" if the tension gets too thick.

The phone rang first thing in the morning and I answered with my headache returned and eyes glossed over.

"Hello?" I rubbed my face and ran a hand through my hair.

"Joel Powell?" a gravelly voice said on the other end. It wasn't familiar.

"Yeah. Who's this?"

"This is Ms. Vickers. I live next door to Meg."

"Hi Ms. Vickers." I paused and she didn't say anything. "Is everything alright?"

"Not exactly. It's Meg."

"What about Meg?" I sat up on the edge of the bed, my curiosity peaked, my gut feeling on alert.

"She may have fallen off the deep end last night. She left the house and still hasn't returned."

"Where's Damian?" I swallowed hard.

"He's with me now. I heard him crying this morning. He was there alone, Joel. He woke up crying because he couldn't find his mother."

"Jesus Christ." It was nothing new for Meg to leave, but she never left Damian unattended. "You haven't heard anything from her? From anyone?"

"No. There was a note, though."

"What did it say?"

"I think you'd better come for Damian. He's still upset."

"I'm leaving right away." I hung up the phone and stared at the wall, attempting to contain my rage the best I could. My disgust for Meg grew instantly to hate. I never thought I could hate a person I'd once loved so much but I did. I felt sorry for her most of the time, excusing her actions because the drugs controlled her, weakened her. Because she was the mother of my son. I had excused it for Damian's sake. But right now, I could excuse nothing. I could almost hear Damian's cries in my head, feel his fear and torment as he sat alone on the floor, no one to look out for him. And I hated her for leaving him, for fighting me for custody when we both knew he belonged here.

The rage finally reached its threshold. Pressure built behind my eyes and the emotion welled with intense anger, near madness. I heaved the phone against the wall and heard it crash to the floor at my feet. The room echoed, mostly with thoughts of Damian and anger at Meg circling through my head. Still coping through the haze of emotion, I pulled on a pair of jeans, stuffed a few clothes into a duffle bag to prepare for the drive to get Damian and the few days it might take to straighten this mess out and find Meg.

I made a quick call to Trey to watch my place then to Raif who'd arrange with my mother to take over my spot at the ranch for a few days. My life was falling apart. Again.

I left without a shower, grabbed a shirt and made my way out the door half dressed. Eve sat on her front porch when I stormed down the steps. I saw her out of the corner of my eye and kept walking.

"Good morning, Joel," she said, her voice a comfort. It pulled at a softer side of me that had been forced pretty deep at the moment.

I stopped mid-stride and turned to look at her. Her hair moved with the morning breeze as natural as falling leaves. She cupped a coffee mug in her hands, blowing at the edge where steam rose around her nose, her feet propped up on the rail in front of her.

"Good morning," I grumbled, my head still focused on Meg. I didn't want to let my anger filter to Eve or share this part of my complicated life with her; I wanted to deal with it on my own.

"Is everything alright?" she asked, brows bent together.

I hated how expressive she could be. It didn't make walking away any easier. "Fine. Everything's fine. Can you let Trey in the house for me? He's on his way over. I'll be gone for a few days and he's staying."

"Oh?" she stood, still cupping her coffee in her hands. "Sure. Anything I can do while you're gone?"

"No." I turned to leave, focusing on nothing but my son and the estranged ex-wife I held such a loathing for I couldn't think straight.

# Chapter 8

## *Eve* ♀

Trey sauntered up the walk an hour after Joel left. I still felt befuddled after what happened between us on the dance floor the night before; by my own reactions to Joel and by the feelings that seemed to mount every time I saw him. Like, for example, when I saw him fly out of the house this morning carrying a shirt in his hands. He'd tossed a bag into the truck and slipped his arms through the shirt as he walked to the driver's side. My eyes, of course, went straight to his exposed chest. My eyes had stayed glued, my heart pounded and I'd started to undress the rest of him in my mind. But he'd turned with a stone cold glare when I greeted him.

An abrupt change in personality, but whatever. It's not as if I had any feelings there to be hurt in the first place. Jerk.

I hadn't moved from my spot on the veranda in the next hour that passed. I sat and stewed over Joel's morning pleasantries, my initial and obviously unwarranted concern, and tried my best to brush it off as a good excuse to stop thinking about him. Which still wasn't working when Trey pulled up in front of the house. He waved at me as he walked toward Joel's porch.

"Hey, Eve," he said. "You're up early."

"I know. Something in the air here, I can't sleep in. Like I'm going to miss something if I sleep too long. Not that there's anything to miss around here. I just get up and stare at the road. And nothing."

"Yeah, well. I don't have that problem. I could sleep all day. But Joel called this morning and woke me up to come over."

"Right." I jumped up. I'd forgotten about letting him into the house. "I'm supposed to let you in." I walked toward the house and met Trey at the door.

"Thanks. He usually just leaves it open. I don't think he's thinking straight this morning."

"Uh huh. He wasn't exactly his usual smiling self, either. You want a coffee?"

"Sure. I could use one."

Trey lazed himself on the porch at Joel's house and I walked back to my place to fill him a cup, then back again to hand it to him, like the little housewife I wasn't. This small town stuff must getting to me.

"Thanks."

"So, not working today?" I asked, wondering if Trey even had another job yet. Between him and Tal, they'd have to move on to another town to find any work.

"Nope. I was supposed to give Joel a hand today."

"At the ranch?"

"Nope. At his shop."

"I'm surprised he hasn't had you working there before. Not that it's any of my business, but if you've been looking for a job and you're interested in mechanics, why not work with Joel more often?"

"I have from time to time, but he fires me when I'm late or slacking off. Then it takes a while before I can earn my way back again. Same as house key privileges." Trey smiled as if this was all okay with him. He obviously didn't mind his lack of occupation.

"That's good. I mean not for you, but that Joel takes his job seriously."

"He has to. It's his company. He started it from the ground up and he needs to keep it running. If it wasn't for Meg, he wouldn't have to worry so much. Even though he probably still would anyway because that's the kind of guy his is. Now, he's kind of stuck here instead of at the ranch where he ought to be."

"Why can't he be at the ranch anyway? I thought they were divorced."

"Because Joel takes care of everyone. But even he'd have left by now if he could have. She's got him trapped for life. And she keeps screwing up just to bring him back. At least that's my take on it."

"What do you mean, screwing up?"

"Meg's in trouble in a big way. I probably shouldn't be talking to you about it an' all. Personal, you know."

"Yeah. He mentioned Meg. I didn't realize how bad things were."

"That's why he left this morning. To rescue Damian."

"He mentioned Damian last night, too. Who is he? Her new man or something?"

"No," Trey laughed. It seemed I was out of the loop. As if I even wanted to be in the loop.

"Damian's his kid."

"Joel's kid?"

"Yeah, his kid. Meg's kid. I thought he'd have told you about that part at least. Meg took off sometime last night and Joel has to get Damian from the neighbor's place. That's where he's headed now."

"Oh my God. How old is Damian?"

"He just turned three."

"Oh. That explains why he left in a hurry. He looked so distracted."

"He's been fighting for full custody since Damian was born. The best he can do is work his ass off to support the both of them so that Damian has a decent life until things work out more in Joel's favor."

"Does Damian ever come here?"

"Yeah. They have joint custody so Joel gets him half the time, sometimes more sometimes less. When Meg goes away he stays longer. And he's a pretty cute little kid. He's like a miniature Joel. He calls me Uncle Trey," he smiled as pride puffed his chest out.

I sipped my coffee. My heart raced with a mixture of feelings; anger toward Joel's ex wife, sympathy for Joel and for his son who seemed out of his reach most of the time. I wasn't a kid kind of person. They were like dogs. Messy and too much work. I supposed that one day I'd have kids but for now, children were something as far away as another relationship. Still, I couldn't imagine having to divide time with my own kid.

"So how long is Joel gone for?" I asked.

"Until the weekend. He'll prob'ly be back for the barn raising at the ranch. At least that's the plan. So are you coming?"

"Yeah, I guess so. Anything I should do, or bring? I've never been to one before."

"Well, I don't know where you'd fit in, Eve. The women usually bake and cook and gab and nag all morning in the house, and the men build and raise the barn. Unless you're Tal and you just try to move back and forth scrounging for food and avoiding the heavy work."

"Great. I certainly don't belong in the kitchen with the local gossip group. They'd eat me alive. And I doubt you guys would know what to do with me, either."

"You could hang out with us, it you want. Ever do any construction?"

"No. But I can handle tools and I'm familiar enough on a farm. At least, I used to be."

"Really? How so?"

"I didn't exactly grow up as a little lady. My dad and a couple of farm hands raised me most of the time. To be outside and getting dirty came more naturally to me than being in the house doing girl stuff, much to my mother's dismay."

"Then I'm sure you could do somethin'. Joel's mom always makes a huge feast anyway and I can't blame you for avoiding the kitchen. I steer clear of all ladies clubs."

"It sounds like a blast. But I don't know how well I'll like hanging with the country bumpkins. No offence."

"None taken. We just need to get you some shit kickers."

"I don't think so. I could borrow your hat, though."

"No one borrows my hat," said Trey, and he pushed it deeper onto his forehead with a grin. I could picture him sitting with a boot propped up on a fence rung, a piece of grass sticking out of his mouth, staring into the sunset across a field of hay. I wondered where the gold chain with the peace sign—which last time I checked wasn't even the "thing" for the city boys lately—and baggy jeans fit in, but I suppose that was Trey's unique style. Or something.

And no one borrowed his hat. We'd see about that.

# JOEL ♂

I drove up the street to Meg's house, cringing at how unpleasant their living arrangements were. I gave everything I could so that Damian would have a good life, a decent upbringing, the best he could have considering he wasn't with me. I know I could do better. And I would. This was over.

She lived in a town a four-hour drive away. The houses on the street were small; some up-kept, none well kept, bungalows mixed with duplexes. Meg lived in the left half of a duplex that needed to be re-sided and the front lawn needed mowing a month ago; what wasn't covered in dead patches from the decrepit animal they called a dog. She rarely fed the poor thing and it usually crept around the front yard on a rope, cringing at whoever walked past. The rest of the time, it roamed the streets in search of a meal.

As I strode up the walk, the one-eyed dog started to growl—it had two eyes on my last visit four months ago—and limped as always on the three legs it had left.

The windows of the house were dirt brown from the outside, as if a mud storm had blown through and they hadn't been washed since. Part of my taking care of Meg and Damian meant hiring a housekeeper to come in once a week and do a thorough cleaning top to bottom. We were on our eleventh girl in less than a year, most of them chased out by Meg at the other end of a broom.

Dan was harmless as boyfriends went, but he looked like a cross between a bear and gypsy. He took better care of Damian than Meg did most of the time and her mother did the rest; a godsend for Damian but also the sole reason I wasn't getting custody. She did all she could to lie and cover-up for her daughter at whatever cost, making Meg out to be the solid, nurturing parent she wasn't.

I stood on the front porch facing the door and pulled a piece of crumpled paper from the screen.

*Had to go. Emergency.*
*Meg.*

"You had time to leave a note, but you left your son alone in the house," I muttered. I was in complete disbelief.

## EVE ♀

Tal showed up the next morning, arms folded across his chest and a frown deepening on his face. His eyebrows were set low as he trudged up the walk. I sat back with my coffee in the uncomfortable willow chair, which I made tolerable with a few of Maggie's sofa cushions and Grandma's multicolored knit afghan. I sipped my coffee and grinned at Tal.

He stopped in front of me, still holding the scowl, not saying a word.

"Hey, Tal. What's up?"

"I want to talk to you," he mumbled and stuffed his hands into his pockets.

"Uh huh. Did I do something to piss you off already? Because I'm sure I've been doing a good job keeping myself under the radar around here," I smiled.

"No. You didn't do nothin'."

"Okay. But it seems someone put that scowl on your face."

"Cammy."

"Who's Cammy?"

"Cammy is the girl I was dating. Again. Until last night. When I found her with Skeeter."

I nearly bit my lip off trying to contain the laughter about to spill out. It truly was the last piece of the puzzle: This hick town, my hometown, finally had a resident named "Skeeter".

"Who's Skeeter?" I asked.

"An ass."

"A friend?"

"Definitely not a friend. Distant cousin, I think. Way distant. Either way, he just about died last night when I chased him out of Kasey's."

"Who's Kasey?"

"The pub. Remember the pub?"

"So you went to the pub and found Skeeter there with your girlfriend."

"Uh huh."

"And you didn't kill him?"

"Not yet."

"Are you are telling me because you need to borrow a shotgun?"

"No, Eve," he yelled and slumped into the chair next to me. "I'm telling you because Trey told me not to kill him, Raif held me back and Joel's not home. I need you to tell me what to do. Or else I *will* kill him. You're a girl. You know about these things 'bout as much as Joel does."

'Bout as much as Joel does? I thought. I was local therapist now, was I? "Okay. I'm not the best at relationship advice, Tal, but I'll do my best. You should be talking to my mother," I muttered and repositioned myself in the chair to face him.

"Your mother?"

"Never mind. So you really like this Cammy, huh?"

"Yup."

"And do you want advice on how to kill...Skeeter..."—dear God—"or how to get Cammy back? Because I could give you both."

He stared with a dropped jaw and a flash of excitement brushed past his pupils. Curbing the sarcasm for Tal might be a good idea. "Maybe not kill, but revenge. I can do revenge."

"Like what?"

"Let's worry about Cammy first. You have two choices. You can tell her how you feel about her. Girls like that. But be prepared for the long haul or a big slap in the face. If you both really care about each other you can't just turn around and ditch her. You talk to her because you want her back or else you let her go."

"Huh."

"So, what are you prepared for, here? Relationship material?"

"Yup. I am."

"How long have you guys been dating?"

"A week."

"A week?"

"Yeah. But she's different and we've dated before for a year. We broke up six months ago, got together again and broke up a couple weeks ago after a few days."

"Wait. Why'd you break up?"

"Which time?"

"Whichever."

"Mostly, because of Skeeter. Skeeter kept comin' around and I was watchin' after this other girl at the time. But that's all changed now."

"Sounds like you two need some time to play the field a little longer."

"No way. Not any more. She wanted to get married and I wasn't ready. That's where Skeeter came in six months ago. And Cammy's sister."

"Cammy's si—ugh. Alright. So, are you ready to get married, Tal?"

"I don't know about that. One day, I guess. But there's no one else, Eve. No one. I just want Cammy."

"That sounds like it has some potential. So here's what you do: go to her house, bring her some wild flowers you picked yourself and a bottle of wine. You don't mention Skeeter, or even think about Skeeter. And you don't say anything to her. No hello, no conversation. Just smile wide and wrap her up in your arms with a kiss."

"What if Skeeter is there?"

"You kick his ass out the door first. Then kiss Cammy."

"What if she doesn't want me?"

"Then you hope she doesn't kick your ass out the door. Tell her you are *asking* her to listen to one important thing you have to say. That's all. And she can ask you to leave after that if she wants to."

"What do I want to tell her?"

"That you care about her and you want to make things work this time. With no Skeeter and no one else. Just you and her. Because she is the only girl you ever think about and you want to be her only guy."

Tal just stared at a spot on the ground.

"Tal, is Cammy the only girl you ever think about?"

"Yeah. But Cammy doesn't drink wine. She has a lot of expectations."

"Tell me more about Cammy."

"She's beautiful. She's curvy and wears this top—it's low cut and tight and shows her boobs really good—and she loves her high heels and her lips are pouty; she got some work done on 'em in the city—"

"Oh dear God," I sighed. This just got better. I wondered how Joel would have handled this one. Probably just gave the poor guy a case of beer and sent him to bed with a headache. "Is Cammy a pretty high maintenance kind of girl, Tal? Lots of make-up, curvy, high hair, not particularly the innocent and sweet type."

"Yeah. But she grew up in town here. She lives over in the trailer park next door to Skeeter's brother. That's where the problem started, I think. Asshole."

"Then skip the wild flowers, go straight to two dozen red roses and a six pack of beer."

"Cammy'd like that," he grinned.

"Is there a flower shop in town?"

"Yeah. But I'm not working right now Eve, so you can't send me out to buy roses if they're more than a few bucks. Can I get just a couple?"

"I'll go with you. You definitely need two dozen."

"What about Skeeter and the revenge part?"

"If Cammy kisses you back, that'll be revenge enough."

"If Skeeter comes back, can I whoop him?"

"Yeah. Then you can whoop him."

"Good. Then if I have to beat the shit out of Trey and Raif to get to him this time, you'll know why. Let's go."

"Go where?"

"Flowers."

"Now?"

"Yeah. Cammy won't expect it now and Skeeter's workin' so he won't be home."

"Where does Skeeter work?"

"Pawn shop. Next door to the flower shop."

"Of course."

I spent sixty bucks on flowers and beer, but like a lost puppy sniffing his way through life in circles, Tal needed all the help he could get.

The trailer park didn't come as any surprise as far as small town trailer parks go. It had gone up the year I moved away but had fast become more run down than the older houses built thirty years before. Old cars sat in gravel driving pads which on second glance seemed to be just the gravel road between rows of trailers. An elderly man rocked all Deliverance-like in a creaky rocking chair on his front porch, eyeing us from beneath bushy eyebrows. His eyes held on us even as he paused to spit a mouthful of tobacco on the ground while I took a moment to shudder to myself.

A group of kids ran across the road in front of us kicking a soccer ball and shooting off cap guns in the air with hoots and hollers.

I parked the Jeep and Tal took a deep breath. He opened the door and stepped out.

"Do you want me to wait for you?" I asked.

"Maybe just a minute. In case we don't get to the talking part and she sets Skeeter's brother on me. Skeeter I can handle. Eddie I can't. He's a seven-foot tall gorilla with a collection of shotguns. And he doesn't use 'em for huntin'."

I had stepped a little too deep into Tal's love life and really wished Joel had been here in my place.

"Okay," I whispered to myself and ducked back inside the Jeep. Then I locked my doors, rolled up the windows tight and prayed my air conditioning worked, because I would suffocate to death in the sweltering heat before the seven-foot gorilla got me. I jammed my finger on the door locks a few more times.

Tal knocked on the door and a girl wearing a tight shirt and cutoff daisy dukes answered. She looked about a foot shorter than Tal and I could see her huge hair and shiny lip-gloss from where I sat. I probably could have seen those lips coming if I'd been parked three blocks down. Wowsers.

Cammy took the flowers with a wide grin then peered around Tal's shoulder toward me sitting in the Jeep. Her eyes narrowed. Things were looking pretty good until Cammy scowled and Tal hesitated ten seconds too long. She kicked over the beer and smacked him in the shoulder—with the sixty dollar roses!—and petals and leaves flew everywhere. I opened the door, jumped out on natural reaction to save the roses and heard Tal screaming, "She's just a friend! She's Joel's neighbor, Cammy!"

Shit. I ran up the walk and grabbed the flowers in a desperate attempt to save them before they were too mangled to salvage.

"Hey!" she screamed. "Those are my flowers, bitch!"

"Hey, hey. Relax, sister. I'm just saving you wrecking something before you regret it. Do you know how many women would kill to get flowers like that? I never get flowers like that."

"And just what are you doing here with him?" she huffed with her hands set rigidly on her big curvy hips. And Tal was right. She had great cleavage, the kind most women aspire to and them some.

"Listen, Cammy. Tal has something to say to you. I just gave him a ride. Trust me. I am not interested in this guy. I have enough man problems and a long history of failed relationships, I don't need any more. Tell her, Tal." I set my hands on my hips to match her stance and moved in with a glare.

He stared, mortified.

Cammy glanced back and forth between us and I had an inkling she almost believed me. Almost.

Tal didn't say a word. Instead, he lunged forward, grabbed her and planted a big wet one on her lips. I could see the lip-gloss smear and Cammy's arms fly around his neck; her leg wound around his, then the other, and she climbed up higher. Tal pushed past the screen door. It banged against a wall, challenging the hinges with a deafening whine and the two of them tumbled to the floor. I could hear their faces sucking together, saw a pink shirt go flying and doubted they'd make it past the front door, much less close it.

I bee-lined it for the Jeep.

## JOEL ♂

I crumpled up the note into a tight fist and flung it at Meg's house. I wish it had been a big stone. Mrs. Vickers poked her head out of the house next door.

"Joel?" Her face looked long, her expression frustrated and weary.

"Yeah. Damian's with you?" I forgot instantly about Meg and tore across the front lawn to the Vickers place for my son.

"Yes. He's sleeping now. Joel, I don't like this situation one bit. I'm a working parent. A single mom, you know. I don't have time to watch over Meg. I just can't do this all the time. But there is no one else. She hasn't been at her mothers as often lately and that poor boy is going to suffer for it."

I could hear children running around the house, laughing voices and noise echoed through the back yard that Mrs. Vickers shared with Meg. I'm sure there were far too many children under one small roof. Toys littered the living room between old newspapers and dirty dishes. Mrs. Vickers wore a tattered apron, hair net and bright yellow rubber kitchen gloves. Her clothes were faded, the blouse so old it was almost transparent, and her shoes were held together with duct tape. She could barely make it on her own with no one to help her out yet here she stood, doing all she could for her neighbor's kid. My heart sank to the floor.

"I know, Mrs. Vickers. I wish this kind of thing didn't keep happening."

"You need to get this boy out of here, Joel. I'm not telling you anything you don't already know, and I'm not threatening you. I know you've been trying. When will that family judge see the light? That boy is much better off with you. And Meg is worse than she was before. She's always been a mess but its never affected Damian like this."

"What's been going on?" Mrs. Vickers knew more than I'd expected about the situation. Most people watched from afar and refused to get involved when it came to Meg's behavior. Up until now, I'd been on my own in that department.

"She's back to the drugs. I saw her note and I left it for you."

"I got it."

"She was planning to come back, I don't doubt that. I thought I saw her early this morning sauntering down the street toward home. Then a truck pulled up and she got in. Meg was crying and she looked like she was coming down from her high. I know about it cuz my ex is a piece of work. Went through it for years before he overdosed. That's when I went to check on things next door. I got to wonderin' where Damian was. And I heard him crying for his mother, poor thing. I tried getting hold of Dan. He's usually only a few minutes away but he must be outta town working again."

"Mrs. Vickers, I am fighting this. Again. And I hope Damian will be coming to live with me. Permanently. I'm still trying to get custody, but Meg is good at cleaning up for court. The last time she went into rehab she set up a restraining order against me and her mother backed up every part of her story. No one else came forward."

"A restraining order?"

"Yeah, because I tried to take Damian out of here. Then she covered up what she was doing and by the time she went into rehab, they wouldn't give me custody either. Damian stayed with her parents for a few months. Since then, she's shown the court she's a good mother and lifted the restraint on me, but it's on my record and she uses it to fight me every time. I need to know if you'll back me up, Mrs. Vickers. It's a lot to ask but no one else sees what's going on and Meg has everything covered up by the time they come to investigate her. I need someone to tell Damian's story. I need you to help me get Damian back." My voice cracked.

"I'll do whatever you need, Joel. Damian is a good boy. And you are a good man. A good father." Her smile lightened the tone a little. "He was talking about you this afternoon. I told him you were coming. It was all that would calm him down."

"Can I see him? Where is he?"

"Napping inside. Stay for dinner. I'm just about to round up the kids. They should all be home from school now. Then you can let Damian sleep for a while."

"Thank you."

I did my best to make myself at home. I didn't want to intrude and this woman's kindness just didn't stop. I started running ideas through my head of the upcoming weeks and after. What would happen to Damian, to all of us?

"Mrs. Vickers?" I called into the back of the house where she rounded up children from the yard. So far, I counted five, another six or so still in the yard and I wondered how many were her own. The smallest child sat in a high chair smearing a cookie across his face with a wide smile. There were two toddlers making their way into the house, both taking one step at a time, very slowly. A tall kid, a boy with long locks of hair that hung in his eyes, came behind them, rushing them along with a gruff look on his face but smiling as his sister stumbled to her knees and he helped her back up to a stand.

"Yes, Joel," said Mrs. Vickers, appearing again from the kitchen.

"I'm going to run next door to gather a few of Damian's things together. I'll be right back. And if two extra people to feed is a problem, I—"

"It's no problem. We'll manage. I haven't started much for dinner just yet. Julian! Come in here and get a pot on the stove!"

"Wait," I said, "Do you know any good pizza places around here? On me."

"Pizza, Joel? I don't know."

"Yeah, Mom! We never get pizza!" yelled the longhaired boy.

"Don't even think twice about it. You, Julian is it?" I asked. "Grab a phonebook and order a bunch of large pizzas, whatever you like. I'll be right back."

"Thanks, mister!" he called and ran toward the living room.

Damian woke as the pizza deliveryman pulled up to the curb. After a big yawn and a moment of disorientation, Damian reached up and wrapped his arms around my neck. We stood alone in the living room, away from the bustle of Mrs. Vickers' house, and hugged each other, me as much as him, holding on for dear life.

After dinner, I tried to contact Meg and finally tracked down a few numbers where I might get a hold of her. I decided to wait until morning and spend the day tracking her after we spent the night in a motel. It would be a four-hour drive back to town in the already black night and my energy had been drained. More emotionally than anything, I think.

We prepared to leave for the motel, Damian's bag packed in the truck with a few of his favorite toys. I had a room set up for him at my place, so he wouldn't need much from here to get by as long as we needed. Mrs. Vickers stood at the door, holding it open as we stepped outside and Damian clung to my chest, afraid to let go.

"Joel, take care," she said.

"We will. Thank you for everything. And here," I said and handed her an envelope of money.

"No, Joel this is too much. There's nearly—Good God—there's more than two hundred dollars in here."

"It's all I have on me. I wish I could do more. You've been a big help, and not just today. You deserve more than that."

"Thank you," she said with a tear in her eye. I kissed her on the cheek and walked toward the truck.

"Joel!"

"Yeah."

"Please call if there is anything I can do to help with...well, with anything. I'll be there."

"I will. Thank you."

# Chapter 9

## *EVE* ♀

I sat on Joel's front porch, drinking a late evening beer and wondering when I had become comfortable here in this town. Trey sat next to me watching the heat waves from the sun alter the air as it began its descent into a magenta colored sky, listening to the lone bark of a dog.

And I wore Trey's hat.

We heard the wheels of a truck kick up gravel from down the road and watched until an old blue pick up pulled up out front. It was Joel. He killed the engine and opened the door, not taking notice of us sitting on his porch. He walked around the truck, leaned inside the passenger door, threw a duffle bag over his shoulder and emerged with a young sleeping child cradled in his arms. My uterus flipped and my ovaries started to dance. They were salivating for the first time in my life. I told them to settle down. Really bad timing. I wasn't even looking for a man yet.

Joel smiled and without a word, walked past Trey and I on the porch and into the house.

Trey stood up. "Well, I need to get going. Look for a job. Or something."

Job? Was he actually heeding my advice? "I can give you a hand with a resume if you want," I called after him, ready to join Trey in an escape from Joel's private moment.

"Yeah? Huh. Maybe. Maybe not." He kept going. The smartass just wanted a quick escape off of Joel's porch.

Crap. I needed my own escape. I stumbled up from the chair. I certainly couldn't ask Trey for a ride. I lived next door. "Don't you need your hat, Trey?"

"No, keep it. I've got more. You'll need it more than I do this weekend."

I had no idea what that meant. Probably so I'd fit in with the country bumpkins, but I wasn't sure how Trey fit in with the hat so I sure didn't know how I would. Regardless, I appreciated the gesture.

I turned toward the steps and heard the screen door to Joel's house open behind me. Trey drove off in his car, sputtering dust behind him.

"Hey," said Joel.

"Hey. I thought you maybe needed some time."

He grinned, and I suddenly felt trapped. He looked as if he wanted someone to talk to. I couldn't leave with a good conscience so sat down on the loveseat instead.

"Do you want a beer or something?" I asked.

"Sure. I'll get it. What are you drinking?"

"I don't know. Some swill Trey brought over."

"Nice hat," he said and tipped the edge of the brim while eyeing me up and down with a lazy grin.

"Thanks."

I pulled the hat off and set it into my lap. Joel sat down next to me and forgot about the beer altogether.

"How have you been Joel?"

"Good. I guess." He twirled a battered old toy car in his fingers and spun the wobbly wheels with his thumb.

"How is Meg?"

"I don't know. I haven't talked to her."

"And Damian?"

"He's okay. He's scared. Did Trey fill you in on everything?" He shone me a weak smile.

"No. He told me about Damian. That's all. And I'm not trying to pry, I just thought you looked like you needed someone to talk to."

Joel stared ahead of him, spinning the wheels of the little car around and around. "Meg and I got together for a couple of nights four years back. I thought we would try to work things out but she didn't want to.

And in the end, it was better that it didn't. Then she showed up at my door a year later with a two month old baby in her arms."

"Damian."

"Yeah. Since then, Meg has had a few problems of her own that I have since made my responsibility for Damian's sake. One of which is her lack of concern. I left yesterday morning because I got a call from the neighbor. Damian was alone at Meg's place. When I got there he was scared to death and I haven't been able to track Meg down."

"Do you think something has happened to her?"

"This isn't anything new. Only this time, she didn't leave him with her mother first. I gave up waiting for her and took Damian home with me."

"Well, that's good isn't it? Can he stay with you now?"

"I've been trying to make that happen for the past two years, but Meg has fought me on it and won. She's had problems with drugs and rehab and still, she manages to make herself look better than I am as a parent. With the help of her mother and a whole pile of lies."

"Oh my God, Joel. What are you going to do?"

"I don't know." He sat back into the loveseat. "He was so scared, Eve. The poor kid doesn't know what's going on, he's so confused. Life for a three-year-old shouldn't be like this. He needs stability and love and Meg can't give him that anymore. I don't want to let him go this time. I can't let him go."

He looked up at me with glassy eyes. I could feel the pain rip through him and I couldn't imagine what it must be like to be so close to a child and unable to protect him as hard as you tried. Joel Powell had more layers of integrity and strength than I had seen yet.

I reached my hand out and set it over both of his where they clasped the toy car. "It'll work itself out."

"I know. But now I have to figure out work. I can't just leave him here. I could take a few days off." He ran a weary hand through his hair.

"Do you want me to watch him?"

"What?"

I swallowed hard at the proposition I just laid out there. Shit, Eve. You've never taken care of children before. You don't even like them.

And I knew I should ignore my feelings of sympathy and the motherly instinct that kept nudging me forward, but I couldn't shut up.

"Well, I've never really taken care of kids before. But if you need a hand, I could watch him for a while. If you trust me. I don't know if you should trust me. I don't know if I trust myself. What do you have to do with him?"

"I just get him lunch and keep him occupied. A nap in the afternoon. Snacks in between. Don't let him drown or run into the street or stick something in the electrical socket and he's fine."

"That doesn't sound bad."

"I don't know. It's a lot to ask."

"Who else is going to do it?"

"My mom used to help out with him, but with everything at the ranch I can't burden her right now."

"Then it looks like me or Trey. Quite honestly, it's your call. I don't know if I'd want to flip that coin."

"Why don't I bring him over for a while tomorrow morning? I'd tell you to come here, but I don't want him around the renovation work until the nails at the windows are pulled up. I'll go to work after lunch and we can spend the morning getting you used to the idea. And Damian. He doesn't always adapt well to new situations or strangers."

"Sure."

"If you aren't up for it by tomorrow afternoon, I'll make other arrangements."

I just smiled like an idiot.

"Are you sure about this?"

Last chance to back out. This was it, Eve. "Yeah, I am." Then I remembered where my hand rested.

He looked down to my fingers entwined in his and began rubbing them with his thumb. It was a gentle caress, a comfort to the both of us.

"Thanks, Eve. For everything."

"No problem." I grinned and for a moment, lost in Joel's eyes, I thought he might lean in and kiss me. I think I wanted him to. My heart beat faster, pounding heavily in my chest, and I squeezed his hand tighter. He squeezed mine, the tender moment growing into something more. Or was that just my imagination?

We'd never know, because a wailing cry sounded from inside the house and Joel leapt to his feet. I followed him, running, into the house toward Damian's room. I watched from the doorway as Joel leaned over and scooped the crying child into his arms.

"Hey, buddy, it's okay. Daddy's here," he whispered, kissing his cheek to calm him. The child gripped Joel's shoulders and snuggled his head in, squishing his eyes tightly shut until he settled to a whimper. I watched, locked in a stare of awe that this virile, strong man could move with such ease and confidence to being gentle and tender; the love for his son was painted so plainly, so openly across his face. I wondered what it must feel like to have that kind of love for a child and my ovaries panged again.

Joel's strong hand brushed lightly through Damian's hair, tugging softly on the dark locks. He shushed him quietly and Damian settled to the sound. Joel could have started singing a lullaby right now and I would have stood there listening as if in the midst of a completely ordinary event.

"Blanket," he whispered to his dad.

Joel reached toward the bed and ruffled through the sheets to find it. It rested in a heap on the floor and he hadn't seen it fall. I took a few steps into the room and reached to the floor. I lifted it toward him and held Joel's stare.

"Thank you," Joel said and I knew then that the kiss on the porch wouldn't have been just my imagination. We could both feel it now. I knew because this wasn't the friction of one person alone; it took two to ignite the electricity that moved through me. But now wasn't the time.

"I'll walk you out," he said and followed me toward the door with Damian in his arms, wrapped in his blanket, head resting on his father's shoulder.

"He looks like an angel, sleeping. Does he always look so peaceful?"

"Not always," he smiled. I imagined I would see why "not always" tomorrow when I had a three-year-old to handle all on my own.

"Is there anything I can do?" I asked, feeling a little out of place and awkward.

"No. I think it was just a nightmare. I'll sit up with him for a while and he'll go to bed."

"I'll see you in the morning, then."

"Goodnight, Eve."

I waved at the door and sauntered back to the house with more mixed emotions. I didn't know a thing about babysitting a three-year-old and had a sudden inclination to phone my mother for advice. Then I thought against it and focused on the thought of kissing Joel, which brought nice warm fuzzies to my stomach. I wouldn't be sleeping tonight.

Wednesday morning came and I dragged myself out of bed to start a pot of coffee brewing. I puttered around the house to baby proof, though I had no idea what to baby proof, or if I needed to at all. Should I still consider a three-year-old a baby? How much supervision did he still need? I'd watch him like a hawk to be safe and block all of the electrical outlets.

I remember slugging back a shot of Windex as a kid so decided to hide the cleaners on the top shelf of the linen closet. And then there's the knife block in the kitchen, electrical outlets, stairs…those were the things I knew about. I was not cut out for this. And Joel said something about lunch and snacks and a nap. Where would he sleep? What would I feed him? Grilled cheese worked for me; hopefully it worked for Damian. Does Damian eat ketchup?

I checked the clock on the wall and wondered when they'd be here. Nine thirty. I wanted as much babysitting time with Joel as I could get before he left me to fend for myself.

I decided to walk over and see if he needed a hand. Maybe he'd forgotten he would come by.

I knocked lightly on the door and waited for an answer. None came, so I peered in through the window at a shadow of Joel on the sofa in the living room. I opened the front door and walked inside— probably not the best use of the neighbor's key, I know—and stood at the foot of the sofa.

Joel reclined into the back cushions with Damian, still cradled in his arms wearing Spider-Man pajamas and holding his tattered blanket. Joel had his feet flat on the floor, leaning an arm on the armrest, his head tipped to the side opposite Damian's who nuzzled into his dad's chest.

Now if that didn't set any healthy woman's ovaries to skyrocketing, I don't know what would.

"Joel," I said, unsure if I should wake him or just walk back out the door.

He opened his eyes and looked up at me.

"Hi. Shit, what time is it?"

"Nine forty. AM. Looks like you had a rough night."

"Yeah. He wouldn't settle, so I sat down with him. I must have fallen asleep."

Damian stirred and opened his eyes, still huddled against the safe and warm chest.

"Good morning, buddy," said Joel, tilting his head down toward his son.

"Who's that?" he asked quietly and pointed at me.

"This is my friend Eve. We are going next door to visit her today."

"Oh."

"Hi, Damian," I said and he stared at me without an answer.

"Come on, let's get you dressed," said Joel.

"Where's Mommy?" he asked. Joel set him down on the ground and took his hand to walk to the bedroom.

"Mommy had to go away for a few days. But Daddy is here. I'm not going anywhere, okay?"

"Kay. Can I bring blanket?"

"Yep. What else do you want to bring?"

"Ele*p*ant."

I watched from the door again with my arms crossed, unsure of how I could be of any help besides gawking at Joel in his pajama bottoms and bare chest.

"Where is Elephant?"

"Don't know," said Damian.

Joel turned toward me. "Do you mind watching him for a few minutes so I can have a shower?"

"Sure. Damian, why don't I help you find your Elephant?"

Damian wrapped an arm around Joel's leg and buried his face in his dad's knee.

"You know, I might have heard an elephant out there, Damian," I said and crouched down to his level. "What does an elephant sound like?"

Still nothing, so I barked like a dog. He giggled.

"Hmmm. Not like that, huh? What about..." I said and quacked like a duck. "Did you hear that one? Was that the elephant?"

He laughed again. "She's *punny*," he said and looked up at Joel.

"Well, I won't know how to find the elephant if I don't know what it sounds like."

Damian made a wail of a sound through his teeth and sputtered saliva all over my face.

"Well, that sounds more like an elephant. A wet elephant," I said and wiped my face. "Want to help me look?"

Damian nodded and followed me into the living room.

## JOEL ♂

The hot water washed over every tense muscle and I finally felt my body relax, the stress begin to release. What a remarkable sight to see Eve interact with Damian; her inner child emerged when she approached him. I could see it in her face, feel it radiate from her and yet her eyes remained nervous. She feared Damian as much as he feared her. The only difference being that as an adult, Eve faced her fears for the first time in a while. And Damian froze beneath them.

When I'd opened my eyes this morning, forgetting I held Damian in my arms, that we spent a long night on the sofa in the middle of my unassembled living room, I saw Eve looking down at me with wide eyes and her angelic smile. I melted. Goddamn it, I wished I had kissed her the night before. And now, standing here in the shower, I couldn't fight off my own body's reaction to the thought of her.

I had kept women and relationships low on the list of life's priorities for years. There had been moments of weakness, times of male urges and needs, but those went as fast as they came, satiated rarely; I've had enough chaos in my life to keep my thoughts focused elsewhere. This was different. I felt like a teenager again, raging hormones encouraging me to rip her clothes off and satisfy whatever urges had long built up and been forced inside.

I banged my head against the wall of the shower and turned the nozzle to cold. Ice. I needed freaking ice.

I shaved for the first time in days and pulled on a clean pair of jeans. I held a t-shirt in my hands but didn't get to putting it on when a loud shriek from Damian came from the other room, followed by Eve in a panicked cry.

"Joel!"

I yanked open the door, having second thoughts about leaving him alone with her for the afternoon. I ran down the hall, shirt in hand.

"What, what is it?"

"He wants *ju-ju!*" she yelled over Damian's shrill cry. "What the hell is *ju-ju*? He won't stop! I'm so sorry. I swear I didn't do anything. He just started saying *ju-ju* and freaked out." Her eyes were swelling with tears and terror, lit with both concern and confusion. I grabbed her by the shoulders, ready to slap her calm.

"Eve, relax. He wants juice."

"Juice? Why is he freaking out?" she yelled.

"He's still upset about everything going on. Damian," I said, focusing on my son wailing tears and bursting so hard with frustration his face had turned the color of tomato sauce. "Damian, settle down. I'll get you a juice. Come on, stop crying. Eve didn't know and you're making her cry, too." He stopped to look up at Eve and I swear I saw a satisfied grin behind his eyes. Definitely my son, little manipulator that he was.

"Look, I'll pour a juice and we can help Eve stop crying. Okay? What do we do to make someone stop crying?"

Eve stared aghast, hiding the fact that tears of panic, the adrenaline wave now settling, were sitting heavy behind her eyes.

"Big hugs," said Damian and he wrapped his tiny arms around Eve's calf, nearly knocking her to the floor.

"It's okay, Damian," she said. "I'm sorry I upset you. I didn't know what *ju-ju* was."

Damian looked her straight in the eyes and said, "*Ju-ju* is juice, Ee*b*ie."

Eve glanced to me with a look that asked, *is this some kind of joke?* I laughed and handed Damian his juice.

"He totally knew what he was doing! He is such a man already." She spoke under her breath. "I thought I did something wrong."

"Damian," I said, turning my attention back to him. "You can't play games like that with Eve. She's new at this and doesn't know these games. Be nice, or she won't help take care of you."

"Kay."

I wiped his tears with a paper towel and hunched down to his level. "Would it be okay if Eve took care of you after lunch today?"

"Where are you going?"

"Daddy has to go to work. But I won't be long and we'll have supper when I get home. We can order something for supper if you want."

"Pizza!"

"You want pizza? I'll get you pizza. But I need you to listen to me, carefully. Eve is very special. And you need to be nice to her today."

"I will."

"Thanks, buddy."

"Where's Mommy?"

"I'm going to call Mommy from work and figure out a plan for us. And we'll see Mommy again as soon as we can. You might be staying with Daddy for a little while."

"Why?"

"Because I love you and I haven't seen you for a long time. I miss you so much. Will you stay with me for a while?"

He nodded and my heart nearly broke in two it ached so hard. I smothered him with a hug and felt his little hands squeeze my neck.

"I *wub* you," he said into my ear and I squeezed my eyes as tight as his.

"Let's go over to Eve's now, okay? I'm going to stay with you for a while and then go to work when you think it'll be okay to stay with her by yourself?"

"Kay. I need ele*p*ant!"

"Did you find him?"

"Yep. Ee*b*ie *p*ound him under the pirate ship!" He talked in the only other volume he knew: three notches above high.

119

"The pirate ship?"

"Yeah! And we sa*b*ed him before he went into the water!"

"Into the water?"

"Uh huh. And the *pyranites* almost ate him."

"What are *pyranites*?" I asked Eve, completely baffled.

"Piranha's," she said with an eye roll. "You know, the one's that swim around your pirate ship,"—she motioned to the sofa—"in search of elephants. Catch up papa."

"Right. The ele*p*ant *pyranites*. I forgot to tell you about those."

"And Ee*b*ie's house has a treasure hunt in it!" he screeched.

"A treasure hunt?"

"Yep! Hurry, hurry, so you get to come on it wi*p* us!"

"Okay, okay. Daddy needs to get dressed. And so do you, Spidey."

"Kay." He took off down the hall to his room to dig through the dresser.

When I stood back up to adult level, Eve stared with her hands over her mouth and eyes wide.

"What?" I asked.

"Nothing. It's just…he's so…I've never been around kids much. I didn't know I could freak them out so bad. He screamed bloody murder. I thought he was choking or something. I don't know if I can do this, Joel."

"Eve," I said and took her shoulders in my hands again. "If he'd been choking, he wouldn't be able to scream bloody murder. And that is a three-year-old not getting his way. It's what they do and Damian is a pro. Above all else, you have him excited to go to your house after spending all of about fifteen minutes entertaining him. For him, that's a huge step. You're a miracle worker."

Eve took a deep breath and grinned. "I am?"

"Almost. We'll see how the morning goes."

"You love him so much, Joel."

"I do." Then I started something I wanted to the night before. I moved toward her, like one magnet pulling toward another, the heat between us reigniting instantly from last night. Our eyes held. I could feel her lips drawing mine closer, even without the physical connection. The emotional reached frightening levels—

And Damian flew back into the room wearing a pair of backwards underwear, rubber boots and a red cape, carrying Elephant at his side.

I drew back, dumb-assed flushed cheeks and all, and stared at Eve, my arms falling to my sides. "Damian, I thought you were getting dressed," I said, trying to keep my eyes locked on the fast moving target that was my son.

"I am!" he said and he flew around the kitchen table with his arms at his sides like an airplane.

"You really need to put a shirt on," said Eve and I felt her eyes drift over my bare chest then to my crotch before she walked toward the kitchen.

I really needed to get to work.

Eve and I sat on the porch with a cup of coffee and watched Damian run around the front yard in his superhero cape and racecar sweat suit I finally convinced him to wear, however long it lasted.

She sat with her feet perched up on the railing, slouching into the chair and cupping her hands around the warm mug. I could still see my breath in the air as I watched her through it. She'd hate to hear it, but she looked somewhat comfortable in our *Small Town Nowhere*. More comfortable than she would likely admit.

"Is this what my afternoon will be like?" she asked. "I'm dizzy already watching him spin in circles."

"He has a lot of energy to burn. Don't feed him any sugar."

"Sugar would make him busier than this? How could he be any busier?"

"Trust me. He can be much busier. And I brought a huge bucket of cars and trucks. If all else fails, you can have races. He likes to race cars."

"And what about nap time? When is nap time?"

"Depends. Sometimes he won't nap."

"You should have told me that before I agreed to this. I might need a nap," she laughed.

"Probably. I'll leave you my cell number if you run into trouble. And Mom's number at the ranch."

"So, Damian's coming this weekend to the barn raising?"

"I hope so. Meg was supposed to bring him out. It's my turn to have him. This is a bit early, so I hope she doesn't want him back right away. Then the fight will begin."

"So Trey says the men build the barn and the women make food in the kitchen."

"Yep."

"Hmm."

"What?"

"Still trying to figure out where I'm going to fit in."

"Good question. Welcome to small town life. You either join a quilting bee or learn to run a tractor."

"I can run a tractor. And I can rope a cow."

"I can't see you roping a cow. But I can see you quilting even less. So how are you with a nail gun?"

"Prob'ly pretty good."

"Bet you'd shoot a hole in your foot."

"No I wouldn't, smart ass. I could build the crap out of that barn. If I wanted to."

"Yeah?"

"Yeah."

"As good as you play poker? And what do you mean if you wanted to?"

"As opposed to hanging out in the kitchen I won't have many options, will I? I was thinking of not going."

"Why? You should come. It'll be fun. You can meet my mother." What the hell did I just say? Meet my mother? Meg had been the last woman I introduced to my mother.

"I guess that would be okay. And my mother is going?"

"I think so. Oh, this *will* be fun," I said, unable to hold back a grin again.

"Don't laugh. I'll tell her how much you enjoyed her lemon cake and that you would love to talk about the recipe. And that you needed some advice about getting stains out of your upholstery. She'll keep you busy for a good three hours."

"You wouldn't."

"I would," she laughed and sipped her coffee.

I glanced over and a comfortable silence fell over us. I watched and listened to Damian squeal around the yard, Eve's giggle in the background and felt more content than I'd been in a long time. "It's nice having a neighbor I can talk to again."

"What, you didn't strike up conversations with Maggie all the time?" She raised her eyebrows in feigned surprise.

"No. I love Maggie. She's very sweet, just not the kind of person you can sit and talk to about everything."

"So you feel you can talk to me about everything?"

"Sort of. You're like one of the guys."

Eve went silent after that and a wall went up between us for the next hour while we watched Damian play with his breakfast and run circles around the living room in front of the television.

After lunch, I stood at the door in my work boots and a ball cap. My heart pounded.

"Damian, buddy, I have to go to work. And you're going to stay with Eve for a while. Only until tonight."

"And we'll have pizza?" he asked.

"Yes. Only if you behave."

"And can Ee*b*ie have pizza?"

"If Eve wants pizza, she can have pizza, too."

"At Ee*b*ie's house?"

"Maybe."

"Kay." I could tell he held back tears to be brave for Ee*b*ie.

I leaned down to whisper in his ear, "Be nice for Eve, okay. And no tears. We don't want to make her to cry, do we?"

He shook his head no and grinned with flushed cheeks into my eyes.

"Have a good day," said Eve from the door.

God, I didn't want to leave either of them. "You too. Good luck. If you need me for anything, call. You'll be fine."

She nodded and closed the door behind me. My shortened day at work already felt a few seconds too long.

# Chapter 10

## *Eve* ♀

We had five minutes left until Joel returned home. Five freaking long minutes. I thought I could handle a three-year-old. Did I actually say, *How hard could this be*? I jinxed it is what I did.

The minute Joel left the games began. We had another treasure hunt, this one a covert operation planned and organized by a three-year-old. He found a box of my feminine products, which he called *torpedoes*, three of which are still missing and one of which had been jammed down the kitchen drain. No garbage disposal, remember?

Next, he hid Stumpy. When I found him, the poor cat was head to tail in canned pasta and tomato sauce from lunch. And he wasn't purring at my feet, I can tell you that.

We didn't get to the nap because we were on clean up duty, which didn't amuse Damian in the least when I made him help scrub the floor where the grape juice mixed with sauce mixed with mystery fridge liquid mingled on the carpet.

When we'd finished clean up, I sent Damian to wash his hands. *Not* to play with my make-up or eat my lipstick, which he did. I only figured it out because I heard a loud giggle from the bathroom from where I stood just now on the kitchen stool to put away the cleaning products high into the cabinet and Damian surprised me with what he called an Ee*bie* clown face.

"Damian," I called from the stool and tucked away the last bottle of Pine-Sol then turned back around. "Damian!" I screeched, stepped backward and landed on my ass on the hard linoleum. "Shit."

"Shit!" he repeated back. Loudly.

"No! Don't say that...it's a bad word...Damian." I gasped for air, winded from my fall. "Eve shouldn't have...said it...and I'm sorry," I said in a near whisper.

"Shit!" he yelled in Damian volume and continued to run in circles around me.

I wanted to cry.

I wanted to rip my hair out.

I wanted my tubes tied.

"Shit, shit, shit," he said. Then, "Daddy!" he yelled with laughter and ran toward Joel who stood in the kitchen entrance. I lay still sprawled across the floor in a most ungraceful pose.

"What did you just say?" asked Joel.

"I said—" he started.

"Joel, I'm sorry...He heard me...this looks so bad." I held a hand to my throbbing butt cheek and struggled to catch my breath.

"Damian go to the bathroom and wash your face," his dad commanded.

"Crap," I whimpered and felt a tear roll down my cheek. I couldn't breath.

"Are you okay?"

"Just...winded."

He took my hand in his and I felt the pressure of his arm at my lower back as he raised me to sit.

"Take a deep breath," he said.

"I'm alright. Thanks."

"No you're not. Sit down." I sat back on the floor.

"I'll be fine. I'm sorry. I suck as a babysitter. I'll never be a good mother and I want my tubes tied," I whined. He laughed and only then did my tears pour. "It's not funny."

"Tell me what happened. Start with why you're on the floor."

"I fell off the stool. I was putting away the cleaners—up high because I thought I was kid proofing—and he scared the crap out of me so I fell. That's when he learned the new word."

"It's okay. And the make-up?" I tried his best not to laugh but his eyes flashed amusement at me.

"After he covered the cat in pasta sauce, I sent him to wash his hands. And by the looks of things, that's when he ate my lipstick and painted his face."

"The cat?" Joel stood up to search for his demon child.

"There's more, Joel," I said and pulled him back down to crouch next to me. I needed to spill it all to someone. "We had a bit of a search and rescue of my things. He hid...some stuff...around the house and I had to find it."

"Uh oh."

"And he might tell you I was mean to him because I made him clean the kitchen floor with me."

"Pasta sauce?"

"And grape juice and something else he pulled out of the fridge. I can't tell what it is because he mixed it all together to make mud pies."

"I am so sorry. He's not usually like this all at once."

I started to sob again.

"Is it still hurting? Your back?" Joel set his hand at my lower back and brushed away a strand of hair that clung to my damp cheek.

"No."

"Then what's wrong? Something else is hurting."

"No, no. Nothing's hurting."

"Then what is it?" he actually looked concerned.

"I thought I had a connection going with him. And—"

"What?"

"You must be so disappointed. Trey would have done a better job."

"Trey showed Damian how to open a beer can with his teeth."

"Did he teach him how to swear? And put on make-up?"

"No, but he's well versed in curses from his mother. *Shit* was probably not a new one. You don't suck. Damian is just going through a lot of stuff right now and you were his outlet."

"Great. Glad to be of assistance." I had to laugh now at my pathetic need to impress Joel with my kid watching capabilities. Since when did I feel a need to prove anything to him or to myself about it? "I guess

I thought I wanted kids one day and now I'm not sure I'll ever make it."

"You'd do fine. Look at me. Do you think I figured it all out in one day?"

"Uh oh," I said, staring blankly in the direction of the washroom. "What?"

"Oh my God. This is the most embarrassing day of my life."

We watched Damian walk down the hallway wearing a pink thong on his head with the last two "torpedoes" sticking out of his ears. Half of the make-up he'd worn on his face now streaked bright red and blue across the bra around his waist. My black lace bra; the one I tend *not* to parade around for the neighbors.

"Damian, put that stuff down!" yelled Joel. "Give it back to Eve."

"Ee*b*ie, I'm playing dress up!" he yelled, looking for my appreciation. I jumped up in horror to grab the bra, Joel pulled the thong off Damian's head and we stood there in awe. Neither of us wanted to make the first move toward the *torpedoes*. I pulled the *feminine hygiene products* out of his ears and stuffed them quickly into my back pocket. Oh, dear God.

Joel stared, unsure of what to say. He flushed red in the face, as much as I had I'm sure; I felt the temperature rising higher in my cheeks as we stood there.

"Damian, go sit down in the living room," he said, his voice low and commanding. "And don't touch anything! Eve, I'm so sorry."

"Well, there can't be anything worse than my neighbor yanking a pair of my panties off his son's head."

Joel shoved the pink thong at me with a look of mortification. "Sorry," he said quietly and we stood there in awkward silence.

"When are we having pizza?" Damian yelled from the sofa.

"We aren't having pizza!" Joel shot back and glared into the living room. I could see him mustering all of his parental control in that moment while he took deep breaths. I didn't feel so bad for myself as I watched his embarrassment and frustration rise in a symphony around us.

"I want pizza wi*p* Ee*b*ie!"

"Now way. No pizza and no more Evie! We're going home for time out and a very long nap," said Joel.

"No!" he wailed and ran toward me. I could see the increasing panic as the knowledge of how much trouble he might be in began to come clearer in his little mind. "I want to stay with Ee*bie*!"

"*Evie* did not have fun today. I told you to be nice for her."

"But we did have *p*un! We played dress up and treasure hunt and Ee*bie* got almost all the torpedoes, cuz she's good at that game! And you don't *have* torpedoes! And we painted wi*p* the cat. Cat's *p*unny. And she got me yummy lunch. Except she made me wash up. And, and, and I'm sorry I said a bad word!!"

From a three-year-old's perspective, I guess we did have a pretty cool day. I could only laugh while Joel stared aghast at the both of us.

Damian threw himself against my legs and reached to be picked up. "Hug, hug, hug!" he yelled. I scooped him up and sucked all of the love from him that I could. No kid had ever wanted me before. It made my fallopian tubes beg to stay untied. His squishy pudgy cheeks and tummy were like soft little pillows full of unconditional love.

"Damian," I said. "Did you have fun today?"

"Yep. Didn't you have *p*un, Ee*bie*?"

"Yeah, tons of fun. So, can we have pizza papa?" I asked Joel and shone him a look through my puffy eyes.

He shook his head with a grin and picked up the phone to order.

# JOEL ♂

I don't know which was more convincing, Damian's affection for Eve or Eve's helpless—but sexy—pout. I know she did it for show but it got the point across and had me aching again to rip her clothes off. I needed to gain control of my hormones. Fast.

I had called and located Meg this morning. She accused me of kidnapping our son but she still sounded drunk. I convinced her that this was the best arrangement, that she needed some alone time. Part of the convincing meant telling her it was well deserved alone time for being a hard working mother. But it kept her calm and avoided her making another call to the police.

It had happened before. I had agreed to take Damian for a week, my week, to spend some father son time. Meg, either in her drunken state at the time of the arrangement, or in one when she'd discovered Damian wasn't home, called the police to have me arrested for taking our son without her consent.

It took me an overnight stay in the slammer and a night of sobering up on her part to convince the authorities I was not in the wrong. Even then, there'd been a restraining order against me for four months until Meg had had enough of taking care of Damian on her own. She dropped it and we were back to square one, as if none of it had happened.

Now, I pretty much risk arrest every time I bring Damian home. So I live life cautiously. And I hold my breath that the cops won't show up at my door this week just like I do all of the others. And that I won't have to explain our strange situation. I feel more sorry for Meg every time, and angrier that she continues to fight me.

The difference this week is that I did take him from her house without her permission but her neighbor witnessed her leaving him alone. This time I would fight, with Mrs. Vickers on my side. But not today. Meg still wasn't "herself" this morning so there was little she could do about us in her current condition.

The barn raising would come in three days time. So I had a few days to get ahead at work and Damian would be spending the days with Eve. She wanted to do it, though I understood if she didn't want to speak to either of us ever again after round one. I have a feeling she might call in reinforcements this time around.

The air felt cool tonight, a chill washing over town as the summer days began to dwindle away. Damian slept peacefully—he conked out the minute he hit the pillow—and I could hear Eve through the screen next door. She paced the window and talked on the phone. And I pictured her in the pink thong and black lace bra. Then with only the thong, breasts bare, the sleek curve of her hip all the way down her leg to her toes. Painted pink toes, so I'd noticed this morning. Then...well, you get the picture.

She walked out onto the porch with a wine glass in her hand and the phone propped between her shoulder and chin. At the same time,

Tal pulled up in front of my house with Trey in the beat up shit-trap of a car. I felt too stressed to deal with their crap right now but I needed an excuse to stop thinking about Eve naked.

"Hey, Powell," called Trey. Tal followed and waved toward Eve. She waved back and smiled at me, locking her stare for a moment as she ended her call and went back into the house. I could swear she felt the same energy. It would be best to get it out of our systems as soon as possible before I kill myself.

"Hey," I called back to the guys and they sat down on the front step.

"So, we up for a game of poker?" asked Tal.

"I don't know. I have Damian here and he's sleeping."

"Raif's on his way over. Maybe we can play at Eve's place," said Trey. "She won't mind."

"Eve was watching Damian all day. I'm sure she needs a break."

"Ooh. How'd that go?" asked Trey.

"Worse than your first time with him. But don't tell her that. He's been especially strung out."

"No wonder. Poor kid's so confused right now."

"I know. He's staying with me for a while."

"So, are we playing or what?" asked Tal, completely insensitive to the situation. At least he helped avoid talking about it.

"I don't know." I hesitated, afraid to wake Damian and not willing to disturb Eve again. Or have to watch her all night.

"I'll go ask," said Trey and he hopped across the railing to her house to pound on the front door.

"Hey farm girl," he said when she answered.

"Hey, Trey. What's up?"

"We're playing poker, want to join us?"

"No, but I'll watch. I can't afford to lose any more money on you guys."

"Great. We're playing at your house. Damian's sleeping."

"I'm not leaving Damian alone in the house, Trey!" I called across the lawn.

"Then we'll play on the front porch," he called back.

"I'll grab a sweater," said Eve and stepped into the house again.

"Eve's not in for the game but she's coming over. See how good I am with women?"

"Oh so convincing, Trey!" yelled Eve from behind him, running to catch up.

"So, Tal," I stared with a wry grin, "how the hell did you get Cammy back crawling all over you?"

"I just did," he grinned. I swear he was blushing.

"Have you heard from Skeeter?" asked Eve. We all did a double take on Eve. How the hell did she know Skeeter?

"Yep. Beat the shit out of him."

"Tal! You were supposed to be nice. You got the girl, so no beating on Skeeter. Remember?"

"He started it. But this time, Cammy told him to leave. Without even a word from me, I swear; I did what you said. But he wouldn't go so I kicked his ass out the door."

"Then good for you," said Eve. "He probably deserved it."

"You're the relationship expert now, Evie?" I asked.

"I'm the pro around these parts," she said with a wide grin. "Just not in the Eve department. Those don't usually go so smoothly. If you can call Cammy and Tal smoothly. She did beat the crap out of some roses and call me a bitch."

"So, she finally making a man of you, Tal? Getting hitched?" asked Trey.

"No. We just got back together and got Skeeter out of the picture."

"That's a start," I said. "Sounds like I missed all the fun."

"So I hear you had a fun day with Damian," said Trey, eyeing Eve with raised eyebrows.

"Yep. I did. We had a treasure hunt and played dress up."

I couldn't hold back a laugh when I thought of Damian's dress up game.

"What's so funny about dress up?" asked Tal.

"I got to see Eve's underwear for one."

"Shut up, Joel," she shot back. "And I didn't plan that. Damian helped himself. I'm just not so good at kid proofing the house yet."

"Her underwear? What kind of underwear?" asked Raif. He'd come up from behind us mid conversation.

"Black lacy ones. See through and edible," said Eve. "Black rubber suits, whips, dog collars—" started Eve.

"Okay, okay, that's enough," I said.

"What's wrong Joel, can't handle it? Not getting enough lately?"

"No, thanks very much. And it wasn't dog collars and rubber suits." I felt my face flushing. "Are we going to play, or what?"

"You deal," said Raif and handed the cards to Trey.

So the game started. Eve watched and laughed, relaxed among our group of men with her sneakers propped up on the rail swaying lazily back and forth. She swore along with us and no one held back with the jokes and laughter. When things got out of hand, Eve didn't hesitate to cuff us one or put us back in line with a smart assed comment. She even made a beer run. I think it would be safe to say we enjoyed having her around.

## EVE ♂

By the end of three days with Damian things had improved. We've now come to the understanding that if he does anything to wreck my stuff, I get to keep one of his toys. I am now the proud owner of a Ninja Turtle with nun chucks, a well used and abused red dinky car and a superhero cape. And Maggie's house has not been destroyed. Yet. We have also learned to play dress up with Daddy's clothes instead of my lingerie drawer, much to the dismay of Joel, who mentioned yesterday afternoon that he missed seeing the underpants.

When Joel returned home tonight—impressed, I have to say, that Damian slept quietly on the sofa—I was close to relaxed. Though I had frantically started searching for a missing earring just the right size to look like candy and fit down a three-year-old's mouth. At least he wasn't choking.

"Good evening," said Joel. "How did it go? Is he actually sleeping?"

"Yep." I tore open a few cupboards at three-foot accessibility level and searched for the earring.

"What are you looking for?"

"Nothing."

"Eve?"

I paced the floor with my hands on my hips and stopped above the litter box. Kitty litter had been spread around the floor in the lovely pattern of a true Zen artist. And something sparkled in the light from inside the box.

I fished it out without a second thought and brushed my hands on my pants. "Here it is. I thought he swallowed it." Huge sigh of relief.

"Well, as long as everything went smoothly."

"It did. Except for the earring. Which I only just noticed was gone. No choking or hacking up jewelry today."

"Good. Thanks for watching Damian all week. I owe you."

"No you don't. It kept me busy at least. And it turned out to be not so bad. He's a sweet boy."

Joel smiled and walked toward Damian who lay sprawled across the sofa.

We stared at him, in awe of the childhood innocence—innocence that came out mainly while he slept—and I yawned.

"He looks just like you, Joel."

Joel smiled and I felt him staring at me. "You're good with him, you know. You'll make a great mother one day."

"Thank you. But the cards are still out on that one."

"Why?"

"I need a man before kids and I still don't want a man."

"I see. Well, at least you know what you want. Does your mother know about your plans for not having a family any time soon?"

"Not exactly."

"You coming to the ranch, then?"

"Yep. I'll drive out behind you. When are you leaving?"

"Sun up. Raif's coming with me."

"I told Trey and Tal I'd give them a ride."

"I like that someone else is taking care of them for once. Should I be paying you for babysitting them, too?"

"No. And you should be nice. They're your friends."

"I know. I've just have a lot on my mind right now. The extra worry isn't easy and it's strange to hear you defending them."

I smiled and led the way to the door. The sexual tension ignited again and I felt the urge to move him out of my personal space or else pounce on him. Joel leaned Damian over his shoulder. Damian stirred, then settled again with a sigh.

"Well, I'll see you tomorrow," he said and held my stare at the door. I moved in toward him and ran a hand through Damian's hair.

"Goodnight Joel," I whispered and backed away.

# Chapter 11

## JOEL ♂

I opened the door to a knock and let Raif inside. The morning had been frantic already, just with the addition of Damian to get ready. He wouldn't eat his cereal, wouldn't get dressed and I finally just gave up. We had hotdogs and grape pop and he was going to wear his Spider-Man pajamas come hell or high water.

"Hey, buddy," said Raif as Damian came running toward him.

"Uncle Ray, Uncle Ray, Uncle Ray!" he chanted at the top of his lungs.

"Are you putting your clothes on, little dude, or what?" asked Raif.

"NO!"

"Yes! No one else is wearing their pajamas."

"I am!"

"You are?"

"Yep."

"Okay, then let's go," I said, pulling him to go out the door. "We'll wait on the porch until everyone is here. You can run around the yard."

"Run, run, run!" he screamed and tore down the steps.

We looked up to Maggie's house and watched the door shut behind Eve. And stared. I couldn't look away. Lucky for me, Damian still distracted Raif.

She wore a sleeveless top, fitted over her breasts—very perfectly— loose and flowing in white lacy fabric. She wore jeans that flared at the bottom with a pair of sneakers. Her hips swayed when she walked and all of this would have been bad enough, but she wore Trey's beat up cowboy hat over relaxed waves of blonde hair. And lip-gloss that made her lips look wet and juicy.

"Mornin' cowboy," she said and walkwed toward me. I would have grabbed her and run straight into the house if she came much closer but Damian ran to her instead. Saved by a two-and-a-half-foot Spider-Man.

"Ee*b*ie, Ee*b*ie, Ee*b*ie!" he yelled. "Uncle Ray is here!"

"No way! Hi Uncle Ray!" she yelled, matching his enthusiastic grin just as wide and keeping pace with Damian's bursting excitement.

My mother and the rest of the women were inside when we arrived, the men already setting up tools and lumber. I couldn't believe all the people that turned out to help. I led Eve inside with Damian and made introductions all around. The room fell quiet at the mention of her name, then at the fact that she stood at my side. Every female in town seemed anxious to marry me off or in the least, check in with the state of my love life. Any hint of a member of the opposite sex within a two-foot radius meant good news. Unless, of course, that person was Eve.

"So, Eve, nice to have you here. Your mother told us about your staying at Maggie's. How is Maggie doing, anyway?" asked Mrs. Richards.

"Fine, I suppose. I haven't heard from her. She is on her honeymoon after all. But all the same, she does seem to be lacking in the area of postcards."

"We barely saw you at the wedding. Where did you run off to so fast?"

"No where, really. I wanted to get a start on the drive into town."

I leaned over Eve's shoulder. "One of the gossip group leaders. Keep your eyes open."

"Thanks."

"You going to be okay?" I asked.

"I hope so. I'll raise a white flag and sent out for reinforcements if I need you."

I laughed. She was toast.

## EVE ♀

Before I could take cover the welcome wagon ambushed me, my mother in the lead, brandishing her weapons and calling for reinforcements.

"Dolly," she said, waving her hand behind her but keeping her eyes locked on me; she knew better than to assume I wouldn't make a break for it if she broke eye contact for even a second. "Meet my Eve. Dolly wasn't at the wedding on account of her father's in the hospital, poor man."

Here we go. At least I had some back up of my own. I turned around for just one warm, supportive glance from Joel. The bastard had left.

"Hi, Mom," I sighed.

"Eve, I am so glad you came to help out. You could learn a thing or two from us women. Though I'm surprised you aren't out in the barn."

"Uh huh."

"And who is this little fella?" she asked, crouching down to Damian's level. Damian shied away and clung to my leg. I couldn't blame him. "Now aren't you just a doll."

"This is Damian."

"Of course it is. Joel's little man. What's he doing with you, Eve?" My mother came back to my level and stared in utter confusion.

"I told Joel I'd look after him today while he worked outside. And I figured Mrs. Powell would have her hands full with the food and all you nice ladies in her kitchen."

That got the attention of everyone in the room. My mother looked genuinely shocked that an innocent child would be left in my potentially incapable hands, while the rest of the women watched in wonderment at the mention of Joel's name from my mouth. Mrs. Powell approached.

"You don't have to do that, Eve. I suppose, though, it would make things easier for me." She smiled, set a hand on my shoulder and said with a wink, "He's really taken to you. It's absolutely amazing." I could tell by the looks around the room, the "nice ladies" were trying to decide if she spoke about Damian taking to me so well or Joel.

"We're buddies," I said and shone him a smile of comfort. "And we're going to have fun today, aren't we, Spidey?" With my acknowledgement of Damian, not Joel, a look of disappointment took the glee out of the ladies' glee club.

"Yep. Gramma," Damian started and motioned for Mrs. Powell to come down to his level. "Can I show E*ebie* Daddy's toys upstairs?"

"Of course."

"Did you need me to help out in here?" I asked Mrs. Powell, only because I felt a pang of guilt shoot through me at getting out of helping in the kitchen. Leave it to a three-year-old to save the day.

"Not at all. I'll show you upstairs, Eve, and Damian can show you the rest. He knows where everything is."

I followed, giving my mother a wave as I turned around. "Bye everyone," I called.

"Eve, you come and call for help if you need it," I heard my mother say from the kitchen. I could feel her nerves start to simmer.

"I'll be fine. I can handle a three-year-old for a few hours."

"Huh," someone commented to my mother. "What's going on with Joel and Eve?"

"Nothing. I don't think Eve and Joel would—no, I'm sure it's nothing. And just wait. She'll never handle more than a half hour with that boy."

At the top of the stairs, Damian broke free from my hand and tore across the hall to an open doorway.

"Eve, don't let them bother you. Joel gets this all the time. He makes everyone curious."

"So I gather. Really, Mrs. Powell, there's nothing going on. I was just trying to help Joel out with everything being so hectic right now."

"There's no need to explain. He'd be lost without you there this week and I know he appreciates it; something going on or not. I'll iron out the rumors before they start multiplying, because they will. And fast."

"Thank you."

"Call if you need anything, and help yourself to some food in a while. We're putting out snacks."

"Snacks?" yelled Damian from inside the room.

"Yes, love, snacks. I'll send some up for you and Eve."

"Pie?" he yelled.

"Not until after supper."

"Chips!"

"No chips."

"Ice cream with chocolate hunks and ras-*perries* and *smarsh*-mellows!"

"I'll see what I can find," she smiled. "Don't know what that father has been feeding you."

I smiled and winked at Damian. *Smarsh*-mellows sounded pretty good right about now. It's no wonder Damian and I got along so well. He knew how to pack in the junk food and did it without second thought to the waistline.

When I walked into the room my eyes couldn't decide what to look at first and an overwhelming feeling of nostalgia—and a warm fluttery sensation because it was Joel's room—ripped through me. There were medals hanging from red-white-and-blue ribbons tacked into the wall, a photo of a cowboy roping a calf hung next to them; stacks of children's picture books, tattered and well read, sat in a pile in the opposite corner next to a single bed piled with blankets and stuffed bears. I ran my fingers along the edge of a small dresser, the rough edges and peeling white paint tickling my fingertips. A recent picture of Joel with Damian sat atop an old yearbook, a bronze statue of a bucking bronco next to it.

I lifted the frame from atop the yearbooks and ran my fingers across the inside photo: Joel, smiling as wide as I've ever seen him smile, hugging Damian from behind. His arms nearly smothering him with the love I could feel spilling out of the picture. Damian's eyes were squeezed shut with laughter. Complete and utter happiness. His brightness made me want to laugh with him.

"What's that, Ee*bie*?"

"A picture of you and your daddy."

"Can I see?"

"Sure." I crouched down and he leaned into my arm.

"That's me!" he yelled. "And Daddy!"

"Do you remember that picture?"

"Yep. The horses' day. And swimming. And we were running and running and running. And Daddy caught a cow! A baby cow what's called a ca*p*! By his legs. And he *p*ell down!" Damian mimicked the cow lying on the ground, three legs together with one kicking in the air.

"Wow. Does your dad rope calves?"

"Yep! He's there," he said and pointed to the picture on the wall next to the medals. "And he got shiny medals because he's so good."

I inspected the photo, and sure enough, there stood Joel; a handsome young cowboy.

"When did he win those?"

"When he was littler. Gramma says Daddy won lots. Be*p*ore I was even born."

"Wow."

"And me, too! I can rope 'em, too."

"You're a calf roper are you?"

"Yep. I roped Daddy and he *p*ell on the ground."

"Wow."

"Ee*b*ie," he said and climbed back into my lap. I sat cross-legged on the floor and Damian leaned his cheek on my shoulder, a touch of serious suddenly seeping from his little voice. "Is Mommy going to take me away?"

"What?" I drew in a breath and ran the palm of my hand over his forehead. "Damian, no one is going to take you away."

"Because I want to stay wi*p* Daddy. And we can do fun stuff."

"I know." I kissed his head with a sigh. "Oh, buddy. Daddy will work out what's the best for you. Like always. Do you know why?"

"Why?"

"Because he loves you so much. And your Mommy loves you very much, too."

He nodded.

"You are the luckiest little boy in the whole wide world because you have so many people to love you."

"Do you lu*b* me too, Ee*b*ie?"

"Of course I do. I love you very very much."

"What if I could stay wi*p* Daddy? And Gramma. And Mommy. And what if you could stay wi*p* me, too?"

"Well, for now, I am staying in the house next door to your daddy. So for as long as you are staying with your daddy, and as long as I am staying at Maggie's, I'll only be a few jumps away."

"How many jumps?"

"It depends how big you can jump."

"I can jump *really* big!" he bounded off my lap and started bouncing around the room. I sighed deep as the conversation moved on and my heart broke into about a million pieces. Then I heard a soft knock at the door.

## JOEL ♂

I stood outside the door with a tray of cookies and milk. My legs wouldn't move. My heart sped and I felt my chest tighten. Damian's unusually soft voice filtered through the door. He asked Eve if his Mommy was going to take him away and I nearly let the tray fall to the floor, ready to bound into the room and cradle him. My fatherly urge to fix everything wanted to take over but I waited when I heard Eve's voice, lending him comfort, speaking honestly but gently, reassuring his innocent doubts.

I watched this beautiful woman through the door. She sat with her back to the door, Damian in her lap with his little head resting on her shoulder. She rocked him slightly and it reminded me of the unconscious sway I'd developed from the moment I held him in my arms, the sway every parent inherits with a child.

I wanted to go in. I wanted to share the moment with my son. With Eve. But I didn't. He needed to know there were other comforts out there, other people that cared for him, too, not just me. I wanted Damian's world to be safe, the people around him offering the love and protection he needed in his life.

I knew Eve had misgivings about children, questioned her own capabilities as a mother if that's what her future held. But in that moment, as I watched her with my son, I trusted her more than I trusted anyone. My respect for her grew mountains in those few seconds.

I held back a lump in my throat as Damian bounded up from the floor, back to his typically bouncing, loud self. Eve's laughter trickled out of the room and crawled up my spine sending my heart to throbbing again, the lump getting harder to hold down.

I knocked on the door and they both turned toward me.

"Hi," she said.

"Daddy!"

"Hey, bud. I came in for a bathroom break and Grandma sent me up with cookies."

"My cookies?"

"Nope. Just for me and Eve. Yum, yum."

"Oooh. I love cookies," she said. "And chocolate chip. My favorite."

"Awww, they're my *pay-borite*, too!" he whined.

I rubbed the top of his head and lowered the tray. "I'll share them with you if you make me a promise."

"What, what, what?" he asked. He hadn't stopped bouncing.

"After we eat them you have to come out and see the barn."

"Can I help?"

"A little."

"Can Ee*bie* come wi*p* us?"

"Yes. Evie can come with us." I glanced toward her then quickly away.

"I can show you the new place where the horses are going to sleep, Ee*bie*. Daddy is buildin' it."

"I'd like that," she said and swigged down a whole glass of milk. I could tell her emotions had gone limp after her conversation with Damian and she held it inside about as well as I did.

I sat down on the floor next to Eve and we watched Damian jump around between bites of cookies and gulps of milk, both of us trying to keep him still long enough to swallow without choking. We laughed and I enjoyed the moment together, just the three of us, a natural place to be.

When the cookies were gone and Damian's face wiped clean of chocolate crumbs and a very manly milk mustache, I shuffled him into the washroom.

"I don't *have* to pee!" he yelled.

"You have to try or we can't go outside."

"I want to pee like the horses! Outside!" he said and stomped his foot on the ground with a scowl across his face. "In the bushes. *B*emember, you showed me to point it in the trees and—"

"Hey, hey, hey. You're giving away my secrets, bud," I laughed. Eve let out a whoop of laughter from outside the washroom door. "Horses go outside. Little boys go inside."

"But today I'm a horse."

"Well, in this house, the horses pee in the toilet."

He fought hard, as he did with everything, but I won in the end and sat him down with his pants around his ankles, balancing himself with his hands on the edge of the seat.

"Shut the door!" he yelled and shot me a smile. "No girls allowed!"

So I shut the door.

I let out a huge sigh and ran a hand through my hair when I turned back to face Eve. "Let's pretend you didn't hear that conversation."

"Don't worry about it. I heard about the *smarsh*-mellows and chocolate *hunks*, too."

"Uh huh."

"He's a really special kid, Joel."

"I know."

We stood in silence until the toilet flushed and Eve started speaking in a quiet voice. "Did you hear what Damian said about—"

"Daddy! I'm *p*inished!"

"Okay, let's go," I said and nodded toward Eve. We'd finish that conversation later. I took Damian's hand as we walked down the stairs.

"Joel," said Eve and she grabbed my arm. "Is there any way out of the house besides through the swarm of chatty Cathy's down there?"

"Why? Afraid?"

"Deathly."

I peered around the corner at the bottom of the stairs, Eve stealth-like at my shoulder, and held Damian back behind me.

"Follow me." We tiptoed through the living room and around the back hallway, making a narrow escape. Almost. Dolly Emerson materialized through the back door.

"Well, hello there, Joel. And Eve. Aren't sneaking off are you?" she tittered.

"Yes, I am. Back to work. I just wanted to bring Damian out for a while."

"I hope he hasn't been too hard on you, Eve. Damian I mean," she said and flushed before continuing with her point. I could tell she aimed to make one. "You're mother says you aren't usually all too comfortable with children. My Samantha wasn't neither. Not the type naturally cut out for kids. Then she gone and got pregnant, year and a half ago. Now it's like she was born for having babies." She oinked like an old sow.

I felt Eve tense at my side. She cleared her throat to tamp down the fire. "Actually, Damian and I have been getting along quite well. I don't know about natural, but we manage okay."

"Mrs. Emerson, you can tell Mrs. Whitting that Damian hasn't been so well behaved since Eve started watching him. And she is a natural. Just too damn full of pride to admit it." I poured on the country twang. "Don't you think, buddy?" I asked Damian.

"Yep. Ee*b*ie is a nat-*oor*-al."

We brushed past her, the three of us all smiles.

"What's a nat-*oor*-al, Daddy?"

"That means you and Evie are best buddies."

"Oh. We are. Right, Ee*b*ie?"

"You betcha. Thanks Joel," Eve whispered. "But you don't need to sweeten me up to her. I'll hear all about it tomorrow, I'm sure. She and all the ladies still think I've only watched him for a few hours today."

"Let them think what they want. And you're still as coarse as salt," I smirked.

## EVE ♀

I set Damian down on the swinging chair on the front porch. The end of a long day and he dozed, flushed from the sun and the attention he'd received from everyone around him. I could relate, though the attention I received came more in the form of gossip—which bad road my life did or did not steer down, questions about Maggie's whereabouts. I felt like I should have been sitting under Maggie's wedding bed making notes and details about her honeymoon to appease these people. Or filling out a women's magazine questionnaire called, *What Kind of Kisser Are You?* The only person aside from the guys I really felt comfortable holding a conversation with was Mrs. Powell.

She was a lifesaver. I spent the afternoon in the yard with Damian, then in Joel's old room playing with old toys, trucks and cars, racetracks made of old lumber that he and his dad had put together. Everything at the ranch reminded me of what home was supposed to be and for once, I didn't cringe and try to get away. I loved it here.

When I glanced up, Damian now asleep behind me on the swinging chair and the road ahead bare—the truck beds empty and most everyone gone home after the long dinner and clean up—I eyed Joel walking toward the house. His jeans, tattered and dusty, fit tight to his thighs. He pushed a dusty white cowboy hat, less tattered and shaped than the one I wore, over his eyes. His tanned unshaven face set a perfect backdrop for the white smile he shone. He even wore chaps. And I hated cowboys.

But I'd never seen Joel look so much like a cowboy and the electricity he sent off lately already had me buzzing. More as I stared at those chaps and the patch of denim above them, than I had yet. I drew in a deep breath and my knees were actually weak. I always thought that a figure of speech, one I refuse to use, but there it was. They were weak and I was swooning.

"Hey," he said.

"Hey. You actually look like a cowboy tonight."

"Guess I do," he said, emphasizing his drawl. "Whadaya think? Should I mosey on down to the old sa-loon?"

"I don't know if I'd go that far, Gary Cooper. But it looks good on you," I laughed. "So, you finished the barn at last?"

"Yep. Been a long day. Where's Damian?"

"Sleeping on the porch swing. Your mom said she'd watch him for a while."

"Thank you for taking care of him."

"You're welcome. We had a good day."

"The sun will be setting in an hour. Do you want to go for a ride?"

"A ride?"

"I need to run a couple of the horses."

"Cowboy's day is never done, is it?"

"Never. You know how to ride, I assume."

"I haven't in a long time, like everything else ranch related, but I used to live on horseback as a kid."

"Come on. Raif's coming and Trey if we can track him down." We started a slow walk away from the house.

"Sounds good. I saw Trey found a new hat."

"Yep. I never thought I'd see the day Trey would give up that one." He tugged at the one on my head.

"He likes me," I grinned, very proud of myself to have claimed the hat. And I kind of liked it, in a city girl meets country kind of way.

"Everyone likes you. You fit in here better than you think you do."

"Really? Maybe not the people liking me part. I think they're more interested in what gossip I'm bringing to town. But I am almost fitting in, much to my dismay. I even bought a county music compilation CD and have listened to it twice since yesterday."

"I'm impressed," he said with a chuckle.

"There's Raif."

"I'm going to find Trey and take him home. He's plastered somewhere out back," said Raif.

"You're not coming for a ride?"

"No. Not this time. You two go. Is Tal around?"

"I saw him at the house," I said. Please tell me Tal is riding. "Is he coming?"

"Nope. Tal refused to get back on a horse since he was bucked last summer," said Raif. "See you guys tomorrow."

"Bye," we said in unison.

"Do you still want me to go with you, Joel, or would it be easier to go alone, because—"

"I could use the company." He paused as he started to walk and looked back at me with a grin. "Afraid of the bucking horses, Eve?"

"Not the horses," I muttered to myself and followed him to the stables.

# JOEL ♂

We rode in silence for an hour, appreciating the surroundings. Eve sat quietly in the saddle while I clacked my tongue at the horses, guided them through the rougher parts of the terrain.

Tranquility overcame me and a sense of renewal to have the barn up, the smell of fresh lumber and paint taking place of smoldering timbers; the horses returned, even if only until we sold the place. I have yet to find the same feeling of serenity anywhere else but on the back of a horse, the sun setting in my wake.

We followed a path cut through thick trees, splashed gently through a creek. Hooves clacked over the pebbles and the sound of the trickling water made me smile and breathe the cool, moist air into my lungs. The biggest of life's content came to me in the saddle.

I glanced back at Eve with a smile every now and then to make sure she handled the ride okay; I admit I hadn't expected her to do so well atop a horse. But as with everything life threw at her, Eve found her niche and slid into it with ease.

"You all right?" I asked.

"Yeah, managing at least. It's been a while," she said with a carefree laugh.

"I'm impressed."

"Just like riding a bike, right?"

We stopped at the edge of a clearing and climbed down from the horses, gathering reins to walk side-by-side toward the cliff's edge. The sun lowered in the sky casting orange, purple and pink across it's canvass, warming the ground with a soft glow. I watched as Eve sucked in the air again, air undisturbed by pollution and noise, or the smell of exhaust fumes and refuse like the city streets. Only the smell of earth, grass and horse droppings hung in the air here. So different from her life in the city.

"This is so beautiful," she muttered, caught up in the beauty as I had always been in the same surroundings. Tonight I watched her.

"Still miss the city?" I asked and tied the horses to a tree to rest and graze on the grass of the hilltop.

"At this very moment, I could forget cities even exist and believe all there is in the world is this."

"This is what I want. Sunsets undisturbed by buildings, quiet the way quiet should be when you can only hear the crickets and the rustle of the trees and the flow of the river."

"Wow. Very idyllic, Joel. It is nice. Did you spend your whole childhood here on the ranch?"

"Yep. In the same farmhouse my mother still lives in. But we moved it up from the valley years ago. It used to sit right down there." I pointed it out with an outstretched arm, an excuse to lean closer. "In that nook of trees."

"Why did you move it?"

"We were flooded. So, when the ground dried, my dad had this brilliant idea to move the whole house to a high point, instead of building a new one. It was a nightmare. But I'm glad now he did."

"Well, it's a beautiful place, the ranch and all of the land, I mean."

"Eve."

She glanced up to catch my eyes on hers with a deep blue intensity.

"I heard what you said to Damian in the bedroom. About Meg."

"Oh." She looked down, then back again. "I didn't know what to say. I just wanted to hug him."

"I know. It hasn't been easy for him. Thank you."

"For what?" she half laughed.

"For your honesty with him. For not trying to smooth it over. For not bashing Meg, even though I would have wanted to. For letting him know how much people care about him. That you care about him."

"You're welcome."

"He means the world to me. I couldn't have handled it better than you did this morning. I just wanted you to know."

"Thanks. That means a lot. I'm still new at this kid thing. But I feel the smallest bit closer to being confident in motherhood one day. Though it's probably a long way off."

She looked to the ground with a nervous anxiety. I could feel it oozing from her. We stood close, watching the sun slowly dip into the horizon. The night whispered a beautiful song on the breeze, the sky a backdrop of lilacs, blues and crimson as the day changed to night.

She looked back and I met her eyes, both of us caught in an unguarded moment. I moved toward her, nothing out here to interrupt whatever electricity had been buzzing between us, and pushed my lips into hers. It started gently then moved to tasting and exploring as we began to devour. She felt so soft and inviting.

Her hair tangled in my fingers as I held her head in my hands. She leaned closer, her body against my chest and my arms instinctively came around her. We held the moment, drank each other in, until I came suddenly to my senses. I pulled away, fighting with fast-paced breaths.

"I'm sorry, Eve, I—"

"It's okay. It's just…sexual tension. Neither of us have had much lately, from what I gather, and it's just…bursting to come out."

"That's putting it bluntly, but yeah."

"Let's get back." She walked around the other side of the horse and didn't look back. At least we seemed to be on the same page; nothing more than sexual tension. I didn't want it to be more than that, either. Neither of us needed another complication in our already complicated lives.

We rode back at a faster pace, racing the sun before it pooled completely beneath the horizon. We unsaddled the horses, brushed them down and walked in silence toward the house to retrieve Damian and the other boys.

"Trey and Raif are probably gone by now. In my truck," I said, the realization it was gone just hitting me now. I stared at the dirt pad, Eve's Jeep the only lone vehicle.

"That's okay. I can drive you home. And Tal if Raif didn't find him."

"He did," said my mom from the door. She cradled a sleepy Damian in her arms, but looked like she needed it as much as he did. "And I have a proposition for you, Joel. Why don't I keep Damian here for the week until things are worked out with Meg and you can catch up at work. Come for dinner to see him if you want. All of you are invited. You, too, Eve. Tell Raif and the others."

"You've been so busy, Mom, with selling and—"

"I won't hear anything of it, Joel. You look like you're ready to keel over you've been working so hard. If Meg is concerned, tell her she can take it up with Damian's grandmother."

"Damian, do you want to stay at Grandma's for a while, with the horses?" I asked.

He nodded a sleepy smile. "Are you comin' back?"

"Soon, yeah. I'll come for dinner every day if you want. We can go riding."

"Will you bring Ee*b*ie?"

"If Evie can come."

"And Uncle Ray?"

"And Uncle Ray. And Trey and Tal."

"Kay."

I kissed his forehead then walked toward Eve on the step.

"Ee*b*ie, too."

"What?" she asked.

"He wants a kiss," I said, shining a smile toward her. My heart burst like a mob of teary-eyed women at the sight of his little arms stretching out for Eve.

She planted a kiss on his forehead and thanked my mom for the food and hospitality; her mother would have been so pleased with her manners.

She started up the Jeep and I sat in the passenger seat. "So," I began, our kiss being the one thing on my mind. "I won't lose control again."

"That would be for the best on both our parts. And we shouldn't mention it to the guys."

"Yeah, you're right. It would be weird."

I'm not sure how it would be weird, but she was probably right. It was weird enough to the two of us. Maybe not mentioning it to the guys simply made for the perfect excuse to ignore it ourselves.

We drove silently back to town, exchanged neighborly goodnights and went our separate ways. I had a feeling I wouldn't be seeing much of Eve the next few days.

# Chapter 12

## *Eve* ♀

I intended to avoid Joel for a while but the reminder of our kiss just wouldn't leave me. I still felt his warm lips on mine, the heat lingering there in a tingle; it was so clearly etched in my mind. I liked the way the day smelled on him, the feel of his hands running through my hair, his fingers intertwine and tangle as he pulled me closer.

Besides, with Damian away for the week, I thought I'd better finish his living room. It was only fair, right? And it could be done in an afternoon. I still had his house key and could be in and out before he came home, Joel none the wiser. And if he wasn't there, there would be no chance of repeating the accidental kiss.

Then I lost track of time.

Joel pulled his truck into the driving pad at the back of the house and stomped up the walk. The door flew open and banged shut on rebound off the wall as I finished the last stroke of the paint in the living room. The floor had been polished, the window seat in place, not yet attached to the wall, and I had moved the furniture back, taking a little creative license on my part.

I squished the lid closed on the last can of paint and looked up at Joel standing in the doorway to the living room. He wore a scowl across his face. And grubby, dirty, sexy work clothes.

"Hi. Sorry to intrude, Joel."

He didn't answer.

"I didn't mean to be here. But it's all finished."

Still nothing more than a cold scowl. I could feel the emotion seeping from him.

"Bad day at the office?"

"I talked to Meg," he finally said. His mood didn't improve and his tone went quiet, yet built with anger; anger he seemed to be trying to curb. "She's threatening to come and get Damian. I threatened her back and she says she's seeking another restraining order. I reminded her she was the one to leave our son unattended and she hung up on me."

"Uh oh."

"Damian is still at my mom's. I called and she hasn't heard anything, and Meg sounded pretty strung out so I doubt I'll hear from her again today. Here's to hoping."

"Anything I can do?" I took a step closer wanting to help but cautioned still by his steady frown.

"No. I just want peace and quiet. Is that too much to ask? Then Tal and Trey said they're coming over. To make noise."

"Coming over to make noise?"

"They will. As usual."

"And you haven't got enough patience to take it today, huh?"

"Nope."

"Do you want to hide at my house?"

"Normally, I wouldn't hide, but under the circumstances I'm afraid I might kill someone—" And Trey's car pulled up outside. They were already hollering and Tal stumbled up the walk.

"Get down," said Joel. He tugged me to slide with him down the wall. We sat with our backs against it, facing away from the door.

"They're coming up the walk," I whispered. Joel put his finger to my mouth and shushed me. Tal pounded on the door, Trey peered in the window and all went quiet.

Joel heaved a deep sigh, most of his anger leaving with it and he smiled, nearly starting to laugh.

"What?" I mouthed. He surprised me with the sudden change of mood.

He leaned in close to my ear. "The last time we did this we were hiding from your mother."

"So?"

"I don't think Trey will be leaving us a lemon cake," he said.

"So, you had a really shitty day, huh?"

"Yeah."

"Want to talk about it?"

"Not really," he smiled. "There's just so way too much going on."

"Well, if you need a shoulder—"

"I probably do."

We sat in silence. And I wasn't sure what more to say until Trey and Tal stopped making so much noise and Joel started talking again.

"My marriage to Meg was a mess. We were going to reconcile after a few years, even after the cheating incident. I was stupid. I thought I could trust her again and I did. We slept together, she was ready to move back in and then she started back with the drugs. Our relationship was on its way back to familiar chaos after a short week, not even." He paused.

"Then what happened?" I set a hand on his arm, wanting to fix everything. His eyes glossed over and he drew in a deep breath. I felt the air thicken, nearly suffocating me and understood how Joel must have felt.

"I came home from work and she was shooting up in the bathroom. Her drug dealer was there, one of the guys she'd been sleeping with three years before. She told me she hadn't seen him since the incident, but it turned out she hadn't stopped."

"Oh, Joel."

"To top it off, I'm sure she's still seeing this guy, behind Dan's back now, doing the same thing to that poor bastard. But thank God for Dan or Meg would have had Damian really screwed up. Dan's a good guy. Somehow, he loves her despite all this. I never could."

"I don't know what to say."

He continued, a need to get it off his chest now urging him forward. "I'm long over all of that. I don't give a shit about Meg and I'm glad things didn't work out with her and me. That's not what's eating at me." His hands shook, skin paled.

"Then what is it?"

"Damian."

"What about Damian?"

"I've questioned, Eve." He looked into my eyes and his soul opened from within them. "I've questioned from the beginning, but never to Meg, never to family. Just wondered to myself."

"Wondered?—about Damian."

He nodded and I realized the significance of what he said.

"Meg asked me today for a DNA test."

"Oh, Joel." I turned toward him. "Listen. Damian is your son. Look at him. Look at his eyes. His hair, his face."

"And who knows what these other guys looked like. God, I'd thought it. Out of lack of trust for Meg, I thought it. But I pushed it away and just prayed it wouldn't haunt me."

"Stop, Joel. You can't question. You can't do this to yourself."

"I'm afraid. I don't want to know, Eve." He stared at me with damp eyes, searching for an easy answer that he knew wasn't there. I heard the desperation in his voice. "I just want him to be mine. I can't lose him. I just can't."

I felt a lump form in my throat, tears threatening to fall, and knew that Joel must be feeling the same, only magnified by a thousand.

"I've got so much energy pent up right now. And anger. So much. I don't know what to do with myself." His entire body vibrated. I took his shaking hand in mine and held it tight. He searched my eyes for something to ease the pain while the emotions bled from him. I could feel it in his hand, see it in his dark eyes. "What am I going to do? What—"

I kissed him. I didn't know what else to do, so I kissed him.

And before I could think about what I was doing, what I really wanted or needed, what Joel needed, his arms came around my neck, pulled me closer, tighter, our lips pressed together and the emotions began to explode.

His hands moved down my neck, one on either side of my chest, grazing the swell of my breasts. It was one of those moments when your woman-ness feels like it's on full blast, sensuality is at its peak and my insides nearly fried they were so hot.

"Eve," he started and pulled my face away, leaning his forehead against mine.

"What?"

"I'm not looking for a relationship thing right now. I won't do this if you're looking—"

"I know. I'm not looking."

"I need you, Eve." He said it with a gruff voice in my ear. His eyes glazed over with a look that told me we couldn't push the energy aside this time. It needed a release or it would keep building until we exploded.

I grabbed the sides of his shirt and pushed him to the ground. We rolled around on the new floor, bodies entwined, hot and ready for release.

He stood to his feet and pulled me toward his room by my shoulders, then my waist, as his hands continued to roam across my body and he pulled off my shirt, then bra, flinging it to the floor in a heap of pink lace.

I felt a shiver roll over me when I realized I would see more of Joel than the bare chest I already had. But when he started pulling off clothes, I didn't take a lot of time to notice. He had a muscular build but softer than the mirror-obsessed playboy boyfriend I had before Jackson. I remember feeling like Bruce would break me in two he was so like a rock from head to toe. Joel felt muscular but he knew how to hold a woman in a strong, warm, reassuring embrace without feeling like or acting like a stone.

The rest of my clothes lay in heaps with his on the floor, on the edge of the bed, in a chair next to us. He snapped the strap of my panties, sending a thrill of urgency. I bit his lip, pulled his hair and fell onto the bed. He lay on top of me, I stared into his eyes, then he moved inside of me and our energy burst like fireworks. I think I actually saw stars.

## JOEL ♂

I was satiated. For the first time as long as I could remember. And that feeling lasted all of about thirty seconds before I wanted more. I had to put an end to this insanity, but I wasn't in a position to make those kinds of rational decisions just now. Eve lay naked and breathing heavily next to me. I wanted to be in other positions. She read my mind and pounced on top of me this time, smothering me with her naked body.

For now, the heat, sex and energy between us seemed all that mattered; all on levels I'd not experienced with any woman before. I brushed it off to the time and quality of sex I'd been lacking and dove in for more.

"Joel," she said in the same neighborly Eve voice I'd come to know. She lay next to me at three in the morning, both of us feeling satisfied. "About what we said yesterday in the Jeep—"

"Yeah I know. We didn't do well at avoiding each other, did we?"

"Nope. Are we still keeping this a secret?"

"That would be best."

"See you tomorrow then?"

With that awkward moment, I walked her to the door.

And I slept like a hibernating bear.

# Chapter 13

## *Eve* ♀

We'd had the workout of a lifetime, but from the moment I woke and felt him next to me, things were weird. Not I-made-a-horrible-mistake weird, but where-does-this-leave-things weird. I'd learned another side to Joel; a side I'd envision with a flush every time I saw him across the proverbial neighbor's fence and I wasn't sure what any of it meant. And I'd arrived home minus one pink lace bra.

I'd been avoiding a relationship because of Jackson. Not that I considered this a relationship. I didn't want it to be a relationship. But since when did I jump into someone's bed for casual sex? And if I dug way down inside of me to where I hide all of my honest feelings—the ones I also avoid—I would have to say it would be easier if it felt like just casual sex. But though that's technically what this was, it felt different. Like somewhere in between.

Probably because we were friends. We were all friends. Trey, Tal, Raif. They'd either laugh their asses off at the big joke of a situation or look at me like a groupie to share around. Both good reasons to keep this a secret like Joel and I had decided.

All said and done, I lay in my own bed, the sun had come up hours ago and I remember doing a lot of wall watching since I'd hit the pillow; I still only had a few hours of sleep aside from what I had at his place. I really needed a coffee, some headache pills and a swift kick in the ass.

What the hell did you get yourself into, Eve?

I knocked on the door and Joel answered, wearing a pair of jeans and no shirt. I was beginning to think Joel didn't like shirts much.

"Did I wake you?' I asked.

"No. I just got up." A pregnant pause stalled our conversation like a tractor moving through thick mud. I stared into his eyes. They were heavy and dark and the lump returned to my throat when I thought about Damian.

"What's up?" he asked.

"I just wanted to make sure you were okay after last night." I fiddled with the fabric of my sweater at my wrist.

"Yeah, I feel pretty *okay* after last night," he grinned and glanced up and down my body.

"No. About Damian."

"I'll be alright."

"I wanted you to know that this whole…thing…it wasn't meant for anything more than consoling, Joel. No strings."

"I know."

"Just something we both needed."

"Release of emotions. It's okay, Eve. Come here." He pulled me into his arms and I felt the warmth radiate through me.

"I'll see you later, then," I said and pulled away after one deep inhale of Joel.

I walked across the grass and back to my warm bed.

I heard a knock at the door. Whoever came behind that knock also asked for a swift kick in the ass. I sighed and rolled over to squint at the alarm clock. It was almost noon.

I pulled on a pair of track pants and a t-shirt and ran a hand through my hair on the way to the door. I opened it to find Trey and Raif standing on the porch, Tal reclining in the willow torture chair.

"Good morning," I said with a yawn.

"You look like shit, Eve," said Trey. Lucky for me, Trey seemed comfortable enough now to give me his opinions on things

"Thank you," I said with a snide grin. "Nice hat." He wore the newer version of the hat he'd given me a few days back. He pulled it down over his forehead and grinned wider.

"Have you heard from Joel?" asked Raif.

"No. Do I look like I've heard from anyone today? Why?"

"He isn't answering the door and we were supposed to start a game tonight."

"Well," I hesitated, waiting for one of them to get some brains. "It is to*day* right now, not tonight, so I don't suppose he expected you so soon."

"Thanks, brainiac, but we've figured that out." said Trey. "Usually he's still home at this time."

"Usually he's working, isn't he? Maybe he's working," I said and made to close the door.

"Nope. He took the day off."

"So, wait for him or come back later."

"But you have a key. We could go inside and wait."

"And one of you should have a key, too." My mood told me it was too early be having this conversation. I wasn't ready for the Trey-mindset just yet.

"I used to have a key. Lost the privilege, remember. I had another one cut but gave it to Tal," he said.

"So…?"

"So, Tal lost it."

"I'm not giving you guys a key to Joel's house. That's *not* why I have a key."

"Come on Eve, we need to get in there. I brought beer for tonight and it's getting warm in my car."

"That's why neighbor's exchange keys. So they can help each other out," said Tal.

"No. We didn't exchange keys because we're neighbors," I argued.

"Oooh. It's like a sex thing, isn't it?" said Tal from the chair. "So you can be naked and ready for when Joel comes home." They all chuckled, Raif raised his eyebrows and whistled, Trey winked and nudged my arm. My jaw dropped and I prayed I wasn't turning red in the face.

Poker face, poker face, poker face, I chanted in my head. "It's *not* a sex thing! I was decorating! Remember?" God! Damn!

"Aww, come on, we're just teasing. Jeez, you're a grumpy sonofabitch in the morning." Trey huffed then asked, "Please can you open the door?"

"The magic word and everything, huh?" I asked, reaching for a better excuse to give them. My head pounded and honestly, I just wanted them off my porch.

"Can you just give me the key, Eve? Then we don't even have to disturb you," said Trey.

"No way. I do not trust you with the key. Are you sure Joel's not home?"

"I've been pounding on the door for ten minutes. Please. Help us, Eve. You're our only hope," he said, hunched down on one knee with his arms outstretched.

"Alright, alright, *princess*," I said and walked back into the house. It had better be some special beer.

I returned with a robe over my shoulders, floppy untied runners on my feet and Joel's house key dangling in my hand. I glanced in the mirror on the way by—hair in matted knots on one side, smashed down on the other, bags under the eyes—and groaned. I hoped I didn't smell like sex. "You realize I haven't even showered or done my hair yet," I said with a scowl.

"Yeah, we couldn't tell at all," said Raif with a sarcastic smirk.

"I thought you were supposed to be one of the mature ones. Now I'm not so sure." I trudged across the lawn, tramped up the stairs of Joel's porch and jammed the key into the door.

I walked in first, followed by Tal and Trey, then Raif who carried a case of oh-so-precious beer in each hand.

"You guys drink like fishes, you know that?" I said.

"I know. But it's poker night. It'll be a long one. You joining us?" asked Raif.

"I don't know. I didn't know it was poker night."

"Joel was supposed to tell you."

"Yeah," said Trey. "I even came by after he was off work last night. He wasn't here, so I stopped by your place to let you know. You weren't home either."

"I was at my mother's," I said, feeling the need for no reason at all to find an excuse for my absence. Anything to lead them away from the idea I'd been here, making out with Joel on the floor as they peered through the window.

My eyes instinctively glanced to the place where it all began, then to the edge of the living room where the clothing started to peel away. My cheeks felt warm and I secretly wished these guys would leave, Joel would walk through the door and we could go at it like rabbits. I really needed to quiet those thoughts.

Then I looked down. To the same spot on the floor where clothes started to come off. Where a pink lace bra came off, apparently, because there it was, staring up at Trey in all its glory. Shit!

"Well, well, well," said Trey. He reached down and picked it up, dangled it by the strap over his index finger. "Looks like Powell's been busier than we all thought."

"No fuckin' way," said Tal and walked toward Trey.

"Unbelievable," said Raif.

"He didn't even tell you?" asked Trey.

"Nope. Not a word."

They huddled around it as if it were some kind of long lost treasure. Then they all looked at me. They knew. How did they know? I watched them, like three little boys standing around the evidence, their eyes burning holes into my bra still dangling at Trey's finger.

"Eve," said Trey and he walked toward me. "You must know what's going on."

"What? No!" I said, startled into using my scowling face.

"Yes you do. You live next door. Any women making house calls?"

"How would I know?" I felt the panic subside. At least they weren't making me the guilty party. Yet.

"She was at her mother's last night. Maybe the mystery girl was here last night and gone before Evie came home."

"Oooh. Wonder if she stayed over," said Tal, mesmerized by my lacy C-cups. He took it from Trey and held it up to his chest with wide eyes and a teasing smile.

"Good God, you guys are so immature," I said and tightened my robe. I felt violated somehow.

Then the back door opened and Joel came into the living room.

"Oh, no," I said. I hadn't intended to say it aloud but it came out that way. Thank God they were watching Joel for a reaction about the bra. Tal still held it up to his chest, batting his lashes and making a kissy face in Joel's direction.

Joel looked perturbed. Then confused. Then his face turned red, his eyes like fire, and he glanced at me.

"Where did you find that?" he said, reaching for the bra. It didn't feel any less awkward seeing it in his hands.

"On the floor. Eve let us in to drop off some beer for tonight. Seems you've got a lady friend we don't know about. Who's the floozy?" asked Tal.

"Even Eve didn't know. And Eve lives next door," said Trey.

"And what about me, jackass? I'm your best friend. How long's this been going on? And we want details. Is she hot?" asked Raif. I could see Joel's nostrils starting to flare.

He stared in awe, caught between questions and watching me blush redder as the long seconds ticked past.

"Long legs? Blonde or brunette or redhead?" Raif continued.

Then Tal chimed in. "Shaved or natural?"

And Trey…"Does the carpet match the drapes?"

"We know she must have nice t—"

"Enough!" yelled Joel. "I'm not telling you guys about my personal life. Now get out."

"Come on. We're going to need something here."

"No."

"Since when are you so modest, Powell?" asked Raif.

"Since it's none of your business."

"Was she good?"

"Fan-fucking-tastic. Now get the hell out. And you," he began, standing inches from my face with a finger pointed at it. He grinned, his back to the others, "just lost your key privileges."

"What?"

He raised his brows and held out his hand.

"Fine. Here." I slapped them in his hand, letting the sexual tension release through being angry. "And the next time you guys decide to wake me up for this type of lovely conversation, consider yourselves a target. You're a bunch of pigs."

"Oh, since when are you such a women's activist?" asked Trey.

"I'm surprised you could even say that word, Trey. And shaved or natural, Tal?" I asked with my nose wrinkled in the air. "Yuck."

They all started to laugh. I decided to leave before I blew a fuse.

"Are you still coming for poker?" called Raif out the door.

"You bet I'm coming! And I'm going to win!"

"Great. She probably will now you've got her all fired up," said Joel. And that was the last of the conversation I heard before slamming Maggie's door shut behind me.

# JOEL ♂

"Alright, now Eve's gone, no women present. Tell us who it was," said Trey

"No."

"Anyone we know?" he prodded. Raif just smiled from behind him. He likely figured I'd tell him sooner or later.

"Cindy Knowles?" asked Trey, then Tal, taking turns with the grilling.

"Jessie Law?"

"No!"

"That's where you went. You were gettin' some this morning. Probably drove her home and banged her again," said Tal. I thanked the god's he didn't say "banged her" before Eve had left. I cringed at the thought of her reaction and everything unfolding in front of the guys.

"No. Today I was working."

"Thought you had the day off," said Trey.

"I was doing a side job for a couple of hours at the Langly's."

"Langly have a daughter?" asked Raif from behind Trey.

"Raif, last warning," I said.

"Okay, but we won't leave this alone until we hear something."

"She's a nice girl. We had a night. Just one night, that's it. So there won't be more to talk about."

"But it was so good you didn't sleep? You look like shit."

"Yes, it was that good. Now get the hell out of my house!" They all fled, finally, and I slammed the door. They'd be back around seven with more ammunition so I figure I'd gotten off easy so far.

And it *was* that good. Fantastic even. I stood frozen in my living room, the pink lace bra lying delicately in my hands. I knew seeing Eve right now, me in a state of tumultuous urges, would not coincide with my plan to avoid further encounters. I wanted to compare this bra to the one she presently wore, imagined the feel of her breasts filling it.

So of course, I found myself on her doorstep five minutes later trying to convince my conscience I just needed to check in.

"Hi," she said and peered around the doorframe, likely looking for the clowns I called friends.

"Hi. I thought I would come by to apologize for them. And make sure you're okay. And bring you this," I said and pulled the bra out of my inside jacket pocket.

"Joel!" said Eve, yanking me into the house for cover. "Someone might be watching."

"And that would be bad because…"

"Because apparently I am now a floozy. God, I can't believe you guys. Typical."

"No. Not typical. Don't group me in with them."

"Come on. As if you wouldn't have been saying the same crap if it was Raif's house and you found this on his floor." She dangled it in front of my face again.

"Probably would. But it wasn't. I was the one with the underwear. So were you." I moved in closer, unable to resist. I pulled open her bathrobe and slid my hands down her sides. "You're naked under there."

"I was going to jump in the shower."

"Need a hand washing?"

"No. And this is exactly why we aren't going to tell them."

"Okay. And I won't tell them about this, either." I kissed her neck. I don't think she realized how beautiful, how incredibly irresistible she was. She pushed me away and glared with those eyes as if she wanted to eat me alive.

I felt her hands at the back of my neck, twirling in my hair as she pulled my face toward hers.

"Damn you, Powell," she said and pressed herself into me—lips, body and every soft naked part of her. Still fantastic.

# Chapter 14

## *Eve* ♀

When Joel stood on the front porch this morning, I had gathered enough strength to keep him from coming inside the house. Then he dangled my underwear in front of me, sneaky bastard, so what choice did I have?

I fell asleep for a much-needed nap, soaking in the warmth of Joel's body next to me. He felt soft and warm and inviting. I ached for his lips again the moment I woke up…still in bed with him. What in God's name was I thinking? How would I be able to keep my hands off this cowboy after today? Cowboy. Crap. I don't like cowboys.

My heart started to race, fueling the panic. The moment things start to happen in a relationship, I sure as shit begin to fall whole-heartedly in love with the guy. Not this time. This wasn't a relationship and nowhere near love just yet. I needed to run away, escape before that happened. Lying here in eternal bliss did not help matters.

I gently lifted Joel's arm from where it rested across my chest, where it squished my breasts against me and set it on the pillow behind me. His sleeping hand brushed the bare skin of my butt cheek, sending shivers over my entire body. I managed to slide out of his grasp and looked back at him. He still breathed the quiet, contended rhythm of sleep.

I studied his face, the strong jaw line and hard contours, the light pink of his lips, their fullness, softness a contrast to the harsh lines. I noticed his lashes then, curled, long, and dark, like an innocent child. Not so innocent a couple of hours ago.

My eyes wandered down his naked body, his shoulders, arms, chest, all muscular but soft and welcoming, not chiseled and hard like he belonged on a fitness magazine. I hated that. Those muscles screamed *artificially enhanced with steroids.* Who'd want to touch those? Joel's were soft, tanned and screamed, *rub your naked self against me.* My eyes widened as they lingered further, reaching the edge of the sheets now wrapped around his waist. There was no concealing what hid under there from my already well-indulged eyes. I had to get away. I turned, slid to the edge of the bed and into my panties.

"Where are you going?" he asked in a groggy voice and reached his arm around my waist to pull me back.

"I didn't mean to wake you. I just…wanted to get a drink. Or something."

"You wanted to run away," he said. I turned to see he smiled but his eyes were still closed. He always sounded so confident when he spoke. As if he knew what I was up to and instead of feeling vulnerable at my leaving, he faced it as he faced everything else: head on. I wish I had his strength sometimes.

"I wasn't running away. Not really. Where would I run to anyway? You live next door. And we're at my place."

"Still, you're running."

"I'm not trying to—ugh."

"Just lie down with me and enjoy the quiet. Please."

"Alright. But no funny business."

"No funny business."

I lay down and we faced each other with a few inches between us. He draped his arm over my waist and twirled a finger at my lower back. His eyes were open now and he watched me with a lazy grin.

"Listen. No noise. Almost normal," he said.

"Uh huh. You're in a strange girl's bed with whom you are secretly having casual sex. Very normal."

"That's not what I meant. And you aren't that strange. It's just nice to pretend the chaos doesn't exist."

"Chaos like Trey and Tal and Raif."

"Yep. And the ranch. And Meg."

"And my mother. And my falling apart life."

"See? It's much better to just lay here and forget the world."

"It is. But what do we do when seven o'clock comes around?"

"What's at seven o'clock?"

"Poker."

"What?" Joel jerked his head up and stared at me with wide eyes, the sexy lazy expression faded. "Shit."

"So, we're back to rushing through the crazy life?"

"No. You know what, we aren't. I say we just walk over there and tell them what's going on."

"Yeah, right. That I am the floozy you spent the night with. That will be great. No discomfort in that conversation at all."

"So what?"

"So where is this going, Joel?"

"Why does it have to be *going* somewhere?"

The anger heightened. "It's one thing to tell them about a new relationship and introduce me as a girlfriend and continue on as is. It's entirely another to spill our secret and tell everyone in town that I'm your booty call! Because that's what'll happen!"

"Eve," he said, trying to console me into something more sane.

"What are you going to tell Damian? And Meg."

"Shit. I didn't think about Meg. So what about Meg? Why can't I move on, or have a life? She sure the hell has. Look at her life."

"And how will this whole situation look to her and her lawyers and the court, Joel, if it goes that far? You can't lose Damian over this. I know I don't know Meg at all and won't pretend to know your situation, but I can guess how hard she will push and fight against you with whatever ammunition she can get her hands on."

"So what? I'm tired of fighting her and living my life so goddamn carefully."

"What is this between us then, Joel? Two days of great sex. I don't want this to be a relationship and neither do you. Do you?"

"No." He paused. "No, I don't. Meg will use it I know she will and before long, the rumor will be that I'm sleeping with everything I can get my hands on."

"Not exactly what I would have said but that's the gist of it I suppose." Crap, was that all this was, really?

"No, I didn't mean it like that Eve."

"No, but that's what it is, Joel. I'm a booty call. There's no sense in painting a pretty picture here. I'm not a sensitive, gentle soul. Not anymore. It just is what it is."

"So what do we do?"

"We get dressed. We go over to your house and we play poker. And I win. I've been practicing."

"You've been practicing? With who?"

"On the computer. And I've been reading books. I'm quite the poker shark now."

"Really?" He crossed his arms and stared at me with a wry grin. "We could use this to our advantage then."

"What do you mean "our advantage"?"

"We could work together and pull one over on—"

"No way. You're an ass when you play poker. I'm playing to win like everyone else. Not with you, Joel. Against you." I grinned back at him and the game was on. We were both teasing again, but only half teasing and more a convenient distraction from previous conversation we both jumped on to get the hell out while we still could.

We were both dressed and standing at the door. Then staring at the door and the walkway and Trey's car parked out front.

"Now what?" he asked.

"Well, if we're keeping this all secret, then here's what we have to do. First, I'll go over and pretend as if you aren't here. I'll ask why everyone's sitting on the front porch and not going in. Then you go through the back and meet us out front while I distract them. And have an excuse ready for where you've been because you know they'll assume you were with your floozy."

"I was." He brushed his lips across my neck.

"Shut up, Joel," I smacked his chest and he pulled away laughing. "And this has to stop."

"Why does this have to stop?"

"Because I don't want to be a floozy."

"You aren't a floozy. I was only joking."

"Still, this is casual sex and I get labeled as a floozy. They said it themselves and you admitted you'd think the same if it was Raif in the reverse situation."

"I only admitted I'd question him if I found pink lace underwear in his house. I said nothing about a floozy."

"Whatever. Just get over there. We'll talk about the sex later."

"Just *talk* about the sex?"

"Joel!"

"Okay, okay."

I walked out the front door and bounded across the front lawn to Joel's house. Trey turned his head to look at me. I saw Tal reclined on the loveseat on the porch and Raif leaning against the rail.

"Hey, Eve. You gonna let us in?"

"Why, isn't Joel home?"

"Nope," said Trey and Tal gave a whistle. I saw him grinning in the light from the street lamp.

"Then I guess we'll wait."

"You have a key. I want to see if there's any more underwear in there. Maybe something black and see through this time. Or edible. Or some kind of sex toy," said Trey.

"Joel confiscated my key thanks to you. And don't be rude, dumbass. You're in the presence of a lady. Besides, it was just a bra. Not a big deal."

"Then you obviously don't know Joel very well."

I rolled my eyes and laughed inwardly at how well I knew Joel. "And why is that? Is it so strange to find women's underwear in a single man's house?"

"No. It's strange to find women's underwear in *Joel's* house."

"Why?"

"He hasn't exactly been busy since Meg."

"Well," started Tal, "There were a few since Meg. Just none he's been secretive about."

"You're right. There was Maxine a year ago," said Trey.

"Yeah, Maxine. She was hot. Like Cammy."

Oh, yeah. Hot like Cammy. Now I had to worry. Ugh. "A year ago? There's been none since then?" I asked. *Like* I even cared.

"Nope. And then, he wasn't keeping secrets. We got details."

"Details. Nice to know locker room conversations really do go on. Do you ever consider the women's reputations you're destroying?"

"I don't know. Maxine's did a good job destroying her reputation all by herself. And I think Joel was nicer than what she was in her circles," said Raif.

"Maybe he's being secretive because this is a nice girl."

"Maybe. So why are you so concerned?"

"She's jealous," said Trey.

Crap. I said way too much. Shut up, Eve. This could not be the green head of jealousy rearing itself, could it? Or did I want to be more than a mere escapade? Of course I did. Just not anymore. I wanted no part of this anymore, that's all. And a woman always has to stand up for another woman. It's some sort of code, I'm sure. Especially if secretly, that woman is me.

"She is jealous. She hasn't been getting any, either, and she hates hearing about it."

"How do you know what I do in my free time?"

"Don't get defensive Eve," said Raif, brushing it off. "Besides, we do know what you do in your free time. You hang out with us."

"Right. Well, guess that tells us what all of you get in your spare time, too. Nothing. That's what. And you're all a bunch of jealous men, hard pressed for anything close to what Joel's getting so you have to grate him about it."

"I'm getting some," said Tal with a wiseass grin.

"Shut up, Tal," we all said in unison.

"You guys are pathetic," I said. "Did I call you pathetic yet?"

"Hey, settle down. We should know better than to get into with you, anyway," said Raif.

"And why is that?"

"Because you're the best I've ever seen at getting her back up about everything, even if it doesn't involve you. You need to lighten up, Eve," said Trey.

I would have slugged him one if I hadn't had a few heart-to-heart's with Trey. But it turned out he knew me better than I imagined and there was something far deeper and more intuitive embedded in that thick head of his after all. So he'd been right. Except the part about

Joel's sex life *not* involving me but I couldn't hold what they didn't know against them.

"Are we going inside, or what?" I asked, tromped toward the front door and knocked.

# JOEL ♂

I opened the front door before anyone could jam a freshly cut key into it and glanced at Eve with a grin. Her eyes danced and the sour expression on her face changed to pissed off when she saw me. Obviously, the guys had gotten to her first. Chances are, my floozy came up in conversation again, maybe something worse. And Eve's temper had been forcefully subdued which meant she had also held off slugging someone. Or all three of them.

"Powell!" yelled Raif.

"Hey," I said and let them inside. Eve slumped down in a chair at the kitchen table away from us and started shuffling cards.

"So, Joel," said Trey. "Where were you tonight?" he asked, still laughing as he walked past me.

"Nowhere."

"Which means somewhere. And somewhere means you were out banging your new found sex machine."

I shot around toward Eve who stared with a hot glare in Trey's direction.

"Before you get your back up, Evie, that was purely for your benefit. No hard feelings. I'm sure Joel's love interest is pure and innocent and wonderful and he should ask her to marry him because they had sex once. Is that better?"

"That's closer to what the women want to hear, isn't it?" asked Tal.

"No. Actually, I would prefer the other. You make it sound like we're all out to snag men into our trap and tie them down in a relationship. Not all of us, including myself, want a relationship. Maybe never. We're not evil and we have desires beyond being the ball and chain. Including hot naked sex. Now can we just play poker?"

Everyone stared aghast. And something about what she said made me want her again. Something else made my chest hurt, like she'd crushed my heart with her fist. I tried to avoid eye contact and walked into the kitchen. I knew this was pure intent to make her point about ending things between us but did she have to be so coldhearted, and dare I say, bitchy?

Eve dealt the cards while Raif set out the poker chips and I handed everyone a beer. And that was the last of conversations about anyone's love life for the next hour. Until Trey started things up again, this time with Eve as the target.

"So, Eve, you really don't want a relationship, huh?"

"Nope. Why is that so hard to believe?" she asked and placed her chips on the table. "I call."

"I just thought all women wanted relationships; husbands and kids and baby seats and little tiny socks." He winced, eyes closed and voice climbing an octave higher.

"Not this one."

"So then you're out looking for something like what Joel has," he grinned wide. "And I fold."

"And what exactly does Joel have, Trey?" Eve stared him down for an answer.

"Meaningless sex."

She scowled again and I felt the urge to defend her. I don't know why; she ignored me more than usual and my game was off tonight.

"What?" she asked.

"I raise," said Raif, doubling up the betting. Tal matched.

"Yeah. Meaningless sex," Trey continued.

"It's not meaningless sex," I muttered, hoping no one but Eve paid any attention. "I call."

She shot me a glance, her eyes wide and cheeks flushed. So did Raif who stared curiously for more information.

"No?" he asked.

"Not exactly," I said. "Would you just play the river card?" I prodded.

"What then, Joel, if not meaningless?" asked Eve. I stared her down and everyone's eyes shot between us.

"Incredible," I said, my heart pounding and angry. "But just sex, nonetheless."

"Are you seeing her again?" asked Tal.

"Nope. Apparently not."

"Why not if it was so incredible?"

"It's too complicated."

"See, complicated means she wanted a relationship and you didn't. Right?" asked Raif. "Full house. I win."

"No. She doesn't. And neither do I. To put it bluntly—and to use Eve's own words earlier—she didn't want to trap me in a relationship. Just hot naked sex. Which didn't mean anything and is now over." I felt guilty throwing it back in her face but she deserved it for saying it first. Maybe she felt a twinge of something close to what I did.

"Well, Joel, at least you're being honest in your relationship," said Eve.

"Yep. But it isn't a relationship, remember. It was nothing."

"And we still don't get to know who it was?" asked Tal as he dealt another round.

"Nope. But we're side tracking. Eve didn't answer her question."

"What question was that, *Powell?*" she asked. I hated it when she fit in so well as one of the guys. It made her stand out from other women I'd been attracted to. I liked her boldness and it pulled me in deeper because as much as my anger and hurt grew, so did the excitement. And the bulge in my pants.

"Trey asked if you wanted something like what I had. Meaningless sex."

She stared at me, our eyes caught again then hers shifted to everyone else around the table, I assumed to cover up the tension between us, apprehensive someone find out.

"No. I don't. I would and I have before, but not right now."

"Why not?" I asked, grilling her still.

"She hasn't found the right guy," said Raif.

"How can there be a right guy for casual sex?" asked Trey.

"He's right, Raif," said Tal. "There is only a right guy for relationships. Any guy would do for casual sex."

"Really? I disagree," argued Raif.

"Why? It's just sex. I raise you ten."

"Yeah, but the guy still has to be decent. Everyone has standards. Even for casual sex."

"No way. Sex is sex is sex. He could be a greasy bum, unemployed and it wouldn't matter. It's not like you have to worry about him supporting you or somethin'. You're move," said Tal and motioned to me to bet.

Eve looked like she wanted to speak, to argue the point.

"It could be just anybody for some women," she said, hesitating.

"But not for you, right?" said Raif.

"No, I think it could be anyone," said Trey. "If it's casual, then it's fun. You'd probably go for rugged, right Eve? The more mussed up, the sexier he is. Until you enter a relationship. Then it's all about changing him and making him a neat and tidy yuppie."

We all checked after the flop, the same at the turn card and Tal dealt the river.

"No it's not," she argued with a grin. "I can't believe you guys are having a conversation like this. You do realize you're arguing over what kind of guy you'd be in a relationship with versus casual sex. What kind of guy for you again, Trey?"

"Shut up, that's not what I was sayin' at all. I was speaking on your behalf, Eve."

"Well, you were wrong, hotshot. It would matter what the guy was like, relationship or not. I have standards."

"Like employment, right?"

"No, like I would never go home with any guy from a bar that I met an hour before. I'd want to know something about him and be able to have a conversation and like his personality at least. And don't even get me started on looks."

"He'd have to be a hottie, is that what you're saying?"

"No. Actually," she said and glared at me with a challenging grin. "He could be the ugliest son of a bitch I ever met."

I fumed inside even though I knew she was joking. She was joking, wasn't she?

"See, it's opposite for men. Men would take home anything with a pulse, the hotter and the less you know about her the better. No personality is good." Tal slugged back some beer.

"Does that go for Cammy, too?" I asked.

"No. Cammy is not casual sex. No personality, hot, warm body: casual sex."

"Very nice, Tal," said Raif as he dealt the last card. "And I disagree. She'd have to have a personality of some kind."

"You're a pussy."

"No, I'm not. The better the personality, the more imaginative she is in bed." He shone Eve a grin.

A few beers later, someone—I can't remember which of the guys because we were all sloshed—asked Eve about her last boyfriend. Of course, we all perked up with great interest to know more.

"Me and Jackson were boring so there's not much to tell. I was with him because it was comfortable. I decided to get out because I would have eventually married the immature bastard and lived my life married to a keg party as barf bucket girl."

"That's not as strange as I would have expected," said Raif.

"No? I turned a guy gay once."

"What?"

"Yep."

"You didn't actually turn him gay, Eve," I said.

"No, I just helped him out of the closet. We dated for a while and I was really in love with that one. He was nice, polite, a great dresser, the kind of guy you could take home to your mother."

"Like me, right?" asked Trey.

"No, you aren't the take home to anybody kind of guy."

"Why not?" Trey asked, almost offended except that he was plastered.

"You don't have any clue what you want to do for a career. No offence, but women need that in a relationship situation. And you'd probably offer my mother a joint as you ogled her boobs."

I couldn't have been more shocked at her comment and we all burst out laughing.

"So, what kind of guy does Eve Whitting look for, then. In an "actual relationship". You obviously don't like potheads," I said.

"Or gay guys," said Trey. She rolled her eyes at both of us, and our bad humor.

"I don't know. He needs a nice package," she said and we stared aghast. Again. Then she started laughing. "I don't know."

"A nice package?" I asked with raised eyebrows. She can't be serious.

"See, you thought I was going to say a sense of humor, someone caring and nice and sweet," she said.

"Isn't that what women want?" asked Trey.

"That's not all of what women want, cowboy." She winked at Trey. "You guys are so easy to get. I'm just kidding, jeez. Though a nice package helps."

"Well, that's all men think about in women. All joking aside," said Trey.

"That's because you're all pigs," she laughed.

"No, we're just honest. Unlike Joel here who still won't spill the beans. Was she at least full of personality, Joel? Fill us in for Eve's sake, so she doesn't beat the shit out of us one at a time for slamming women again."

"She is definitely full of personality."

"I'm all in," said Tal, shoving his chips to the center of the table.

"Shit," said Trey.

"You too, Trey, if you want to keep goin'. I'm calling you all in."

Trey considered it and shoved his chips to the center.

"Explain, Joel," said Eve. "Remember that I am waiting to beat the shit out of all of you."

"I'm not getting into this conversation."

"I think it's because he likes this one more than he's letting on," said Raif.

"Really?" asked Trey.

"No, I don't," I argued. And they were all back to staring me down again. "It was sex. Nothing more. Who wants another beer?" I stood up and walked into the kitchen, listening to them banter back and forth at my expense.

"No, Joel. See, if you don't care and the sex was that great, then why stop it? So, you must like her. Or she really likes you and you're pushing her away before she digs her claws into you."

"Okay!" yelled Eve. "This conversation is back to degrading women. Actually, it never left, but I'm not in it anymore if we don't talk about something else." She laid her cards on the table. "Full House. I take you all out, and the pot. And I believe, Trey and Tal, I just beat your asses. You're out of chips and you both owe me fifty bucks."

"Shit," said Trey.

I laughed from the kitchen. Served the buggers right.

"Joel, your deal," called Raif.

I walked back into the living room and set a beer in front of everyone. I dealt and lost the next round to Raif who bluffed on a five of clubs and eight of diamonds. Then Eve took me out of the game.

"Sorry, Joel," she sang as she gathered my chips into a pile. "It's down to us, Raif. And looks like I'm winning."

"Things can change awful quick lady," he said and dealt the cards.

# Chapter 15

*EVE* ♂

I thought about the night at Joel's, while sitting alone with my pile of poker money, and winced at the entire conversation; mine and Joel's input in particular. Of course, he'd meant what he said. So did I, didn't I? And as far as I could tell, neither of us felt any sort of attraction beyond a mere lusting after the opposite sex. I pretty much told him he was ugly, he told me I was a means to hot naked sex. Or had I said that?

Didn't I tell him earlier in my bedroom I didn't want a relationship and made sure he felt the same? Could it be more plain? And what had he said? Everything had blurred, and the words of our strange conversations ran together with the words of Trey, Tal and Raif.

What *had* he said? *No, no I don't.* There. He said no. But he had hesitated.

Shit. He hesitated.

What did it matter if Joel did want more? I didn't. That was clear. I couldn't be more clear and I'd have to stick to my gut feeling, though right now my gut twisted and turned and I couldn't stop thinking about Joel naked next to me. Was that so bad? Lots of people have sex just for the sake of sex.

A knock came to the door as I pulled on my pajamas. I answered with my guard up; chances were it would be Joel and I needed my best defenses to keep the emotions at bay. Or sexual tension. Emotions would be insinuating there were feelings and feelings leaned uncomfortably close to talk of a relationship.

Of course, it was him.

"Hi," he said.

"What's up?"

"Not much."

"What do you want?"

"I wanted to talk."

"About what?" Yes. I was snappy.

"Aren't you the ice queen tonight?"

"What is that supposed to mean?"

"You were cold hearted, Eve. I thought we were at least supposed to be friends."

"We are. I'm just blocking right now. Imagine there is a wall in front of me that you aren't allowed to climb over."

"I know. I got the gist of how you feel about that. Can I still come in? If I promise to not try to conquer that wall."

"No. You can't come in."

"Because Trey is on his way back with another case of beer pretty soon and if he sees me standing on your porch—"

"Oh, for Pete's sake!" I said and hauled him in the house by his jacket. "What more could we possibly say to each other?"

"Look, can we at least talk civilly? I know I said a few hurtful things tonight, and I'm sorry."

"You came to apologize?"

"Yes. I came to apologize. I feel like shit."

"Oh." Crap. He broke me without even trying. "I'm sorry, too. I didn't mean to call you whatever it was I'd called you." Hopefully he didn't remember.

"An ugly son of a bitch?"

"Yep. That was it," I winced. He grinned.

Joel stood in front of me, only inches of safety between us. I could feel his breath, smell his cologne. His eyes sparkled and I felt them pulling me into an abyss again. The tension swelling. A tension I thought had long since been released after the first and especially the second time we'd slept together, but it only seemed to be growing, as if the tension had become more than a simple need of release. Instead, there lived and breathed an unavoidable attraction between us; a monster with traitorous eyes and teeth that dug right in and held on.

"Listen, Joel, I do want to be friends, I just—" And I was cut off by the ring of the phone. I paused as he opened his mouth to speak then looked to the floor. The tension broke and I walked into the kitchen to answer while Joel made himself at home in the living room. I glanced over as I picked up the receiver. He sat on the edge of the sofa, arms dangling over his knees, hands clasped together, eyes bouncing across the floor in front of him.

"Hello?" I answered with hesitation.

"Eve! It's Maggie."

"Maggie?" I asked, shocked.

Joel's head came up. He could hear me talking, not that it helped that I almost yelled with surprise. "Are you calling me from the middle of the ocean? You are still in the middle of the ocean aren't you?"

"No. Not right now."

My heart fell to my toes as a fleeting thought passed through my brain. Maggie was calling to come home. I would be leaving early. I wouldn't see Joel again.

## JOEL ♂

Eve grinned and turned away. She talked to her sister with a heartfelt warmth like only girlfriends and sisters could—another side of Eve I hadn't seen but liked. I thought about leaving with a quick wave, leaving her to her private call. Then the conversation changed, the tone changed in Eve's voice to an inkling of unease.

"You are in the middle of the ocean, aren't you?"

Panic set in for some reason. Was Maggie coming home?

"Then how are you phoning if—" she questioned her sister. Her eyes looked confused as she leaned against the counter top. I wished I could hear the other side of the conversation, but had to rely on Eve's alone. "Oh," she said and listened some more.

"I'm glad you're having a great time. How long are you at port?" She leaned her head toward the receiver and started biting her nails, her eyes scanning the room. A small grin turned up at the sides of her mouth and her eyes looked like they were laughing. She looked happy and content. I really needed to go. I inched forward, trying to ignore her private conversation while Maggie told her about the trip so far—I could hear her talking through the phone, her voice excited and laughing—and stopped when I heard Eve speak again.

"Yeah, I met him…yes, he's very cute, Mags."

Who were they talking about now? A man, no doubt. A love interest for Eve. Her family never gave up, did they?

"No. He's been over for dinner with the other guys…no, Trey and Tal and Raif. Don't tell me you've never met them; they're practically joined at Joel's hip…Yeah, they're nice. We've been playing poker… no, just poker—which I won—and dinner. And thanks to Joel, I have managed to avoid Mom a few times. Thanks for sending her over, by the way." Her tone changed to accusatory and I heard Maggie argue; something about "it's for your own good".

"It is not. It's because you're so nosey. And if Joel hadn't rescued me, Mom would be over here every day at least twice. She even brought me a book on relationships that I promptly tossed out the front door… Yeah, I met Damian. We've been spending a lot of time together. He's very sweet. I could eat him up…No, Maggie! Damian, not—never mind. So you aren't coming home yet, huh?…Yes, I miss you to pieces, but you can stay away as long as you want and never come back to your house if you're going to be giving me more relationship advice…No, Jackson's still back home and I haven't heard from him. I'd like to keep it that way…it makes Mom happy, too, though I'm further than I was from grandchildren which is a negative in her books…Talk you in a couple of months, okay? Love you, too."

I sat back into the cushions as Eve hung up the phone and approached the living room.

"So, how is Maggie?"

"She's fine. And you can wipe that smug-ass grin off your face."

"What? You could eat me alive."

"No. I was talking about Damian. He's a sweet, cute little boy. Unlike his father who is a rat."

"I'm not a rat."

"Have you heard any more from Meg?" she asked and I could feel her ask with hesitation. It was a touchy subject. But when Eve asked I knew she was truly concerned.

"No. I haven't heard from her since the threatening conversation. She might even forget about the DNA testing."

"Do you want her to?"

"Mostly. I want to take it, but only if it comes back positive. So I don't know."

"I doubt the test works like that, huh?"

"I doubt it," I smiled. "So, your mother isn't the only one swooping in on your love life?" I asked, referring again to the phone conversation with her sister.

"No. Maggie does her fair share. Except she does it out of pure love and compassion for me. Mom does it because she wants grandkids and because she thinks her and Dr. Phil need to team up and fix me."

"Do you need fixing?"

"No. I don't think so. Mostly."

"You said you were lonely once."

"I don't recall saying that. It's only been two months away from Jackson."

"More than two months now. And that's long enough when your relationship is destructive." I leaned in toward her, instinctively wanting to fix her family issues again. She leaned into my arms and I hugged her. "I should know. I've been lonely for years."

Eve sighed and closed her eyes into my chest. I could smell her hair; feel her breath above the edge of my shirt and down my neck.

"Did you know you smell like strawberries?" I muttered in her hair.

"No." I felt her smile against my chest. "Joel?"

"Yeah."

"Remember what I said about the wall in front of me?"

"Uh huh."

"You can climb over it now if you want." Her soft voice, wanting to be cradled and comforted and satisfied all at the same time, made my heart beat faster and my body throb.

"Maybe we need to rethink this sex thing," she said.

"Like we should continue it?"

I slid a finger underneath the elastic of her panties, popped open the top button on her jeans and smiled, unsure of where I really wanted things to go. Toward satisfying my Eve urges for starters. Then, suddenly, the picture became clear as day. This urge for Eve was for her and only her, not just a pent up emotion I could release with anyone. Eve was something more.

"We need some rules, then. This has to be just casual, with no strings," she said.

I could make due with rules. For now. "Okay. I think both of us agree this is nothing more than sexual tension." My lips found her neck and she whimpered against my ear as she gave in completely to the urges.

"Good. And this needs to be just between us, Joel."

"I wasn't thinking of sharing you with Trey or anything," I grinned against her skin.

"You know what I mean," she said and cuffed me in the shoulder.

"Ow! Yes. I know what you mean. You kiss like no other woman I've known, but Jesus, you still punch like a guy."

She slugged me again.

## EVE ♀

This time, we got right to business, satiated our urges and Joel left for his house after two in the morning. Very impersonal on both our parts, just the way we wanted it to be.

By early afternoon, I woke to the sound of pounding on the front door. The door bell had been ringing for a while, but I worked the damn sound into my dreams without realizing there really was someone there and not Jackson in a pink bunny suit pounding the door down while I made out with Joel on a bright neon sofa wearing only sunglasses from the eighties. All of it was a bit strange, but what wasn't in my life?

Had I said something about my life being calm again? I must have been delusional.

I did that half asleep Frankenstein walk to the door wearing a matching set of black panties and a bra, my housecoat open in front, hoping that Joel returned and not only for a good morning coffee between neighbors. I was turning into an animal.

It was my mother. I tied the housecoat closed and stood at the door peering through the window.

"Eve, open up this instant! I can see you in there. You can't hide from your mother any longer!"

"Okay, okay," I said, opened the door and squinted as the sunlight poured into my sex domain.

"Eve, it's after twelve thirty in the afternoon. Are you just getting up? You're depressed aren't you?"

"No. I'm not depressed. I'm just tired."

"My God, look at you. You're a mess. Your hair's all matted and tangled. Your eye make-up is smeared all over your face." —confirmation I was doing a good imitation of the classic monster walk. Call me Frank.— "And, Eve, is that a *black* bra strap under there? And what is that pile of money on the—" she drew in a deep breath and covered her mouth with surprise. "Oh, dear God! You're *whor*ing!"

"What? No!"

"You've turned into a harlot! A harlot! This is worse than suicidal!"

"I'm not—wait, worse than suicidal? You'd rather I was trying to off myself than sleeping with men for money?"

"Of course that's not what I mean. Oh, Eve, where did I go wrong?" She started spinning around the room.

"Mom! Calm down. I was just playing poker next door. We played late and I won."

"You're *gambling*?"

"Just with a few friends."

"Which friends?"

"Raif and Trey and Tal and…Joel."

"Joel is a gambler? Maggie's neighbor?"

"Not just a gambler. We're all friends."

"And Raif. That boy is trouble. He's a womanizer. I never should have trusted my girls living next to that bunch of—"

"Mom, stop being so dramatic."

"I'm not being dramatic, Eve. I know Raif's mother. And as much as I am sure she loves that boy, he's trouble. All of them are. Good Lord in heaven," she muttered. "A womanizer and a gambler infesting my daughter's life and—"

"How do you know Raif's mother?" This was too much. Really. "Is she in your gossip circle?"

"It's not a gossip circle, Eve," she said with her hands set firmly on her hips.

"Right. Just a place to get together so all you hens can talk about everyone in town. And Raif is a nice guy. So is Joel." I can't believe this turned to me defending this bunch of bums.

"They're all a bunch of bums."

"Joel is not a bum! Trey and Tal might *act* like bums sometimes, but Joel is not. He works hard—"

"And what about the sex? Tell me you're not servicing all of them over there, too, Eve."

"Not *all* of them." I was pure evil. But technically, I wasn't lying either.

"Joel Powell? Joel Powell? And he's roped you into it, too, I bet. Well. Wait until I speak with his mother. Wait until she hears he's running a brothel over there. And those other boys—"

"He's not running a—never mind." I rolled my eyes and walked toward the front door. Trey trudged up the walk. Great. Just what I needed. Now what did *he* want?

"Look, Mom, here's one of my latest conquests now," I mocked and opened the door. "Hey, Trey. What's up?"

"Sorry to bug you, Eve. Oh, Hi Mrs. Whitting," he said and tipped his hat toward my mother who now stood in astonished horror, unsure of what to think. Mostly hoping I wasn't banging this guy. "Eve, I still owe you the rest for last night." He handed me a wad of five's. "You gave me the ride of a lifetime, Eve. You're more experienced than you were letting on at first. Have you been practicing with Joel behind our backs?" There were so many double meanings in there I didn't know where to begin. My mother did.

"Eve!" she yelled.

"Oh, Mom, he's talking about poker!"

"I'll be going, then," said Trey.

"Smart man," I mumbled and shut the door.

Five minutes later Joel strolled up the walk. I hadn't quite managed to explain any of this further to my mother. Instead, I just let her vent for a while, so she was still ranting away when Joel opened the door.

She didn't waste any time and pushed me aside to get to the door. "How dare you Mr. Powell!" she shouted. "I have a few bones to pick with you."

"Joel, run away fast. You should not be here." I moved fast to regain my spot by the front entrance, took him by the shoulders, spun him around and pushed him toward the door.

"You told your mother?" he asked, mortified.

"No!"

"Told me what? And Eve, you keep quiet. I want to hear about this from him first."

We both froze and my heart raced. Shit.

"Mrs. Whitting, we were just—it was innocent and I—"

"We were just gambling Mom!" I shouted, desperate to shut him up. He did look priceless, though, stammering and turning three shades of red. "I was trying to explain to her why I look so tired and "used", for lack of a better word," I eyed him with raised eyebrows, "and that the money on my coffee table did *not* come from my providing favors for you or your friends at your brothel next door." I raised my brows and gritted my teeth at him.

"Oh," he said and smiled, nearly laughing.

"Now you really need to get out of here before I smack you, Powell!" I yelled and Joel backed out the door.

"I was just home for lunch and wanted to ask you a favor about Damian. I can come back later."

"What favor? Do you trust me to baby-sit again? I thought I'd have tarnished him after a whole week with me. Forget just the barn raising." Really, I missed Damian like crazy.

"No. I mean, yes, I do trust you, but I wondered if you wanted to come over for a movie with us. Damian asked that I invite you and the guys over tonight. Mom's in town for the evening so she's dropping him off. We're watching Spider-Man. Again."

"Sure. Call me later."

When he left, my mother, having been convinced of the gambling and no sex after all, broke into the next bit of traumatizing information.

"Good God, Eve. You were babysitting?"

# Chapter 16

## *JOEL* ♂

Damian had already found a spot on the sofa between Trey and Raif when Eve came through the door. Nice to know she was above knocking.

"Hey," she said. "So someone told me it's movie night."

"Yeah!" yelled Damian. He bounced up and down on the sofa, shaking everyone with his excitement. "Ee*bie*'s here! Ee*bie*, Ee*bie*, Ee*bie*!"

"Hey there little man. How's it going at Grandma's house?"

"Good. We made pie and cookies and had sleepovers! And Uncle Trey and Uncle Ray are here!"

"I know. What movie are we watching?"

"Spider-Man!" He stuck his wrists out in the air to shoot "webs" at Eve complete with sound effects.

"I love Spider-Man! Where's Joel?"

"I'm in the kitchen. What do you want to drink?"

"It's a dry night, Eve," said Trey. "No drinking when Damian's here." Trey looked disappointed and Tal sat quietly in the corner, bored already. A night without beer would do these two good. Doubtful they'd get through an entire movie. Lucky for Tal, Cammy sat perched on his knee in an overstuffed chair, boobs in his face, to distract from the lack of alcohol.

"Anything. Doesn't matter," she said. "Hi guys."

"Eve," they mumbled back.

"Hi, Cammy."

"S'up, Eve. Nice to see you again. Hey, totally love what you did with your hair. Looks kinda like mine."

"Thank you."

Cammy had pulled her hair into a tight ponytail smeared back at the sides with bangs that stood four inches above her hairline. I'm sure Eve contemplated a buzz cut at that moment. In the least, yanking the elastic from her own head.

"When's it starting?" asked Damian.

"Hang on, bud," I called. "Wait for Daddy."

"Hurry up!" shouted Damian. "Can I tell you a secret, Ee*bie*?"

"Of course."

"I'm coming, I'm coming." I carried the drinks into the living room, cradling two bags of nachos under my arms. Damian leaned up to Eve, cupped his hands to her ear. My heart melted watching them.

When Damian finished his secret, he hugged her and slunk back into the cushions between Raif and Trey. Eve went pale. Then her cheeks flushed, her eyes glossed over and she covered her mouth with her hand. I saw a tear roll down her cheek and Trey stood to his feet.

"Eve, you okay?" he asked.

She left toward the hall and Trey turned to me with a confused glance.

"I'll see what's wrong," I said. I was as surprised as everyone else.

I set the drinks on the table, dropped the nachos and rushed out of the room. I found her in the bedroom, wiping at damp eyes, and closed the door behind us.

## EVE ♀

"Hey, what's wrong?" Joel asked with gentle concern. He followed me into the room and with arms outstretched, set his hands on my shoulders to pull me closer. "What happened out there?"

"Nothing. I just needed a minute. I'm fine now."

"No, you're not. What's going on?"

I heaved a deep breath and sigh all at once. I really didn't want to talk about it and definitely not with Joel. He cupped my face in his hands and stared into my eyes.

"Was it something Damian said?"

I nodded and took another huge breath. "He said he liked it better here than at his mom's. And he has a secret wish that he wants to—"

"What?" Joel's face started to fall and I knew the moment understood my meaning.

"He wants to stay with his *real* daddy." Tears started to well again, damn it. I held them back for Joel's sake. How dare I need comforting over his distressing situation. He needed the warm wrap of comfort. Not me. "Sorry, Joel. I just lost it."

"It's okay. He'll be okay. So will I." He set his hands on my shoulders.

I nodded and felt Joel's hands squeeze me tighter. I needed to kiss him; he wanted to kiss me. I could feel it. Then the door opened. It was Trey.

"Everything alright?" he asked with one hand on the door's edge, peeking carefully around the corner.

"Yeah, everything's fine. I was just, um…" I didn't know what to say, or how to explain any of this.

"We were just talking about Damian," said Joel.

"Everything okay with Damian? Is it Meg again, because I'll ring her neck if—"

"Trey, come in and shut the door," said Joel. He did. He sat down next to me on Joel's bed. "Meg asked me for a DNA test to see if Damian is mine."

"Shit," said Trey with a dropped jaw.

"Eve was there the day Meg asked for my sample so she knows what I've been going through. Now, Damian just told her he wanted to stay here with his real daddy. I'm sure he didn't mean it in the context we're thinking but it upset her."

"Oh, Joel, man, this is not good. What are you—"

"Everything is at a stand still for now until I hear from Meg. For now we all need to calm down. Damian's out there and as far as I'm concerned, he doesn't need to know about any of this. Not yet."

We both nodded and my tears started to well up again.

"Eve, please calm down," said Joel. Trey put his arm around my shoulder.

"It's not that. I just feel like I'm...intruding...on something and getting too involved." What more could I say with Trey sitting there? I only hope Joel understood my meaning and that Trey didn't.

"Hey, Eve, we're all friends here. And even though you're new around here, we've all got Joel's back. Without intruding. You're one of the guys now," said Trey. "No offense. At least you're the hottest one of us."

"Thanks Trey," I said and looked at Joel with a smile. He stared, unsure of what to say.

Damian started to yell from the living room to summon us back for the movie; it was a familiar mouth-full-of-chips yell. Trey walked out of the room singing the Spider-Man theme song at the top of his lungs. I followed and Joel pulled me back with his hands on my shoulders from behind.

He kissed my cheek near my earlobe and whispered, "You're not intruding."

## JOEL ♂

Chips flew from Damian's mouth as laughter took precedent over chewing. Trey won their tickle fight and Raif set a hand on my shoulder. He understood something was up and likely knew the gist of it without me saying. Whether Trey filled him in or he just put together a few of the pieces, he knew there was something going on with Damian.

"So, did anyone notice my new shoes?" asked Eve.

"No. We're guys," Raif simply stated and didn't bother to look.

"I did some shopping today. With a bit of extra money I came into last night."

"You spent the poker money already? On shoes?" Asked Trey.

"Yep. I'm loaded. Or at least I was until I went shopping."

"Yeah, yeah, no need to rub it in."

"Sorry," she said and all fell quiet while Tal stuck the DVD into the machine. None of us liked losing, but no one less than I did. "And my new shirt. How do you like my shirt?" she continued and zipped open a sweater to reveal her t-shirt.

Raif and Trey both scowled at her. I stood up and gawked at the shirt; pink, fitted, covered in sparkles, jewels and faux fur. Something Eve would never consider wearing normally. I cringed to think that our poker money funded a wardrobe from Munchkin Land but knowing Eve, our reaction fueled the reason for buying it and parading around my living room in the first place. When I glanced to the floor near the door, I saw the sparkly white runners with curly neon-pink laces she'd kicked into the corner.

"Very…nice?" asked Raif, his face twisted.

"I BeDazzled it myself," she said with an enormous grin, pirouetting in front of the TV.

"Great. Matches your lip-gloss. I'm sure you'll be the envy of the playground at recess," I said.

She stuck out her tongue.

"Oh. My. God," said Cammy, smacking her gum and staring at Eve's chest where a rainbow of jewels highlighted her breasts. "You so totally could have borrowed my BeDazzler."

"Don't suppose you bought us anything?" I asked. Eve stood and reached for her purse.

"I bought something for one of the men in this room."

We all exchanged glances and watched Eve reach into her purse. We waited like dumb idiots in anticipation, as if it would be for any of us. She pulled out a small box and set it in Damian's lap.

"This is for the movie," she said and crouched down next to him. He opened the box and pulled out a *Dock Ock* figurine from inside.

"He's the bad guy!" Damian yelled and showed everyone in the room, a mix of surprise and glee filling his eyes. "Wi*p* octopus arms but they're robots!"

"So, you've picked a favorite. I see how it is," said Trey feigning disappointment.

"Oh, Trey," she said and tousled his hair. "I'll get you a toy next time I win."

Eve walked back toward the kitchen and grazed past me with a whisper that no one else could hear over the sound of the opening credits. "And I bought something for you, too, Joel," she grinned and kept walking. Then she casually lowered the waist of her pants an inch, as if adjusting them, and let a line of lime green underwear stick out above. It was a thong.

The thong sort of made up for the BeDazzled pink.

She set me up for an excruciating two hours, teasing with what she wore, and everything delectable underneath meant for my hands.

# Chapter 17

## *Eve* ♀

I *did* buy underwear. And it *was* a thong. My mother would be writing in to Dr. Phil by this afternoon if she knew the dirty thoughts tromping through my mind right now. It wasn't as if I hadn't thought them before, or acted on them before, but this was my first time in a casual sex relationship so the second-guessing began to overwhelm me; one of those guilt things that every mother drills into a proper young lady. This had become another conflicting situation in my life but at this same time, I wanted no part of a cease-fire on Joel's part.

I sat in my bathroom on the closed toilet seat thinking about Joel, who now sat in my living room. Confusion and Mayhem—or less dramatically, the roller coaster ups and downs—were supposed to have made their way out of my life by now. Or so I had planned. So I had to wonder why most days felt like I sat next to Confusion in the front of that long coaster-train, racing at light speed around a bend to swoop up yet another endless hill next to Mayhem, egging us all on. Or maybe the ride was over and I had stepped off only to find myself in the calm eye of a hurricane, waiting for the storm to hit again.

I came up with some ideas in bed last night while I lay there not sleeping and here I sat reviewing them again. This time on the closed seat of the porcelain throne.

My actual list of men I'd slept with was short, considering. And all but one were serious relationships that I had made certain were serious before things actually got *serious*. There were good things about casual sex: No ties. No spending the night and explaining feelings to each other. No rules and no pressure on when you would see each other next, what family function you would drag each other to. The trouble was, most of those things that were avoidable in a casual relationship were already there between Joel and I and it scared the hell out of me.

The biggest obstacle in my life—because my mother says there is always an obstacle; something one has to overcome inwardly before committing seriously to a partner, yada yada yada—was that my relationships inevitably ended with me running in the other direction, tail between my legs.

It seemed that while running from normal, I quickly found myself chasing it. And my roller coaster life had followed me. I couldn't get away from it. I was in that last fast decline down the slope, my car fast approaching the carnie at the exit that held the key to stopping the ride, then WHOOSH! I was going around again.

One of those "whoosh!"-s was my mother. The other was Joel. I thought about him now more often than one is supposed to while in a casual relationship. He popped into my thoughts even when I wasn't just thinking about sex, even though it usually ended up about sex. At first, I just passed it off as intrigue by a new friend and neighbor. But I didn't think about Trey or Tal or Raif nearly as much and thoughts of the country bumpkins certainly went nowhere near naked or heavy breathing.

Joel and I made chemistry that couldn't be denied. Sparks. Reactions. Multicolored explosions. It had been present from the start, beginning with an attraction that gained momentum, became sexual and tense, leading me to cravings. Now the cravings were changing into need. A need to know if he was drinking coffee at his house the same time as me; if he was mapping out my little quirks and physical attributes in his head the way I was of him. I knew exactly what he looked like as his smile started to stretch from a sedate grin to a wide one so I'd be melting instantaneously. I think I could trace every one of the sexy lines on his face when he smiled.

Just when I thought things had escalated to the highest peak, that mountain grew bigger.

The end of Damian's week with Mrs. Powell—aside from our date with Spider-Man—had arrived. Joel came over in the morning before he picked up Damian in the afternoon. We had joked a few days ago that it would be our last moment to unleash our raging selves before Damian returned so I had a hunch why he was there.

I had opened the door with a wide grin and a sweet hello. Then he had kissed me gently on the lips, squeezed my shoulder and walked toward the sofa. He sat down and I found it difficult to picture a world without Joel in it. Joel was becoming a permanent fixture—his kiss, that hello smile. Did I want this to become routine? Did I need more of Joel, more emotions, more connections?

That was the exact moment I retreated to the washroom to freshen up. I actually used the line like they do in the movies though I had no idea what "freshen up" was going to accomplish. But here I sit. On the bathroom throne in thinking pose.

## JOEL ♂

I don't know what I thought I was doing coming by Eve's this morning. I knew my intentions when I left the house, but they changed the moment she opened the door. Her smile invited me to smile with her. Or beam like an idiot. And in what was now a constant primary thought, I wondered what she wore under her clothes. Mostly, I just wanted to hear her voice and see how her day was going. Living next door to her and not with her had become aggravating.

I wanted to wake up being the first thing on her mind, the first thing she saw. I wanted to look into her eyes in the morning and know that everything else would somehow fall into place. This casual sex thing wasn't exactly working as planned and the only saving grace was the knowledge it worked for her. Eve would keep us sane.

She felt a change in me this morning and ran to the bathroom as soon as I got here, retreating as usual when faced with an emotion that might be more than just friendship. The best thing to do, short of walking out of her life before things got much worse, was to have sex—carnal, physical, detached sex—and leave; to prove to myself and her this was the level of our relationship. Nothing more.

"So" she said as she walked out of the washroom.

"So."

"Big plans for today?"

"No." I leaned in to run my fingers through her hair, to turn this into a mere sexual craving, which wasn't that hard at first because the craving never subsided. It wasn't long before we were in her bedroom and we didn't say another word to each other until I stood at the front door to leave.

"So, that was all you needed, huh?" she joked.

"Yeah, I guess so." I felt a tug then in my chest. I held off the urge to pull her against me, touch her gently, bring her back to the bedroom and spend the day loving each other. Really loving and caring. Even sitting over a coffee just talking would have been better than using her for my own satisfaction. It killed me and I needed to get the hell out of there. "I'll see you later."

"Sure."

And I walked away.

## *Eve* ♀

"Oh, God. This sucks." Losing my grip on staying vertical, my body slid down the closed door. For the first time in our casual relationship, we had "just sex". And I know that's what Joel and I were fronting about this "thing" of ours, but it was horrible. No feeling, no meaning. And the look in his eyes tugged at an inner weakness.

If I had to guess, which I did because neither of us had been open about emotions deeper than sex when it came to each other, I'd have guessed Joel was beginning to cave into those deeper emotions alongside me. Until today.

I thought we'd been getting close, that Joel felt those urges grow at least a little. At first, I thought a good session without emotion would be good medicine. God knows I wasn't ready for a relationship and Joel was in no position to have another woman to worry about. Not a broken down one like me who'd left her job and couldn't function in a solid relationship, much less a casual one.

Now, I think I may have guessed wrong.

The doorbell rang and the lump in my throat fell back inside my twisting stomach. "Pull yourself together Eve," I said to myself and opened the door. It was Trey.

"Hey, Eve. Seen Joel?"

"No. Why?"

"I thought I'd catch him before he left, see if he needed a hand today."

"Still desperate for a job, huh?"

"Pretty much. Either that or keep lookin' for one in town. Again. I've about gone through them all," he grinned.

"Coffee?"

"Sure." He sat at the kitchen table with his lanky arms folded in front of him. I set two mugs down and took a seat across from him.

"Something wrong? You look like hell."

I felt sorry for myself and didn't hide it well, apparently. "No. Life just sucks, that's all."

"Oh, Evie, buck up little girl," said Trey. He reached for my recently claimed cowboy hat off the kitchen counter and shoved it on over my eyebrows.

He adjusted it with a grin and I let out an enormous sigh. It just felt like a huge sigh day.

"So, you gonna tell me about it, or should I leave you to be depressed all by yourself?"

"No, you don't have to go. I've just been thinking about relationships and all the crap that comes along with them."

"Like what?"

"I don't know. Why is it that I can't hold down a relationship? At first, I thought it was that I was picking losers, but I don't think that's it. It think it's me."

"Why, what did you do, go all psycho on their asses? Stalker or somethin'?"

"No. I'm serious, Trey."

"Then stop talking like you're an idiot. You're a good catch when you take away the new found poker skills—guys hate losing, especially to women—and the punching; God knows where you learned to hit like a guy."

"Thank you. I think. But what's happened with me, Trey, is every one of the guys I've dated has chosen something else instead of me. Jackson chose his beer keg; the egomaniac chose—well that one's obvious. One of them even chose men over me. I'm too outspoken and too opinionated and too…brash. I'm just "one of the guys", not the nice, pretty, sweet and sensitive girl that a guy wants to marry. That kind of a girl, my mother says, would find her man. Like Maggie."

"So why do you need to find a man all of a sudden?"

"It's not that I need to find a man. But what if I do find one? What if I start to fall in love again and he doesn't because it kind of has to be a two way street."

"You're asking me for relationship advice?"

"Not really. I'm just venting and feeling especially sorry for myself today."

"What happened that's so different today?"

"Never mind, Trey. Sorry for bringing you down, too."

"What you need is to come with us tonight to the bar and have some fun. You need to get laid is what you need to do."

"And I suppose that's what you'd do for one of your guy friends. Take him to the bar to get laid."

"Yep. Always works."

"It won't. Trust me. Casual sex is exactly what I don't need right now."

"Well, then just come out for some drinks and a round of pool or something."

"No poker?"

"No way. Not with you. So, you coming?"

"I'll think about it."

"I'll take that as a yes because I know you have nothing better to do, and I'll be here to pick you up at nine."

"Is everyone going?"

"Tal is, that's a given. With Cammy," he rolled his eyes. "And Raif will be there with his brother-in-law. Don't know yet about Joel. But I'll see you later." Trey pulled me in for a brotherly hug and I let my head rest on his shoulder, sucking as much sympathy and warmth that I could. He kissed my forehead and banged the hat down tighter over my eyes.

"Thanks, Trey," I said and walked him to the door. At least he had me smiling.

The bar proved to be a good time. Joel stayed home with Damian so I found it easier to keep my mind off him for a while. The guys kept me amused, too, watching Trey try to entertain his brother-in-law, Doug. Doug made Tal and Trey look like a couple of politicians.

"So, Doug, you've been married for how long?" I asked, for lack of a better conversation opener. Tal and Raif played pool while Trey refilled drinks, leaving me face to face with the joy-of-all-men.

"Six years."

"Well, that's nice."

"You married?"

"Nope. No plans as of yet."

"Yeah, you don't want to get trapped in that hole."

"No?"

"Nope. Then comes the kids. Then there goes your chances of getting out and having fun with the guys."

"You're here now."

"This is my one day a week. Which sucks."

"I can see that." I regretted striking up a conversation with this buffoon and swallowed the last of my beer. I scanned the bar for an escape. In my search, I met eye to eye with the biggest brute of a drunk guy in the corner of the bar and his peepers feasted on me, like I was fresh meat on the market. Huge shudder.

"Me and Lacy were married cuz we were young and stupid. Look at Raif. He's still free and he's got women all over him."

"Well, Raif is an unusual case. You don't want to be like that. Guys like Raif don't settle down and eventually there comes a time when you've run out of time. You're lucky you've got…Lacy. I'm sure she's a nice girl and a good mother."

"She's still pretty hot. Big boobs."

"Nice. Well, I need a pee break," I said and stood up, looking for the fastest route to the ladies room.

I nearly bumped into Raif on the way there as he stood away from the table to admire the game he'd won.

"Hey, Eve, where you going? Want to play a game?"

"Maybe later. Gotta pee."

En route to the washroom I bumped into Tal. Literally. And I got another eye up and down from Cammy who was sucked up against his arm. Good thing she wasn't holding roses.

"Eve," she said, smacking a wad of Double Bubble between her teeth; I could smell the overly sweet bubble gum and thought of the huge packs of it we bought as kids. Nothing better than a wad of gum so big it makes your jaws hurt and saliva shoot out of your mouth and before you know it, you're slobbering all over and blowing bubbles the size of cantaloupes.

"Hi Cammy," I said, trying to be sociable.

"Sorry 'bout calling you a bitch before. I meant to apologize the other night—you know, Spider-Man—but was kinda distracted by Tal." She winked at Tal and popped a giant bubble with her fingers. I had always been fascinated at how people could talk and chew gum and blow bubbles all at the same time. A lot of practice, I supposed.

"No problem," I said.

"Tal said you explained how to talk to women for him."

"Sort of. But he did most of it on his own."

"Well, thanks anyway. We should go get our nails done sometime."

"Sure. Sometime."

She smiled wide, smacking her gum and sloshed a kiss against Tal's cheek. "You going to the can?" she asked. "I'll come with you. I gotta pee."

Cammy followed me into the washroom and I took the cleanest stall I could find. After all, we were already a few hours into intoxicated patrons relieving themselves.

"So, Tal's a pretty great guy, huh?" asked Cammy through the stall wall.

"Yeah, he is. Are things better with you guys?"

"Yep. Happens that Skeeter was a mistake. But I just wanted to make Tal jealous. He kinda deserved it after last time with my sister."

"So, now you're even," I said. I supposed that was Cammy's kind of reasoning.

"I really owe you one, you know Eve. There's this guy I should set you up with."

"Really?" Huge sigh. "I'm kind of just getting over a relationship and I don't think I want another one right now."

"Yeah, I know what you mean. A girl's got to hang onto her independence sometimes. My sister's trying that right now. The whole no sex thing. She's lasted like, at least a week now. I don't know if I could go that long."

"Uh huh."

"You know, men are always talkin' 'bout their manly urges and us women are supposed to be there to satisfy them. But we have urges, too, and there ain't nothin' wrong with that. We all need some satisfying. Not that you need to be satisfying yourself with every hot guy that comes around, but satisfying nonetheless. You know?"

"Yep." And in Cammy's own way, she was right.

"I just count myself lucky Tal's the man of my dreams an' all."

"You know, you are lucky, Cammy. I hope things work out for you guys. And Tal is a really good guy."

I flushed the toilet and met her at the sink. She leaned back against the chipped and stained sink cabinet, twirling her hair between her long pink fingernails.

"I am lucky. And it'll will work out this time. I can feel it, you know. No more cheatin' for me and Tal." She grinned wide and I followed her out of the washroom.

Cammy didn't miss a beat on our return to the table and was back to slobbering over Tal. Trey eyed a girl behind the bar and Doug slouched in a pathetic mound over his beer in the corner a few seats away.

"Bought you another beer," said Trey.

"Thanks. So the next round's on me, huh?" I asked.

"Yep. You aren't getting off easy just cuz you're a chick, cupcake."

"I'm not a chick. Or a cupcake."

"A hussy, then."

I punched him hard on the arm.

"Ow! Alright, a beautiful young lady," he said and batted his eyelashes.

"That's better."

"So, I think I figured out your trouble."

"You have, have you?"

"Yep. You said you aren't the kind of girl your mother tried to make you. And I'll tell you what. *That* kind of girl is one that worries so much about how to please a guy that he doesn't have to choose her, she chooses him. Then she's so worried about keeping him that she's giving him the attention."

"That doesn't make sense."

"Sure it does. Look at that guy over there in the circle of women. He married a girl named Susan because Susan wanted to please her man and would do anything to keep him happy. She drives him insane with wanting him around her all the time. Now look at the son of a bitch. He spends his time watching every other woman and trying to forget about his wife sitting at home."

"Crap. That's not great, huh?"

"Nope, but she started out a nice girl like your sister."

"Yeah?"

"Or, you could find yourself a guy like Doug."

"No thanks. What's Lacey like, anyway?"

"She used to be the hottest thing around here. Until she married Doug. They're both really nice, just in their own little world. You could say they're a perfect match. But as much as they bitch 'bout each other, I've never seen any two that happy around here. Not since things didn't work out with Joel and Meg."

"Why, were they all sunshine and butterflies?"

"Everyone thought so at one time. She was a nice enough girl. And you know Joel."

I knew Joel.

"Raif and Tal and I knew her differently, though. Something was always off about her. Like you thought she was up to something but couldn't put a finger on what. Then every other guy this side of the tracks entered the picture."

"So what happened that she'd screw up with a guy like Joel?"

"Who the hell knows. But I'm glad she's gone. Don't tell Joel that, but it's a miracle it never worked out cause Joel tried real damn hard."

"What about you, Mr. Relationship Guru? Why aren't you with some nice girl?"

"I never met the right girl until I met you, Evie," he said and tousled my hair again. I liked Trey because he acted like a big brother and I always knew he was joking. "Want to play a game?" he asked and motioned to the pool table.

"I told Raif I'd play a game with him."

"Sure, they always go for Raif."

Sure enough, a mob of women surrounded him, cheering him on. "I noticed that. Does it bug you?"

"Nope. I usually get his leftovers."

"Men are such pigs."

## JOEL ♂

After dinner and a late visit at the ranch, I took Damian home. Part of me hoped to see Eve on the front porch and the other wanted to walk past her with a neighborly wave and ignore the fact anything had happened that morning. I felt like an ass, too, the way I had treated her. I used her, or at least made her feel used. Even though we agreed to keep things casual, I had never acted so heartless before today. I was a complete jackass.

One thought picked at my brain all day: for a brief moment, as I started to back out the door, there was a glimmer of hurt in Eve's eyes. I had let both of us down.

Eve's Jeep was in front of the house when I pulled up. The lights were out inside, the porch empty. It was nearing midnight and she was probably asleep, curled up in bed and alone.

I tucked Damian in for the night and made my sheepish way across the lawn to see Eve. What else could I do? I was an ass and needed to make an attempt at an explanation of my behavior.

I knocked on the door and waited for her answer. There wasn't one so I jiggled the knob. Locked. I had just started to knock again when I heard Trey's El Camino pull up in front of my house.

"Shit." He'd be wondering what my sorry ass was doing on Eve's porch after midnight. Borrowing laundry detergent…Damian's favorite car was inside and just couldn't sleep without it…I was locked out of my house. None of those excuses were plausible enough, even to Trey, so I took a few steps down the porch to sneak through the back when I heard my name.

"Joel!" called Trey from the passenger's side. He stepped out and stumbled onto the curb.

"Shit," I said again. Raif waved from the driver's side window.

"Give me a hand!" he called and opened the back door on the driver's side.

"What's going on?"

"Just dropping the local drunkards back home. Get in, Trey, this isn't your stop!" he yelled and pushed Trey's head back inside. "Tal get out!"

Raif stood back, Tal stumbled out to the road and I rolled my eyes, thinking only of Eve sleeping alone in her bed. My heart panged with guilt again, calling me to go to her, crawl in with her maybe. Watching this display or babysitting my teenage-like friends was the last thing on my mind.

"I have to throw up," mumbled Tal.

"Not on my watch. Puke in front of your own house," said Raif and continued pulling the next one out of the back seat.

It was Eve.

My jaw dropped. She stumbled out after Tal and then around the car balancing on the bumper for much needed support. She missed noticing the curb and tripped over it, landing on her knees.

"Ow!" she cried out. "Mother f—"

"Jesus," I said and ran to help her up.

"Hey, Joel," said Trey. He was half way out of the car again. "You missed an awesome fucking night, dude. Eve was table dancing. She had all of Raif's enter—entor—ant—"

"Entourage," said Raif.

"Yeah. One of them. About six women up there on the bar doing the line dance we showed her. Well, what she could do while balancing."

"You don't say," I said, completely shocked and unsure of what else to say. "Come on, Eve," I pulled her to her feet again. "Are you all right?"

"I am soooo drunk," she said with particular emphasis on the "k" and walked toward Trey who was now fully out of the car and ignoring Raif's demands to get back in. "Thanks, Baby Cakes," she said to Trey and kissed his cheek.

"Anytime, Sugar." He lifted her into his arms and fell back over onto the front lawn with Eve on top of him.

Eve shrieked out with laughter. "You are such an ass. And you are no longer my boyfriend."

"Come on, I thought we were perfect for each other."

"We were. Not anymore. You can't even hold me up. You're too wasted."

"So are you."

"Yeah, but we made a good pair, didn't we?"

"Yup. Match made in heaven."

I stood in awe watching them. So disgusted at the flirtatious banter coming out of their mouths, fire might have shot from my eyes.

"Joel, get her inside. Here's her purse," said Raif and tossed it to me.

"What the hell happened?" I asked, fire smoldering.

"After Eve's little strip tease—"

"Strip tease?"

"I never," started Eve with a hiccup, her finger pointed at no one in particular to make her point, "did a strip tease. Jody—Judy—*Julie* took off her top first. I just inched mine higher." She held out her hand, fingers measuring out a few inches to demonstrate, which she squinted through at us.

Raif rolled his eyes, completely frustrated that he was still the one sober and taking care of the bunch by himself. "One of the guys at the bar started flirting with Eve and Trey stepped in to save her by acting the boyfriend. By then, they were both pretty loopy and thought it would be fun to keep the charade going all night, walking arm in arm around the bar introducing themselves as Mr. and Mrs. Evie. Which was annoying." He sent the two of them a glare which set off another round of laughter and falling in the grass from the two.

"We decided to take my name," Eve said, sitting herself upright on the lawn next to Mr. Evie. "Didn't we, Sweet Cheeks?" She winked at Trey and blew him a kiss.

"Mr. Evie," Trey repeated then belched and his eyes rolled in the back of his head.

Raif shoved Tal back into the car and started around the other side to work on Trey. "Next time, you're coming with us. Then you can deal with them." He gave Trey a nudge with his boot to wake him up.

"Sorry I wasn't there," I said and glared at Trey on the ground with Eve who giggled like a little girl in the grass.

"Nothing happened. Just innocent fun. Immature, but innocent," said Raif.

"And annoying," I said, laughing to cover my emotions. Here I thought she was home crying her eyes out.

"Oh God, I want to throw up," said Eve, teetering forward over her legs sprawled out in front of her, Trey's old hat set low over her forehead, her hair in wet clumps around her flushed cheeks.

"How much did you have to drink?" I asked.

"I don't remember. No more than a couple of... (hiccup) ... pitchers."

"Come on, let's get you into bed."

"Who's bed, Joel?" she giggled.

"Eve," I warned with a grin I couldn't help but let out.

"Mine?" called Trey. "There's always a space for Mrs. Evie."

"Not tonight," said Eve. "You can come by Joel's sometime, cowboy, and I'll try to fit you in."

I eyed Raif and he rolled his eyes again. "We heard all about her mother's idea of the sort of house you were running."

I nodded, thankful they hadn't heard more. Hopeful they hadn't heard more.

"I'll get these two home if you can get the princess inside," said Raif.

"Sure. I don't know who got the worse end of the deal."

"Me either. Later."

Raif shoved Trey into the car and drove away, Trey blowing kisses out the window, which left me with Eve on the front lawn. I scooped her into my arms and walked toward her house.

I set her down at the door and she stood there staring at the lock. "Well," she said and let out a not so lady-like belch. "Won't open with magic, will it?" she asked.

"Where are your keys, Eve?"

"Hmm. Had them when I left. Then Raif took them away when Tal and I wanted to drag race in the parking lot. What a freakin' party pooper."

I searched through her purse. "They aren't here, Eve."

"Uh oh. Guess I'll have to sleep here," she said and started a slide down the wall to lie down on the porch.

"Come on, Sunshine. You're coming with me," I said and picked her up in a cradle hold.

"No funny business," she said with a sexy smile.

"No funny business," I grinned back.

"Unless you want to use me some more, Powell," she said.

I felt my insides twist and my smile faded. "Let's just get in the house, Eve."

"Yes sir."

She shuffled through the living room and landed on the sofa with a flop into the cushions.

"Eve, you can't sleep in your clothes, they're covered in beer."

"I know. I spilled some."

"Some?" I asked. More than half of her shirt was soaked.

"I spilled lots."

I peeled her out of her shirt, leaving her on the sofa in a tank top and blue jeans. She tossed the hat behind her. I left the room to check on Damian and grab Eve one of my t-shirts.

"Joel," she began when I came back.

"What?"

"There was nothing going on between me and Trey, you know. Not that it would matter if there was."

"I know. And why wouldn't it matter?"

"Because it's not like I'm dating anyone right now. Not really."

"Not really, no." I hated Trey about now, hated that I wasn't there to protect Eve. "Who was this guy hitting on you?"

"Don't know. A really big huge cowboy." She held her arms out as wide as she could in a drunk over exaggeration to show me just how big the guy was. "He wanted some *sugar*."

"Did he hurt you?"

"Nope. The guys rounded on him fast and made him leave the pub. He didn't get any *sugar*."

"What's this bruise on your arm?" I asked and ran my fingers across her skin where it had turned purple.

"I fell off the bar."

"You fell off—Jesus Eve, you need to be careful."

"Are you worried about me, Joely?"

"Of course I'm worried about you. You're—never mind. Come on, pull this shirt on."

"Your shirt?"

"Yes."

"I like this one." I slid the faded green John Deere t-shirt over her head and she sniffed it.

"I missed you, Joel," she said in a deep sexy voice, and leaned in toward my face. I couldn't help but stare as a blaze of heat moved through me from head to toe. She pressed her lips against mine then passed out.

"Jesus." I said and picked her up. I couldn't leave her on the sofa for Damian to find in the morning so I carried her into my bed and tucked her in. "Goodnight, Mrs. Evie." I ran a finger across her closed eyes. She looked like an angel. A drunk angel, but an angel nonetheless.

"Love you, Joel," she said and rolled over.

I knew she didn't know what she was saying—this was the incoherent alcohol daze speaking—but closed my eyes tight and wished for a moment that she had. It would be a long night.

# Chapter 18

## *EVE* ♂

I woke up in Joel's bed. My heart hammered in my chest then my head began to pound from the inside and I thought my brains might start leaking out of my ears. "Oh, crap."

Then I remembered the drinking. "Oh. Crap." And dancing on the bar. I felt my arm for the welt when I remembered hitting the floor after hitting a chair and whatever else helped break my fall. "Shit." And put two and two together that I was now in Joel's bed. Wearing his t-shirt. "Oh. My. God." I couldn't remember anything else.

I got out of bed and the room started to spin—definitely a hang over—and walked toward the kitchen. Damian sat at the table and Joel sat next to him eating a bowl of cereal. Joel smelled fresh showered and Damian didn't see me there until Joel looked up at me standing in the hallway. I must have looked like a peach.

"Eebie, Eebie, Eebie!" yelled Damian and he bolted toward me. Joel didn't try to keep him quiet or warn him of my full-bore headache that he must have known about. I winced and prepared for the bounding hug of a three-year-old whose volume switch was stuck eternally on high.

"Hey, bud," I said, voice scratchy and mouth like sandpaper.

"You look yucky."

"Thank you."

"Eebie, are you sick? Why are you at Daddy's house? Are you staying here? Want some breakfast?"

"I'm just a touch sick. Evie's head is pounding. And maybe your dad can tell you why I'm at his house because I don't remember."

"Did you hit your head? Sometimes if you hit your head you can't *be*member."

"Eve didn't hit her head, Damian," said Joel. "She was locked out of her house last night because she lost her keys so I let her sleep here. Daddy slept on the sofa and, no, she's not staying." Joel eyed me carefully and yesterday morning's episode of sex-without-feeling came flashing back with the reminder of the stoic expression in his eyes again now. I couldn't read his thoughts.

"I'll just grab my stuff and get out of here," I said.

"You can't. You don't have your keys." Joel took a sip of coffee and looked back toward Damian. He acted as if he didn't care if I left or not.

"Fine. I can sit on my front porch, then."

"Wearing that?"

"I'll put my own shirt on." As if I could let this smart-ass win a game of wits with me. What the hell was his problem?

"Go ahead. It's in the washing machine."

"You washed it?" I asked, feeling a touch guilty now.

"It smelled like beer," he bit back.

"Fine. I'll just go look for my keys. They're probably in my purse somewhere."

"No, they aren't."

"Did you check?"

"Yep. And I know where they are."

"Where?"

He sipped his coffee again without a reply.

"Joel," I warned.

"They're in Raif's car. He's on his way over to pick up Damian and drop off your keys."

"Where's Damian going?" I had a sudden nauseated feeling things were about to get bad and I had a hunch it had something to do with last night and most of the parts I didn't remember. Somewhere between falling off the bar and waking up in Joel's bed.

"Uncle Raif is taking him to the graveyard."

"The graveyard?"

"To see some cars and trucks and mud and splashing!" yelled Damian, smacking his hands together. He stood on his chair making car crash noises. "And then we get to watch them pull the trucks out if the mud sucks 'em in!" He pulled his hands down to his sides, his whole body demonstrating the "suck 'em in" part. Spit flew and his eyes bugged out like a fish. He was the most expressive kid I'd ever met.

"I see. *That* graveyard."

"Can Ee*b*ie come?" he asked.

"Sounds like it might be fun," I started, my only chance at an escape.

"No. *Evie* is staying here."

I scowled at Joel and he held a firm glare. The doorbell rang and Joel rose to answer it, keeping his eyes on mine. "Get a coffee. And sit down," he said in a low voice. Damian already stood at the door yelling for "Uncle Ray".

"Hey, buddy," he said. "Joel. How's our princess?"

"Fine."

"I'll see you later. We won't be late."

"Have fun," said Joel, then in a sweet, fatherly tone, "Damian, doesn't Daddy get a hug?" Damian ran into his arms and Joel let out a bear growl. "Agh, that's too tight! I'm choking!"

"No your not!" laughed Damian.

"Almost. You're getting too strong."

"Bye Daddy! Bye Ee*b*ie!" he yelled as he ran down the walkway.

I stood to grab my keys. Joel walked past me and set them down on the kitchen table. I reached for them and he stared me down. Jesus, he could be intimidating. And mere seconds ago he'd been in sweet, lovable daddy mode with Damian.

"Alright, I give. What's with the attitude? Tell me what I did last night and get it over with. And I apologize in advance."

"You don't remember anything you did?"

"No."

"Well, for starters, you did some table dancing and danced on a bar with Raif's circle of friends—his lady friends—nearly stripped, but not all the way. You only "lifted your top a little", or so you said."

"Oh, God." I covered my face with my hands.

"Then you fell off the bar. You were nearly hogtied by a giant ogre cowboy until the guys came to your rescue." He sipped his coffee while I watched in awe. "Oh, and you and Trey had some "thing" going on."

"What?" I asked, mouth gaping.

"Does Mr. and Mrs. Evie ring a bell, because you made rounds to the entire bar with introductions. There were plenty of "honey"-s and "sugar"-s between you. Cupcake."

"No way. I would remember that."

"Well, you don't. Then, in front of all the guys, and whichever other neighbors were watching the midnight show in the front yard, you asked if you were sleeping in your bed or in mine."

"But everyone was drinking and wouldn't have—"

"Raif wasn't drinking. Neither was I. Then you asked me if I wanted to "use" you again."

"Oh. I'm sure I didn't mean—"

"That's what I wanted to talk to you about."

"Shit," I muttered. Things snowballed quickly as I mentally searched for a dark hole to crawl into.

"Eve, I'm really sorry," he said after an annoyingly long dramatic pause.

"What?"

"For using you yesterday morning."

"You weren't using me, Joel. I never should have said "use". That was the beer talking. I didn't mean it."

"I was using you and I knew it. That was my misguided intention and I'm sorry."

Just then, the door flung open and Trey tumbled through in his usual jolly mood.

"Then why are *you* so mad?" I asked, ignoring Trey and starting to fume. Used me? Like, on purpose? Now I was confused.

"I'm not mad." Joel stood against the countertop with his arms folded in front of him, looking more than just mad.

"Yes you are."

"He's jealous," said Trey.

"I'm not jealous," said Joel.

Was he jealous?

"He just wishes he could have had you all to himself last night like I did. How are you, Cupcake?"

"Back off Trey!" I yelled. Anger reared back, fangs at the ready to bite.

"She doesn't remember last night," said Joel, smiling a smug little grin from behind his damn coffee cup like this was some kind of joke.

"Uh oh," said Trey. He poured himself a coffee. "I was just kidding Eve. Nothing happened. Trust me, you aren't my type."

"And what is that supposed to mean?"

"Nothing," he laughed. "You just aren't the kind of girl I go for. You're like...one of the guys."

"Not enough make-up and slutty tight clothes, huh?" I huffed. No, actually, I yelled and kept right on yelling. "Should I get a boob job or poofier hair, or what?"

Trey glanced me up and down. "No, maybe just the slutty clothes. The boobs are big enough if you push 'em up under a tight shirt or somethin'."

I picked up a spoon from the table and flung it at him.

"Ow!" he said, still laughing. "What the hell is going on?"

"And as for you, *Sunshine*," I glared at Joel. "I take back the apology for whatever it was you did to put yourself into a grumpy mood this morning. Hope you two have a nice day together." I nearly took his front door off the hinges as I left for Maggie's.

## JOEL ♂

"Well, at least she's back to her old self," said Trey with a chuckle. He spread a thick lump of peanut butter on a piece of bread he'd grabbed from the counter and slurped back half a cup of coffee.

"What do you mean? When isn't Eve herself? Besides last night when she was drunk."

"She was talking about relationships and how screwed up her love life is all day yesterday. I thought taking her out to the bar would fix that, which it did, but thanks to you, she's gotten all spunky again this morning." He licked his fingers with a slurp and tossed the knife in the sink.

"Why was she so upset about her love life?"

"Somethin' about being just one of the guys and screwing up all her relationships. Not that she "wants one right now"," he rose his eyebrows, mocking Eve. "So...she's upset."

"Is this about Jackson? I thought she was over Jackson."

"Oh, she's over Jackson. I think she's got someone else on her mind. See ya'," he said as he eyed me suspiciously and stuffed the sandwich into his mouth as he went out the door.

"Why the hell is my life turning upside down now?" I asked. Of course, no one listened. And the apology to Eve didn't go so well. And jealous? Yeah right. I was far from jealous. Nowhere near jealous, for Christ's sake.

I let the screen door bang closed behind me and aimed across the lawn to Eve's house. The time had come to put an end to everything. She came to the door but didn't invite me inside. Instead, she walked away and sat on the sofa.

"What do you want?" she asked when I wasn't leaving.

"I just wanted to talk." I opened the door myself.

"I figured we were done talking."

"We were."

"But..."

"But I wanted to apologize again. I wasn't trying to be mad."

"You were acting like a jerk."

"You were out with my friends, having a blast while I was feeling like shit for treating you the way I did yesterday morning."

"The point is, Joel, what happened, happened. And you knew what you were doing. So did I. I wanted things to be emotionless as much as you did. And if you were feeling bad that's not my problem."

"You're right. It isn't."

"And what's wrong with me going out with your friends? I thought we were all friends. I like being just one of the guys and being treated like just one of the guys by everyone, maybe even you."

"Fine. I have no problem treating you like one of the guys."

"Fine."

"So what is this Trey says about you having relationship problems?"

"That idiot can't keep his mouth shut, can he?"

"Nope."

She heaved a sigh. "I was just thinking about all my exes and how since I am nowhere near wanting another relationship, if I would ever find one. Which I don't want anyway. So I am destined to be a spinster and was only upset debating which kind of decrepit old cat will be sitting at my window."

"And what conclusion did you come to?"

"I decided that if Maggie didn't mind, since she has scratched herself from the spinster list, I would take Stumpy with me when I go. Unless he finds a nice lady cat with a nice set of legs to steal him away. Then I suppose I'll get a fish."

"Sounds like you have it all figured out," I let out a laugh. I couldn't help it. She wallowed in something I knew would never happen. Some guy would eventually sweep her off her feet and I'd still be alone on Vine Street.

"Now you're laughing," she said with a grin.

"So are you."

"Want to watch TV?"

"Sure. What are you watching?"

"Family Feud."

"Who's winning?"

"The Simpson family. They got the last round with *Things you keep in the back of your fridge.*"

# Chapter 19

## EVE ♂

I told so many lies to Joel yesterday morning I knew I'd burn in hell. I needed to repent at church this Sunday even if it meant voluntarily facing my mother; the fear of God slunk into me the more I tried to talk myself around Joel.

We'd ended yesterday afternoon's TV watching with him asking, "So, where does this leave us?" and me answering, "I don't know. Not where it was headed and not where it started, either."

I know, it made no sense even to me, but something had to be said without telling him how I felt. At this point, he believed I didn't want anything more than friendship. Neither did he. Honestly, we were both confused about what we wanted or if we'd ever get to where we both needed to be.

At seven thirty in the morning, a knock sounded at the front door. I had just jumped out of the shower, my hair dripping wet spots on my bathrobe. I cinched the robe around my waist and opened the door. Joel gave me a quick up and down glance and I grinned at him. Damian had his arms wrapped around Joel's leg, eyes tired and glossy and he didn't look to be in a particularly good-kid mood this morning. But then, I couldn't say I felt much better after no sleep.

I had watched the hours on the clock tick slowly by as my mother and I argued into the night on the phone. She had a list. The most horrible of my past relationships all lined up against those with potential to start up again—a prime example of my mother preparing for the worst case scenario (my spinsterhood); tactics worthy of an army sergeant—just in case I lost all hope of a new venture. Jackson was on the potential go list, so was my gay ex-fiancé, which made no sense. I don't know how we got into these conversations.

At the front door, I eyed Damian's scowl. "Uh oh," I said and raised my eyebrows at him.

"Sorry to bother you, Eve. I need a big favor. My mom is coming by the shop to pick up Damian for a couple of hours but she can't be there until later."

"So, you need me to watch him for a bit?"

"Yeah, but I need you to come with me to the shop to do it."

"Why?"

"Because I promised to take him, then my mom called to say she'd be late. Now there's no talking him out of it."

I glanced down to Damian, trying to hold back a smile and look serious for his sake. "Hey buddy, you don't want to hang out at Evie's today?" I asked him, crouching to his level.

"No!" he yelled in the biggest voice yet. "I'm going wip Daddy to work so we can build stuff!"

"Oh. We could have fun here and make popcorn and—"

"No, no, no!" He started jumping up and down at this point and I could see tears filling his eyes. Really, I just wanted to see how much pull I had on this kid and avoid having to do my hair today.

"I'll get changed."

When I returned, Joel sat on the sofa and Damian had fallen asleep over the other end. Joel got up and came toward me.

"Sorry, Eve. I wouldn't normally give in so easy but he's had a rough time lately."

"That's okay."

"He's sleeping now. Do you want me to just go and leave him with you here?"

"No. He sounds like he really wants to see you today. I'll come along with you boys."

"Thanks. I owe you."

"No you don't. It's not like I have a job or a family or a life or anything that you're taking me away from," I grumbled. Well I'm sure the sofa will miss me and maybe, just maybe, Stumpy too.

"Talking to your mother last night?"

Where did this man find the innate ability to tell what was going on in my life?

"Yeah." Big huge sigh.

Joel didn't say anything more, just set his hand at the back of my neck and pulled my face toward his grinning lips and shining eyes. He kissed me, careful not to let it become hot and bothered, but it was our most romantic kiss yet which couldn't have confused me more. Then he pulled away and knocked his forehead on mine.

"Let's go," he said and scooped Damian up in his arms.

Things were getting weird. We were turning into a couple, or at least we could have been under normal circumstances. Joel had different ideas I'm sure, so I tried to keep myself grounded. But how could you expect a girl to stay grounded with a kiss like that? I'd be feeling it for the entire week. At least.

## JOEL ♂

I had been preparing to walk away and leave it as friends. Eve didn't want more than that and the sex was getting us into trouble. But when I saw her this morning, I kissed her. I kissed her as if it were just a normal part of an average day. And that's what this had become. A completely unintentional, natural feeling without pretenses. I was in trouble.

We drove to the shop with Damian between us in the truck. Eve sat quietly and Damian talked the whole way, telling us a mangled story with multiple ideas running together from one to the next. Most of it came out clear but a lot of it sounded like words he made up or didn't know how to pronounce; one of his best personality traits—he wasn't afraid to say what he wanted even if it didn't come out right—and I hoped he'd always hang on to that.

Just sitting this close to Eve and not touching her tested my last hope of restraint. Working in the shop with her would be worse. She followed me inside and Damian introduced her to Mac, my only employee at present and the only other permanent fixture besides me.

Mac stood five-foot-two, could grow a full beard in a week and always spoke with a muffled grumble due in part to the toothpick always propped at the corner of his mouth. When he spoke, he scared the hell out of most people because he didn't mince words—rarely *used* words—and never glossed anything over with kindness or even a grin. He stared through his one good eye, the other one glass that shifted about in its socket like something out of a horror movie. Eve didn't flinch.

"Nice to meet you, Mac." She held out her hand and Mac just nodded a hello and wiped his grubby socket wrench on his coveralls, blackened with years of oil and grease.

"Huh," he said in admiration of her firm grip.

"This is Daddy's girl*p*end!" screamed Damian.

"This is Daddy's *friend*, Damian," I corrected with a grin. Eve smiled with an embarrassed laugh.

"You helpin'?" asked Mac and he stared Eve down. It wasn't a tool for conversation or a joke. He was serious.

"Yep. What do you need me to do?"

"Take this," he said, handing her the wrench. "And tighten that, so as I can get the rest of this shit done."

"Right," she said and raised her eyebrows in my direction.

"Mac, she's here to watch Damian. Not fix stuff."

"Put 'em both to work, then," he muttered and shuffled toward the back of the shop.

"Listen, I've got a few things to do. First is fix this piece of crap," I said and pointed to an old car along the side of the shop.

"I thought you did heavy duty stuff."

"I do. And I get stuck doing these crap favors for people who know I'm a sucker."

"What do you want me to do?"

"Ee*b*ie, come see what Daddy's doing!" yelled Damian.

"Okay. Guess we're watching. If that's okay."

"Sure."

I slipped into a pair of dirty coveralls and pulled a smaller pair onto Damian. "Sorry you had to come, Eve. I've done this before with Damian here but I'm so backed up, I don't have time to chase him around the shop."

"Not a problem."

"Put on a pair of coveralls if you want. There's a clear pair over there."

"Thanks. Damian, let's go see what's over there. Show me something cool. Like that," she said and pointed to a tractor through the window in the back. Fortunately for business, a field of empty space sat behind the shop to store anything that could be brought in. Everything else meant a house call.

Damian led her through the back garage bay.

Two hours later, my mom arrived to take Damian for a day of lunch and ice cream and whatever else she could think of to occupy a three-year-old between now and dinnertime.

"Hi, Eve," she said.

"Hi Mrs. Powell. Nice to see you."

"You, too. It was good of you to come with Damian."

"Well, anything to help out. I don't mind. He's a good kid. I'll see you later, buddy, okay?"

"Bye Ee*b*ie!" he yelled and started to walk toward my mom. "Ee*b*ie, Ee*b*ie, Ee*b*ie!" he yelled and ran back. "Hug!"

"Big hug," said Eve and feigned choking.

"Daddy says I'm getting too strong!"

"You are! Wow."

"Bye Daddy!" he yelled and slammed his little self into me.

"Bye Damian. Love you. Hey, take off your coveralls so you don't mess up Grandma's car."

"Kay!" He took off running out the door and I have no idea what happened to the coveralls.

"So," said Eve, inching her way toward the car. Her dark blue coveralls hung loose at her shoulders and she'd rolled the sleeves and legs into cuffs. I eyed her quickly and slid back underneath the car.

"Whacha' working on?" she asked.

"This piece of crap Chevy."

"Don't like Chevy's?"

"I just don't like this one. It belongs to the Watson's eighteen year old hellion of a kid."

"Say no more. So, anything I can do?"

I slid back out on the dolly. "What do you know about cars?"

"Not much, but enough to get by. I can at least give you a hand because I would rather get my hands dirty than stand here like a pretty princess and bat my eyes at you big strong men."

I watched her in awe, doing my best not to picture Eve under the car naked and covered in engine grease.

# EVE ♂

There were grease stains on his cheeks already. And of course, I found that irresistibly attractive. And the coveralls fit him perfectly and I knew first hand what hid beneath them. We were under the car, the car up on a hoist, and it took all of my strength to lie next to him and keep my hands to myself.

I knew nothing about cars. Not really. I had worked on tractors back home as a kid but the years had grown between now and then and in my fight to morph into City Girl, one of the things I lost was the knack with tools under a vehicle. But it came back quickly with Joel's help. Just handling a socket wrench brought back visions of greasy tractor parts and helping put things back together in the barn.

"So, you don't know what you're doing? I thought you'd be a pro at this stuff, tomboy."

"No. I was around stuff, but never a pro. But it feels good to be tinkering again. I would have made a good son."

"No you wouldn't have. Trust me. You make a better girl."

"Thank you." Huge pause, which I filled with a nagging question I'd had. "So, have you heard back about your DNA test?" Joel dropped a wrench with a sudden clang to the floor and froze before focusing back on the car. He shook his head with a grin.

"Sorry. I was just curious. And worried. I wanted to make sure you'd been doing okay with everything but it's none of my business, so tell me to shut the hell up if you want. And I won't hit you in the shoulder. Promise."

He paused without a word. For a brief moment, I had the feeling he would rather I just leave and never show my face again for bringing up the subject. Then he spoke in a low, uneasy tone.

"I'm going tomorrow for the test. I'll hear back in a week."

"Are you scared?"

"I'm cared as hell about the results. And I hate needles."

"You'll be okay with the needles. You're a big strong man remember? And everything else will be okay. No matter what the results, you love Damian. That's what counts."

"I know. And I keep trying to tell myself that but it'll never be the same. If he's not mine, I'm pretty much out of his life with this custody battle and Meg's issues. At best, I'll stay a part of his life, but not as a parent. We'll grow apart."

"But all kids grow apart. Then they come back again."

"But if he's mine, he won't have a choice but to come back. I'll make him. And hug him 'til he can't breathe if I have to because he's my kid. If he isn't, there's nothing I can say or do about anything. Chances are, Meg won't let me have any contact and I won't be able to do a damn thing about it."

Joel continued to work on the car, focusing his attention on his hands and the mechanical parts and the grease.

"What are the chances do you think?" I asked.

"No idea. That's what's so scary. At first I thought if he's not mine, he must be the drug dealer's—which makes me shudder—but I don't know what Meg was up to at that time, or with who."

"Well, if you need any moral support, or you want me to kick anyone's ass, I'm there for you. I can come in handy for bitch slapping if Meg needs a good smack upside the head. Which she probably does."

"I'll let you know," he grinned.

"I could totally take her. Or maybe I can schmooze the lab guys to fix the results."

"That wouldn't get me anywhere, now would it?"

"No, I suppose not. But I bet you'd feel better."

"I feel better just knowing you're here. Even if it's for slugging Meg."

He looked over with a grin and brushed his greasy hand across my cheek. I reached for his neck and we kissed with the pent up zeal we'd been cautiously avoiding. Since this morning.

Joel broke away from the lip-lock and I backed onto the dolly beneath me.

"I thought we were trying to avoid that kind of thing from happening," I said.

"Yeah, we were. And we should be. Sorry. And sorry about this morning, too. I don't know what I was thinking."

Or, I'd have accepted, *no, Eve, I want you, Eve, let's stop avoiding our feelings and go do it on this greasy floor like rabbits, Eve. Don't you hear wedding bells? I do.*

Jesus Christ. I *so* did not hear wedding bells, so why expect Joel to hear wedding bells? The panic rose. This was the Joel in my imagination doing the talking; his pretend thoughts, not mine. That's all. Imaginary Joel definitely needed some work or he'd be getting me into trouble.

"I'll finish up here by lunch in another hour and take you back home. I have some house calls to make this afternoon."

"Alright. Do you need someone to watch Damian while you're getting the blood work done tomorrow?"

"I think Mom is going to keep him overnight tonight. My appointment is in the morning, then I'll head to work."

"Let me know if you need anything."

"I will."

# Chapter 20

## JOEL ♂

The lab felt eerily quiet. I wasn't sure what to expect, but it wasn't sitting in a room full of people waiting like cattle at a slaughterhouse. A chill of pending death floated through the room though I had no idea what the rest of them were here for and didn't care. But I felt like a goddamn cow ready to have a spike shot into my head.

I hated needles, and maybe if I concentrated hard enough on that panic, the other panic would lift. But Damian stayed forefront in my mind. With Eve. I had been picturing us as a happy little family, even though at this moment, both of those relationships held an uncertain future. Back to delirium again.

I had to wonder why all of this now. Why had Meg decided, three years down the road, to question Damian's paternity? I nailed most of her reasons down to simple malice, bringing the thoughts of her infidelity fresh in my mind. I didn't love her anymore, had moved on from the past, but it had always been like a thorn in the side and a huge mountain to climb to get to where things in my life had finally settled. Meg was out of control. Her drugs controlled her, controlled her life. Maybe this was her way of getting some of it back; by stringing me along.

Whatever her thoughts, it didn't feel sincere. And in some way, that had to be the better of two options. If this was sincere questioning on her part, if she really didn't know who Damian's father was, the chances for me where shit. If this was merely a game, then I had a fair prospect at winning.

I heard my name called, but it didn't register. I saw the woman behind the desk. I watched my name roll off her lips as if in slow motion, but it only echoed through my head. My head pounded from the inside, the rest of me completely numb.

"Mr. Powell," she said again and I stood. I faced my last chance to bail and run the other way. Maybe it was better not knowing. I could continue as is, acting father to Damian even if I wasn't biologically, and move on. Like Eve said, I loved him. That's what counted. Still, I had to know or else question it all my life. And there would come a time he'd want to know. Or need to know, like those horrible made-for-TV movies where some kid finds out he has some kind of bizarre disease but because he's adopted, they'll never know which rare, mutating strain it is or find a cure before time slowly ticks away.

"Mr. Powell? Are you alright?"

"Yeah." I stood motionless in the waiting room, a copy of *Road and Track* dangling at my side by a single page. I followed the woman in the white lab coat toward a small room, my heart pounding so hard the Tech's voices sounded like hollow, wordless echoes. Another tech waited in the room, a young kid more like it, preparing vials while they idly chatted.

That's the last thing I remember. The rest became a blur until I found myself at my mom's, sitting on my old bedroom floor and cradling Damian in my arms as if we'd just been reunited after years of devastating separation. And I cried like a baby.

## EVE ♀

Joel had gone to his appointment this morning and I'd half hoped he'd come over for the company, or at least someone to drive into the city with for moral support. I knew he needed to do this on his own, but a girl can hold out hope, can't she? It wasn't as if these maternal fix-you instincts had kicked in intentionally; I wanted to hold Joel's head in my hands and wipe away his frustration and pain. I wanted to pat Damian on the head and know he belonged to his dad without question. I wanted to kick Meg's ass to fucking Alaska and back and—

"Eve? You okay?" My father's voice echoed in my head. "You've barely eaten a bite and you look like you could rip someone a new assh—"

"Not at the dinner table! We're eating supper for Pete's sake," my mother scolded. Fortunately, she hadn't learned the art of mind reading but I knew that day would come.

"I'm fine. I'm just not that hungry," I said, staring at the peas on my plate where they swam in a pool of butter.

"Have you been reading that book I gave you, Eve?" she asked, pausing her meal to lean closer across the table. "That one about when relationships go wrong?" And she turned back to her meal, conversation still directed at me but now with a disappointed shake of her head. "I really hope you haven't slipped into a satanic slump or something. It's not good for you, this not eating or sleeping. You look like heck-fire."

"Thanks, Mom. And we've been through the satanic ritual thing. I don't have them. Lesbian, Satan, Depression—I didn't sign up with any of those clubs. I just didn't sleep well last night. I have stuff on my mind."

"What kind of stuff? Maybe I can help."

"Doubtful," I mumbled into my corned beef hash. "It's not something I want to talk about."

Silence followed for a moment. My mother looked awkward, my father and I just relieved for the peace while it lasted.

I had hoped dinner with my parents would take my mind off Joel for the evening, but my mother had a way of directing me right back to what I was trying to forget even when it wasn't intentional on her part.

"You know, I saw Amy Powell yesterday. They still haven't sold that ranch. I sure thought Joel was going to buy it. Or at least take over running it. I don't know why he's still at that house but I reckon it has something to do with Meg and that boy. Have you still been babysitting the boy?"

"His name's Damian, Mom, not "that boy". And yes, I've been watching him here and there."

"I don't know how a child can grow up with one parent, one dysfunctional parent no less, and hardly a father there."

"Well, I doubt it would matter how dysfunctional Meg is, Joel makes up for it a thousand times with Damian. He's a good father and he's there for him. A lot. And Joel's mom spends a lot of time making sure he gets a healthy woman's perspective on things, too."

"Uh, huh," she muttered and stuffed a hunk potato into her mouth with raised brows.

"What is that supposed to mean?"

"I think you know a lot more than you're letting on about Joel Powell."

"I'm his freakin' neighbor, Mom! Of course I know about him. We practically share a room those houses are so close."

"Maggie was his neighbor and she didn't know him that well. And what do you mean share a room? And don't say freakin' at the dinner table."

"Maggie isn't me. I get along with those guys better than she would and "share a room" was a *freakin'* figure of speech."

"Joel's a decent guy, Vivian. Everybody knows that," my father said and sent a scowl across the table. "Leave him alone. This whole damn town gets their panties in a knot over everyone else's business too damn often. And when there's nothing' to gripe about, y'all find something wrong to raise the roof to a stink."

"All's I'm saying is that I'd be leery about Joel Powell because of his history. Otherwise, I'm sure he's a good man. And if Eve says he's a good father, he's a good father. I'm sure Amy did a fine job raising Joel." She smiled then added, "Except that he's a womanizer."

"Mom!"

My father shook his head and I sighed. Then we moved into safer conversation.

"I heard from Maggie," my mother said. "They were in port again and sailed out this morning."

She continued talking and I zoned out, sipping on a glass of water to wash down the supper that wasn't sitting so well. Her voice wove through the background dialogue of my own thoughts like a snake through tall grass until I made a move for the sofa.

A sort of comfort often came over me being back at Mom and Dad's place—even though I could do without the lectures—but it was still home. It made me want to curl into that old floral-print sofa and dated family heirloom furniture; fall asleep the minute I walked through the door.

I woke up to a peaceful house, an afghan pulled to my waist and the dim glow of light in the corner where my father read the paper. He always kept the sports section for before bed when he could relax with his feet up without interruption.

"Hey girlie," he said when I stirred.

"What time is it, Dad?"

"Late. After ten. Your mom went to bed."

"Oh. Sorry I passed out."

"That's okay. You needed the rest is all. Well," he rose to his feet and stretched into the air like a big bear. "I'm gonna pack 'er in. Why don't you spend the night, Eve?"

"I think I'll head home. I've got a lot of things to work out in the morning."

He rubbed a hand across my head. "Drive careful, then. And take care of yourself."

"I will, Daddy."

I pulled up to Maggie's house, stumbled up the walk in my half-asleep state and opened the door. I didn't look through the window next door to see if Joel was awake or more than glance at his house. A light flicked on somewhere inside but I kept walking and went to bed. If he needed me, he'd come.

## JOEL ♂

I left the ranch late that night and crashed the second I had Damian settled. I woke on the sofa the next morning to another day of just forcing myself through the week. I did this for three days, locked myself away from the world, from everything except Damian. We spent time just the two of us. I hadn't even seen Eve and though I missed having her around, it was for the better if we let things slide. Especially this week. Except that *this week* I probably needed her more than ever; for that small piece of comfort, her care and concern, just lying next to me in contentment at night. But what guy was going to admit that?

I didn't expect today to be any different than the last few. My mom had taken Damian for the night so I could work all morning. And as the sun crept through a crimson painted sky, I stretched on the sofa, not ready to face the day just yet.

But Trey pounded on my front door. He'd been yelling and for God knows how long. He likely woke the neighborhood.

I opened the door and rubbed my eyes.

"Wake up Powell," he said, far too energetic and springy for this early. Or for Trey period.

"What the hell for? Go home Trey."

"Nope. You're taking the day off work and we're hanging out."

"Why is today so special?"

"Don't argue; just follow me, will ya? Or Eve'll have my head in a noose."

I pulled on a clean shirt and walked across the front lawn after Trey toward Eve's place. He knocked and walked in. I followed in confusion, then with annoyance for being woken and apprehension because I'd be seeing Eve in a few seconds. I hadn't thought about what I'd say after avoiding her for a few days.

When I walked inside, Raif and Trey stood in the doorway, Tal in a chair next to them with Cammy in his lap smacking her gum. My mom bounced Damian on her knee at the kitchen table. Then Eve approached holding a cake decorated with thick chocolate icing and sporadic sprinkles, one lopsided candle sticking out the top that burned a waxy scent through the room.

She wore a red paper party hat on her head.

"Happy Birthday, Joel," she said with a wide smile, her voice speaking softly, intimately to me.

"Shit," I said under my breath.

"You didn't actually forget your own birthday, did you?"

"I actually forgot my own birthday," I grinned back.

"Well, you've had a lot on your mind. You doing alright, cowboy?"

"Yeah. I'm okay."

The entire room and everyone in it could have disappeared, just for that brief slice of time, and I wouldn't have noticed.

She bit the corner of her lip and I held her stare before turning to everyone else to say, "I can't believe you all got up so early for this."

"There's more. We're going for a picnic. And we have presents," said Eve.

"No presents."

"Well, sort of presents. Remote control cars and monster trucks, actually. First, you have to make a wish." Eve leaned in closer and whispered, "And wish really hard so it comes true, Joel. Okay?"

I nodded, glanced toward Damian at the kitchen table, Eve in front of me, then blew out the candle. I didn't have to think hard for this one. "I can't believe you did this."

"I had a lot of help. I didn't even know it was your birthday for one. You can thank Raif for that and Trey for letting me in on it. I'm glad to be here, anyway. And I blew out about a hundred candles for you this morning."

"Thanks."

Raif came forward to pat me hard on the back as we all walked into the kitchen. "I talked to Mac in the shop. He'll manage everything for today and Trey and Tal and I are going in with you tomorrow to catch up."

"Daddy, Daddy, Daddy!" yelled Damian from the kitchen. He ran toward me with open arms, finally distracted long enough from his bowl of Count Chocula and Grandma's comfortable lap.

"Hey bud. So, looks like we get to spend the whole day together, huh?"

"Yep! And we're gonna race trucks!"

"Sounds like fun."

"Uh huh."

"Damian, I talked to Mommy last night. You're going to go with her to Grandma Reese's on Sunday night for a few days."

"When is Sunday?"

"The day after tomorrow."

"Aw, how come?"

"Because they miss you, too. Mommy is staying with Grandma for a while and you get to go, too. It'll be fun. And you can come see me again and stay for a long time. Alright?"

He nodded and I could feel his little fingers clench tightly to the back of my neck. "Can you take me or is Mommy coming here?"

"I'll take you. And I'll stay a bit to visit. And Grandma Reese isn't very far away from here. Not as far as Mommy's place. So I'll be close by if you need me. Okay?"

"Kay." And at that, he ran around Maggie's kitchen table making engine noises.

## EVE ♀

You could hear Joel's voice break as he spoke with Damian; the uncertainty in Joel's eyes, the love in Damian's, they were both trying to be so brave. And we all felt it. We all knew it would come, the pending test results and heights of emotion when it did, but no one knew when. It felt as if a cloud hovered above all our heads, darkening even as we watched Joel and Damian together, the same thoughts running between us.

Mrs. Powell let out a sigh from behind me. I turned to smile at her, wishing I could give her more support. Here she sat, watching her own son in a tight embrace with a boy we all hoped was his own by blood. Mrs. Powell walked into the entranceway where we all huddled around and took my hand with a squeeze. The two women in Joel's life. Awkward. I couldn't wait to start racing monster trucks.

I'd fought Trey for the red one the entire drive to the ranch. Neither of us would give in and Tal decided he'd take the red one just to shut us up. The five of us, Raif, Trey, Tal, Cammy and I drove in the Jeep. Joel, Damian and his mom went in the truck.

We all got pieces of the story while away from Damian's ears in the afternoon. Meg had been up to her old habit of trying to convince everyone she would commit to rehab and make a valiant effort this time around. Until then, until Joel and her mother saw proof of a change, Meg wasn't allowed time alone with Damian. So her time with Damian would only be in the presence of others.

Due only to Joel's selfless heart, he gave up the time with his son, the time Damian used to spend with Meg, to Mrs. Reese. He still held out hope that Meg could clean up for Damian's sake; Joel held out for the day she'd come out again, bury the other Meg, the drug infested one, for good. Until then, Damian still needed his mother on some level so would have her with his grandmother present. Joel had more strength than any man this side of my father than I have ever known.

No one else seemed too hopeful. I decided not to form an opinion because mine was tainted. I still held the Alaska and kicking-her-butt-there thought in the forefront of my mind.

Once again, Joel and my control went out the window the first moment we were alone. I stood out at the Jeep, packing up leftovers to head back home with the boys while Joel settled a sleeping Damian into his truck. The others were saying their goodbyes to Mrs. Powell inside, i.e., scrounging for food.

When I turned to close the trunk Joel closed in fast. His hands came to my neck, his face toward me and his lips smashed into mine with a craving needing to be satiated. We didn't speak a word, just stood lip-locked, aching to be wrapped up in each other. We were in the shadows, but close to the house, so all we could do was fumble hands over clothes and the body parts hidden beneath and resist falling into the bushes next to us.

I arrived home late and jumped into my comfy clothes. The phone rang when I walked out of the bedroom. It was my mother.

"Hi, Eve. Sorry to call so late."

"Hi Mom."

"How are you?"

"I'm doing okay."

"So what have you been up to?" she asked and I was a bit astonished at this point. No jibes or cut-downs? No gossip?

"Well, nothing much. We had a party for Joel Powell's birthday today. That was nice. Amy was there. And the guys."

"The guys? As in Raif and Trey?"

"And Tal." I waited for it.

"Hmm. That's nice."

"Yeah." You've got to be kidding me.

"You know, Eve, I wanted to invite you for dinner tomorrow night. And Joel."

"And Joel? Why Joel?"

"Well, I got to thinking, he's a nice young man." She paused.

"Uh huh."

"And Amy says he's been lonely and working so hard. She thinks you starting up a friendship with him has done him some good. I thought I'd do what I could to help, that's all."

I was stupefied, so answered the only way I could think of with, "Okay. What time?" Instead, I should have said, *What? Is this some kind of ploy to be part of your matchmaking?*

"Seven thirty. We'll see you then."

"K. Bye." I hung up the phone in complete shock and ran straight to Joel's house to kill myself laughing.

# JOEL ♂

I rummaged through a basket of clean clothes to prepare for an extra day at work the next morning, and Eve showed up at my door. She stood on the porch wearing slippers, baggy pajama bottoms and a t-shirt; a housecoat hung open and loose at her sides. Regardless of her mussed hair, make-up blurred and fading, she still looked beautiful. More beautiful than ever. And she was giggling.

"Hey. What's going on?" I asked.

"I just had the oddest conversation with my mother. She called to see how I was doing, what I've been up to and to invite me to dinner tomorrow." She stared with an odd grin, waiting for me to answer while I waited for the punch line.

"That's it?" I asked.

"That's *it.*"

"Huh. No bashing, no relationship talk?"

"Nope."

"Not even a jab about grandkids?"

"Not even."

"Wow. Is everything all right?"

"I guess so. I'm just amazed. And impressed. And happy. Maybe we can start to have a normal mother-daughter relationship. Or not." She paused and I saw the moment her suspicious mind took over. "This is almost creepier. I kind of want my old mom back."

"Are you sure? It was only one conversation. I'm sure not all is lost."

"Well, there's more. You're invited, too."

"Me?"

"Yep."

"Uh uh. You told her to invite me so you didn't have to sit through supper alone with your parents."

"No, I swear I didn't. She was actually talking to your mom."

"That's even worse."

"Not really. You're mom said she thought I was making a good impression on you as your new friend and my mother wants to encourage it. For your sake."

"This is only getting stranger. You've been a good influence all right. But not for why my mother thinks so," I said and grinned wide.

"Joel, you have to do this. I'm thinking it might be strange to sit through a pleasant conversation at dinner with my mom. I need you there to walk me through it."

"Ugh."

"Please." She bounced on the balls of her feet.

The thought of dinner with Eve's parents would be daunting to any man.

"What time?" I asked, already sure I was going.

"Seven. We can leave around six."

"Okay. I'll go."

"Thanks, Joel."

"No problem. And Eve," I called as she stepped outside the door. "Thanks for today."

"You're welcome."

While her face said she thought this situation hilarious, I knew that couldn't be further from the truth. Panic rose inside of her, hurt stepping temporarily aside while she awaited her mother's pokes and jibes. Eve needed a pillar and I wanted to be the man she could lean on.

I stood on her doorstep the following evening wearing khaki pants and a dress shirt, some of the church clothes that I took out for special occasions when jeans weren't appropriate. I decided not to wear a tie, keep it casual.

Eve answered the door wearing the same white flowing blouse she'd worn to the barn raising that made me want her then. It fit her tight around the chest, tied beneath her breast with a string, draping down to just touch the top of her low riding pants. Her hair, the bold blonde with dark stripes mellowed by curls, bounced when she walked and she smelled like a garden.

"Hi," I said.

"Hey."

"I brought flowers for your mom. And some for you." I handed her a bouquet and she sniffed inside the paper.

"Roses."

"I didn't know if you liked roses. Or if your mom does."

"I do. Thank you. I'll just put them in some water before we go." She walked into the kitchen, leaving the door swinging open and me on the porch. "You look nice. Sorry about dragging you to my parent's house," she called from inside.

"I don't mind."

"It should be eventful, anyway. I can drive if you want."

I nodded and followed her to the Jeep. We drove in silence the first ten minutes until Eve started singing along to a George Strait song on the CD player. Which meant she knew the words to a country music song.

"What are you listening to?" I asked, dumbfounded.

"What do you mean?"

"You actually know the words to *All My Exes Live in Texas?*"

"Yeah. Got a problem with that, cowboy?"

"No. It just surprised me. A good surprise. And you can sing, too."

"I used to be in the choir, remember?"

"No. I don't remember."

"No? My parents made me join because Maggie wanted to but she was too shy. And I hated the idea in the beginning."

"I don't remember seeing you in the choir."

"I was in the middle row. And I always sat down so no one would see me. Funny thing is, I could sing and Maggie couldn't, so she gave up and dropped out."

"And you?"

"I dropped out with her and kept up singing on my own at home. When people didn't listen. Except my dad. I knew he liked it when I sang so I didn't let on I knew he was there and he didn't let on that he stood just around the corner."

"That's very nice."

"Thank you," she grinned. "These, by the way, are the only two country songs I actually remember some of the words to. The rest I'm working on. Do you want to hear my favorite song? I used to sing it all the time as a young teenager when he pretended not to listen."

"Sure. Let's here it."

She flicked through the songs until she came to one in particular and the track started to play.

"Do you know it? It's called, *A Love Without End, Amen*."

"Yeah. I know it." And the words started to come through the speakers. *...Daddy's don't love their little children just every now and then...it's a love without end amen...*

Eve reached to turn it down when she realized it hit home with me. I grabbed her hand before she turned the dial and held it.

"Leave it Eve. It's okay."

"I wasn't thinking."

We listened, both of us holding deep meaning for the same song in our own ways. As it ended we pulled up to the house and she turned off the car. We sat quietly in the dark.

"Thanks," I said.

"For what?"

"For making me see that everything will be alright. You always do."

"I wasn't trying to."

"You didn't have to try." I smiled, squeezed her hand and looked through the window at her mother waving from the doorstep.

"Here we go," she said and stepped out of the Jeep. I followed and met her mom with a kiss on the cheek and handed her the bouquet of flowers.

# EVE ♂

Dinner went well over all. My mom wasn't too terrible at first and only let a few accusing questions slide to fill her gossip needs while my dad shook his head and protected the both of us when he needed to.

Joel acted more proper than I had seen before. Well mannered, a gentle smile stretched across his face at just the right times, polite and warm...a perfect gentleman. If I'd been introducing him as my latest boyfriend, I'd have been cashing in with a huge "cha-ching!" of a win with my parents. But he wasn't and my stomach turned a little at the reminder.

We'd been sharing moments. Not just hot and bothered moments, but those moments when I could feel both of us wanted to admit to more. I nearly blurted out that I cared about him as we left the house. The words clung to the tip of my tongue and I wanted to tell him everything.

I didn't. I couldn't. And I reasoned with myself; as much as my body and my heart thought I was ready for a relationship, even one I wanted to pursue with Joel, my mind disagreed. And I had better make sure my whole body fell in line before plunging into dangerous waters. I had, after all, fallen in love a few times too many and sunk each time. With Joel, I wanted to float, not drown.

I watched Joel walk toward his house, me up my sidewalk, he up his, and we exchanged a glance and a wave goodnight. Even without a kiss or the hesitation in one, I had to bite back the deep sighs of a young girl with an eyelash fluttering-cotton candy sweet-i's dotted with hearts crush. Still my Adonis neighbor—handsome, sexy, anything else cliché you want to throw in there—Joel had put up with my family, stuck up for me against my mother, yet I could sit back with a beer and curse with Raif on one side of me, Trey on the other and Joel joined right in on the banter.

Who was this guy?

# JOEL ♂

I still couldn't figure Eve out even as I peeled off my shirt and pants and fell into bed. We laughed. We cried. We had sex. My heart pounded and blood flowed through my body fast enough to ignite every sensation and set me on fire; her smell in my nose, the glint in her eyes, the touch of her skin when she brushed past all made me want to roar inside. But it stayed a suffocated roar because I couldn't do anything about it. And my excuse? My life was already too complicated.

Complicated. How just like a guy avoiding a relationship is that? For now, that's what I had to keep telling myself. I had been planning a move in the direction of a relationship, but I needed to work on Meg first. As much as it would be easier for me to have Eve permanently on my side for the support—not just emotionally; especially not just emotionally—it wouldn't be fair to stick her in the middle of me and my drug-addicted ex-wife.

Great, Joel. You'd just better hope she's around long enough for you to get your life figured out.

# Chapter 21

*Eve* ♀

I woke up with tingling body parts.

Somewhere along the line I lost focus. Church seemed to be the perfect solution this morning, seeing as how my mother would drag me there anyway. My mother had become a solution, shoving me back into reality and out of this fantasy dream world where my sexy Adonis next door and I used our lack of control to fix the problems lying beneath the surface.

The cars lined up around the church's gravel lot and down the dirt road, people were filing into pews and I searched for a glimpse of him. He probably wasn't even here. I suppose that would give me enough time to focus on repenting, since that's just what I needed to do.

My mother's need for me to attend church seemed more urgent than usual this morning and I had a feeling she knew something was up since dinner the night before. Twice in the last two days, my mother stirred up suspicious thoughts in my mind. Something was amiss in this here ol' town of Tayton and my Spidey senses were tingling.

I'd had invitations to the ladies group for prayer night and coffee— likely hoping to be the first to get the juicy details straight from the source. Or better yet the chance to join a real life exorcism of evil spirits from *that Whitting girl*—and offers for dates from most of the single male population who'd heard of my line dancing technique at the bar. (On the bar.) Man, stories really took forever to die.

I smiled nicely to the congregation as they stared at us walking through the parking lot. All the while muttering nasty thoughts under my breath.

"What's that, honey?" asked my mother.

"Nothing. I just said I stepped in some *glass* and did you hear that *duck*?"

"I think you might be going mad, Eve."

"Might be?"

## JOEL ♂

I searched the churchyard for Eve. I received a few odd looks from the crowd which likely had something to do with the rapidly spreading rumors of my high-strung neighbor and why we were spending so much time together.

Then she appeared as if out of nowhere, looking awkward as usual and lacking her mother's choice of attire this morning. She wore nothing near small town church clothes but instead, a fitted blouse and tight black pants that flared at the bottom.

As I walked toward her, she caught me staring and gave me a warning glare with one raised eyebrow.

"Good morning. I see you chose your own wardrobe today," I said.

"I did. I decided that what, with the rumors going around, I'm already in everyone's black books. Why bother fighting it?"

"Uh huh. Well, you look hot."

"Thank you."

"What are you doing after church?" I whispered in her ear.

"Back off, cowboy. Those thoughts are not for church. God might hear you."

"God can see your outfit, too. I'm sure he'd understand."

"Here comes my mother. Want to stay and chat?"

"See you later," I said and walked away. The last "chat" I had with Mrs. Whitting happened over meatloaf and a heavy conversation about how I could help Eve turn her life around. I remember the words: *do you know any decent boys to introduce her to? Not the type you run with* which I assumed included me. Funny how the invitation began as sweet and innocent...

I positioned us in a pew three rows behind Eve on the opposite side. Her family always sat behind mine so I had to maneuver this one by getting an early seat and dragging my mother in ahead of me. It seemed Eve thought the same thing because I heard her shuffling the Whitting's quickly down the aisle. They didn't get far and sat in the last row against the back wall.

As the music started, my mom leaned toward me. "Joel, I don't know why you don't just go over and sit with her."

"What?"

"Instead of playing these games."

"There are no games," I huffed. My mother's keen sense of observation had always been annoying. She made me feel like a thirteen-year-old kid who'd just figured out the opposite sex was good for more than dodge ball.

"We haven't sat this far back in over ten years," she continued.

"So, live a little."

"Neither have the Whitting's. And I have a feeling Eve has pulled them into the back corner."

"Maybe Mr. Whitting decided to sit in the back."

She gave me a "tsk" and shuffled Damian into the pew between us. "Damian, sit still, honey," she said, maneuvering him away from the hymnals.

"Buddy," I eyed him. "Remember what I said. Lips closed. No bouncing."

"'Kay," he said and snuggled into the other side of my mom.

"Good morning, Joel," said a voice next to me. It came from Raif's sister Lacy and she wore a tight orange blouse, giving me the money shot.

"Hi, Lace. How are you and Doug?"

"Just fine. Hi Mrs. Powell. Hi Damian."

"Hi Lacy."

Raif followed and sat behind me on the other side of the aisle. It had been years since Raif showed up for church. And I could have sworn I heard Trey shuffle in behind him.

242

The service began with the pastor's announcements and he wasn't more than five minutes into the sermon when Damian started turning around and waving at the familiar faces. I heard muted laughter and whispers behind us.

"Damian, sit down," I whispered and pulled him to sit on my lap.

"Uncle Ray is here!" he yelled.

"Shhh. Quiet."

"Uncle Ray is here," he whispered.

"I know. You have to listen now, okay. Sit nice."

"Kay." He set his head down on my shoulder and squeezed his arms tight around my neck. The congregation closed their eyes to pray. I prayed Damian would fall asleep.

"Daddy," he whispered.

"Shhh."

"Uncle Trey is here, too. And Tal. And Cammy. *Be*member Cammy?"

"I know. The whole town is here this morning." And it was weird. The church hadn't been this full since Sue Ann Grady got married and that became the event of the season only because she married a rich stockbroker from the city and they had a catered luncheon following the service. Everyone in town weaseled in for a free meal and a quick peek at the rich tycoon.

"Damian, you can sit beside me on the pew if keep quiet, okay?"

"Kay."

He hunched down on his knees, faced the wrong way and leaned his arms over the back of the bench. He started to giggle and wave and covered his mouth when I turned to look at him.

"He reminds me of you as a boy, Joel," said my mother. "Your father had a heck of a time getting you to sit still. Especially in church."

I leaned over and kissed her cheek and the congregation rose for a song. Damian took full advantage of the movement in the pews. When everyone sat again, Damian made faces at the rows behind me. His laughter started to grow in volume and he stuck a finger in each side of his mouth, stretched it wide and crossed his eyes.

Frustrated, I turned and followed his line of sight. Eve mimicked the same face in the back row. She stopped when she saw me and pursed her lips tight, trying not to smile.

Damian turned again. I could see Raif's shoulder's shake with subdued laughter out of the corner of my eye and a few people cleared their throats.

Eve waved and made more faces.

"Okay, we're leaving," I said and scooped him up. I grabbed Eve's hand on my way out the door and she followed, reluctantly.

"What?" she asked when we were outside. Damian giggled as hard and as loud as possible.

"I was trying to keep him quiet, Eve," I said.

"Come on. We were just having fun. I'm sorry Joel. Tell your dad to lighten up, buddy," she said to Damian.

"Light him up, Daddy."

I couldn't help but laugh and Eve's glowing smile kept it going. "Well, now we have to sneak back in."

"You first," she said.

"No way. Then you'll leave and your mother will pounce on me on her way out. She'd probably blame me for abducting you or something."

"Okay. I'll go first. No more playing around, Damian. We have to behave now," she said and leaned in to whisper in Damian's ear. He laughed and clapped his hands. "Do we have a deal?"

"Kay. Bye Ee*b*ie!" He pinched his lips closed and threw away the key.

I heaved a sigh and walked back down the aisle to our seat. Damian sat as quiet as a mouse the rest of the service, his hands folded tightly in his lap, his little legs jittering on the bench. I knew he itched to get up and run around but whatever Eve had told him worked. A miracle.

## *Eve* ♀

Wednesday. I spent last night playing poker with the guys, which sucked because I lost. My mind obviously wandered elsewhere or I would have beat their asses. And I wasn't in a great mood to begin with.

Maggie and Brock were supposed to be rounding whatever part of the world they were in, taking the rest of the three months to linger between ports and make their way home. But something was wrong. I had that sisterly instinct about her reason for calling from the moment I answered. There had been a change of plans. And along with the negative vibes I felt, I wasn't sure I would like the change in plans, even though Maggie sounded ecstatic.

"Tell me about his news then, or did you just call to bounce up and down squealing into the phone receiver?"

"We love it here, Eve. I can't leave. Not yet. We're going to be delayed."

Excitement rushed through me. I thought immediately about Joel and wondered if a few extra weeks would be enough time to turn things around for us. Then I gave myself a slap to the forehead. What the hell was I thinking?

"So, Mags, how long are you thinking of staying? Do I get to deal with Mom an extra few weeks myself?" I grinned into the phone. Maggie sounded happy and I was happy for her. I loved the sound of her voice and loved that she had found her "one true love".

"Actually, we're staying longer than a few weeks."

A few months, I thought. Even better.

I *love* Maggie.

"This is so unlike me, Eve. I've always been the safe one, the one to take the easy road. But not this time. As long as you can do a few things for me."

"Like what? Winterize your rosebushes?" I grew curious and sensed her hesitation. My heart sat just slightly lower than fluffy clouds full of rainbows and butterflies.

"We're staying for a year. At least."

Silence.

"I refuse to burden you with our house. I contacted my realtor, and there are so many people looking to buy, it had two potential buyers in fewer days and is moments away from a sale; they were just chomping at the bit, waiting for a new listing. She's working up papers and there'll be a sign up within the week. Can you believe it? And don't argue and tell me it's okay because I know you, Eve. I've arranged everything already."

My heart plummeted to the floor.

I hated Maggie.

She continued. "I was only hoping to burden you with one thing; be there for the realtor when she comes by. I'll send a moving company for my stuff to pack and store it so you won't need to worry about any of that. Just my personal things like photo albums and my china doll collection. And I need you to soften Mom and Dad up for my news. Eve…

"Are you there, Eve?"

"Uh huh," I said, but my own voice sounded further away than hers.

"We might just spend the next few years traveling and working when we need to. I can teach over here. All over, actually. I'll miss Vine Street, I really will. But this is so beautiful and I am just vibrating!... Eve. Eve? Are you all right? Say something. You're mad, aren't you?"

"No, Maggie. I'm not mad. I'm happy for you. Really happy for you." I bit the skin off my knuckle and choked back a tear. I started to panic, wondering if there were other places in town for sale. I liked it here. Loved it here. This was home. In the midst of running from disaster and chasing something close to normal, I'd found some comfort. For the first time in my life, it felt good to be belong somewhere. Sort of. And Joel was here. Next door. On Vine Street.

Maggie's house gave me a reason, a need to be here. Not only somewhere to stay, but a reason I had to stay. It was part of my plan of not having a plan and here it was, slowly crumbling to pieces at my feet. Now I needed a new one. A real one.

"Are you sure you don't mind, Eve? You don't sound so sure. I was afraid you'd be mad about helping with the realtor but I hoped you'd be okay considering I was letting you out of this housesitting thing early. I know you didn't want to do it, really. And I really want to do this, Eve. I need to do it."

"Then do it Maggie. You deserve to be happy and live a little." And she did. I sucked back my selfish thoughts, restricting my own lack of happiness for the sake of Maggie's and forced a smile. "So what are you going to do if I get married or something?"

"What? You're getting married?"

"Not even close. I just wanted a reaction. For old times sake." I slid to the floor along the cupboards feeling a sudden urge to curl up with my sister under the covers with a box of tissues on the sofa and have a crying session. A lump formed in my throat. I brushed away a tear. "I'm only teasing, Maggie."

"Well, if you were I'd be there as soon as I could, at least to send you off on a honeymoon. You'd have to give me enough notice, hon." She laughed into the phone.

"Well, when it happens you'll have enough notice. You'll be sending your kids to college by then and you could fly home in an hour from anywhere around the world because planes will fly that fast when we live on Mars."

"Poor Eve," she sighed. I heard her heart breaking for me, somewhere in the recesses beneath all of her ecstatic happiness.

"Can I take Stumpy?" I asked, stifling a whimper.

"What? The cat? You hate cats."

"I kinda like 'im."

"Of course."

"Take care. I love you, Mags. And I'll try to convince Mom it's a good idea."

"Thanks Eve. I really owe you one. I'll send along details with the realtor, okay?"

And that was it. Maggie would sell her house. I'd be leaving within the next couple of weeks. Or sooner. I should likely count on days, just in case. I had no idea how long things like this took, but there wouldn't be much time.

I stood in the kitchen stewing about what would happen next. I contemplated calling Joel and confessing my feelings despite the fact my body and mind weren't exactly on the same team yet. Except that my heart had switched sides. It was my body, twitching and shaking with nerves, that wasn't so sure now.

I sucked it up, because that's what I'd tell someone else to do in my situation, and stood to lean on the countertop.

I could see Joel through the kitchen window, standing over his sink rinsing dishes. He glanced up and smiled. I waved and that was all I saw of Joel until Sunday morning.

# Chapter 22

## *Joel* ♂

I stood in the churchyard with Trey, Tal, Cammy and Raif while everyone else mingled. The pending lab results consumed my thoughts; I had hardly seen Eve and never alone, and scanned the crowd now feeling lost in a place I'd always felt comfortable. As if something or someone was missing from my side which left a deep dent to be filled.

This was the second Sunday in a row the entire town showed up for a service and I still had to wonder what had enticed them there. I spotted Eve in the distance with her mom—her dad had already made an early escape—and my mom visited a few groups over.

"Why are there so many people here this morning? And why are you guys here two Sundays in a row?" I asked.

"Rumor has it Joel Powell found himself a woman and we're all here to catch a glimpse," said Raif.

"What?" I laughed.

"Well, that's the story. I figured since you won't tell us about it, we'd come check it out ourselves."

"Along with everyone else in town," said Trey with a laugh.

"There's nothing exciting about me and a relationship, even if the rumor were true."

"There's a lot exciting when the relationship is with Eve Whitting."

"What?"

Cammy punched Tal in the arm. "See! It's because I told Eve she needed to get herself satisfied. She took my advice. 'Cause we're friends now. Us women stick together."

"Eve's not really getting some, Cammy," said Tal. Then to me, "I know it's a load of shit, Joel, but it makes for a funny story."

"Where did this one stir up from? You, no doubt!" I glared at Trey.

"Me?" he grinned.

"Dumb ass."

"What's the big deal? There needs to be some sort of excitement around here. And I never really started it. Lace asked me if I was seeing Eve and I said no. She heard about the bar scene a couple weeks ago."

"And how did my name come up?" I demanded. I felt the rage begin to boil.

"I said she wasn't with me, it must be someone else. Lace mentioned your name. I didn't agree with her."

"Did you disagree?"

"Not exactly," he grinned. He knew exactly what he was doing; Trey was a shit disturber to the core and always had been. I just didn't like that it involved messing with Eve's life.

"So that's why she asked me who I was seeing lately," said Raif. "I said no one in particular. And she knows Tal's dating Cammy so she asked about Joel."

"And you said what?" I asked with a glare.

"I said I knew you were having some fun with someone but I didn't know who. Shit, Trey!"

"Did either of you think about Eve in all of this? Do you really think she needs another rumor for this town to feed on?"

"Did I hear my name?" asked Eve, strolling up behind us.

"Shit," I said.

"There's a lot of profanity flying around over here for church on a Sunday." A hush fell over the crowd around us. "What's going on?"

"Nothing. Apparently Trey started a rumor." I folded my arms, preparing for a brawl between Eve and whoever got in her way first.

"Really? A juicy one I hope," she grinned and rubbed her hands together.

"A good juicy one," said Cammy.

"It's about you, Eve," I said with much less excitement than the rest held.

"Me? Great. What did I do now?" she scoffed, preparing to let it roll off her as most others did.

"Joel," said Tal with a chuckle. "Get it? Not *what* you did Eve, but *who*."

"What?" She turned beet red and stared at me. "Oh, God."

"It wasn't on purpose," said Trey.

"You're an idiot, Trey!" she said and cuffed him in the shoulder. "I suppose things look really bad since everyone saw us walk out of the service together last week with Damian."

"Hey, that wasn't my fault," said Trey.

"This is all your fault," I said and cuffed him in his other shoulder. Then the murmurs behind us grew into laughter coming from a group of women a few feet away. Lacey and her friends stood in a trio looking like glammed up pageant queens, the kind that didn't make it into the running any more. This was their collective second appearance at church in years.

"That's her," she said to one in pink. "She's the one I was telling you about. I just can't believe Joel would be interested in her; she's not his type at all. Do you remember her from high school?"

"I know. He usually goes for the sweet tarts; those pretty little things. I'd of pegged him for one of those, not a tomboy."

"From the rumors I've heard, she's a tease and a flirt," said one with big teased and bleached hair.

"She only hangs out with Joel and his crew. Did you notice? No one else."

"She'll probably go through all of the idiots eventually, if she hasn't already." This came from the one in half-inch thick make-up. "I wondered why they were keeping her around. I guess now we have our answer."

"Be nice, Cindy, one of those idiots is my brother," said Lacy and she turned as an aside to us with a smile before continuing back with a snort to her friends, "I hope he's got higher standards at least."

Raif made a move to lunge toward Lacy and I stepped in front of him. No way was he getting the first word. But Eve stepped in and quieted the both of us.

"Nobody move," she said as she tromped across the ground between churchgoers, knocking Jack Tilly into Mrs. Ellis, the seventy-eight year old choir director, to get to Lacey.

"I'll back you up, honey," said Cammy and trudged after Eve.

Eve stopped in front of Lacy and stared with the harshest scowl I'd seen yet. Her eyes didn't leave Lacy's. They filled with anger and hurt; she tried her hardest to control it and had met her limit. Her fists became tight at her sides and the four of us guys held our breath, inching back out of instinct because we all knew what was coming.

"First of all, I can be a "pretty little thing" when I want to be. Sweet. Tart." Eve pulled her arm back in the air. "Second, I'm full of sass and can throw a damn good punch." Her fist met the right side of Lacy's face and landed her with a thud on the ground, knocked senseless, blood dripping from a cut beneath her eye. Cammy spit on her.

Lacy's friends cringed, the crowd gasped, obviously more surprised than the four of us who'd simply winced because we all knew what Eve threw behind her punches. By the look of Lacy on the ground, she was more than stunned.

Eve marched off toward her car and I followed. "Are you okay?"

"Fine." She shook the pain from her now swelling hand dangling at her side and drew in fast-paced breaths attempting to control her anger. When she glanced up at me, I saw she tried even harder to control the tears.

"Let me drive," I said.

I could tell she wanted to argue against my coming along, but her hand bled at the knuckles.

"You don't have to come with me. It'll just fuel the rumors."

"I don't care about rumors."

I turned to see Raif cross his arms and stare after us. "Nice work," he said to Trey with a scowl.

"Just a little nudge Joel!" yelled Trey.

"Bastard," I said and got into the car.

"What?" asked Eve. She had already sat into the passenger side.

"Nothing."

"Where are we going?"

"Home." I peeled out of the driveway and down the road toward home without another word.

## EVE ♀

"Do you think Raif's mad that I punched his sister?" I asked as Joel wrapped my hand in a bandage. We sat on the sofa in Maggie's living room.

"No. He's probably mad you didn't hit her again."

He hunched down, bent at the knees and leaned over my hand where it draped across his lap. I could smell his cologne and watched the waves in his hair as I spoke.

"I didn't mean to go off like that, but it was either that or break into tears. And I'm not good at crying in public."

"Why tears? Don't let what they said bother you. It's all based on rumors and lies." He wrapped a strip of gauze around my knuckles, stuck the end down with a piece of tape and massaged my palm.

Tears threatened again. I was not typically an emotional person and don't know what had come over me. "No it's not. Not all rumors."

He looked up with surprise. "What do you mean?"

"It's all based on truth, Joel. It's just Trey who thinks he started a rumor."

"Well, you aren't a sleaze."

"Then what am I Joel?" I needed to hear it from him again.

We heard Raif's truck pull up out front, Trey's car behind it. Joel looked back toward me with a clenched jaw. "I'll be right back." I could feel his temper flaring. This whole situation angered him as much as it did me but I hadn't noticed it in his eyes until now.

He left and I jumped to the window to see what would happen next. Joel rarely lost his temper, but I had a feeling this was one of those rare occasions.

He strode across the lawn toward Trey and grabbed him by either side of his shirt collar. Trey argued, with a grin as usual, but it only lasted until Joel put a fist to his face. I winced and Trey stood up from the ground. I really liked Trey. I didn't want to see anyone get hurt. But right about now, I wanted Joel to sock him again. Maybe it was the tomboy in me looking for a good fight. Maybe it was because Trey was the dumb ass that started this whole thing.

I moved closer to the window and listened through the screen with my good hand on the door handle.

"Okay, I deserved that one," said Trey. Joel hit him again.

"That was a cheap shot. Now you're dead, Powell." Trey threw a punch that hit Joel in the stomach and they both went to the ground in a grappling tangle.

Joel drew back his arm, bicep tight and fist clenched. His legs held Trey on the ground; his fist hit him in the jaw. I flinched as Trey retaliated and broke open Joel's bottom lip. Raif moved in before a knockout and ripped Joel off of his opponent.

Raif held Joel back, though it took all of his strength. Trey stepped back and hunched over his knees to catch his breath.

"Joel, go talk to Eve." Raif used his strength to *encourage* Joel toward the house. "I'll deal with him."

Joel paused, his stare locked on Trey, his chest heaving with frustrated breaths. I could tell he debated it in his head, even though the look on his face mirrored my own thoughts.

I wanted him to hit Trey again, even urged him in my mind to do it, but I knew it wouldn't solve anything; just something that came from wanting someone else to pay for my embarrassment. Great. Now I felt guilty.

I sighed, slouched into the sofa and just plain wanted Joel. But that wasn't going to happen. I was his floozy and the whole town knew it including the friends around us, our families, my mother. My father. Ugh.

The screen door swung open and Joel walked in. I wanted to curl up in bed and forget this day ever happened. Instead, I stood, walked silently to the kitchen to run a cloth under cold water for his face and met him in the living room.

"Are you okay?" he asked. He hadn't moved from the front door.

"Yeah. You?"

He nodded. A cut marked the side of his lip and blood trickled down his chin. He wiped it with his hand and sat down next to me on the sofa. I could feel his heart pounding hard from within every one of his muscles that connected with mine at our shoulders, legs, arms.

I dabbed the cut with the cloth while he stared at me through an awkward silence.

"You aren't a floozy, Eve. You are so much more than that." He shook his head with an exasperated glance to the floor and wiped his chin with his shirt. His eyes shot back to mine and held with more meaning than I'd felt from him yet. "I've never thought of you as a floozy. Nothing between us was cheap or meaningless. Ever. And I'll beat the shit out of Trey again tomorrow for starting the rumor in the first place."

"Thanks, but that isn't necessary. I just don't know where I stand on this right now."

"Eve," he said and took my shoulders in his hands. "You mean more to me than sex. If it makes you feel better, we can stop with this for good and just hang out, you and me, as friends or...whatever." His expression humbled on the last word.

"What do you mean, whatever?"

He smiled then. His eyes shone. I could palpate the tension between us, one I had been hoping would play out just as it was; that same tender look in his eyes, the hint of a smile, our happiness joining in an actual—dare I think relationship. We were at least on the same page. And I knew then I wanted more from Joel. I needed more. And he might need that, too.

He began again after a hard swallow. "Eve. I—" And he was interrupted by a pounding on the front door. Then it opened and my entire body froze in anticipation of what he had started to say.

"What?" I asked him, pleading with my wide eyes that he ignore the door and Raif, now standing at it.

"Joel, sorry to interrupt, but Meg is knocking the shit out of your door and she's mighty pissed off."

"What?" Joel stood and followed the noise coming from outside.

Agh! Don't freakin' leave!

I followed Raif out of the house and watched Joel stride across our front lawns. Meg stood there, or some woman I assumed to be Meg, banging a fist on his front door with as much passion I must have had when I socked Lacey in the face.

"Joel!" she yelled, scratchy voice carrying through both yards and down the street.

"Meg, I'm not home!" Joel called across the lawn, making slow strides toward her.

"I can see that." She smacked gum between her teeth and flopped toward Joel in high-heeled mules—very inappropriate to walk across grass in, I might add, but she seemed to manage like a pro—and a crap-load of make-up smeared across her face. I wasn't sure if she put it on that way, or if she'd put it on that way two days ago and hadn't taken it off yet. What a piece of work, I thought. But I had sort of a biased opinion; what, with me wanting Joel and wanting her to go f—Well, anyway, I imagine the glare on my face didn't hide my true feelings for Meg.

I lowered myself to sit on the front porch next to Raif. Neither of us wanted to intrude but I couldn't peel myself away from the scene.

"Joel, I need you," she said and threw her arms around his neck.

"What?" he asked, reluctant to hug her at first, but his arms came around her waist and he pulled her closer toward him.

I closed my eyes and drew in long calming breaths. I really wanted to cry. Or hit something. I wasn't sure which would be more beneficial just now. Probably both.

I couldn't hear all of what they were saying, though Raif and I made a solid effort of straining toward them for a better earful. Trey and Tal mimicked our positions on Joel's front porch. Cammy stood at the ready on the front lawn, prepared to get a shot at Meg for my sake and my heart swelled just a little for her.

"I'm going through a lot of crap right now Joel. I am really trying. I'm going into rehab and my mom is helping out still, until then. But I need you Joel. I need you to come home. Damian is freaking out and he won't listen to anything I say."

"What's he freaking out about? He was fine when I left."

"I know. But I told him about the DNA test and he took it real hard."

"You what?"

"He doesn't believe me when I tell him you're his dad."

"We don't even know if I am his dad! Why the hell did you tell him? He doesn't need to know until we find out what's going on. I wanted to talk to him myself...I wanted to...I can't believe even you would do this!"

"Joel. The results came back. They're positive. Damian is yours."

"What?"

She nodded. And then it happened. Everything fell apart. For me anyway. For Meg—well, Joel swung her around in his arms and laughed aloud. He had forgotten we were all sitting there, forgotten about the conversation we were having moments before. This was a significant moment for him and I didn't want to take that away for the world, but this really sucked.

Then Meg chimed in, "It's just like we're a family again. I can feel it, Joel. Can't you feel it?"

He nodded, still spinning her around and chanting, "He's mine. Thank God, he's mine."

I was going to be sick.

I ran into the house, made a beeline for the washroom and threw up in the toilet. My stomach twisted in knots. It wasn't the end of the world. I knew it wasn't, just that we were no further ahead or back from where we began.

But it felt exactly like the end of the world. Damian was his son. Meg spun with Joel on the front lawn. It was a nightmare. A bittersweet fucking nightmare.

# JOEL ♂

'Damian is yours'. The words clattered around in my head, shuffling every other thought aside as I tried to process the facts. I had my son. Nothing else mattered in the world. Everything around me began to blur behind my eyes; they were damp with tears of utter happiness. A huge weight had been lifted and I couldn't help but throw my arms around Meg, because no one else stood in front of me. I would have grabbed hold of a tree had it been the closest thing there.

I was floating. The words froze in my throat; I wanted to share every emotion I had with those around me. I could have screamed from one end of the earth to the other.

Then things began to settle. I stopped chanting like a lunatic. I came back to level ground, my head cleared and I began to focus. My house. Trey and Tal just walking inside with Cammy. The El Camino sat parked on the street. I could feel Meg in my arms, in a loving embrace and everything felt so suddenly wrong; like an out of body experience. But when I floated back to reality I wasn't holding Eve as I imagined; everything hit like a cold stone falling to the ground. I felt the thud, a shiver and stopped dead. I wanted no one else, needed Eve there to share the moment. I turned to search for her at her Maggie's but the porch was empty.

Then Meg whispered into my ear, "Just like old times, Joel. It was meant to be this way. In time, things always work out."

I pushed her away and held her shoulders at arms length. I knew she read my expression correctly because she winced with a hope that I'd fallen into some kind of trance, under her spell. I spoke in a near whisper. "What? No, it's not like a family again. It was you, Meg, that did this; you that caused so much animosity and lies and hurt. For Damian. For our families. For *me*."

"It could have been more." She stared with glossy eyes then the hate came through, reminding me of the Meg I knew so well. She'd lost. She had given it one last try then morphed back to the same old Meg. "Look, Joel. I don't give a shit about you, either. And the games are over. Okay? I promise. I only want you to come with me, hate me or not, and make Damian stop crying. I can't calm the kid down. Neither can Mom. I need you. Your *son* needs you."

I fought to find a way to send Meg away for the last time. Right here, right now. But taking Damian when he was upset with his mother would add more confusion for him. We needed to sit him down, iron things out, and then we'd leave. Me and him. I was done with Meg. Done with her games. Damian was better off without her.

"I will go with you for Damian's sake, nothing more. We aren't a family. We never will be. Damian will always be my son. You will never be anything more to me, Meg, than pain and hurt and someone I can't get rid of because Damian needs a mother. However pathetic you are. I will go with you. And he is coming back with me. For good. When you're out of rehab and clean long enough that I'm satisfied he's safe around you again, then, and only then, can you start seeing him again."

"You can't do that to me Joel. You can't take him."

"I can, Meg. If you cared about Damian the way you should, nothing would matter but him. You wouldn't have told him about the DNA test. Not now. You'd be trying harder to keep clean and you wouldn't have left your three-year-old son alone in the house while you were out looking for a fix!" I let go of her shoulders and stared at her. "Wait for me in the car."

I walked across the front porch and into the house to pack a bag.

## EVE ♀

I heard the screen door bang closed. Joel. I washed up, wiped my face—now the pale look of death warming over—and walked out of the washroom. Raif stood in the living room leaning a hip against the sofa. I glanced up at him and slouched into the cushions.

"So good news, then, about the test, huh?" I said, feeling the need to say something. I let out an enormous sigh. My voice even quivered.

Raif sat next to me and nodded.

"So, what's going on out there?" I dared to ask.

"I don't know. I followed you inside and the others went into Joel's place to give them some privacy."

I didn't respond, only ran my hands through my hair, trying not to look desperate.

"Eve, you'll be okay. Joel won't go back to Meg."

"What?"

"Just trust him and give him space to do this and he'll come back to you."

I eyed him suspiciously. "He told you about us?"

"No. No one told me anything. I just know."

"How? Was it that freakin' obvious? Oh, God, so everyone knows and now I will be the sleaze bag of Vine Street and—"

"Eve, relax. Jesus. I expected you to be crying, not yelling."

"Why is that, Raif?" I scowled harder, back to wanting to punch someone.

"Because Joel is leaving and you love him. Which, by the way, doesn't make you a sleaze bag."

"Well it might—Okay. Wait, what's the difference?"

"The difference is that I know you, for one thing, and you aren't that type of woman. And when two people love each other, they are supposed to want to be together instead of playing these stupid games and—"

"When what two people love each other? I never said anything about love."

"You and Joel, dumb ass. Jesus, Eve, are you two the last to figure it out?"

"Maybe," I huffed and crossed my arms at my chest. Defense mechanisms were breaking. "So, *are* we the very last to figure it out?"

"Probably. Trey knows."

"How does Trey know?" I yelled.

"Trey knows because he seems to share a brain with you more than he ever has with anyone else and it probably filtered over. And everyone else eventually figured it out. You can practically see the tension between you two."

"Everyone else like who, Raif?"

"Like Joel's mother. I'm sure he told her. And my mother asked me about it so she heard from someone in the gossip circle—"

"Your mother? That means my mother—oh God! This is so embarrassing."

"No, what's embarrassing is that you just figured it out and that Joel still doesn't have a clue."

"I have to talk to him," I said, nearing a state of panic and running for the front door.

"Eve, no. Let him go."

"I need him."

"You need to let him go. He needs to do this, whatever happens now. For Damian."

"Shit." Then the water works began.

"Finally. See, when you start yelling, I'm lost. This I can handle. I know how to fix emotional. Come here," he said and pulled my head onto his shoulder.

## JOEL ♂

My plan to scoop Damian out of his mother's grip and steal for home failed miserably. There were appointments with a social worker, another with lawyers and it seemed we'd be stuck at the Reese's until Wednesday at least, attempting to clear things up. In the meantime, Damian and I had a lot of talking ahead of us and I needed to see Meg checked into rehab immediately following our appointments. I wanted nothing left undone. I wanted to get home when this was over and make sure it stayed over. I wanted plans made for when Meg returned in six to eight months so that nothing she could say or do would change Damian living with me permanently.

I stood from the rocking chair in his room at the Reese's after watching him sleep for over an hour and walked across the hall to the spare room Meg's mom fixed up for me. Mrs. Reese had always been good to Damian. She had a good heart. But until now, it had been overshadowed by her daughter and she wouldn't admit her daughter was an addict. I guess she felt she'd made up for the lies by protecting Damian through it the best she knew how.

I couldn't blame her as a mother. I don't know that I could be strong enough to do what she did to her own daughter tonight. With Damian settled to bed, the three of us sat down for a heavy conversation and forced Meg into treatment.

She had already agreed to going, said she'd signed in to show up in two days time, but she hadn't planned to go through with any of it. There were no bags packed and Mrs. Reese overheard her on the phone making plans for the following week with friends; as if the chaos continued outside her realm, Meg protected in a little shell of a world. Just like a child.

When confronted, Meg looked immediately to her mother for support, her eyes glazing over with pained tears. Mrs. Reese swallowed hard and as I held my breath, bracing myself for the two to team up on me again, Meg and her mother faced off.

"I can't lie anymore, Meg. I can't protect you. All my support has done is create this tension and pain for everyone else. And it isn't helping Damian. It isn't helping you. You have lied to me, Meg, and told me you would get better. You have lost my trust with your lies and are close to losing your life. I will not be part of that. Not anymore."

"But mama," said Meg, full out pitiful put on tears. I could see a thick string of contempt in her eyes toward her mother now; just another person blocking her road to a fix.

"No Meg. Joel is a good man, a good father, and Damian needs to stay with him. You are not being a mother to that boy. Joel," she had said, tears filling her eyes as she faced me. I was dumbfounded. "You go to that meeting with the social worker and lawyers. And you tell them what you need to tell them. I will stand behind you. I'll do whatever it takes. I can never…never tell you in the right words how sorry I am for any hurt and trouble I've been a part of. I wish I had seen it sooner. I really thought I was helping my daughter and my grandson."

"You can't do that, Mom," said Meg, sucking back tears as they continued to pour down her cheeks.

"I can. And I will." She stood and took Meg, who now sobbed uncontrollably, into her arms. "I love you Meg and I am doing this for you. And for Damian. I will always love you because I am your mother. But I will not support what you're doing anymore." She let her go and left the room.

It must have been the hardest few steps Mrs. Reese had ever taken in her life. I heard her sobbing in the other room for hours afterward.

Meg turned to furious, screaming and flailing her arms. "You can't do this to me!"

I stood from the chair and left the room.

I lay awake in bed across the hall from Damian, staring at the wall and thinking about the week ahead. The worst of my worries were behind me and things would be moving forward, but not without many hills and obstacles along the way. Meg was only part of them.

# Chapter 23

*Eve* ♀

As expected, the realtor knocked on the door within a week of Maggie's call. The woman stood four-foot-two, her hair a jumble of curls to her neck, pink pencil-skirt suit popping at the seams from her plump figure. She wore a bright smile and the dimple in her fifty-year-old yet nearly wrinkle-free face puckered when she squinted a cute hello. She reminded me more of one of my mother's cronies in her days as a Mary Kay Rep than a realtor. She introduced herself as Ruth-Ann.

Ruth-Ann proficiently organized papers in neat piles, things I needed to sign that Maggie had arranged from overseas; movers, packers, signing over the house. I watched in awe, waiting for the dream to end. Maggie had given me rights to do everything and it killed me. I wanted to toss Ruth-Ann's *1997's Top Realtor* engraved gold-plated pen down the garbage disposal then remembered Maggie didn't have one.

"You do know there is no garbage disposal, right?" I asked, hopeful. "Will the new owners still want to buy, or should we—"

"Yes, I should say so," she said and tittered which turned to a loud giddy laugh and little snort. She tapped my shoulder. "Such a card you are Miss Whitting. Funny you aren't snatched up yet and looking for a place to settle down yourself."

"I could buy this one."

"Oh, honey. This is a done deal. But you come on down to my office when you're ready and I'll set you up a real nice place to start a family."

I nodded. And swallowed. And hesitated. And signed the papers.

I stared at the sign for two hours straight after it went up but it didn't go away no matter how much I willed it to happen. I even prayed for a miraculous thunderbolt to strike it down but it didn't come through. No rain clouds in the forecast.

I licked my finger and pointed it in the air. "Not even a friggin' wind."

I waited three days, quietly hopeful, but heard nothing from Joel. I had a week to get out of the house so the packers and movers and cleaners and whoever the hell else wanted to stop in besides me could do their thing.

I checked, too, casually, with everyone I could think of around town, my family. No one had heard from Joel. So I packed my things, loaded up the Jeep and drove to the only place where I might find hope of a real reason to spend the few remaining days of my time on Vine Street, waiting for him to come home.

Mrs. Powell answered the door with a surprised look in her eye and a comforting smile on her face.

"Eve? How are you doing?"

"Fine. Can I come in?"

"Of course. Sit down and I'll make some tea."

"Thank you." I walked inside and prepared for a long, sincere but difficult conversation. "I'm sorry to bother you and I won't take up too much of your time, but I needed to know something before I leave."

"You're leaving?" She set the kettle on the stove and turned to face me, leaning against the countertop with surveying eyes. They were exactly Joel's eyes.

"Yes. I'm going back to the city. Well, eventually I'm going back to the city. I'll probably stay at Mom and Dad's for a few days while I line up a place. And a job."

"Is Maggie back so soon?"

"Maggie is selling the house. *Sold* the house. They're staying in—I forget where—but she's in the middle of nowhere right now, making plans to live abroad for a year or so. Anyway, the realtor stopped by with the papers, and between cleaners and movers getting the house ready for the new owners, I only had this week before I needed to be out.

"I didn't think I should stay the rest of the four days. I have my own things to take care of. I was surprised it sold this quickly, but hey, there is apparently a market for growing families and new couples in small towns like this one. Moving from the big city. To little old Tayton. Where everything is just quiet and peaceful. And normal.

"And for Maggie, she's happy living—wherever it is she's living for now. And she's never been the one to live on the edge and take chances. So, here I am, bags packed and waiting."

"Eve."

"Uh huh," I said over my cup of tea. I could feel the steam on my cheeks and my heart beat like clopping hooves at the Kentucky Derby. It hurt to swallow and for some strange reason, my eyes were burning. My throat felt like it would close over.

"Did you come by to talk about Maggie's house and realtors?" She sat next to me and set a hand over mine on the table.

"No." Damn, his mother was good. I heaved a breath. "Actually, I don't know why I came. I'm a little...confused? Maybe. And..." I cleared my throat to fix the sudden squeak in my voice. "Have you heard anything from Joel?"

"He hasn't called you?"

"No. And I'm supposing that's a bad sign."

"Not a bad sign. I think he just has so much on his mind right now." She stirred her tea as it steeped. "He called the day he left Tayton to say he was with Meg and Damian. He mentioned that the DNA test was good. Damian was upset and he went to straighten things out."

"Meg came by. And they hugged. And they cried together. And he left. She wants her family back together. That's what she said."

"What did Joel say?"

"Nothing. He swung her around in his arms with a beaming smile. And looked happy some more."

"Oh. Did he say anything else?"

"I don't know. I went into the house at that point to throw up in the toilet."

"Oh, Eve. I hadn't realized you were in love with him. I thought it was just a...closeness. And Joel had better wake up and see what he has here waiting for him."

"Raif said you knew. About us. About what's been going on. Oh, God. I hope you do or you're about to find out some things, Mrs. Powell." I shook my head. I couldn't shut myself up. I hadn't cried in three days, well practiced at holding it inside, so I supposed it just all came out in blubbering nonsense now.

"I know. And I'm glad you aren't shy. I just wish these "things" you two were doing were more honest."

"What do you mean?"

"You've both been lying to yourselves about deep rooted feelings and when people do that things get worse before they get better."

"When does the get better part happen?"

"All I can tell you honey, is nothing can happen if neither of you make a move."

"I can't make that move, Mrs. Powell. Trust me, I am a pro at running away from things but I wouldn't be running away from this if it weren't for the fact that Joel needs to concentrate on Damian right now. Whether he works things out with Meg or not doesn't matter. It sucks and would be the biggest crap sandwich ever of a situation for me, but I'm trying my best not to be selfish about this. He needs to work things out with his son and get their lives straightened out before someone like me comes bursting in to complicate things."

"You're right, you know. You're a smart girl. Though I wish I could disagree with you and send you racing after him. I know he must need you, Eve."

"How do you know?" A tear leaked down my cheek. God, I was a sucker.

"Because he's my son. And mothers just know. That's what being a parent is all about."

"Do you think Damian will be okay?" My heart broke at that moment; that I might not see Damian again, either. Another few tears fell for that little boy. Then some more for all of the dreams I'd been having and hiding from, even from myself; about Joel and me together, about taking care of Damian, wanting to be there for the kid as if he were my—Oh crap. It had happened. My ovaries really were at that place and so was I. My timing was the pits.

"Damian is strong. I can't say as he won't be affected by all of this. He already is. But if Joel can work things out the best for his son,

I think he'll manage just fine. They'll manage together. They're both tough."

"I hope so. So, I guess I have to leave the me-and-Joel part up to him to act on. Unless he decides to sit back and just hope."

Mrs. Powell only nodded in agreement. I admired her for her strength and honesty. But a little bit of false hope would have been nice right about now.

"I would love to tell you more, honey. He hasn't talked to me in detail about his plans, just that he and Damian are okay for now. I could give you the number at Meg's place. Maybe you could call—"

"No. I think it's best if I leave him to deal with this first." I took a breath, a deep one that brought a coolness to my lungs. And the pressure in my head seemed to release. "Thank you for the tea. And for talking. I feel better for the moment."

She stood and pulled me into her arms.

"Mrs. Powell, please don't say anything to Joel about me coming by."

"Whatever you think is best, Eve. But—"

"I think it's best. Please. I don't want to deter his focus from what's important right now. I don't want him worrying about me."

"What can I tell him if he calls?"

"Just that I hope things are going well for him and Damian. I'll be at my mom's for a while before I go home."

"If you need anything at all, you just call, okay?"

"I will."

I planned to see Trey next on my way through town toward the farm. And there he sat on Joel's doorstep, as if waiting for me. (Okay, so I took one last swing by Vine Street on the off chance Joel had returned so I could run with wide open arms, we'd declare our undying love and live happily ever after.)

Joel wasn't there.

Just Trey and his beat up El Camino.

"Hey, Eve," he said, rising from the stoop. "I knocked and you weren't home. And there's this sign on the front lawn." He nodded to the realtor's sold sign and looked curiously back to me. He looked hurt that I hadn't told him.

"I know."

"You're leaving, then."

I nodded with a grin that I hope he understood. "Maggie sold the house. She's staying abroad for a while. And I'm going back to the city."

"Everyone's just up and gone, huh?" asked Trey. "First Joel. Now you."

I shrugged.

"When you leaving?" asked Trey.

"About now." I grinned and heaved a sigh. "So, have you heard from Joel?" I blurted out.

"No. I thought maybe you had."

"No."

"He looked pretty angry when he left with Meg."

"Yeah. Did he say anything?"

"Not much. We went inside about the same time you did. Then Joel came in, packed up a couple of bags and left. Said he'd only be a couple of days. And he wanted me to check in on you, make sure you were all right. That's why I'm here."

"Oh. No message."

"No, but he wasn't himself, Eve. Far from it. He was so angry with Meg, and happy and confused all at once. He wasn't thinking straight about anything."

I nodded. "Maybe he needs Meg."

"He doesn't need Meg."

"But it seems they've got a better chance right now than he does with me."

"Then he's a big fucking idiot and I'll kick his ass."

"Thank you."

"Welcome." He grinned and adjusted his hat with an awkwardness that said he wasn't happy to see me leave. "I can't believe you're really leaving. It's like you've been here forever, then poof. Gone again like a—"

"Like an Angel?" I grinned.

"No, I was thinking more like the Wicked Witch of the West, but whatever."

I slugged him on the shoulder and he laughed.

Tal and Cammy walked hand in hand toward us down the street. They were sweet. They were annoying at times and a bit too "into each other" in public, but sweet and my heart panged that I didn't have a chance to have what they did. Love was love no matter which form it came in.

"You leaving, Eve?" asked Tal, eyeing the sign.

"Yep."

"Really?" asked Cammy. "Are you going far? Because I was hoping we could get together for a girls day or somethin'."

"That sounds nice, Cammy," I smiled and squeezed her hand. I truly did wish we could get to know each other better. When you chiseled off the make-up and bubble gum, Cammy had a unique and loving heart.

"Keep in touch, Cupcake," said Trey and he hugged me tight. We held it for a moment, and I didn't want to let go. I really liked Trey; my big brother from Vine Street. It wasn't just leaving Joel. Leaving all of this broke me into a thousand pieces.

"Take care of yourself, okay?" He pulled away from the hug.

"I will. Mr. Evie. If you ever decide to follow your dreams to the big city look me up, 'kay?"

"You bet."

"Sure you will. You'll forget I ever existed."

"Of course. Like I said: Poof. Gone."

"Goodbye Tal. Cammy." I hugged them both then glanced back at Trey with a squeeze of his hand. "Say goodbye to Joel for me, will ya?" I swallowed back the tears. Jeez I turned into a bigger baby the longer I stayed in this old town.

They all waved and I walked toward the Jeep without looking back.


I stewed for three more days, mostly as an unidentifiable lump on my parents' sofa, until my dad kicked my ass off of it in the wee hours of the morning. The time had come to get my life in order and stop sulking over a relationship that need never even started. It just wasn't meant to be. The rest of the plans, well, those all panned out just as I had figured.

Watch Maggie's place. Tolerate my mother. Get a break from my messed up life in the city. Return to start over. That had been the plan. Everything accomplished.

I just wasn't supposed to meet Joel Powell.

I called my old apartment building and found a place one floor higher than my last. I had a home. And I could move in that week. Fortunately for me, most people were squeamish about the previous rat infestation, but I had lived through it before I'd left for Vine Street, so I could live through it again if it came to that. And maybe, though it was a reach, Stumpy was a closet pro-mouser.

I felt dejected at first that I hadn't heard from Joel before I left and that he hadn't tried to contact his friends or my family or anyone. It had now been a week. Not that I felt particularly sorry for myself anymore. The sadness worked its way into hurt and naturally, toward anger which now bit at me the hardest of all the emotions rolling around in my head.

The first thing I did when I moved in was *not* hook up phone service, and I wouldn't for a couple of weeks. Thankfully, the anger had set in which made me hard as nails on the outside, gave me the gumption to trudge ahead, with or without my happy ending, and I had myself convinced I wanted solitude.

I didn't handle the ending of relationships well and phone service would only give me something to sit next to, endlessly waiting for a call that may never come.

Next, I sent a postcard to my mother. It said something like, *Tell everyone I'm fine, but I don't want any letters or crap sent to the apartment just yet. I won't hook up the phone and I won't answer my cell. I have caller ID. Mom, that means I can tell by the number who it is and won't answer. Just everyone leave me be for a couple of weeks. Love y'all. Eve.* A bit pissy, but that's exactly how I felt.

I did call Trey. We talked, only a short conversation, but it felt good to hear his voice and let at least one person know I was still alive.

I had also finally figured out my problem with men and relationships. While my mother did share her "expert" advice on the subject, the answer didn't come from her. Or from Dr. Phil even though, also thanks to my mother, I am now an avid Dr. Phil fan. No, the answer hit me smack in the face as I walked up the stairs to my new/old apartment building.

I want a guy to need me as much as I need him instead of always being chosen last in the relationship. I had talked to Trey about it once before and hadn't really thought about it again until now. Not one of them ever chose me first. In priority, I fell somewhere after Jackson's keg of beer and on the same level as every mirror in Bruce's apartment, car, store window—you get the picture.

Until someone wanted me over every other meaningless thing in their life, I didn't want them back. The trouble was, Joel's "things" were far from meaningless and I couldn't and wouldn't expect Joel to set them aside. So I was stuck.

A week had passed since moving in. I'd had a week by myself, two job interviews without follow up phone calls and I lived off beer, ice cream and anything packaged and microwavable.

I curled up in a large chair—my only piece of furniture not being stored at my parents—where I planned to hunker in with a bucket of self-pity ice cream and what was left of a six-pack of beer. I apparently went through four in the last hour and a half.

I shoved Trey's hat over my eyes and Stumpy jumped into my lap after hitting a wall and stumbling over the open box in the middle of the floor. I stroked his soft fur while he purred and rubbed his cold nose on my arm.

"See, Stumpy, it's just you and me. I told you we'd be happy. And I'm okay with being a spinster. But you have to promise not to go tromping around town looking for a nice lady cat. We're in this together, like it or not. And I gotta tell you something about the girls in the big city. See, they're easy because there's more competition. It's a faster market, buddy." I leaned down to whisper in his ear. "I know what you're thinking. Easy would be nice. Especially for you; you probably haven't been laid in a long time. But it's no good." Huge yawn and everything spun. "Nope. We're gonna stick together you and me." I closed my eyes and felt myself drifting off to the melodious sound of Stumpy's loud purring motor. I had already become quite accustomed to that sound.

I woke up to pounding in my head. Stumpy meowed, leapt from my lap, hit a wall and high tailed it around the corner when I stood to attention, my heart banging. It wasn't only my head pounding. It was the door. I scowled at it because I wasn't exactly expecting company. The beer had long worn off, morning had arrived and I'd passed out, not so gracefully, on the living room chair. I had a huge headache. Not to mention I still wore Trey's hat, a pair of baggy pajama bottoms and a t-shirt with no bra.

"Shit," I said under my breath and walked to the door in a daze. I looked through the peephole at Joel standing in the hall.

"Double shit," I said and set my ear to the door, my hands carefully placed for balance, quiet as a mouse so he wouldn't know I was there. Maybe he'd go away. Maybe he'd—

He knocked louder and I screamed at the noise echoing through my head.

"Eve?" he called. "Open up. I know you're there."

I opened the door. "Joel?" I asked with a curled up lip and the best look of annoyance I could muster; one usually reserved for dates that decided to show up weeks later after no phone call.

"Eve. I've been trying to reach you."

"I don't have a phone yet. And I sent specific instructions to my mother via post card. Maybe you didn't get the memo. What are you doing here?"

"Can I come in?" he asked and eyed my hat with a grin. Then my shirt where I should have been wearing a bra and where my nipples were poking out from beneath the clingy fabric because I wasn't.

I quickly took off the hat and used it cover my chest. He walked inside as I blew a few strands of tangled, unwashed hair from my eyes.

If my apartment looked like one storm after another had hit, my hair was the cyclone carrying them. I ran a hand briskly through it and shuffled the comforter off the chair.

"Sorry, there's no where to sit. I've barely settled in yet. And Stumpy and I kind of crashed last night. How's things?" I asked with an out of breath sigh.

He smiled and stared at me. I cleared my throat and busied myself in the kitchen looking for a glass of water. My heart banged so hard in my chest I thought it may bruise my chest wall. My head would soon follow and I didn't know if I should follow my instincts to hug him or smack him across the face.

"So, how did you find me?" I asked.

"Your mom. The guys didn't know where to find you, so I talked to my mom, then to your mom—"

"Trey knew where I was."

"Well, Trey wasn't exactly happy when I saw him."

"No? Why not?" I stood frozen in the kitchen, Joel hadn't come any closer, likely due to the pissed off vibes I sent him. I couldn't even look at him.

"He was mad that I'd go back to Meg, not phone you and told me to go to hell. Then he slammed the door in my face."

"Oh?" I turned to grin at him.

"He likes you more than he likes me."

"Uh huh. I'm his Cupcake."

His tone grew more serious. "Why did you leave, Eve?"

"Didn't you ask Raif or someone about it?"

"No one knew much. Just that Maggie's house was sold and you'd gone."

"Jesus, those guys are idiots. They knew why I left. Maggie sold the house on a whim. I left because I didn't want to stick around for a week of movers and cleaners. Besides, I accomplished my goal in coming to Tayton in the first place: watch Maggie's house then return to the city to start my life over. Done. It isn't as if I was going to wait around for something that wasn't going to—" I quickly reoriented my thoughts and turned back toward Joel. "Why did you come here, Joel?"

"I assumed you left because you never wanted to see me again. I wanted to know if it was true or if I would be standing here like a dumb hopeful idiot chasing a woman who really thought what we were doing meant nothing."

I crossed my arms. "Do you want it to mean nothing?" He didn't say anything. The tears started to well so I put up my defenses. "I guess that's my answer, then." I felt him move closer, my back still turned.

His arm gripped my elbow and he turned me to face him. He stood inches from me now, forcing me to look up into his eyes. "What I want is for you to come back home."

"This is home, Joel. Vine Street isn't my home, it never was. It isn't even Maggie's home anymore."

"A lot has happened, Eve. There's so much going on and you're the only one I want to talk to about it, the only one I want to tell everything, to share every single emotion and every feeling I have inside of me ready to explode."

"What are you feeling?"

"Afraid. Angry. Out of fucking control." He was shaking.

"Okay, okay, tell me what's going on." And I really wanted to listen; as a friend or whatever he needed me to be right now. It felt as if everything that had fallen between our once trusting friendship, and now, where we stood figuratively alone, had vanished. And I now faced the same Joel who first confided in me about Damian, about Meg, about the DNA testing.

"I don't know where to begin, there's so much." He sighed and washed his hands over his face. "I met with social services and our lawyers. Meg has signed over full custody of Damian. She's letting him go, going into rehab and starting her life over. Again. So we're starting our lives over again, too. Me and him."

"Oh my God."

"And my mom sold the ranch."

"Oh. My God. Is that...is that okay with you? And Damian is staying with you? For good?" I started to smile despite myself. Nothing about me seemed to matter for the moment. "And the ranch. But you love the ranch."

"Yeah. With Meg in rehab and me not supporting her anymore, things are changing. I bought it Eve. The ranch is mine. All of it." A wide smiled stretched across that hard jaw and Joel's eyes shone.

# Chapter 24

## JOEL ♂

I wanted to pull her into my arms. We stood in her small, rundown apartment, the same place she'd left months ago. And Eve's face told me the pain she felt, though she did her damnedest to keep it tamped down inside.

Eve had come to the city as a young girl and quickly found herself stuck in a life that eventually began to crumble around her. Her chance at escape on Vine Street seemed fruitless now; she'd stolen a moment of sanity in Tayton and though she'd never admit it, she didn't want to come back. Not to this. Yet here she stood, in the same building, the same position in life—perhaps even lower now without a job or a relationship—and here I was, talking of the ranch and Damian and my life's panning out. My happy ending.

Eve didn't know if or how she fit into that happy ending. I wasn't sure she *wanted* to fit into it and though my mother and Raif seemed sure she would, nothing felt certain when I looked into her eyes right now. She obviously didn't know the details of why I'd left, why I'd taken so long with Meg and—just a hunch—she was more than a little bit angry that I hadn't reached her until now.

"You bought the ranch?" She swallowed hard, dumbfounded, and the hurt swam beneath the surface. "That's so…that's great Joel. Really great. Everything's working out so perfect. You deserve the best and—you know what?" Her tone changed and with a snap, that feisty tempter made its escape. Tears began to pour and I feared what would follow. "You are a really big huge giant—ASS!"

"What? Eve, listen—"

"No, you listen, Cowboy. I am happy for you. I'm happy for Damian because he is the most important piece in all of this. I couldn't *be* happier the way everything worked out for you, Joel. But it's pretty damn hard to feel all peachy keen jubilant when you have everything you ever wanted and I am sitting here in this *shit-hole* apartment waiting for my next job interview that I have a less than fifty percent chance at getting because I told my old boss to go fuck himself. And I know I am being super selfish and bitchy and I hate myself for saying all of this because of what you are going through, but that's just the way it is! *A phone call*, Joel, would have been nice. So it's time for Eve to feel sorry for Eve and worry about just me! And Stumpy. We're a team now. I made him a promise. Him and me! And that's all I have to worry about anymore."

"Eve, listen—"

"Me. And the *cat*, Joel."

"Okay. So bring him with you. I never said Stumpy couldn't come."

"What do you mean? Come where?"

"To the ranch. I want you to come home. I know Vine Street isn't your home. It isn't my home, it never was. My home is at the ranch. I want you with me, Eve."

"You want me to live at the ranch? With you and Damian?"

"Yes."

"Like a family?" I could see her welling with tears again. This would either climb in the direction of happiness or descend into a cesspool of angry. "You want me to live there?"

"Not just live there, Eve. Marry me." I cupped her cheeks in my hands and my face lit up. She did that to a guy. "Please marry me, so I can keep my sanity. I'm sorry I didn't call. You were already gone when I tried and I didn't know you'd left so I just kept trying and I made a few plans while I tracked you down. A lot of plans, actually. My mom never said anything about you visiting her until I came back. No one did."

"I don't know what to—wow. I thought—"

"I know what you thought. Had I known you thought I'd ever consider staying with Meg, I would have called that day. There will always be ups and downs with Meg and her issues. And I plan on working hard at the shop and at the ranch and we'll probably only make ends meet for a while. I can't promise you it'll be easy or anywhere close to a dream. It'll be a boring small town ranch life, Eve, at least close to a normal life. I know you never wanted normal, you left normal years ago. But we want you in it. I need you in it."

She waited before saying anything and just stared at me, all of her emotion pouring from her eyes. I held my breath until she spoke.

"I want normal." She smiled. Thank God she smiled. "I've been so busy chasing normal while running from everything else I didn't realize I'd found exactly where I want to be."

"Thank the good Lord," I muttered. And I kissed her. Everything came together in that moment; my life was perfect. Perfect with all of its imperfections. The time had come to put all of the plans into action and just pray she didn't turn back to hating me again for making them without her.

"Joel, what about Damian? What will he say about this?"

"I sort of already told him you were coming so he won't take no for an answer. And I had to make a few promises."

"Like what?"

"Like he gets his own huge room and he wondered where you were going to sleep which I had a hard time explaining. I told him you were going to sleep in the same room with me after the wedding."

"After the…"

"And that he could carry the rings if he walked down the aisle without making faces. But you have to help me on that one by not starting anything with him. Promise Eve, you won't get him gong at the wedding."

"Wedding?"

## EVE ♀

That one word stuck in my head. It was all I heard, all that would come out of my lips. "Wedding? Wedding. Wedding." I said it over every way

I could but it still didn't make sense. Me? A wedding? That just didn't fit. Marriage yes, but this word hit me upside the head like the end of a rake lying upside down in the grass.

"Yeah, a wedding." Joel still held my shoulders in his hands. "Now don't freak out, Eve."

"Freak out? About what?" I stared, eyes laced with suspicion. "What did you do?"

"Do you have a nice dress you can put on?"

"For what?" I asked with a scrunched up face.

"Everyone's waiting for an answer."

"What?"

"Your mom is there and your dad."

"You planned a wedding, didn't you? Oh my God. You actually planned a wedding. An entire wedding? My wedding?"

"Yeah," he said. "And you keep saying it."

"Because I'm waiting for it to sound like it's supposed to be coming out of my mouth but it isn't. Is it?"

"Yes."

"A wedding. A wedding when?"

He chuckled with a smirk. "Today."

"Today?" I screamed and slugged him in the arm. "What if I said no?"

"Don't say no," he said and pulled my lips against his. The warmth I'd missed and the strong but gentle caress I'd longed for flowed over every part of me. As *if* I could ever say no.

"But a wedding *today*?"

"You don't like half the town, so I didn't think you'd care if the entire population wasn't there on such short notice."

"No, but I wouldn't mind a chance to rub their faces in it."

"Well you can at the reception tonight."

"What reception?"

"My mom has been spreading the word and you and I are apparently the hot topic of town. No one wants to miss it. People are canceling other events and arranging their schedules around this big day in history. And I don't know how many are coming to the wedding but it grows by the hour. You know how fast the Ladies Social spreads a rumor. And they can make it sound damn juicy, too."

"Oh my God."

"So, you still haven't given me an answer."

"Sorry, Mr. Powell, if I'm feeling a bit overwhelmed here. Guest list? And what about the whole cake, flowers, catering thing…it takes longer than a freakin' week to plan a wedding. Did you just fall off a turnip truck, Joel?"

"I know. I'm sorry. But everything is taken care of. You just have to trust me."

"We've only known each other for—what, a month and a half?"

"Fifty three days."

"Fifty three days and "just trust me"? What about a license? You need a license to get married."

"I got one."

My eyes bugged out, my jaw dropped.

"I was hopeful," he said and shrugged his shoulders.

"But how did you get it without me? Don't you need—"

"Just trust me."

"And I made a promise to Stumpy."

"You can break a promise to Stumpy. He can wait in the truck and we'll find him a girlfriend after the "I do"-s."

"I'm about to get dressed for my own wedding, which I didn't plan. And break the news to my family that I am getting married, *after* they watch me walk down the aisle. I suppose I did so much planning at my sisters wedding that I swore I would elope before doing my own. Will there be confetti? I really want confetti."

"Truck loads if you want it."

Another huge sigh and my mind raced. "I have to get my hair and nails done!"

"Cammy's volunteered her services."

"Oh. My. God." My hands went to my face, complete shock. Cammy? Doing my make-up and hair? This I wasn't so sure about.

"Eve."

"What?"

He stared with raised eyebrows and a half grin.

"Yes! Of course I'll marry you!" Tears leaked again, this time the happiest ones to ever stream down my face.

"Was it the kiss or Cammy's beauty treatment that convinced you?"

"It was just you, Joel. Just you convinced me. And I don't ever need more than that."

# Chapter 25

## *Trey* ♠

"Where the hell is he?" I asked.

Raif stood with his arms crossed, Tal next to him, all of us in our best suits. Joel insisted on us renting nice clothes, or me and Tal anyway because we didn't have any and these we only got last minute because Lacy's best friend and fellow bimbo runs a dry cleaners in town. We were wearing other dudes suits. But both of the bimbos owed Joel big time for the comments about his future wife. At least that's what Raif told her.

"I don't know where he is. He wanted us all here an hour ago, Trey, how should I know?"

"You're his best man, Raif. Didn't he tell you anything?"

"No. Just that he hoped she'd say yes. We're all pretty much standing here on a maybe right now."

"Do you think she'll show up?" asked Tal.

"Shut up Tal. Of course she'll show up," I said.

"She has to show up," mumbled Raif. He looked as nervous as the rest of us.

"What if she doesn't?" asked Tal.

We didn't answer, only glared at him.

"I'm just saying!"

"Then we'll all be looking like a couple of losers for haulin' everyone here. And I'll beat the shit out of Joel for making us wear these stupid outfits," I said. And I would.

"It's traditional. It's a wedding. What did you expect? At least they aren't tuxes. Just suits. And you're wearing your stupid hat, so stop complaining."

"Well, all's I can say is Joel better be nice to Eve. And he'd better watch his ass. If he doesn't do this right, she'll send him home in a body bag. And it'd serve him right."

"Do you know everything that went on with Joel while he was gone?" asked Raif.

"No."

"Then shut up."

"He could have phoned her at least."

"Good thing it's not you he's proposing to, then, isn't it?"

"I hope he does it right," said Tal.

"How can he do it wrong? She just needs a simple "Will you marry me?"," I said.

"Yeah right. And since when did Eve do anything simple?" asked Raif.

"You're right. He's fucked."

## TAL ♠

I saw the cloud of dust from the dirt road in the distance long before I saw Joel's truck. Joel was obviously eager to get here and I could only hope it was a rush to make it to the wedding on time, not to call it off. I couldn't believe it, but our three sorry asses were worried about someone else's relationship making it. I suppose being that it was Joel and Eve, it shouldn't surprise me.

"Here he comes," said Raif.

"Is Eve with him?" asked Trey.

"I can't tell."

"Jesus, if she's not there—" I started.

"She'll be there," they both yelled. I didn't think there was any need for yelling at this point. I folded my arms and slouched back, hoping she'd said yes or I'd have three grumpy asses on my hands.

Was that Cammy's car behind the truck?

# RAIF ♠

I walked toward the truck as it came to a stop and grinned wide. Eve stood there smiling and I blew a breath of relief. Joel stepped out and set his hands on my shoulders.

"Hey buddy," he said.

"Hey. So, you ready? Eve's ready I'm assuming."

"Yep. Thanks for getting everyone together."

"How did you convince her so fast?"

"I don't know. I'm just glad I did."

Joel walked past me and opened the passenger side door. Eve stepped out wearing a fitted floor length white dress and heels. Even though it wasn't a formal wedding gown, she sparkled from head to toe and looked like she'd planned this thing right along with us.

"Hi, Eve," I said as she came out of the truck.

"Hi, Raif. You are best man, I presume."

"I am."

"Joel, wait." She stopped and pulled back on his arm. "I don't have anyone to stand for me."

"Yeah you do. Just trust me. Everything will work out just fine." You could almost hear Joel's heart pounding and I'd never seen him happier.

Eve heaved a deep sigh.

"Joel, we need to get going," I said.

"Is everyone here?"

"Yep. And the guys are..." They came up behind us. "Supposed to be inside! What are you doing?"

"Trey!" Eve said and pulled him in for a hug. "Thanks for this. And for backing me up even though Joel didn't deserve the door slammed in his face. Not really," she said. We all rolled our eyes.

"No problem, Cupcake. And you are coming with me. Raif, Joel, you need to get in there."

"Tal," said Joel, "Go inside and tell them I'm here. Where's Damian?"

"He's with your mom."

"We'll get him when we go in," I said and pulled Joel away. He was lip-locked with Eve already. "Come on. Plenty of time for that later."

## JOEL ♂

I sent Raif in after Tal, the announcement being made that I had returned with a bride. Raif sent Damian down the aisle from the front row running like an elephant through the door where I waited outside. I hauled him up in my arms and swung my son around in the air.

"Is Ee*b*ie here?" he asked.

"Yep. Are you ready?"

"Uh huh."

"Do you remember what you have to do?"

"Uh huh."

I plunked him down on the ground and fixed the tiny box into his hand. "Don't drop this, buddy. You have the most important job here."

"I won't, Daddy. Promise." He beamed a smile up at me and bounced on the balls of his feet. I was just as excited.

## EVE ♀

I stood there with Trey feeling a little awkward that I had no idea what to do or what to expect next or who else would be inside the church waiting to watch me walk down the aisle. I could just as easily have been a guest in the back row at someone else's wedding. Trey stood beside me along the church wall where no one could see us out the side window. Then I heard the front doors open, a hush fall across the crowd and a loud rumble of chatter and gasps. And Damian giggled before the doors closed behind them. My heart warmed to the sound.

"You ready?" asked Trey.

"Ready as ever I guess. I didn't ever think I'd be getting married. Not now. Not in this church."

"Well, you deserve the best, Eve. So does Joel."

"Thank you. Guess this makes our break-up official."

"Sorry, Cupcake. You're still my girl."

"Thanks Trey."

"And here. You'll need this." He handed me his old hat, the one I'd brought with me home.

"How'd you get this?"

"Joel brought it back. I told him it was one of the conditions."

"It's perfect. I'll carry it down the aisle. Sort of a symbol of the cowgirl I've fought turning into."

"You've always been a little bit cowgirl."

"So what now?"

"Now we wait for your dad to walk you down the aisle. And your bridesmaid and your maid of honor."

"Who's my maid of honor? Lacy?" I joked. Okay, not a time for joking. Give me a break; my knees were knocking I was so nervous.

Cammy walked toward me with a beaming grin. I smiled back. She'd toned down her hair for the occasion, dimmed her usual glowing lips to neon pink and wore a low cut fitted floral print dress.

"Cammy," I said and hugged her tight. "You look beautiful."

"I'm glad for you, Eve," she whispered.

"Thank you. And thanks for standing for me. And the makeover."

"Anytime, honey." She spit out a wad of gum into the grass and beamed wide.

My dad came around the corner next and I glanced over, my heart beating faster. Maggie clung to his arm, carrying a giant bouquet of pink roses.

"Maggie!"

"Eve!"

"How did you get here?"

"Joel tracked us down through Mom and Dad a week ago, so we flew home for a few days. I wouldn't miss this for the world."

"A week ago? He had this all planned a week ago? I found out this morning."

"Then it's a good thing you said yes. He started planning more than a week ago, so I hear. And I have to say I am surprised. I mean, you and Joel, Eve? Though I couldn't have found you a better guy myself. I wish I'd thought to introduce you ages ago."

"I can't believe he did this. Who else is inside?"

"Everyone. The entire town almost. More people turned out for your wedding than mine after a year of planning."

"They just want a peak at the sleaze marrying Joel Powell. Oh my God. I'm marrying Joel Powell. Me, Maggie." I drew in a deep breath to avoid fainting and felt Dad's arms around my shoulder; I leaned into him to keep upright. "Daddy," I said and couldn't get out any more without the waterworks starting.

"Are you happy?" he asked.

I nodded with a wide smile.

"Then let's go get my girl married. He's a good one, kid, that Joel," he whispered. "It's your cue, Maggie."

"See you inside," she said and walked through the door. I held my flowers in both hands, the cowboy hat tucked alongside it.

"You bringing that?" asked my dad.

"Damn right."

He laughed with a wink. "That's my girl."

For the first time in a long while, my whole body agreed. All of me wanted Joel by my side; body, heart and soul. It felt like hours longer than the few minutes since we'd last kissed. Who cared about all this tradition anyway? I wanted to run down the aisle and meet him, not pace slowly, one foot at a time. Step, pause. Step, pause.

Cammy started the march and Dad and I followed Maggie inside. It felt as if someone plunked me in the middle of a dream. A beautiful fantasy full of adventure, love and a little bit of healthy chaos. Joel stood at the front; my cowboy Adonis. The exhilaration raced so quickly through my veins I forgot to glimpse at the faces in the aisles. But I didn't care who came. Damian bounced up and down next to his dad and they were all that mattered.

"Hi Ee*bie*!" he yelled down the aisle in typical Damian volume. This warranted a few shushes from the audience but I stopped and waved and made a face at him with my tongue sticking out. He made one back and Joel picked him up to keep him still and gave me a glare behind his radiant, wide smile. This was my family. Our family.

# JOEL ♂

She looked beautiful; vibrant, stunning, glowing sunshine, all the words typical to describe a bride on her wedding day. Eve was anything but typical. She emitted more life than any woman I'd ever met, radiating energy to anyone near her. And alongside the sunshine and beauty, existed a fiery, brash, temptress of a tomboy. The perfect compliment.

And she carried Trey's cowboy hat.

She began her slow walk down the aisle, dress swaying around her ankles, and stopped to make a face at Damian when she reached only a quarter of the way down. I scooped Damian up while Eve turned to her father and tugged on his arm to go faster. She dragged him in a near jog the rest of the way.

Mrs. Pollard looked over her shoulder from the organ bench, her smile turning to panic and mortification at the bride almost running down the aisle. She turned back to the keys and tried her best to keep up with Eve's quickened pace. There were a few chuckles from the audience then gasps. Those likely came from Eve's mother. I laughed. Leave it to Eve to ditch the traditional wedding march.

Her father kissed her cheek, shook my hand and took a seat in the front row with our mothers. Eve turned to wave at the guests and then focused back on me. We stood alone, ready to take our vows. It was the second time for me, but felt like the first and only. I swallowed past the lump in my throat and took a deep breath. It was the first one I felt going in since she'd said "yes".

Thank God she did.